Not Really the
PRISONER
OF ZENDA

Books by Joel Rosenberg from Tom Doherty Associates

Home Front
Foreign Land

*Not Exactly the Three Musketeers**
*Not Quite Scaramouche**
*Not Really the Prisoner of Zenda**

*Fantasy

Not Really the
PRISONER
OF ZENDA

A GUARDIANS OF THE
FLAME NOVEL

JOEL ROSENBERG

TOR®

A TOM DOHERTY ASSOCIATES BOOK

NEW YORK

NOT REALLY THE PRISONER OF ZENDA: A GUARDIANS OF THE FLAME NOVEL

Copyright © 2003 by Joel Rosenberg

Edited by Claire Eddy

A Tor Book
Published by Tom Doherty Associates, LLC
175 Fifth Avenue
New York, NY 10010

www.tor.com

Tor® is a registered trademark of Tom Doherty Associates, LLC.

Library of Congress Cataloging-in-Publication Data

Rosenberg, Joel, 1954–
    Not really the prisoner of Zenda : a guardians of the flame novel /
Joel Rosenberg.—1st ed.
        p.   cm.
    "A Tom Doherty Associates book."
    ISBN: 0-765-30046-X (acid-free paper)
    I. Title.

PS3568.O786N66 2003
813'.54—dc21

                                                    2003040213

First Edition: June 2003

Printed in the United States of America

0   9   8   7   6   5   4   3   2   1

For Dave Baker,
owner/operator of http://www.slovotskys-laws.com

Not Really the
PRISONER
OF ZENDA

Prologue
⚜ The Night

I t was, of course, a dark and stormy night.

That was the way that his luck was running.

The gusty wind had let up—just for the moment, probably; life is like that—which merely made the hard rain beat straight down on him as Pirojil limped slowly through the mud down the Street of Two Dogs, looking for trouble.

But he wasn't finding any, not tonight.

Unfortunately.

The dim light leaking out from the tavern windows was the only illumination, and it was scant illumination at that—but there wasn't much to see, anyway, except for the rain and the mud, and that was hardly worth looking at, anyway.

He had already had to give up on the theater district, busy as it had been—and it had been busy: *Birth of an Empire* was still doing a full-house business at the House of Wise Tidings, night after night after night.

Pirojil didn't understand that at all. He had finally forced himself to sit through the whole play; a mugger's pouch had contained a couple of Karlsday Night tokens, and there was no need to let them go to waste. It made no sense that the playwright had received applause after the final curtain, instead of the rapidly thrown rotten fruit—or, better, rocks—that the idiot fully deserved.

It wasn't just this one theater that was doing well, though. The other theaters were crowded, despite the fact that yet another had opened since the last time that Pirojil had been in the capital.

But, despite the threat of rain in the clouds and in the air that had become a promise too well kept, the streets in the theater district had been just this side of lined with not only the capital armsmen, but more than a few nobles' guards. Pirojil had spotted some Imperials that he knew were from the Emperor's Own—Silver Company, he thought, although with the recent shake-up, they could have been moved to Gold or Purple—which meant that the nobility attending theater tonight included more than just a few nobles minor, but some of the major landed nobility, as well.

Shit.

You could pretty much trust the old-line nobility to ruin a good thing, at least for a night. The theater district was often prime hunting ground for footpads and such, but tonight it had been far too well watched for the footpads' purposes, or for Pirojil's own.

So he had moved along, down to less well-off districts, and then the rain had finally hit, driving everybody indoors, apparently.

Rain.

It was more than unfortunate, worse than unfortunate—it was *unprofitable*, as well as being miserably cold and even more miserably wet, and he hoped that it wasn't a harbinger of things to come. He would have to get used to doing this alone sooner or later, and to Pirojil's way of thinking, later was usually worse than sooner.

He and Kethol and Erenor had, until recently, been supplementing their pay with the occasional footpad in much the same way that he and Kethol had when they were partnered with Durine. The Three Swords Inn—if there ever was a Three Swords Inn—would not be built with what three soldiers could save from their pay, despite Pirojil's recent promotion to captain.

Biemestren's wealth, and the trade constantly flowing in and out of the capital, supported the largest criminal class in the Empire, probably in the Middle Lands. You could hang all the thieves you wanted to in the square—and hangings were a standard part of Tenthday entertainment for the masses—but, as far as Pirojil could tell, all that really did was give the pickpockets and pouch slashers a distracted crowd in which to ply their trades.

It had always seemed to Pirojil and particularly to Durine amusing—not to mention profitable, although the profit was the entire point of the whole thing, after all, and the amusement just a bonus—to let that criminal class help support them.

After all, how could a robber complain about being robbed?

What were they going to do? Go pound on the door of the jail and ask the armsmen to arrest the erstwhile victims who, instead, had beaten the robbers and taken everything they had, from their pouches, to their knives, even to their brass belt buckles?

Biemestren armsmen, like armsmen everywhere, weren't renowned for their senses of humor, and besides, Pirojil, Kethol, and Erenor had not lolled about at the scene of the crime either, as Biemestren armsmen probably wouldn't have found their hobby terribly amusing—and neither would Baron Cullinane, which was only part of the reason the three of them had always been careful.

Jewelry was a problem only in that you could never get its full value—but the gems could be pried out and sold separately, and while it was always a shame to ruin some delicately crafted setting or pendant, it was also safer to simply melt it for the value of the gold or silver.

They had once managed to acquire a particularly gorgeous brooch, beautiful enough that Kethol had been tempted to find the rightful owner—some minor lord from Niphael, judging from the filigree work; it would have been easy to find out which visiting noble had been set upon that night—but, for once, it hadn't taken much effort for Pirojil and Durine to talk him out of doing anything stupid.

Common soldiers who were supplementing their pay with a little bit of private enterprise among the criminal class—even if it consisted of stealing from the criminal class—couldn't afford to draw any attention to themselves.

Money was money, of course, and the most they ever had to do was carefully examine the silver coins—or, all too rarely, a gold one—for any distinctive markings that had been scratched on to it. On the rare occasions that they found any, that coin, too, would go into the melting pot. The evening wasn't over until they had melted the silver and gold—separately, of course—and reduced them to unidentifiable metal lumps.

That part Pirojil could do himself, of course. But it really took more than one person to do the rest of it effectively, not to mention safely.

There had to be one person acting as bait, and Pirojil wasn't the best bait. He was above average in size, for one, and a close look—which he hoped would come too late, which *should* come too late in the dark—would reveal that his preposterously ugly face was creased with scars, proclaiming him a less than ideal target.

He did the best he could.

A floppy cap covered where the tip of his left ear had been bitten off even better than his fringe of hair could. His slick oiled canvas rain cloak, with its mirror-polished silver buttons, hid the brace of knives at his hip and the sword that was slung down his back, while the buttons acted as an additional garnish on the bait. His short, heavy dagger was in his right hand, but he had it in a reverse grip, the blade flat along his forearm, and he always made a point, before going out, to be sure that he had fully blackened its surface by holding it over a candle. It would be hard enough to see the blade in daylight, and at night it would be effectively invisible.

Not that he was going to have any use for the knife, unfortunately. Even the pouring rain couldn't wash from the air all of the garlicky smells of roasting meat that mixed with the sounds of laughter from the taverns, but the rain had almost emptied the streets. It lacked an hour of midnight, and even an Imperial soldier who was due to stand the next watch—and who at least thought that his decurion was too lazy to check for the smell of beer on his breath—wouldn't think of leaving the warmth and comfort of the tavern to go out into the storm until either the storm passed or the various stations of the Nightwatch, scattered throughout the city, began to echo the sounding of the warning bell.

Shit, all of the Nightwatch on duty in this part of town were probably inside, somewhere, keeping themselves warm and dry, too, although the fact that none of the lanterns in front of each shop and home were lit was only weak evidence for that, and didn't approach proof. There was no point, after all, in rousting the locals out of their bed to light the lanterns, no matter what the law said, if the next blast of wind was simply going to blow the lantern out again.

A stray dog rooted in a pile of garbage in the alley next to the largest of the taverns, but if there were eyes peering out of the dark at him, Pirojil couldn't see them.

He staggered on down the muddy street, listening, ever hopefully, for quiet splashes behind him, but hearing nothing but the damn rain.

It was useless, and he probably should have quit tonight before beginning. Still, he would have to get used to doing this alone sooner or later, after all, and at least to Pirojil's way of thinking, sooner was better than later.

Durine was dead, his body rotting in that cave in Keranahan under a cairn of rocks; Erenor wasn't trustworthy; and Kethol wasn't even Kethol anymore—he was Forinel.

So if Pirojil was going to work this scheme, he would have to do this by himself, and he might as well get used to it now.

Durine had worked it by himself from time to time, but Pirojil had always thought that you really should have at least two, preferably three men. Beyond the bait—and you had to have good bait—it was just this side of necessary to have at least another one, or preferably two, in case you actually struck gold. Or, more commonly, silver. And sometimes only copper.

And tonight, apparently, nothing except mud, and if mud was valuable, peasants would be princes.

The streets were more than due for a good cleaning; his boots sunk almost to the calf in spots, and it was just as well, at least while he was struggling to get himself clear, that he was alone.

Of course, he could have walked along the wooden sidewalks, which were raised up just out of the mud of the street, but he was supposed to be scared—a merchant, perhaps a frightened horse trader from the territories, hurrying back to his inn after closing a deal, constantly clutching at his pouch, visibly patting at it to be sure that it still was there, while unintentionally reassuring anybody watching that here there was money for the taking.

Pirojil had learned some useful things from Erenor about maintaining a disguise. Erenor was a wizard, granted, and much of what he did in creating a seeming was magic—but not all of it, not always. He said that putting on a seeming was always more than just magic, and sometimes didn't require magic at all, and could be utterly ruined if, say, you looked like a bent, wizened wizard but carried yourself with the easy grace and bold strides of a young man.

For this, you needed to do more than act like you were a victim, looking for a place to be victimized—you had to *be* the victim, to know yourself the victim, to believe with every move you made that you were the victim, curse yourself for finding yourself in Dogtown too late on a night when even the Nightwatch barely ventured out into the rain.

Pirojil was, he hoped, putting on a good show, but there was nobody watching, and, of course, his new rain cloak leaked.

Shit. He should have expected that. There should have been a flap of cloth over the shoulder seams, because no matter how much you oiled the seams, they always leaked, and Pirojil's old ragged rain cloak, which hung in the bureau in his quarters, was of better construction than this—it just looked cheap. This poor excuse for a slicker had left him soaked and miserable, and his teeth were starting to chatter with the cold.

He hurried along.

Just one more trip up Dog Street, then down Blacksmith's Way—although why they called it that Pirojil didn't know; there were no smithies along that twisting street, and had been none the first time he had been in Biemestren, years ago—and then he would give up.

Which he did, wet, cold, muddy, and empty-handed.

He paused for a moment under an overhang and wrung his floppy hat out just as a matter of good practice, although the point of it escaped him. The hat, even wrung-out, was still soggy, and when he walked out into the rain it would become instantly soaked, once again. Which, of course, wouldn't have made it any less useful for flinging up and into a face while he went in low behind his knife, but he clearly wasn't going to be having the opportunity to do that, not tonight.

It seemed that the armies of thieves and footpads and muggers and such that infested the capital were taking the night off, at least until the rain let up, and Pirojil should probably have been smart enough to do the same in the first place, rather than spending a couple of hours tromping through mud, with nothing to show for it but wet clothes.

Well, so much for this. . . .

He made his way back up the hill to the outer gate of Biemestren Castle, and cursed his luck when the rain finally stopped just at the very moment that he reached the top of the hill.

It was one of those nights.

He thought for a moment about going back down into the town, but decided against it. He was getting tired, and tired men made mistakes, and it was bad enough a night without ending up beaten and dead in some alleyway.

He stripped off his floppy hat, and twisted it once again until he got most of the water out, then folded it and his slicker across his arm, revealing the tunic underneath.

Not that the guards would need to see the tunic—his face was, unfortunately, so distinctively ugly that he would be instantly recognized.

Surprisingly, he didn't have to knock on the small door in the main gate, as it swung open at his approach. He was reaching for the pass that he had put into what he hoped was a sufficiently waterproof packet under his tunic, but the guard didn't challenge him.

"A pleasant evening to you, Captain Pirojil," the guard said. "A little wet out tonight, if you don't mind my saying so."

Well, in fact, Pirojil *did* mind his saying so—Pirojil was soaked like a drowned rat, and he hardly needed any comments from some lucky soldier who had been fortunate enough to be able to spend *his* evening warm and dry in shelter of the guardhouse, with a warm brazier of coals to keep him company—but it didn't seem like a good idea to put the man at a brace and explain that in detail, despite the strong temptation.

You made enough enemies in this life, as it was, and shouting at the lucky sod wouldn't have made Pirojil any warmer or drier.

"Yes," he said, "it's been just a little bit damp, at that."

The soldier surprised him by offering him a folded blanket; it was warm, warm enough that it had probably been sitting next to that brazier, waiting to comfort some officer, or even a noble, who had been foolish enough to go out on a night like this. That was very nice of—

Oh. Pirojil *was* an officer, now, at least technically.

"Thank you," he said. "And a pleasant, dry evening to you, too."

He reslung his sword belt over his shoulder—he didn't want to belt it around his soggy waist—and made his way up the short paved road across the outer bailey, conscious of the eyes watching him from the ramparts of the inner wall.

That was fine with him; he had every right to be here, at least at the moment, and he knew enough to stay on the road, and wondered as to whether it would be a bullet or an arrow that would bring him down if he made a sudden dash into the proscribed outer bailey.

A bow shot, he finally decided—the guards probably wouldn't trust their rifles on such a wet night.

If the guard at the inner gate recognized him, he didn't say anything, and Pirojil actually had to show his pass to be given entry. When the door squeaked shut behind him, he tucked the pass back in its pouch, and the pouch back into his tunic, and he walked quickly across the courtyard to the barracks, not bothering to avoid the puddles. There was no point in it; he couldn't get any wetter.

He scraped off his boots in the mud room. Ignoring the clicking of a game of bones that came from the common room on the first floor, he climbed the stairs all the way to the top, his boots making squishing sounds as he walked. He looked back down the stairs. Between his boots and his dripping clothes, he had left a trail of slime, like a snail. Well, at least cleaning that up wasn't his problem. Let the servants handle it.

Visiting officers were billeted on the third floor, which made life easier for the common soldiers, who didn't have to remove their boots for fear of annoying somebody senior enough to do something about it, and at the moment, he was the only one resident in the west wing.

Which also was just fine with him. One of the few things that

Pirojil prided himself on was not needing any company.

He drew his sword and dagger and laid them out on the table in the common area, and quickly located some soft cloths with which to dry them off thoroughly, even though that would require a complete re-blackening of the dagger the next time he went out. He couldn't find any oil in the common area—except for the lamp oil, which he didn't trust to protect the blades—so he retrieved his own flask of linseed oil from his quarters, and gave both blades not only a good oiling but also a good polishing before setting them down and retrieving a change of clothes from his room.

You had to have a sense of priorities. He might feel like he could have rusted out in the rain, but he couldn't. His sword and his knife definitely could, and he didn't like to take sandcloth to them any more than he had to.

Shivering, he stripped off all of his clothes, and stood naked to warm himself for a moment in front of the fireplace before dressing. While the officers' quarters were serviced—often, in more than domestic ways—by the castle's staff, the majordomo was not so clueless as to send unwitting serving girls into the barracks at night, and body-modesty was not a luxury that Pirojil had been able to afford for longer than he cared to think about, anyway.

His wet clothes, along with the belt and scabbard, he hung up near the fireplace; they would be dry by morning.

The boots, though, would take at least a full day to dry properly, but he would be sure to put them on while still damp in the morning, over a couple of extra pair of thick wool socks to be sure that they didn't shrink too much. It was either that or replace them, and a few days of aching feet were far cheaper than a new pair of boots would have been.

It still made him feel strange, though. He was an officer, now, and could count on traveling on horseback or better, but he had been a line soldier long enough to know that taking care of his feet was no more optional than was taking care of his weapons.

And as to the sword and dagger? They could hardly go back in their wet scabbards, but that was no problem for tonight, and his sword belt could dry in front of the fire, too. Biemestren Castle or no Biemestren Castle, he would sleep with his sword and his dagger unsheathed, next to him, where he could find them in the dark.

He ran a well-bitten thumbnail down both sides of the sword's blade. Still razor sharp; he hadn't had to cut anybody or anything tonight, and hadn't for a long time. No need to get out the whetstone. The dagger, too, was sharp enough to shave the hairs off his forearm—they made that wonderful little popping sound when he located a patch of stubble.

Not that it mattered as much—if you were close enough to use a dagger, you could drive a blunt one hilt deep into a chest, after all. He knew men who worried about the edge being too sharp and brittle, although he never worried about that himself, as a chipped-bladed knife was just fine for killing, if not as good for shaving.

His pistols were still in his room, along with his rifle. It wasn't just the weather, of course—gunshots would have been inconveniently noisy for the sort of thing that Pirojil had hoped to have done this wet, miserable, wet, wasted, wet night.

A freshly polished silver tea service stood on a table in the middle of the common area, and an ancient silver pot, tarnished almost black, was kept warm over a low oil flame. He poured himself a cup and sipped at it—it was stale, and the tannin made his lips pucker, but it wasn't too bad—and added a splash of corn whiskey from a nearby cabinet, then gulped half of it down.

It burned his throat with only a gentle fire, and set up a pleasant warming in his gut. Both the whiskey and the tea were rather a lot better than he was used to. There were definitely some advantages to this new rank.

He sipped at the tea, made a face, then went back and, just for variety, retrieved a different mottled-glass bottle of whiskey, uncorked it, and took a drink directly from it. It burned as it went down, but not enough—somebody had been watering it.

Well, there were two ways to handle it. The simple way would be to just recork it and ignore it—it wasn't his problem, after all.

Instead, he walked to the nearest garderobe and poured all the watered whiskey out, then refilled the bottle with water, and carefully scratched three wavy lines, the Erendra symbol for water, on the bottle. He set it out on the bar, as a warning to whoever was watering the whiskey.

The first bottle, though, was still fine.

Pirojil took another drink, and looked for a long time at the silver tea service, and thought about how, since he was leaving tomorrow, he could steal that—it was worth easily a hundred times what he had hoped to earn in the city, below—and he would be long gone before anybody else noticed that it was missing.

He held the teapot in his hands. The palms of his hands were thick with calluses, and as long as he didn't use his relatively unmarked fingertips, it would warm him rather than burn him.

He *could* steal the pot, but of course he wouldn't, so there was no point in tormenting himself with the thought. He was just being silly; he put the pot back down on its stand over the flame.

Pirojil was, after all, taking the Emperor's pay, and while the stolen possessions of a footpad were fair game, he would no more steal from the Emperor than he would have stolen from the Cullinanes. Pirojil didn't have many compunctions about a lot of things—he had had to lose all those a long time ago—but there were some things that he just wouldn't do.

If you didn't have loyalty, you didn't have anything.

He walked to his room, closed the door and propped a chair in front of it, set his weapons out on the floor, next to the bed, where he could find them easily, and then lay down on the bed.

Sleep came quickly, as it usually did. Insomnia was another one of those luxuries that he had long been utterly unable to afford.

His sleep was filled with the screams of the dying, with visions of terrified white faces, round eyes, open mouths . . . and, always, always, the nauseating shit-stink of the freshly dead.

As usual.

Part 1

OPENING MOVES

1

The Widow's Walk

Put three nobles in a room for lunch, and before
the appetizers are served, you'll have four conspiracies. At least.

—Walter Slovotsky

The wind had begun to howl, threatening still more rain, but
the Dowager Empress neither quickened nor slowed her already sodden pace.

Beralyn Furnael simply refused to be affected; it was no more
and no less than that.

It wouldn't have been accurate to say that threats meant nothing
to her—in fact, the truth was entirely the opposite—but she was far
too old, and had far too long been far too stubborn, to let anything
as unimportant as the wind move her mind or her feet from any
path she had set them on, even if that path was something as familiar
and trivial as that of her nightly walk around the ramparts of Biemestren Castle.

Yes, there was some truth in what she said: that she needed her
exercise, and that the moment that she permitted her traitor body
to deny her that need, it would be time to have servants dig a deep
grave, next to her husband's, on the hilltop behind the castle that
had been theirs, and lie down beside him for all of eternity.

Beralyn didn't mind lying, but she didn't believe in doing so promiscuously.

It was also true—at least when Parliament was in session, or when there were other visiting nobles, which was more common—that her nightly walks gave her son the opportunity to spend some private time with one or more of the lords' and barons' daughters who, through no coincidence, always seemed to be accompanying their fathers to Biemestren Castle.

None of them had any use for a useless old woman, after all. She would just be in the way.

There was always talk, of course, about how the visits were inspired by the cultural life in the capital, about how theater and music and generally better craftsmanship could be found here than out in the baronies, and such. All that was, of course, true enough, and perhaps more than a tiny proportion of the apparently empty-headed young twits really had that as a main reason for coming to Biemestren, unlikely as that seemed.

Their fathers, she was sure, invariably had other goals in mind. There were always commercial bargains to be made, and political ones, as well, besides the obvious hope: the grand prize. Her son. The Emperor.

An unmarried emperor was an obvious prize, as well as both an obvious and subtle threat, and the easiest way for any of the barons to simultaneously gain that prize and neutralize that threat was to have him marry into the baron's family.

She wished one of them would succeed. Any one; it didn't much matter to her, as long as the girl was fertile—and Beralyn would have the Spidersect priest make sure of that, while supposedly examining her for her virginity. Beralyn couldn't have cared less about whether a young girl had spent her years keeping her knees together, or spreading them for every nobleman with a smooth smile—but whoever Thomen married had better be able to produce a son, and quickly, or the poor girl might just have an unfortunate accident, some dark night.

Hmm ... it would be better, come to think of it, if Beralyn didn't like the girl at first. While it wouldn't make a whit of difference in what she did, it would bother her to push somebody she actually liked down the stairs.

Below, in the courtyard surrounding the donjon—what everybody else called the keep, or the Emperor's House, although she preferred the older term—the remains of the Parliament encampment looked like what she remembered from her childhood as the remains of a party.

Biemestren Castle was large and roomy, certainly—easily four times the size of her late husband's keep in Barony Furnael—but it had never been intended to accommodate a meeting of even all of the Biemish barons and their entourages, much less the Holts, as well.

So, once again, despite the local nobles minors' homes being pressed into service, the castle had been painfully overcrowded and cramped during Parliament, and the kitchens had worked day and night to turn the constant flow of every sort of edible beast or vegetable imaginable through the castle gate into meals for those attending, while scullery men plied their trade behind the kitchens and beneath the castle's garderobes to carry the refuse out.

Now it seemed almost empty, and she wondered why that bothered her.

All of the multicolored pavilions had been taken down, and the tents and floors packed away against the next Parliament. The sodden ashes of four cooking fires had yet to be removed from the gravel-covered grounds, and she frowned at that—with the kitchens working night and day, what had the barons needed with their own cooks and cook fires? What *were* those lazy scullery men doing?

It would all be cleaned up and gone within a few days; Beralyn would make sure of that. And then it would be absolutely empty.

No, it would just seem that way—the castle was really never empty of visitors.

There were always delegations from Nyphien and the other of the Middle Lands coming and going—for talks, they said, but mainly to spy—as well as engineers from the Home colony, and the occasional contingent from one or more of the dwarven countries, mainly Endell, always eager to trade for what they saw as the unceasing flow of good iron and better steel from what she still thought of as Adahan City, but which had been renamed New Pittsburgh back when that horrible Karl Cullinane had been emperor. She didn't much like the people from Home—even apprentice engineers treated nobility with shocking informality, and Ranella, the Empire's chief engineer, felt free to walk into Thomen's presence whenever she felt like it—but Beralyn was willing to make allowances, given that it was the Home engineers who had built the blast furnaces in New Pittsburgh, and if the Emperor putting up with a few of the too-loud, too-self-assured swaggerers was part of the price, she could live with that.

And then there were the nobles minor, some from the Emperor's own barony, but even more from Arondael, and Tyrnael, and Niphael, and every other of the Biemish baronies, and increasingly the Holtish ones. They would never have the status of the ancient noble lines, which were tied to landownership, but many of the upstart merchant lords were actually wealthier than all but the richest of the old nobility.

The Imperial court was not only the commercial heart of the Empire, but the social center, as well. Most of the time, at least a dozen of the local nobles minor would be playing host to at least one young visitor from an outlying barony, usually a younger son or daughter of a father who already had an heir, and who had come to the capital for any of the number of declared reasons, and never for the declared but usual reason of seeking some suitable mate, preferably one of good breeding, better lands, and even better wealth, but who often would happily settle on a marriage that would unite some portion of the merchant concerns of the nobles minor.

Ancient laws of primogeniture forbade the division of major nobles' domains, but commercial enterprises were another matter.

It would be interesting to calculate how many marriages had been prematurely consummated—often marriages that had yet to be arranged—in the guest quarters of the donjon alone. And never mind how Lord Lerna's house in Biemestren seemed to regularly have more action going on than a lowertown brothel on payday. There was something about the air in the capital, presumably, that prevented young noblewomen from visiting the Spider for the potions that would have prevented pregnancy.

Pity that Thomen's own quarters were far too well guarded for that to happen there.

Yet another thing to blame Walter Slovotsky for, she decided.

Not that there weren't enough already.

She looked out, past the town below, toward the dark horizon, and for a moment she thought she could see a speck that might be the dragon, Ellegon, carrying that horrible Jason Cullinane back toward what was now known as Barony Cullinane, but which, to her, would always be Barony Furnael.

No, it wasn't. It was just some speck in her eye. Jason Cullinane and the dragon had left early in the morning, and were long gone.

She had heard that the dragon would soon be back to carry the new Baron Keranahan back to his barony, as well—the Cullinanes were awfully friendly with Forinel, suspiciously so—but any time that Ellegon was gone from Biemestren was a good time, from her point of view.

She had heard the dragon say, more than once, that it didn't like peeling back the mind of somebody that it didn't know, but that didn't mean it was true, and she kept iron control over her thoughts whenever the dragon was around, just as she kept the same iron control over her actions at all times.

Jason Cullinane was gone, and he would not be back soon. Not gone nearly far enough, nor permanently enough, but there was nothing that she could do about that.

At the moment.

She shook her head as she walked. Others would say that Jason Cullinane had been generous in abdicating, in giving the Imperial crown to her son, Thomen, accepting only the Furnael barony in exchange. Others believed that Jason Cullinane meant what he said: that Thomen was better suited to rule the Empire of Holtun-Bieme than Jason was.

Others were fools.

There was nothing generous in it. Thomen *had* been running the Empire, while Jason Cullinane, then the heir apparent, gallivanted about the Middle Lands, enjoying himself. Thomen had not only deserved the crown by birth—he had *earned* the crown, by hard work, over years, serving first that horrible Karl Cullinane, and then as Regent for that even more dangerous Jason Cullinane.

She had discussed that with him, many times, and he had always said the same thing: "Well, then, Mother, you should be very happy, because now I *have* the crown." And then, he would smile and would tap at the place on his forehead where the silver crown of Holtun-Bieme would rest on those rare state occasions when it was removed from the castle's strong room.

He ignored the truth. That was all there was to it; he simply chose to ignore the truth.

Thomen could be very bloody-minded when it came to other matters of state—he was wisely resisting too quickly giving control of most of the Holtish baronies back to the barons, and he watched the Treasury very closely, not paying out good gold for works projects of questionable worth, insisting that the barons involved would have to fund the projected rail line between Adahan's New Pittsburgh and Biemestren.

He even said that he had put off marrying for good reason, not out of a lack of time or interest. She believed that the way that little upstairs maid of his made a point of having difficulty sitting down most mornings was a reliable testament to his interest, just as Beralyn's insistence that Derinald regularly take the girl to the Spider had proclaimed loudly to that little piece of common trash that there would be no question, ever, of a bastard to complicate matters.

But, so he said, as long as the Emperor remained unmarried, and made it clear that he would choose his bride, when he did choose a bride, from whichever noble family—Holtish or Biemish— that he decided upon, then he would not have to put up with the conflicts that any choice would of necessity instigate.

There was, he said, no need to rush.

She disagreed, but his wasn't a stupid position to take. In the short run. Particularly if he had been sensible enough to be sure that the major danger to his throne was dead and buried.

Jason Cullinane was a real threat.

The awful truth—the truth that simply everybody knew, but which was spoken of only in whispers, when it was spoken of at all— was that if Jason Cullinane chose to take the crown back, he could do so overnight.

There was no doubt in her mind that he someday would.

Oh, he certainly could and no doubt would claim to have some noble purpose in mind when he did that.

Perhaps he would decide that Thomen was not removing the military governors and lifting the occupation of the Holtish baronies quickly enough, or perhaps he would convince himself that the Emperor's justice fell too heavily on common thieves or too lightly on some noble's son who had had his way with a few peasant girls.

Perhaps he would decide that the occasional bandito raids along the Kiaran border required a stronger response, or—if Thomen finally decided to bring those Kiaran dogs to heel—Jason Cullinane would decide that it should have been a weaker one.

Or, more than likely, Jason Cullinane would marry that disturbingly masculine little Slovotsky girl, and find that he wanted to gift his own son with an empire, and not just the barony.

Or, perhaps, it would be all of those.

But it was, of course, only a matter of time, not of whether.

She had said that to her son, more than once.

More than once she had explained that he simply had to produce an heir, that he had to intertwine himself and his blood with a noble family of impeccable lineage—Lady Leria Euar'den had been Beralyn's choice, but hers was hardly the only noble womb available for the purpose—and establish not just himself, but his line.

And for the sake of his blood and his lineage—and for the sake of the memory of his dead father and dead brother—he simply had to find some way to eliminate the Cullinane threat that Thomen, sweet Thomen, foolish Thomen, saw as an alliance rather than the danger that it most surely was.

Taking the barony away from Jason Cullinane would be a good start. There were collateral cousins of the Furnaels that had a claim to it, and while the Emperor would be a fool to promiscuously strip a baron of his title and lands, there was precedent for it in Bieme, as well as in Holtun.

No. That wouldn't do. She could fantasize about it, but for Thomen to take away the Cullinane barony would likely trigger the revolution that she feared, that she knew, would surely come one day.

Why wait for it? Why not simply cut the head off of the snake now?

Thomen would just shake his head, and say that he didn't think of Jason Cullinane as a threat, that Jason Cullinane didn't want to be emperor, anyway, or he wouldn't have abdicated at all, much less in Thomen's favor.

Just wait, he would say. Notice, he would say, time and time again, that Jason Cullinane himself had put off marrying that Slovotsky girl—or anybody else. Jason was waiting for *him*—let the Emperor marry first, let him produce an heir, and Jason Cullinane himself would stand guardian at the boy's naming.

It didn't matter to her if Thomen was right. Did anybody think that she would let Jason Cullinane within a dozen leagues of her grandchild?

In the meantime, what she was supposed to do, of course, was to wait, and be a useless old woman, and occupy herself with fripperies like the needlepoint that her old fingers were far too clumsy for, and managing the servants that were perfectly capable of being managed by the majordomo, and doing anything and everything except remembering that every time Parliament met it was just another convenient opportunity for Jason Cullinane to take her son's place.

Wait?

No. She would not wait for the inevitable ax to inevitably fall.

There was a sense of freedom, she thought with a private smile, in not doing what you were supposed to.

She trudged on.

A head leaned out of the guard shack at the southern rampart, then quickly ducked back in. There was no need for an alarm; it was just that useless old woman on her nightly walk, and if her tongue was still sharp, it was a simple matter to avoid her, after all.

The servants in the castle had taken to calling her the Walking Widow, she had heard, and calling the ramparts the Widow's Walk.

That was just fine with her.

Ahead, just at the top of the stairs that led up from the inner bailey, Baron Willen Tyrnael was waiting for her, as she had half-expected. Usually, he was among the first to leave after Parliament, pleading the exigencies of running a barony on the Nyphien border; this time, though, he was almost the last to go, and she had assumed that it was to find the opportunity to speak to her privately. It wouldn't be the first time that he had caught her on her nightly walk.

She reminded herself that she always had to watch herself around Tyrnael—the misleadingly gentle eyes and the tight, fierce mouth reminded her, far too much, of her dead husband, Zherr. Understandable, really, since all the Biemish barons were distantly related, in many cases having married each other's sisters or daughters. Even more understandable, really, that he would cultivate the resemblance to Zherr Furnael, the more easily to manipulate a lonely, useless old woman whom nobody took seriously.

She forced herself to concentrate on the ways in which he was different: how, for example, his hair and beard were always neatly trimmed, and close-cropped, not like Zherr's, who she had practically had to drag into the barbering chair.

"A good evening to you, my Empress," he said, awkwardly touching a knuckle to his forelock. That was the only awkward thing about him. Understandably, Willen Tyrnael had had little practice in showing obeisance; surprisingly, he had not put in the time or effort to learn how to do so deftly.

"Do you really think so, Willen?" She didn't pause in her pacing, but nodded at him, giving permission for him to walk along with her. "I find it a rather glum and utterly unpleasant evening, myself. Which is why most have turned in for the night, as I thought you had."

Most men would have nodded in agreement—Beralyn had long since become used to insincere agreement—but the baron shook his head.

"I did turn in, but I found myself not particularly sleepy, and I also find myself the last Holtish baron under the Emperor's roof"—he glanced at the dark sky above—"so to speak, and I find it pleasant not to share his attention with any of those Holtish barons in particular, nor, for that matter, others of the Biemish barons."

"Then why," she asked, "are you not spending time with him, and instead waiting here, out in the dark, for a useless old woman?"

"I would never think of you that way, and I am sure that I have never heard anybody call you that, my Empress, but be that as may . . ." Tyrnael eyed her for a moment. "I asked for some time with Thomen this evening, but I was told that he was closeted up with the baron minister and the lord proctor. And I'm told that he has an appointment with Forinel at the tenth hour, as well. Spending some time speaking with the new baron before Forinel takes his leave seems to be of some understandable importance."

If the idea of Thomen giving precedence to spending time with Bren Adahan and that awful Walter Slovotsky bothered the baron, it didn't show in his voice or face, any more than did his irritation at Forinel's presence. The sudden, surprising appearance of Forinel to claim his barony—just as Parliament and the Emperor were about to name Forinel's half-brother, Miron, as Baron Keranahan—seemed to bother him not at all.

It did, of course. But she admired his self-control; his self-control made them kindred spirits.

After all, Miron was obviously a creature of Tyrnael's. Whatever Tyrnael had spent, in promises or gold, to gain a hold over the would-be baron had, the instant that Forinel had appeared in Parliament, become a wasted investment, and Tyrnael didn't seem to be the sort of man who would fail to regret such a lost investment, and he most certainly wasn't the sort of lord who would fail to attempt to recoup such a lost investment, either.

"So you leave tomorrow?" she asked.

"I'd best. Not that I'm utterly indispensable to the running of my barony," he said, with a self-deprecating chuckle that almost seemed genuine. "After all, graveyards are filled with men who thought themselves to be indispensable. Still, I do like to think I'm of some use—and word has reached me that there are some problems on the Nyphien border."

"Oh?" "Problems" could mean anything short of a Nyph invasion.

"It's probably just more orcs, but I'd rather check it out myself. Delegating things is all well and good, but one of the lessons that the Old Emperor taught all of us is that there's no substitute for getting out and seeing for yourself." His smile broadened. "Of course, doing that once too many times killed him, but no policy is perfect, yes? And I did want to leave you with a present before I left."

"Oh?" She fingered the pendant around her neck—a finely polished garnet on a silver chain.

Cautious by policy as much as by temperament, she had had it examined by Henrad, Thomen's pet wizard, before ever putting it around her neck, and indeed it had been as innocuous as Tyrnael had claimed: it was touched with just a minor glamour, just the smallest of spells that tended to make sweet food taste a trifle sweeter, cold water feel a touch cooler, and the like.

"Another gem?" she asked, fingering the garnet.

His face was impassive, no hint that he recognized it as the Tyrnael family heirloom that he had given to her.

Sometimes she thought that he took his self-control too far, although that was something that could safely be said about Beralyn herself, as long as it wasn't said where such words could reach her ears.

"No," he said, smiling. "Something less appealing, I'm afraid, and more subtle. Would it surprise you, my Empress, to know that a couple of men—Nyphs, by the look of them—two days ago showed up in a tavern in the lower city, looking for your aide, Captain Derinald?"

So there it was.

She didn't bother asking him how he had found that out. There was no question that all of the barons—and certainly some of the minor lords, as well as others—had spies in the capital, and it didn't surprise her that Tyrnael's were among the best.

It *did* surprise her that the men Derinald had hired were stupid enough to come back to Biemestren, but it didn't surprise her much. Men were, by and large, such stupid creatures, and men who made their living soldiering for others were among the stupidest of men.

But she didn't let him see any fear in her face. She had realized, long before, that there were risks, and she did have a plan to protect her son from her own exposure.

Still, it was worth trying to see if she could find a way out of the swamp that Derinald's stupidity had put her in.

"Derinald," she said, "has some low-life friends, and that's long been known to me." It had long been useful to her, as well, although the usefulness of that, and of him, was clearly about to end.

It had all made sense at the time. Derinald had been supposed to have traveled incognito in Enkiar, not Nyphien—he was supposed to pass himself off as a Pandathaway Guild slaver, and she had given him enough gold to make that credible—but he was never quite as clever as he seemed to think he was, and this time his stupidity was going to be expensive.

Tyrnael smiled. "I hadn't thought much of it, until then."

"I had nothing to do with it. Everybody knows that it was the Slavers Guild that tried to have Jason Cullinane assassinated, after all."

His smile broadened. "What everybody knows and what is true are so often such different things. Yes, hired assassins trying to kill a Cullinane spoke of the Pandathaway Slavers Guild, after all. But the timing was interesting."

Yes, it was. Just before Parliament. Just before another chance for Jason Cullinane to take back the crown, despite his protestations that he supported Thomen.

Still, she had expected that the blame would fall on the Slavers Guild, and it had, of course.

Until now.

"Yes." She allowed herself a slight nod. "How interesting. And I suppose that these, these thugs have all sorts of interesting stories to tell."

"Stories?" Tyrnael affected to look puzzled. "About what? I'm afraid I don't understand. Surely there will be no stories about the Dowager Empress's aide having solicited them to murder a baron on his way to Parliament, I'd imagine, if that's what you're worrying about."

So: there it was, all out in the open, or, at least, as out in the open as Tyrnael wanted it to be at the moment.

He thought that she was utterly at his mercy, but she wasn't.

Rumors and suspicions were one thing, but let some reliable word leak out that the Emperor—or the Emperor's mother, it would make no difference—had tried to have any one of the barons murdered, and the outcry could shake the crown right off Thomen's head.

Jason Cullinane's father had earned far more than his share of loyalty among the Biemish barons by turning the tide in the war against Holtun, and even more than that among the Holtish barons by letting them keep their titles and most of their properties, even under the occupation. They had expected, after all, that the conquering Biemish would do to them what they had been busily trying to do to the Biemish, before the war had turned. Cart off the excess peasants and sell them to slavers; kill most of the Holtish nobility, and reduce the rest to nobles minor, at most, and distribute lands and titles among the Biemish conquerors.

But Karl Cullinane hadn't done that, and he had not just forced his will on the Biemish barons—although he had—but eventually even persuaded them that welding Holtun and Bieme together would leave the created Empire stronger than would a Bieme that would have to spend the next generations digesting Holtun.

She was glad he was dead, but she was far too honest to deny to herself that he had earned himself some of that loyalty, and that was the way of it—loyalty could be transferred from father to son, and Thomen's father was long gone.

Still, it was hardly just a matter of loyalty. Loyalty was a far weaker staff to lean on than self-interest. If the Emperor could have any one of the barons assassinated, why, he could have any other of the barons assassinated.

It wasn't just their own necks that would concern them, of course. They would be as worried about their own heirs' necks, as well, just as Beralyn was concerned about Thomen's.

There was a simple solution, of course.

The only trail led through Derinald to her. So let it end with her, and let Derinald flee for his life. With any luck, the dolt would fall from his horse and break his neck.

There was no reason to wait, and there were advantages to doing it here and now.

It would just be a matter of flinging herself over the ramparts, to the hard stones below. Then let Tyrnael explain how the Empress had managed to stumble and fall over the stone railing that rose to her mid-chest.

She wished she could be there to see it, but, of course, if she was, there would be nothing to see.

It would have been better to shout out, "Please stop," or "Please don't hurt me," or "He's going to throw me over the railing, help," but not only would that be beneath her dignity, it would also give him a warning.

She regretted that. It would be good to be sure to take him with her, and that cry would surely do it.

There was much to regret, but no time to regret it.

But as she started to move, his hand snaked out and gripped her wrist tightly, almost hard enough to break bones.

"No," he said, "you misunderstand me."

She didn't bother to pull against his much greater strength. There wouldn't be any point, and Beralyn never believed in useless gestures.

"Release me, now," she said, forcing herself to keep her voice low and level, "or I'll call for the guard."

"And tell them what? That you tried to kill yourself when I told you I know that you tried to have Baron Cullinane assassinated? Let's not be silly, my Empress." He shook his head. "Ah," Tyrnael said, "you have such admirable bloody-mindedness in you. Your son didn't inherit that from you, more's the pity." He raised a finger. "Promise to stay and hear me out, and I'll release your hand. Let me speak, and then do what you will."

"I said—"

"I want your word. I would have been willing to wager anything on your husband's word, and I know you wouldn't dishonor the word of the Furnaels—so give me your promise, your word, on your family honor. It's not much to ask, after all. Surely, surely you can spare me a moment's attention. Then," he said with a smile, "if you ab-solutely *insist* on shattering your body on the stones below, I'll ask that you at least give me a few moments to make my escape before you do."

After a moment, she nodded. "You have my word. For what it's worth."

"I wouldn't dare to presume that the Dowager Empress's word

was not her bond." He released her wrist, but didn't take a step back. "Don't blame Derinald," he said, "any more than you'd blame the knife you chose because it wasn't sufficiently sharp for the task. Nor were the men he found—in Nyphien, was it?—sufficiently sharp for their task. Still, the poor fellows appear to have disappeared, and I don't think they'll ever be seen again."

"Unless, of course, I don't do whatever you ask me, whenever you ask it."

"You misunderstand me, I think. I meant what I said: I think that they'll never be seen in Biemestren again, regardless of what happens between you and me. You're mistaken if you think I'm trying to blackmail you."

He shook his head. "The truth is I'm trying to protect you. And your son. And the Empire. You have been foolish, my Empress, and that foolishness could redound to the detriment of yourself, of your son, and of the Empire. You seem to trust too little, and when you do, you trust the wrong people. That last is a lethal failing, and one I hope you'll repent of—just as I hope you realize that you'd be unwise to mention to Derinald that we've talked, or he's liable to panic and start saying all sorts of silly things, and not think until it was too late that that would cost him his scrawny neck."

"And your gift is?" she asked. "No, let's not mince about the subject: your price is?"

"No, there is no price." He shook his head, again. "You don't understand me at all, my Empress. I've little fondness for the Cullinanes, and thought—and think—that the crown should have been mine when Jason decided to abdicate. But that is what he decided, and that's how it is, and I'd be a fool to try to change that for my own benefit. I may be many things, but I'm not a fool.

"The thing is, my Empress, that I actually care about the kingdom and the Empire. I'm not a sentimental man—that seems to run in the Furnael line, not mine—but we've had a time of peace, and of power. Still, still the world is a dangerous place, and it seems to me that the Empire itself is the wall that keeps some of that danger out.

"I like walls, my Empress. They have such a nice way of keeping things out, don't you agree?" He waited a moment for her to answer, but when she didn't, he went on: "So it would be a bad thing, I think, if it were to become known what you've done, or what you will do." He smiled knowingly. "So, my gift to you is this: my finger, held to my lips," he said, touching his finger to his lips.

She cocked her head to one side. "Surely, Baron, you're not telling me that there is to be no price to pay for that . . . gift?"

"You wound me to the heart, my Empress, truly you do." He shook his head, sadly. "I'm hardly a merchant, engaged in common trade, balancing favors and obligations on either side of a scale. Yes, when you think your voice will be heard, I'd very much like it raised in support, say, of maintaining the occupation in Holtish baronies, and it would bother me not at all if you were to summon my daughter, Greta, to wait upon your most impressive Imperial person—"

"Ah. So you'd like an Emperor for a son-in-law, wouldn't you?"

"Who would not? If the crown is never to sit on my head, or one of my sons', a grandson's head would surely do." He shook his head, sadly. "Sadly, I doubt you could prevail upon your son to see her in any other light than that he would choose himself. No, I'd not ask you to try to foist her on him—you're his mother, after all, and I'd much rather you explain how unsuitable she is. How she has no grace, does not bathe well or frequently, does not—well, whatever flaws you can find in her, particularly if they are flaws that she does not indeed have." He thought on the matter for a moment. "And it might be best if the Lady Leria were to be here, too—and for you to seem to push her at your son, perhaps?"

"She is here now, and she doesn't do anything but make little calf eyes at that Forinel."

He nodded. "They have been long separated, and that's under-standable—but she is about to leave for Keranahan, with her be-trothed." He pursed his lips. "Let her settle in for a tenday or two, and then send for her, at the same time you send for my Greta. I think my Greta will acquit herself adequately—she's hardly a coun-try lady, untutored in the gentle arts." He spread his hands. "There's no guarantee, but it's worth the effort of writing a letter, is it not?"

She nodded. It might work. "And if my telling Thomen that your Greta is totally unsuitable does not make her more attractive to him—if he picks, instead, this Leria chit, or some other girl . . . ?"

"Friends do not require each other to be successful; but, of course, friends do make efforts on behalf of their friends. Do they not?" His smile broadened. "Regardless, I hope you will still look upon me as a friend and ally, for that I surely am. Not just a mer-chant to whom you owe a debt. A friend, for whom you would willingly do a favor, as a friend often does for another." He bowed slightly. "And I'd ask another favor more of you."

"Yes?"

"The *next* time," he said, quietly, but with some heat, "the next time and *any* time that you find it expedient to have some throat slit, I'd take it as a great personal favor if you'd simply chalk the name, say," he went on, looking around, "here, on this buttress, rather than trusting that idiot Derinald to do better in the future than he has in the past."

She had always assumed that all—or at least most—of the bar-ons had spies in the castle. It would be interesting, if she had any servants that she could trust—Derinald clearly wouldn't do—to keep watch on that buttress, and see who read the scrawl.

"I can do that," she said. "But if the name that I scrawl is Jason Cullinane?"

"No, I don't think it will be." He shook his head. "I think that would be a very bad name to scrawl, and I hope you will trust me on this."

No, she didn't think that would be a bad name to scrawl. She thought it was, in fact, the perfect name to scrawl.

"Very well," she said.

"It's good for friends to trust each other," he said. He scratched his nose, then looked at his finger, as though he had never seen it before. "It may happen someday that I might say something that would frighten you, anger you, but I ask now that you would hear me out, then and always. Perhaps the only warning you will have is me scratching my nose—perhaps there will be none. But always, *always*, I hope, as a friend, my dear Beralyn, you will hear me out, as one friend does for another."

"And if your nose simply itches?"

He shook his head. "My nose never simply itches."

"And the . . . attack on Jason Cullinane? The one that you seem to suggest that I might have had something to do with, but which we all know failed miserably, embarrassingly, totally?"

He reached out and patted her hand. "Why, I'm sure that was just the Slavers Guild, aren't you? Pandathaway is so far away, and even if the Slavers Guildmaster were right here, right now, swearing his innocence on his sword, he wouldn't be believed."

She didn't answer.

"I must finish my walk," she said.

"Then I'll ask you one last favor," he said. "If I may presume again upon our friendship."

"Yes?"

"I think it would be best if we simply forget we had this conversation, don't you?"

There was something overly self-satisfied about the way he asked that, something that seemed very atypical for Tyrnael. He usually concealed his feelings much better.

"I see no problem," she said. "You came to bid me a good night before I turned in, and we exchanged a few pleasantries. In fact, since I've not shown your previous gift to anybody, it might be that you gave it to me tonight." That, of course, was a lie, but not much of one—she had only shown it to Henrad, and the wizard wouldn't talk. "Why would I need to forget that?"

"No reason. No reason at all, dear Beralyn." He touched his finger to his forelock, again. "In that case, I'll bid you a very good night, my dear Empress." He scratched his nose, again, and bowed, once again, this time more deeply, and waited patiently, politely, while she walked away.

Well.

There would have to be another way to deal with the Jason Cullinane problem, but the world was full of throats that her son, her sentimental son, was too weak to have slit.

The only question was where and how to start.

After, of course, she scrawled the name "Derinald" on the buttress.

The trouble with being Emperor, Thomen Furnael decided, and not for the first time, was the hours.

Morning always began too early, with some crisis in the making—whether it was an overnight telegram from Tyrnael, about rumblings on the Nyphien border, and laconic reflections about the relative sizes of the forces just across the border; word from Becca that Ranella had been waiting for hours (she apparently never slept) to harangue him about the need for more dwarven miners in Adahan, complete with sniffs about how *she* didn't think that King Daherrin was actually running out of dwarves, although *somebody* apparently did, given what kind of pay Daherrin was asking; and, always, proctors' and bursars' reports that his minister, Bren Adahan, or the Imperial proctor, Walter Slovotsky, should have caught and handled before they reached the Emperor's desk . . .

And that was just the morning.

The days had a way of filling up, although with Parliament now adjourned until fall, and almost all of the barons back where they should be, his work would be real work, at least for a while, and less balancing off of all those irritating, competing interests and personalities—at least in person—and some of that could be laid off on Bren and Walter.

They had asked for—demanded—the jobs as minister and proctor, and Thomen had no objection to letting them do some of the work.

But Bren Adahan was off in New Pittsburgh, and while there were things that the Emperor could count on his Lord Proctor for, paperwork wasn't among them.

Which was why Thomen Furnael was, well after midnight, still at his desk, even though the exquisitely neat printing of the detailed report as to what Ranella's railroad had already cost—and never mind, for a moment, what it was going to cost before Biemestren and New Pittsburgh were finally linked by rail—was starting to blur in front of his eyes, even before he got to the bottom line.

And without so much as a league of track being laid, except for the short test track outside of New Pittsburgh, and with what she lightheartedly referred to as her Mark III steam engine still barely able to pull its own weight.

I guess it isn't steam engine time, quite yet, eh? sounded in his head.

Ellegon? He raised his head. The dragon sounded nearby.

*No, some *other* dragon. Humans in the Eren regions are so *very* hospitable that I'm stunned that you aren't utterly knee-deep in scales.*

Thomen smiled. "Would a quick apology do?" he asked, quietly. He didn't even have to speak out loud, but he preferred to. A man's thoughts should be his own, and not shared unless he spoke.

I'll try harder not to listen, then, Ellegon said.

Neither Thomen, personally, nor anybody else in Holtun or Bieme, had anything to apologize to Ellegon for—Ellegon had, granted, spent a couple of centuries chained in the sewage pit in Pandathaway, forced to flame the city's wastes into ash or be buried in offal, but that was Pandathaway, not the Empire, after all, and things were different here.

I guess I should admire your detachment, but I'm not sure that I do.

"Well, then, I'm sorry," he said. He set down the papers, stood, stretched, and walked to the window.

It's not your fault, Thomen.

"No, but I'm still sorry. Really," he said.

I know.

Beyond the bars, the dragon stood in the courtyard, stretching his neck out to shoot a gout of flame skyward. Ellegon preened himself, and stretched his wings, then turned his head toward where Thomen stood.

"So," Thomen said. "Last I heard, you were going to fly Baron Keranahan and his party home tomorrow."

Ellegon flicked his wings; a sort of draconic shrug. *Jason asked me to. You have some objection?*

Thomen shook his head. "No, no objection—just some petty jealousy. I'm stuck in this castle, while Jason is back in his barony, probably already out hunting, and—"

And Lady Leria is also returning to Keranahan, with her betrothed. Does that bother you?

Thomen's jaw tightened. "Read my mind if you want to know that badly."

Yes, Thomen had been more than slightly attracted to Leria, and had entertained the possibility of marrying her, which made sense for reasons of state, as well. Thomen's main task, as he saw it, was to bind Holtun and Bieme together, and for him to marry a girl of an old Euar'den family might help to do that.

His private thoughts were none of anyone else's concern.

°My turn to apologize, I expect,° Ellegon said.

Thomen forced himself to unclench. He was just tired, and over-reacting. Complaining about Ellegon reading his mind was silly. It was natural for the dragon to do that—

°At least with friends, and at least on the surface level,° Ellegon said. °I can sense that there are some things you're trying hard not to think about—some painful memories, perhaps, or some things you're ashamed of, possibly—but I'm not looking at those, Thomen. Not that it would matter if I did. And not that I would tell anybody, either.°

Thomen nodded. "So, you're back to carry the baron and his lady home?"

°Yes. But I made it a point to be a little early. They won't be ready to leave until morning, unless I wake them up now, and I'm not of a mind to, for any number of reasons.°

"Such as?"

°Can you keep a secret?°

"Yes."

°Well, so can I. In any case, they're not leaving until morning, and . . . °

"And?"

°And I was wondering if the Emperor can drag himself away from his paperwork for a short ride.°

"For what? Is there something—"

°No, there's nothing wrong. Not everything has to be a problem, or a solution, after all. I just thought you might like a break.°

"No important affair of state?"

°No. No surprise inspection of the guard in Tyrnael; no quick survey of wood stock in Adahan; nobody to talk to except me, and nothing to do, except maybe look at the river from cloud level; it's pretty under the starlight, and the faerie lights over Kernat are lovely tonight. No plans—although I might swoop down and swoop up a sheep, because I'm getting hungry—just for fun.*

Thomen looked back at the stack of paper on his desk. It hadn't gotten any smaller while he had been chatting with the dragon. He was the Emperor, after all, and he had responsibilities. And he was a grown man, and had been, for years, and not a boy, who could simply take off whenever he wanted to, to do whatever he wanted to.

Sure you can. As long as you don't do it very often. I warn you, though: your mother will have a fit.

Thomen smiled. You didn't have to read minds to know that. "You just talked me into it."

A gout of flame roared skyward. *I thought that would do it. Dress warm; it's cold up there.*

2

Homecoming I

> The old saw says that the first time is an acci-
> dent, the second time a coincidence, and the
> third time enemy action. As a matter of policy,
> I'm suspicious of accidents, and I don't believe
> in coincidences.
>
> —Walter Slovotsky

The wind rushed by too fast, too hard, driving tears from his
eyes back into his ears.

Or whoever's ears they really were.

These ears sat too closely to his head, and where there should
have been a ridge of scar tissue at the top of the left one, there was
only smooth skin.

The only way that they felt like his ears was that they felt wet.

At least he had long since stopped throwing up—what little he
had had of breakfast had been spread over three baronies, and even
the dry retching had stopped.

Had he known he would be riding on dragonback, he wouldn't
have had as much as a sip of water that morning. He had ridden on
dragonback before, a few times, and those few times were far too
many, as far as his stomach was concerned.

Fortunately for you, lots of people get airsick. There's nothing distinctive—or revealing—in that. The dragon's mental voice was, for once, at least vaguely sympathetic instead of acidly sarcastic.

No, that's only in your mind, Kethol—or should I be calling you Forinel?

He didn't have a smart answer to that, and if he did, he wouldn't have given it anyway—not to the dragon, of all creatures. Kethol had spent little time around the dragon—as little as possible—and being around Ellegon always made him nervous.

I do have that tendency, don't I?

That was understandable. The dragon was a huge beast, its yellowed teeth the size of daggers, and its fiery breath could incinerate a man in moments—Kethol had seen it do just that—or send a man, or several men, flying through the air, broken like a child's shattered toy, with one blow from a tree-trunk leg.

The physical fear was bad enough for most, but it was different for Kethol.

No, it wasn't a matter of that kind of fear, not really. Kethol was perfectly capable of feeling fear—the bitter, metallic taste in his mouth, the pounding of his heart in his chest, the way that the palms of his hands tended to sweat so that he had to force himself not to grip the hilt of his sword or the shaft of his bow too tightly . . .

Those were all familiar to him.

But he was used to that. That was normal, natural; fear was simply part of the job. He had been a simple soldier since he was barely old enough to shave, and he'd been damn good at it—and damn lucky, as well—in order to have survived this long.

No, he was used to danger, even though he would never have said that out loud, particularly in front of Leria, for fear of sounding boastful.

*Well, yes, it would sound boastful—but I would say that it's true enough, although not so unusual that you should sprain your arm patting yourself on the back over it. Many of your kind have courage. It's a lot more common than, say, wisdom. As for me, I think wisdom is better.°

But what he wasn't used to was pretending to be something that he was not, and the dragon—and only a few others—knew just what a fraud he was.

°Get used to it. Dragons aren't much good at forgetting, either.°

He would have to get used to it, just as he had to get used to looking at fingers that were a trifle shorter and slimmer than they ought to be, or at arms and legs and a chest that were almost devoid of the scars that they should have had, at a face in the mirror that frowned when he frowned, smiled when he smiled, winced when he cut himself, but he could not make himself believe was his.

°You had better start.°

That was easier for Ellegon to say than it was for Kethol to do. The elven wizards in Therranj had changed him, yes, with magic far beyond what any human wizards could do, with spells that didn't merely create a seeming, the way that Erenor could, but which had altered his flesh irrevocably.

He looked just like Forinel.

Physically, he *was* Forinel, from the the widow's peak that stubbornly defied his receding hairline, to the thick black mat of hair that covered his chest and arms, down to the missing toenail on the little toe of his left foot.

He looked like Forinel, but that was only on the outside.

And it was a lie.

Behind him, Leria leaned forward to place her mouth next to his ear. He didn't resent that she had taken naturally to riding on Ellegon's back, and in fact was relieved—there was nothing he could have done to protect her from the nausea that racked his guts.

"There's the Nifet River," she said, pointing, "and the Ulter Hills begin just beyond, right at the horizon. We fly quickly across farmland and over Dereneyl, and we'll be at the Residence before noon."

Or perhaps not. I think it would be a good idea to drop you off in Dereneyl, since we're not expected. Pirojil and Erenor agree.

Nobody had asked him, and that was understandable.

Kethol's jaw clenched so hard that it hurt. He'd been an idiot to agree to take this imposture on.

But it was either that, or let the son and heir of the bitch that murdered Durine become Baron Keranahan. Elanee was dead, but even dead, she would have won. Forinel couldn't return to the Empire to claim the barony, not with the elven woman that he had married in Therranj, and particularly not with their half-breed child.

Parliament and the Emperor had been about to award Barony Keranahan to Miron, Forinel's half-brother—Elanee's son—and if there had been nobody to take Forinel's place, that is just what would have happened.

That was unacceptable.

Kethol didn't mind the thought of dying, but losing?

No.

He had to keep telling himself that, that that was the reason why he had agreed, and that it had nothing to do with the way Leria looked at him, the way that her hands and eyes had rested on his hands and eyes. It had nothing to do with the definite certainty that if he did not agree, Leria would find herself in another man's bed.

It couldn't be that, after all. She was too good, too fine for the likes of him, and she belonged in a better man's bed, in a higher-born man's bed.

No. He had to make it just another way to fight.

He knew fighting, and he was good at it.

And what do you say to the notion of Dereneyl as the destination, Baron? It's your call.

There was no trace at all of sarcasm in Ellegon's mental voice.

But no, it wasn't his choice. He was just an imposter. The others were in charge, not him.

So let it be Dereneyl, he thought.

°I'm so glad you agree,° the dragon said, °because I was going to drop you off in Dereneyl anyway.°

Spiraling down out of the sky so fast that it made Kethol dizzy, the dragon came to a steep, bumpy landing within the inner walls of the keep.

It must have rained much more heavily here last night than it had in Biemestren—the wind from the dragon's buffeting wings sent a spray of water from the ground into the air, soaking Kethol thoroughly.

He'd live; he had been wet before.

°Everybody off, and quickly.°

It was risky for Ellegon to drop them off there at all—the Empire in general and Ellegon in particular had enemies, and there was always the chance that some fool with a dragonbane-tipped arrow or spear would be lurking about. A fool, yes—Pandathaway could offer a hundred times the killer's weight in gold, but collecting it would be another matter, after all.

Kethol quickly unstrapped himself and made his way down the dragon's broad sides, fingers and toes digging into the rough surface of the thick scales for purchase. When he reached the ground, his knees trembled and threatened to buckle beneath him, but he tensed up, and forced them to lock in place.

He quickly handed Leria down, releasing her as soon as he decently could. It wasn't right, after all, that somebody like him should be touching someone like her.

She still took his breath away.

It wasn't just the regular features, the pert little nose and full red lips, the golden hair, bound up for travel, leaving her long neck bare. It wasn't even the way that she had felt in his arms, her tongue warm in his mouth.

No. It was the way that she had always treated him and Pirojil and Durine like they were real people, and not just blood-spattered instruments. More: it was preposterous, silly little things, like how she couldn't keep her hands from tending a campfire at night, or how, when she awoke in the morning to find him asleep—or so she thought—across her doorway, she would shake her head and smile.

(Erenor often said, in muttered conversation with Pirojil that Kethol pretended not to hear, that it had been a foregone conclusion that Kethol would fall in love with the first woman who smiled at him, but that wasn't true. Kethol had been in service to the Cullinane family for years, and had guarded both the late Emperor's adopted daughter and his wife, and all of them had smiled at him, often, and while he certainly had liked them all, not one of them haunted his dreams by night.

(Then again, what Erenor said and what was true only coincided by accident.)

Pirojil was down almost as quickly as Kethol was, and was at his side, with Erenor not far behind. The two of them made an unlikely pair—Pirojil, large, misshapen, and ugly; Erenor almost a caricature of a wizard, with a lined, bearded face partially concealed in the hood of his gray robes.

Appearances were sometimes deceiving.

Kethol *hoped* that appearances were sometimes deceiving, although he couldn't for the life of him understand why somebody didn't take a quick look at him and start shouting, "Imposter!"

There was a commotion along the ramparts, but the soldiers over by the main gate and the stableboys and house girls in their noontime game of touched-you-last quickly disappeared from sight, the soldiers quietly ducking into the guard shack, some of the children running for the darkness of the stable, others disappearing behind the bulk of the keep itself.

Erenor shook his head and laughed. He had an easy laugh, a

laugh that sounded sincere, a laugh that probably was sincere every now and then, if only by accident. Kethol had just had to get used to that about Erenor, although he didn't have to like it, and he didn't.

"Standing orders," Erenor said, "are often obeyed when they consist of making yourself quickly absent when a flame-breathing dragon plops down out of the sky."

"Shut up," Pirojil said. "Just get the bags unhooked," he added, although it was hardly necessary—Erenor's nimble fingers were already working on the straps.

°It wouldn't bother me at all if you were to do that a little more quickly,° Ellegon said. °Or maybe a lot more quickly.°

While there was a good chance that the keep was secure, it was vanishingly unlikely that there was nobody in the town below greedy and reckless enough to try to earn the standing Pandathaway Slavers Guild reward for bringing Ellegon down. Dragons were rare in the Eren regions in general, and unknown—well, almost unknown—in the Middle Lands in particular.

Even now, it was entirely possible that nervous fingers were, somewhere, unwrapping a hidden arrow or crossbow bolt, and dipping its tip in a forbidden pot of dragonbane extract before nervously fitting it to a taut string.

"You're worried about being shot at, I take it?" Erenor asked.

°No.° The dragon's head curled on its long neck to eye the wizard, its dinner-plate–sized eyes yellow and unblinking. °I just love getting poisoned, don't you?°

"I'd say sarcasm ill becomes you, Ellegon, but actually, I must admit that I rather like it." Erenor stepped back. "And, in this, as in so much else, I think I may be of some help. Are you ready to go?"

°I was ready to go before I came.°

"Then . . ."

The dragon straightened, and Kethol put his hand on Leria's arm, urging her back and away, trying not to blush when she smiled, and nodded, and folded her warm, soft hand over his callused one.

Erenor's eyes seem to lose focus, and his smiling face became distant and almost expressionless. His thin, parched lips parted slightly, and harsh, guttural syllables began to issue forth.

This wasn't the first time, or the forty-first time, that Kethol had heard a wizard pronouncing a spell. Despite knowing better, he tried to remember the syllables, to put them together into words—if you could remember the words, you could speak the words, and if you could speak the words, you could pronounce the spell, and if you could pronounce the spell, you could work the magic—but the wizard's words vanished on the surface of his mind, skittering about like drops of water on a hot frying pan before they evaporated . . . gone, forgotten, not merely unremembered but unrememberable.

The spell ended with a sharp, one-syllable exclamation.

The sunlight, flashing on pools of water left from the overnight rain, suddenly became brighter, brighter than the sun itself, a white light that dazzled not only the eyes but the mind.

The wind from the dragon's wings beat hard against Kethol, and it was all he could do to keep from being thrown from his feet. His eyes dazzled, he more felt than saw the dragon take to the air.

Thank you, Erenor, the dragon said, its mental voice already starting to grow more distant.

"My pleasure," Erenor said. "And, of course, it's not merely my pleasure—it would be terribly uncomfortable, at least for a very short moment, to have several tons of dead dragon falling out of the sky and landing on my all-too-fragile flesh."

Yes, it would, at that.

Then, in an eyeblink, the blinding light was gone, and Kethol looked back to see the dragon circling above, gaining altitude as he did, huge leathery wings flapping madly until Ellegon stretched his wings and banked, flying off to the west.

°Good luck,° Ellegon said, his mental voice taking on the muted, formal tone that told Kethol that it was intended for all ears—minds—around, and not only his.

°Welcome home, Forinel, Baron Keranahan—it has been a pleasure serving you. And as Karl Cullinane used to say, 'the next time you fly, please be sure to consider flying on Ellegon Airlines.'°

Whatever that meant. Kethol—and Durine and Pirojil—had been the only ones of the Old Emperor's bodyguards to survive Karl Cullinane's Last Ride, but he had never quite understood half of what the Old Emperor said.

Wings stretched out, the dragon flew low over a far ridge, and then it was gone.

Kethol found that he still had his hand folded over Leria's, so he let his hands drop down by his sides.

Erenor chuckled, leaning his head close to Pirojil. "Not a bad entrance, eh?"

Erenor was far too easily amused, Pirojil decided, with the usual irritation.

Faces were already starting to peek out of windows and doorways, and one immensely fat woman—a cook, by the look of the grease-spattered apron—even went so far as to carry a bucket of something out, to dump it on the slop pile next to the stables before, after a quick glare at the newcomers, scurrying back in.

Whatever it was, Pirojil thought, must have smelled awfully horrid for her to be so willing to venture out. The idea of eating here wasn't at all appealing, if even the cooks couldn't stand the smell.

Pirojil wasn't surprised that none of the soldiers had chosen to come out of the barracks at the far end of the courtyard, or from any of the guard posts at the corner towers. A new arrival was always of some interest in an outlying outpost—and to Imperial troops, an outpost didn't get much more outlying than Barony Keranahan—but arrival by dragonback suggested that the new arrivals were of some great importance, and it never took even a new soldier long to learn that it was wisest to at least try to be in another place when something important was going on.

Pirojil wished he was in another place.

The front door of the keep stood open, cool, dark, and inviting. Normally, there should have been a pair of soldiers on guard, and Pirojil had been wondering whether they would be standing in the black leather corselets that would have them sweating like hogs in the hot sun. Pirojil had stood his share of watches in that leather armor, which never seemed to lose the reek of the boiling vinegar that had turned the leather stone-hard and solid black.

Not that you minded the smell when it caught the edge of an enemy's blade.

He had silently bet with himself that the watchmen wouldn't be in armor, that they would just be dressed in linen tunics and breeches, and he hadn't decided whether that would mean that the discipline among the occupation troops was slack, or that Treseen was smart enough to insist that his men not suffer to no particular end.

It did mean, of course, that they weren't of the elite Emperor's Own, because then they would have been wearing their shiny steel breastplates—or, at least, having them nearby, where lesser men could admire them—although likely not armored head to toe.

Pirojil was beginning to be annoyed at the lack of reception.

Ellegon or no Ellegon, protocol would have called for some-body—somebody important—to come out and greet such visitors, and Pirojil was willing to wait for that to happen . . . until Kethol—until *Forinel* started to stoop to pick up his own rucksack.

Pirojil snatched it away from him.

Idiot.

"Allow me, Your Lordship," he said, only the look in his eyes adding: *You idiot—nobles don't carry their own bags.*

He forced himself not to shake his head in disgust. Leria had been trying to teach Kethol how to be a noble, but beyond getting him to learn how to use an eating prong with a proper flourish, and getting him to stop wiping his nose on his sleeve, she had been less than remarkably successful.

For the time being, his awkwardness could be explained away by Forinel's long absence from Holtun and Bieme, but in the long run, it could easily get them all hanged.

Leria laid a gentle hand on Forinel's arm, and he met her smile with an expression that reminded Pirojil of a well-trained dog waiting for permission to eat from its bowl.

"Bide a moment, please, Forinel," she said. "I'm sure it's just an oversight that you've yet to be greeted properly—do let us wait, and send . . . someone in to announce your presence."

"A servant, perhaps?" Erenor asked. "It's always so very pleasant to have a servant, I've found. And, well, since the closest thing we have to that is Pirojil, here, I guess he'll have to do. You may have the honor of carrying the bags, good Pirojil."

Erenor smiled as he handed his own rucksack to Pirojil, and then loaded Leria's on top of the pile. Wizards didn't carry their own gear, either, save for the small black leather bag that contained Erenor's spell books, and which never seemed to leave his hands.

"I thank you for your help, good Pirojil. We shall meet you inside," Erenor said.

Pirojil didn't have to ask how Erenor felt about their roles having been reversed, about how it was Pirojil playing the servant—a captain of march, in theory, but a servant in practice, at least for the moment—instead of Erenor. Erenor visibly enjoyed it. Too much.

Pirojil would have enjoyed beating Erenor's face into a bloody pulp, but that was not on today's schedule, apparently.

Pirojil tried to act as though he didn't much care, which would have been somewhat easier at the moment if he wasn't trying to balance four bags as he walked.

Cursing silently, unable to see his own feet, Pirojil staggered up the steps, almost falling when he reached the top one.

Old Tarnell was waiting for him just inside the door.

He was overdue for some new clothes: his tunic fit him too loosely over the chest and bulged at the belly enough to threaten popping buttons.

But a shiny new bit of silver braid along his shoulder seam proclaimed him the governor's aide, and it matched the silver captain's braid on his collar. That and the two officers' pistols on his belt were the only changes that Pirojil could see: the deep creases in Tarnell's lined face hadn't deepened, nor had the plain wooden pommel of his sword's wire-wrapped hilt been replaced by something more gaudy.

It was a standard barracks joke that the only thing that moved across the ground faster than a good Nyphien warhorse was a newly made captain on his way to the armorer to buy a proper officer's saber, but Tarnell had kept his own weapon with his new rank.

Pirojil sympathized with that—if he was Tarnell, he wouldn't have fucked with something that had served him that well for that long out of anything this side of necessity.

And, in fact, he hadn't, and he had no intention of doing so. The sword at Pirojil's own waist was still the one he had carried for years: straight and double-edged, not a curved officer's saber. Its hilt was wrapped with brass wire, instead of some flashy lizardskin that might slip under a sweaty palm, and the pommel was made of plain brass shaped like a walnut. Expensive as it had been, it was still a line soldier's weapon, not an officer's. Not flashy, but effective—the blade had been made of good dwarven wootz, and was kept sharp enough to shave with.

You killed with the point much more often than with the edge, of course, but that was no excuse for not having a proper edge. Yes, a sharp edge could chip on armor or steel or even on bone, but if you survived the fight, there was always time to sharpen a chip out.

"I can't decide whether you've come up or gone down in the world, Pirojil," Tarnell said, as he helped to unload the bags to the floor. "Last time I saw you, you were with the other two—" He raised an eyebrow.

"Kethol and Durine."

"Yeah—those two. And then you had your own servant—that big fellow, the one who never smiled. This time, you've no servant or comrades, and if you had some sort of Imperial warrant, you'd have shoved it under my nose by now—which says you've fallen in state. But you're accompanying two nobles and a wizard, which suggests just the opposite. And isn't that a captain's braid on your collar?" he asked, smiling, fondling the captain's braid on his own collar.

The last time Pirojil had seen Tarnell, Tarnell had been the decurion in charge of the stables, not the governor's aide. The governor's aide had been a weasel-faced little man with an annoying way of looking slantwise out of his eyes at you, and Pirojil didn't miss him very much.

"What happened to Ketterling?" he asked.

"You hadn't heard?" Tarnell frowned. "Hanged," he said. "The general—the governor found that he had been peculating." His face was studiously impassive.

Well, that was not much of a surprise.

"Occupation brings opportunities" was an unofficial byword in the Imperial service. Pirojil had never heard of a former occupation officer—particularly not one who acted as a governor's bursar— having to beg in the streets for his next meal, or, for that matter, having to take up service as even a minor noble's retainer after leaving office. Somehow, they all seemed to have saved almost miraculous multiples of their salaries.

It was amazingly sticky stuff, gold and copper and silver.

Minor corruption was commonly acknowledged, but only irregularly, if severely, punished. After all, more than a few of the older occupation officers had already taken retirement in the barony they had occupied, and if nothing else, the hostility that they had earned from the local lords and wardens guaranteed that they would remain loyal to the Empire long after the occupation was ended, and control of the rest of the Holtish baronies restored to the Holtish barons.

Yes, every once in a while, an embezzler would be discovered and hanged, and it was probably hoped that that would keep theft down to a minimum, but Pirojil didn't think that anybody ever got drunk enough to think it would ever be eliminated.

The timing of this was interesting, though.

Coincidental that Ketterling was conveniently dead just as the new baron was returning home?

Pirojil didn't much believe in coincidences. What was it that Walter Slovotsky said? "I don't know whoever said that the first time is an accident, the second time is a coincidence, and the third time is enemy action, but whoever it was must have had one shitload of incompetent enemies, and me, I'd like to trade."

Yes, Keranahan was under occupation, theoretically under the baron's reign but in practice and in law under the governor's rule, but, still, if Forinel wasn't given access to the account books if—when—he requested it, there would be some definite Imperial interest.

The governor had bought himself some time, that was all. No wonder Treseen had scurried home, the first to leave after Parliament had let out.

Treseen hadn't known that it hadn't been necessary, after all.

While Kethol/Forinel was not totally illiterate nor utterly innumerate, he would have been no more capable than Pirojil was of penetrating a maze of account books.

Leria, on the other hand . . .

"Where is he?" Pirojil asked. "And is there some good reason that the governor himself hasn't rushed downstairs to greet the baron?"

Tarnell held up a hand. "Hey, Pirojil—take an even strain, man. He just got in from Parliament four days ago, and he's not only had to try and then hang Ketterling, and *then* start to catch up on his own work—and Ketterling's—but his new jerfalcon has taken sick with some sort of feather rot, and he was up half the night with her. He asked me to see to the bar—to all of the visitors' comforts, and then bring you to his office."

Pirojil didn't believe that, either—more likely, the governor had been out riding an old horse or a new wench, or had just been up drinking himself into a stupor late the night before, and had just crawled out of bed. Tarnell had been with Treseen since the war; loyal old Tarnell was just covering for him.

"Then let's go see him."

"Oh, please—there's no rush. Why not have a bath and a meal first? I can have the cook fry you up a couple of chickens and some turnip cake, and have it all ready by the time you're clean."

"The governor, first."

"But—"

"Will my word do, Tarnell, or do you need to hear it from the baron himself?"

"Argh." Tarnell made a face. "As you wish."

Tarnell ushered Pirojil and the other three in. After making quick introductions—and, indirectly, covering for Forinel if he forgot that *Forinel* hadn't met Tarnell before, even though Kethol had—they followed Tarnell up the main staircase to the governor's

office in what had, Pirojil suspected, been the castle nursery, back
when the Keranahan barons lived in Dereneyl, before the occupation.

There were two men waiting, and they stood as Tarnell led
Pirojil and the rest in.

One was Governor—formerly General—Treseen.

It was easy to underestimate the Treseen that was slowly, painfully, rising from his chair to greet them. Vanity didn't necessarily
mean incompetence, although he was vain; his hair had been carefully blackened, leaving only pompous silver traces at the temples.
There was something wrong, something weak about his eyes, as
though he could never quite focus them properly. What had been
a strong jaw had long since become sagging jowls, and his massive
belly spoke of too much comfort over too much time. His sword
belt—and the sword was, of course, a curved saber, announcing that
Treseen never planned on dismounting while hacking down at foot
soldiers—hung from a coatrack to his left, well out of reach.

Peacetime reflexes.

But Pirojil had heard some of the wartime stories about him,
including the breaking of the siege at Moarin, and it didn't pass his
notice that the bone-handled letter opener on Treseen's desk was
within easy reach of his right hand, and was shaped more like a
dagger than such things usually were, and he would have been happy
to bet that the edge was sharper than it had any business being.

It was the other man, though, that made Pirojil's hands itch for
the hilt of his own sword. Or the pistols on his belt. Or, preferably,
a large, spiked club.

Miron.

Miron—more formally, Lord Miron, Forinel's half-brother, son
of the late, unlamented Elanee, and almost certainly her co-
conspirator, although everybody who could have shed any proof on
that charge was either dead or fled. Pirojil would have resented that

more if he hadn't killed or scattered most of them himself.

"It is good to see you all," Miron said, his smile only a little too broad to be believable—not that Pirojil would have believed it anyway.

Miron always reminded Pirojil of, of—of somebody he had known, a long time ago: a strong, aquiline nose under suspiciously innocuous blue eyes, a generous mouth that smiled far too much. His jaw was too square, the sharpness only slightly relieved by a very carefully trimmed fringe of beard that reminded Pirojil of Baron Tyrnael's.

Miron was tall and lean, but broad-shouldered like a peasant, as though he had spent much of his life in strenuous outdoor labor, an effect heightened by the even, dark tan across his face and neck.

And what was that strenuous outdoor labor? Riding down fleeing peasant girls?

Miron's wrists, though, those were what Pirojil always looked at—both were thick, the muscles well defined and always held in tension, as though he was keeping himself instantly ready to pass a blade from his powerful right hand to an equally powerful left.

There were a few—too few—dueling scars on the right wrist. The scars were to be expected, but did the paucity of them mean that he had rarely been touched, or that his vanity had caused him to let only a few heal naturally?

Pirojil wouldn't have wanted to bet either way, but if Pirojil ever had to fight him, he would be sure to watch Miron's left hand as much as his right, although more than likely what he really should be watching for would be a knife in the back from some accomplice.

Governor Treseen waddled out from around the desk and took Leria's arm, ignoring Forinel's glare as he helped her to a chair.

Pirojil forced himself not to roll his eyes.

Shit, man, it's not like he's the sort to bend her over the desk and yank up her dress, after all.

Treseen was, of course, probably the sort to idly wonder what doing that would be like, but Pirojil had no problem with that, Pirojil being the same way. He wouldn't do it—even if the lady were willing, which was beyond mere unlikelihood—but he didn't mind thinking about it. Wondering didn't hurt anything, as long as Kethol didn't see Pirojil watching the way her hips swayed when she walked, and Pirojil was careful to be sure that he didn't.

What went on in the recesses of your mind didn't matter, as long as you kept it there.

Still, Forinel's glare was perfectly in character for a newly affianced baron, so Pirojil let himself relax. He would just let it be. There was enough for Pirojil to complain about concerning Kethol's inadequacies without bothering Leria or Kethol—or himself, for that matter—about the few things that actually looked right.

"Please, Baron, my lady, be seated. You, too, Erenor." Treseen cocked his head at Miron. "Lord Miron, I don't know if you met Erenor in Biemestren. I don't know him well myself; we had the chance to exchange but a few words—a hello and such." His smile broadened. "And fortunately for me, they were words I can remember, or I'd likely have found myself sprouting feathers from my nose, or some such thing."

"No, I haven't met him," Miron said, his smile still genuine as faerie gold. "I didn't have that pleasure. I was, you'll recall, somewhat preoccupied with other matters when my beloved brother made his *very* dramatic entrance. Erenor, is it?"

"Erenor the Great, he's called."

Not that "the Great" was an uncommon appellation for wizards. Just once, Pirojil would have liked to meet a wizard who billed himself, honestly, as "the Barely Adequate" or "the Not Utterly Incompetent." The closest he could think of was Vair the Uncertain, and Vair was a frighteningly powerful wizard.

"Erenor the Great." Treseen's smile and laugh seemed more

than a little forced. "And, surely enough he deserves that appellation for having been able to locate Baron Forinel, after so many years of absence."

"Please." Erenor spread his hands. "General, you do give me too much credit. It was just a matter of assembling the right tools, and choosing to use them, after all."

There was also the matter of the ring that the real Forinel had given Leria before he had left Holtun, and which she had kept hidden over the years.

The boy Forinel had been given that ring by his late father. As a boy, and he had worn that ring for years, first on his thumb and then on smaller fingers as he grew into it. He had worn it long enough and with enough intent that there was a real connection between Forinel and the ring. It had taken a far more adept wizard than Erenor to exploit it, but it had seemed expedient to let Erenor get the credit.

"A modest wizard." Treseen shook his head.

"Who is it who dares to suggest that we do not live in an age of wonders?" Miron asked the air. "Surely not I. Yes, Erenor the Great does deserve *much* for his accomplishment."

In an eyeblink, the hard look he gave Erenor was replaced by a grin that gave the lie to what that "*much*" that Miron would have liked to give Erenor was. "But I'm disappointed in you, Governor—here the baron and his company have just arrived after a most . . . unusual trip, and you've yet to offer them so much as a drink of water or a crust of bread."

"I'm properly chastened, and I'm far too responsible to lie and claim that I'd already given orders to that effect," Treseen said, raising a hand and gesturing toward Tarnell. "Some refreshments for the baron and his company, Tarnell, if you please."

The flick of Treseen's fingers made it clear that he meant for Tarnell to go and fetch, but he didn't appear surprised when Tarnell simply reached over to the wall and took down a speaking tube, spoke a few words into it, and then replaced it, an impassive look on his face.

Loyalty, Pirojil decided, was sometimes as much a mirror as a shield. Tarnell had been perfectly willing to leave Miron alone with Treseen, but not Pirojil and the others. That was every bit as revealing as Treseen not having blamed Tarnell for having failed to see to the party's needs.

"You seem surprised to see me, brother," Miron said, turning toward Forinel.

"No. It's just that—"

"It's just that," Leria said, laying her hand on Forinel's arm, "we would have thought that you'd not dare to show yourself in Keranahan."

"Me?" Miron laid a spread-fingered hand over his heart. "Why?"

"I think that you know very well why," she said, not taking his light tone.

"Why should I be in any way reluctant to return to my own home? Because of those spurious accusations that I was in some, some sort of conspiracy with my mother? Or some silly, preposterous complaint that I cut down a rude churl or two in Adahan? The former is a lie, spread only in whispers, and the latter is true, but not important."

He waved the accusations away with an effete-looking flutter of his thick wrist. "If there is any evidence, any evidence at all, that I was somehow conspiring with my mother, trot it out, please, and place it before the governor, here, and let him judge me himself."

Pirojil had seen Miron play the innocent dandy before, and he wouldn't have believed it even before he'd met Erenor, and been more thoroughly—and expensively—educated as to how false superficial impressions could be.

"So, Miron," Leria said, "what do you think your mother was doing, raising that dragon in hiding?"

Miron spread his hands. "Knowing her as I did, knowing her to be the woman that she was, I'm sure that she intended to gift the Emperor with it. All this talk about how she had tricked Walter Slovotsky and Ellegon into coming to Keranahan is silly. But she's dead, alas, and I think it's even more unbecoming for me to have to defend her reputation than it is for others to demean her, now that she is not here and cannot speak in her own defense."

That was a preposterous explanation, but that was one of the good things about being a noble, Pirojil decided. You could get away with a preposterous explanation. Most of the time.

Miron turned back to Forinel. "You weren't such a quiet sort in the old days, brother. My late mother used to complain that it was all she could do to get you to pause in your babblings at dinner."

Leria laughed. It sounded phony in Pirojil's ears, but he had heard the lady laugh for real.

"That's silly, Miron," she said. "Old days or new days, Forinel has always been one to say little and do much. Unlike some people I could think of."

Miron's lips tightened, but he didn't say anything to her; he just looked over at Forinel.

Pirojil gave Forinel a nudge. Leria was Forinel's betrothed, and that made him responsible for anything she did. It was Forinel's duty to shut her up.

Of course, knowing Leria, that was exactly why she had made the dig at Miron.

Pirojil nudged Forinel again, harder this time.

"I think, Lady," Miron started, "that—"

"Excuse me." Forinel leaned forward. "I think—I think that my betrothed has been spending too much time around Erenor, and that she lets her tongue wag far too freely," Forinel said. "I'll ask your pardon on her behalf. Brother."

"Now, really, Forinel, there's no need for that." Miron made a face. "Lady Leria is, of course, absolutely charming, as always. There's nothing to apologize for, and so no reason to accept an apology."

"I'm sorry, Lord Miron," Forinel said, rising. "I suppose I wasn't clear enough, so I'll try again. As her betrothed, I'm responsible for her behavior, and I take my responsibilities very seriously. If you take offense, we've a courtyard outside, and we both are wearing swords—I'll be happy to discuss it there, and with them. Will you be satisfied with the first blood?"

"Baron?" Treseen's brow furrowed. "I'm sure I didn't hear you say what I'm sure I just heard you say."

Even Leria looked shocked.

Well, that was the sort of gaffe that Pirojil should have expected. Challenging Miron?

That aside—and that was a lot to put aside—Pirojil was almost impressed with Forinel's manner.

Maybe they could pull this off after all. The awkwardness of Forinel's phrasing could be easily attributed to his long absence from polite society. The rest of it, though, was pure Kethol—if you had an enemy, you cut him down now, and worried about the cost later—but it wasn't a bad line to take, as long as you just talked about it.

Doing it? That would be another matter. That sort of thing was a luxury that they just didn't have, not with Forinel as the baron.

Young noblemen engaging in the occasional duel was more ex-pected than not. While it wasn't impossible to get killed in such a thing, it was extremely rare—most duels were fought to the first blood, after all, with a swordmaster standing by, staff in hand, to knock aside the dueling swords after so much as a scratch. And it was no coincidence that most nobles chose to hold their duels conveniently close to a temple, where even if a healer was not standing by, one could be quickly summoned. The short rapiers that noblemen carried on a daily basis were designed for thrusting, not cutting, and while a thrusting blow was theoretically far more capable of killing instantly than a slash was, that was only true if the thrust went to the heart or head—and any but the best swordsmen would find that well before they had worked themselves close enough to touch their opponent's torso, they would themselves first have been struck on the hand, or arm, or leg, or foot.

It was as much a matter of the mechanics of it as it was of common consent that most duels ended with just a scratch, or, at worst, a wound on the sword arm.

There were safer things than dueling, but deaths were rare, and that was only in part because the local noble authorities—the barons in Bieme, and the governors in Holtun—would occasionally choose to consider that the death was a murder.

It was one thing for a couple of nobles to occasionally square off over some private offense—whether real, or not—but it would be entirely another thing for the baron, of all people, to fight his half-brother and heir.

Besides, Miron was almost certainly better with a short dueling rapier than Kethol was.

Legends to the contrary, few soldiers had time for extensive sword practice, and that would be with sabers, not little noble-stickers. Pirojil and Kethol had more training than most, but put all their hours together—and double the sum—and they still probably hadn't spent a tenth of the time with a sword in hand that Miron, a scion of nobility, had.

Besides, while Forinel and Miron each wore a nobleman's short rapier, Kethol had always carried a saber. It probably wouldn't even occur to Kethol until it was too late that as a dueling weapon a rapier was by far better than the saber that Kethol had always carried, just as the longer, heavier saber was far more useful in a battle than a skinny little poking rod could be.

Yes, Kethol was a fine swordsman, and every bit as good with staff and knife and fists and elbows if need be—but a duelist? Hardly. When you fought for real, and not just sport, the only purpose of a strike to the hand, or leg, or foot—as common as those were—was to set up for a death blow, or, as Pirojil himself had done more times than he cared to count, to disable or at least slow one enemy while you had to turn to deal with another.

Now, if Pirojil was going to take on Miron, the fight would start with a kick to the balls or knee, or an elbow to the too-full mouth or noble neck—or, preferably, a bow shot or rifle shot at great distance—and not a swordmaster's "Make yourselves ready."

Sport was a noble's ideal, and Pirojil was very much not a noble.

Miron had let Treseen's words—and Forinel's stupid words, which they were in reply to—linger in the air long enough.

"Really." Miron made no move to rise; he rested one elbow on the arm of his chair, and his chin on the tips of his fingers, as though studying something unusual and vaguely distasteful. "Perhaps it's been too long since you've been home, brother. It's long been a custom—in Holtun and in less civilized countries—that the ruler, be it a lowly noble landholder, or a baron, or the Emperor himself, is not properly subject to challenge by anybody below his station." His smile was deeply offensive without being obviously offensive. "Which is why, perhaps, rulers' ladies so often are so . . . charmingly outspoken."

Forinel/Kethol didn't have a quick response to that. Which was probably just as well.

Miron went on: "And fond as I am of you, Forinel—and, my brother and baron, please do forgive me for the presumption—I wouldn't want you to think that I've lost any skills in the last years.

Even after your departure, my mother saw to it that we always had a good swordmaster on staff. In fact, I think that you might find that I'm better with a sword than I used to be, and I used to be somewhat better than you, much to your embarrassment, as you may recall."

"I think—" Kethol started.

"Excuse me." Treseen cleared his throat. "*I* think this has gone quite far enough," he said. "I will remind you—*both* of you—that I am the governor of Keranahan, and I absolutely forbid either of you—*either* of you—to engage in any sort of duel with each other." His eyes went from Forinel to Miron, and then back. "Since I feel the need to be very specific: I mean there are to be *no* duels whatsoever between the two of you—either in your own person, or by proxy—and Captain Pirojil, I'm talking to you.

"It's no secret that there's bad blood between the two of you, and I don't believe for a moment that either one of you would be satisfied with a little scratch on the other's sword arm.

"If some duel should happen—no matter how it happens—I can promise that it will not go well for the survivor. Neither the Emperor nor Parliament would consider awarding the title to you, Miron, if you killed your brother. And as for you, Baron, if I were you, I would worry a great deal about explaining to the Emperor and the rest of Parliament how a fratricide should properly remain the baron of Keranahan. Understood?"

Miron nodded easily, lightly, and after a moment, Forinel nodded, as well.

Treseen grunted. "As for me, I'd find it more than slightly embarrassing if I were to be obliged to report that the baron had killed his half-brother and heir, and more embarrassing than that were I obliged to report to the proctor or the Emperor himself that the baron, just confirmed in his estate by the Emperor and Parliament, had been killed *by* his half-brother and heir." He looked from Miron to Forinel, and then to Pirojil. "Have I been utterly clear?"

For once, Treseen didn't come across as the buffoon that Pirojil had always thought of him as.

He looked over toward where Tarnell was eyeing him and nodding, as though to say, *You watch over your baron, man, and I'll watch over my captain.*

Pirojil nodded back, and quietly decided that if he ever had to kill Treseen, he'd be sure to cut Tarnell down first. Not out of anger, but in self-preservation.

Treseen was still staring at both Forinel and Miron. "I know that neither of you has served as a military officer, but it's customary when one gets an order to acknowledge it." He turned to Kethol. "Baron?"

"I understand," Kethol said.

Treseen nodded, accepting that, then turned to Miron, who immediately raised and spread his hands.

"Of course, Governor; you've been most clear. I hope that all will pardon my testiness, and just attribute it to a minor case of indigestion." He patted himself on his flat belly.

"Well," Treseen said, sitting back in his chair, "now that we're done with that little bit of unpleasantness, I imagine that you are eager to return to the Residence, and settle yourselves in. A more formal greeting can wait for, perhaps, Fredensday? I'm sure that I can get invitations out today—" He looked over at Tarnell.

"I can find a scribe who knows one end of a pen from another," Tarnell said. "We supposedly have a pair of them down the hall, although I'd never have believed that such thumb-fingered dolts would call themselves scribes." He bit on a heavily bitten thumbnail in thought. "Fredensday is something of a rush, though . . . perhaps Karlsday, or even Tenthday would be better—"

"Fredensday will do nicely." Treseen nodded in agreement with himself. "The sooner the better, if only for my own sake. While I'm sure that I'll enjoy the company, as always, it will also be a particularly pleasant change to have complaints about the occupation be directed at other ears than mine. The local lords will be more than eager to greet the . . . long-lost baron, I'm sure."

"I can't imagine that they wouldn't," Miron said. "Perhaps I should remain here, and help in the preparations—much as it pains me to delay my own homecoming."

Sure. That was a *great* idea. Let Miron and Treseen have more time to plan and plot in private.

Then again, the truth was that there would be no real way to prevent that from happening, and it was pointless to try. Neutralizing Miron's threat was something that required either a lot more subtlety or a lot less.

"No." Forinel rose. "I wouldn't want you to feel that you weren't welcome at home, brother," he said. "You'd best come with us."

Miron shrugged lightly, and easily rose to his feet. "I'm grateful, of course, brother—and I am at your service, my baron."

Pirojil couldn't figure out who had been doing the manipulating, but he had a suspicion, and he didn't like it very much.

Treseen nodded. "Then I'll see you on Fredensday, and I think that concludes our business for today. Tarnell—horses for the baron's party, if you please."

Rising, Treseen extended a hand to Forinel. "Again, Baron Keranahan: welcome home."

3

⛨ Homecoming II

> You can trust a married man on this: home is
> where *she* is. And if that sounds maudlin—and
> I guess it does—it's maudlin that's been honestly
> come by, although it did take a second marriage
> to come by it.
>
> —Walter Slovotsky

Kethol pulled his horse to a prancing halt on the crest of the
hill, looking down at what the locals had been calling the
Residence ever since the start of the occupation.

Back when the Holtish barons ruled Holtun, it had been the
Keranahan barons' country home, a respite from the sights and
sounds and most particularly the smells of Dereneyl, just an easy
hour's ride to the north and west down an old bricked-stone road
that was even easier on a horse's shod hooves than it would have
been on a carriage's axles.

Kethol had some sympathy for their desire for that respite.
Cities smelled of smoke and stale grease, of rotting timbers and
rotting refuse—and most particularly every city always smelled of
the shit and piss of every man, woman, and beast that had ever set
foot in it.

The Residence itself looked pleasant enough, despite the new-looking wooden walls that had turned it into a compound of sorts: a central stone building that rose an impressive three stories, flanked on either side by a long two-story wing, each wing fronted by a full-length portico.

In contrast to the new walls, the old structure was overgrown with ancient ivy, and twittering birds fluttered in and out of nests hidden in the green tangle. Not a place to hole up in time of war, no, but a nicer place to spend a warm summer than the city.

At the far end of the compound, the stable and the barracks stood side by side, as though to suggest that the builders didn't see much of a difference between horses and soldiers, and the near end of the compound was devoted to a fine garden, filled with flowers. He wasn't sure what kind of flowers they were. Probably some were roses, and Kethol thought he recognized some as roses, and others as snapdragons and lilies, but all were starting to go wild and untamed.

But beyond the castle were the woods.

Thick stands of tall pines stood guard over the game trails that broke on the cleared land. The stream that ran through the floor of the valley and under the Residence walls wound its way across the farmed land to disappear into the lush greenery.

He would have expected the woods to be less thick, at least around the edge. Back in Barony Cullinane, all of the woods had been thoroughly harvested around the edges and well into them, as part of the ongoing rebuilding of the crofts and villages put to the torch during the war, and if harvesting of trees bigger than a man could clasp his hands around wasn't strictly controlled by the village wardens and landholders, the woods there would have quickly turned these into the poor excuses for forests that kept huge tracts of Nyphien looking more like the Waste of Elrood than anything else.

Oh, well—it was just another difference, he supposed.

Were the woods protected here? Or was it just that the lands around the Residence were the baron's, farmed by crofters? As legend had it, all crofters were too lazy to so much as rehang a door for themselves, if the village warden wouldn't pay them for doing it, and would spend two days haggling over the price of a job that would have taken a quick hour.

Kethol didn't know much about crofters, but Kethol liked the woods. Every woods was different, from the thin, scrubby forests of Enkiar to the vast, deep Great Woods that rimmed Osgrad in the north.

But every wood, every forest was wonderful in its own way. Just as living trees would shelter you from a storm and from the heat of day, dead ones would provide wood to cook your food. Even the wettest wood could be quickly made to burn if you started with flint and steel and just a little twist of birch bark. A man who wasn't afraid to work from sunrise to sunset could build himself a modest house in a few tendays, starting with nothing more than an ax and a stand of pines.

A man who knew how to use a bow could feed himself on grouse and deer and elk forever, and absolutely anybody could snare for rabbit. Somebody who had been taught what to look for—and what to avoid—could harvest enough mushrooms, wild onions, and bitter greens to make even a humble meal of spit-roasted rabbit an absolute feast.

Perhaps the nicest thing about woods was the noise. The distant chittering of birds and squirrels was always a notice that there was no danger about, and their sudden silence the loudest of alarms. Kethol could sleep more deeply in the woods than he could anywhere else, only to be awakened instantly when everything went silent.

So he had little sympathy for the Keranahan rulers, who had

been forced, the poor fellows, to live just outside a fine woods, rather than in a smelly city.

He spurred his horse, and rode down to the gates of the Residence, trying as hard as he could to look like a man who had ridden down this road a thousand times before, and utterly sure that he was failing.

"I'm sorry to say," Leria said, again, "that you'll find that almost all of the staff is new to you."

"Miron's mother never did like anybody that my mother had brought on," he said, as she had told him to. "So she finally got rid of the last of them? That's like her."

Miron let that pass without comment, which was a nice change.

"Treseen didn't mention that he was sending a rider out ahead of us," Pirojil said.

"No, he didn't." Erenor's mouth twisted. "Did you ask him if he was?"

"No," Pirojil said.

Shut up, he meant.

Yes, their coming had been announced, something that Kethol could have worked out even if he hadn't noticed the groom walking down an obviously hard-ridden mare over in front of the stables, or the messenger, in Imperial black and silver, dippering water from the well next to the kitchen.

A small troop of eighteen soldiers had formed up in two lines beside the gate, all in the green and gold livery of Keranahan. Not much of a company, but Keranahan was still under occupation, and it would have been more than a little surprising if there were a regiment-sized House Guard.

What did surprise him was the thick-waisted guard captain, who broke into a trot, panting as he ran up the road toward them, a broad smile under a broad, many-times-broken nose threatening to split his face.

"Forinel, Forinel," he said, his voice thick. He took the reins as Kethol halted his horse. "It's been so long, boy. I mean, Baron." He grinned, and beckoned with his free hand. "Would you be so kind as to get yourself down off that sorry, spavined, swaybacked excuse for a mount and greet me properly, boy, or I just might let myself forget for a moment that you're the baron and I'm just a simple soldier, and give you a good blading across the backside."

You could try, Kethol would have said.

But that didn't seem like the sort of thing that the baron would say.

Awkwardly, not knowing quite what to say or do, Kethol levered himself out of the saddle and lowered himself to the ground.

"Captain Thirien," Leria said, formally, as she dismounted easily from the back of her small brown mare. "Are you not happy to see me, as well?" The tone of her voice held only a hint of reproof.

She slipped her arm familiarly about Kethol's waist, and gave him a reassuring squeeze that almost made him forget how adroitly she had given him the captain's name without drawing attention to the fact that she was doing just that.

The captain's smile didn't falter as he drew himself up straight, his ample belly threatening to split his tunic's stitching.

"Lady, I am always happy to see you, and always happy to welcome you to the Residence," he said, his tone no less warm for being formal. "And I'm pleased enough to piss to welcome you as the new mistress-to-be of the Residence, if you don't mind my saying so."

He turned from her to grip Kethol by the shoulders. The captain—Thirien, his name was—had stronger hands than Kethol would have guessed.

"But this one, this man-who-left-here-as-a-boy—him I never expected to see again, and you'll forgive me, I trust, if an old man's joy leaks out and splashes around." He blinked tears from his eyes as he looked Kethol up and down, and nodded, approvingly.

"Filled out a little, you finally did," he said. "Always thought you were too skinny."

He waited for Kethol to say something.

"It's good to see you, too, Thirien," he said. "It has been a long time."

That, at least, wasn't a lie—forever was a long time, after all, and Kethol hadn't met the captain when he had visited the Residence once before as himself, in his own flesh.

"That it has, boy, that it has." Thirien beckoned to a pair of soldiers over at the gate. "Well, what are you clods waiting for? Take the baron's horses and see that they're properly curried and fed, if you please."

He clapped a hand to Kethol's shoulder. "Let's get you settled in, shall we?"

Kethol finished lacing the linen vest tightly over the blousy white shirt, then stooped to put on his boots.

The old cedar wardrobe that stood against the north wall of Forinel's—of *his* bedroom, of *his* bedroom—was far too large to fit through the door, and had certainly been built in place by a long-dead carpenter. Large as it was, it was still utterly crammed full of clothes, and Elda, the fat housekeeper (did any noble ever have a skinny housekeeper?), had told him that most of his clothes were still in storage, carefully sealed in chests in what had been his childhood bedroom.

He didn't press the matter further—but, at least, he knew when he found a room filled with chests and chests of tunics and jerkins, he would know where his childhood bedroom had been.

There was far too much here to choose from, so Kethol had made it simple: a plain white shirt and black linen vest, over trousers and calf-high black boots.

He flexed his feet in the boots. They were a little stiff from years of lack of use, but they had been oiled and polished on a regular basis, and it wouldn't take him long to break them in.

They definitely did need breaking in—from the look of the soles, they couldn't have been worn more that a few times, and there were other shoes and boots in the wardrobe that seemed to never have been worn, or, more likely, had been perfectly restored by the same cobbler who had made them in the first place.

These did fit his feet—even though those feet were slightly smaller than they should have been.

The boots really shouldn't have felt so tight, so constricting.

It wasn't the boots. The whole bedroom suite felt smaller than it should have, what with the way that it was built up against the outer wall of the keep, with nothing but a pair of barred windows letting in the late-afternoon sun.

He pushed his way through the silken netting to lie back on the too-soft bed, reflexively checked to see that the hilt of his sword was within reach, and let himself sigh. His shoulders were tight, and his neck could barely move.

Everything should have been fine. Wonderful, even.

He had had the Residence staff presented to him, from the fat old housekeeper to the hostler's infant children—twin daughters; very cute—and all except the youngest of the children had breathed a visible sigh of relief when he had announced, as Leria had coached him to, that he had no intention of "making any changes," which was a noble's way of saying that they could all stay on.

Yes, they had served Elanee, but it was not their fault that she had attempted a very curious sort of rebellion, and neither Kethol nor Forinel—whoever he was—had any intention of turning out a couple of dozen men, women, and children with nothing but the clothes on their backs and whatever they could steal at the last moment.

A tray of snacks had been brought to his room, and while Erenor had insisted on testing it for poison—Erenor thought that everybody else thought the way he did, perhaps, or, more likely, he simply mistrusted everybody as a matter of policy—the wizard had ruled the food safe, and it was definitely tasty. He had filled up enough on the meatrolls and the very garlicky sausage that he barely touched the turnip compote, and had only eaten half of the pork pie.

Finished with his meal, he had used the garderobe in the washroom off his bedroom that was dedicated to that purpose—both his station and his having a room up against the wall had their virtues—and then he had made a sketchy bath in the washbasin, and now he was dressed, and the right thing to do would be to go downstairs and pretend to refamiliarize himself with the Residence, from the dungeon to the attic.

It would be easy to justify, Leria had explained. A few words about how he had been gone so long, and had missed every room, every mural and tapestry, every stick of furniture. Nobody would believe that, but that was the best part of it: everybody would think that he was trying to see what had disappeared in his absence.

He was looking forward only to part of it: he should be able to find a good bow in the armory.

Sometimes, he thought that giving up his own laminated longbow was the hardest part of all this—he had had to; there were too many people who would have recognized it as Kethol's—although that was silly, from the point of view of a noble.

It was just a bow, after all. That was the way Forinel would have thought of it. For Kethol, it had cost half a year's wages, and it had suited him perfectly, and he doubted that he could find its like here.

Still, he should get to the tour sooner than later, although he didn't mind putting it off.

There was a lot to see. The old baron—his father, his father—had had a private library that was apparently famous through Holtun.

Not that that would do Kethol a whole lot of good—he could read Erendra, although not particularly quickly or well, and could make his way through a page of Englits by sounding out the words if nothing else, but the old languages were something that a woodsman's son had never had any cause or opportunity to learn, and a soldier had neither cause nor time to learn.

Although he would have to, sooner rather than later, at least well enough to pass himself off as literate, if some visiting nobleman were to ask his opinion about a book in the library.

But, instead, he lay back on the bed and closed his eyes. He couldn't relax, although he tried to. He was in another man's room, and another man's bed, wearing another man's clothes, and he could almost feel the walls closing around him.

There was a knock on the door.

"Yes?"

When the door didn't open, he got down from the bed, and pushed his way through the silken blackfly netting that surrounded it, careful not to tear it, and walked to the door, opening it.

Leria stood there, smiling. Her long golden hair, slightly darkened and still damp from her own bath, had been pulled back in a simple overhand knot, not the complex braid that she usually favored. An almost preposterously white shift was belted tightly above the hips, falling to mid-thigh, revealing her riding pants, black leather decorated along the seams with silver trim, below.

"Just out of the bath?" He didn't have any objection, but Leria seemed to spend every spare moment soaking herself in hot water.

She nodded. "I thought I'd bathe before dinner, but Elda says that you don't plan to sit table this evening." Did her light tone conceal or reveal disapproval?

"Yes, that's what I said." He beckoned her inside, and closed the door behind her. "There's a problem."

"Oh?"

"I can't read, anything except a little bit of Englits, and recognize a few Erendra symbols, and maybe a couple of dozen dwarven glyphs, and—"

She touched her finger to his lips. "I already thought of that. That's just one of the things you'll have to learn," she said, smiling, "but I think you'll find the teacher pleasant company."

"Teacher?" He frowned. "But if we get somebody to teach me, he'll know—"

"I will be the teacher," she said, her smile warm, and not vaguely insulting. "I hope you won't mind having to spend time with me?"

"No, but—"

"But save that for later, please—we were talking about you not sitting table this evening."

When the old woman had asked him what time he planned to sit table, he hadn't known quite what to say. Sit table? The nobility seemed to spend most of their lives just eating and talking and eating with each other, while Kethol had always been used to quickly wolfing down a meal before he had to get out and actually do something.

So he had just pleaded travel weariness, and that had been good enough.

There were advantages to being in charge, even if you were an imposter.

He started to say something, but Leria smiled as she again put a finger to his lips.

"There's no need to sit table, not tonight—which is why I had her pack us a light dinner, and have had a couple of horses saddled. I thought we'd go for a ride. As you'll remember, there's a wonderful riding trail down toward Ulter, through the woods."

She took his hand and pulled him close, locking her hands behind him, at the small of his back. It was only then that he noticed that her breasts were bound tightly, as though for riding.

The woods?

Her smile and nod were knowing. "We'll want to be back before it gets dark—it's not like you're an accomplished woodsman or something—so let us be going, shall we? Unless, of course, you mind being alone with me."

How was it that she could tease him and it didn't bother him? Not even a little.

"To the woods, then."

These woods had far too long been underhunted—game trails criss-crossed the riding trail in a preposterous profusion. If it wasn't for the wolves, the barony would probably have been knee-deep in deer, and more than waist-deep in rabbit.

He didn't even have to get down from the back of the overly spirited black gelding that the stableboy had picked out for him in order to spot bear spoor under, as far as he could tell, each and every one of the old oaks that held a beehive, as most of them appeared to.

His mouth watered at the idea of smoking out the bees and sinking his teeth into a fresh honeycomb.

As they cantered down the side of the hill, a covey of grouse exploded out of the bushes beside them, the *fluppeta-fluppeta-fluppeta* as they battered their wings together at least as hard as they beat the air sending him reaching for one of his pistols.

It had been too long since he had been out in the forest. It was embarrassing that he hadn't even spotted the grouse before he had startled them, although who had been doing most of the startling and who had been doing most of the being startled wasn't at all obvious.

She laughed, more at him than with him. "I appreciate your concern for my safety, but I don't think a pack of grouse is very dangerous."

"True enough." But he couldn't help but keep his eyes from

scanning not only the trail in front of them, but the brush to either side. "But it's what I'm used to."

"I know." She nodded, and as the trail widened, kicked her heels against her brown mare's broad sides until they were riding almost knee-to-knee. "Still, you can get used to all this. Good food, clean clothes, a regular bath, and as much leisure as you'd like aren't difficult tastes to acquire, are they?"

He didn't answer. "It's . . . different. I've spent most of my life—"

"Shhh." She looked ahead. "I know we're alone, but please, please don't get in the habit of talking about . . . such things." Her lips pursed tightly. "I can't imagine that Miron would suspect the truth, but he's certain to be looking for an opportunity to discredit you—and he is known to the local landholders, and has allies in Parliament. In fact, I think you ought to make an opportunity to court Lord Moarin—he's a wretched old lecher, but—"

"Please? At least when we're alone, can't I just stop pretending for a few moments?"

When she didn't answer right away, he angrily slapped his reins hard against his thigh. The horse misread that as a signal to break into a canter, and he was easily a dozen manlengths away before he pulled the horse back into a slow walk so that she could catch up.

Ahead, the trail broke on a clearing surrounding a small pond. The ducks that seemed to glide effortlessly across its green-scum–covered surface ignored them, while a skinny heron, propped up on one foot at the far edge, paused for a moment to eye them carefully before knifing its long beak back into the water, emerging with a wriggling fish, its rainbow scales gleaming like jewels in the sunlight.

Heron wasn't the most flavorful of birds, but it wasn't bad. Better than eagle and loon, and there was more meat on one than there was on a duck. Since he hadn't been able to locate a proper bow boot quickly, and hadn't wanted to take the time to find one, he hadn't even strung one of the longbows in the Residence armory; he had simply taken a short horn bow and a small quiver from the armory and strapped them to the back of his saddle.

It would be almost too easy to stop, string the bow, and shoot some supper—and it would have been the natural, the normal thing to do. The woods here were like an open town market without the incessant cries of farmers and merchants hawking their wares.

"No," she said, finally. "I don't think you should stop pretending, as you put it. But we can make an exception, just this once. Since it's just you and me."

"Thank you."

"Would you mind stopping for a moment? I'm finding that bouncing up and down on a saddle is beginning to tire me."

"Of course."

He pulled his horse to a halt, quickly bolted to the ground, and went to help her dismount. He could barely feel the ground through the thick soles of his boots. If he had still been himself, he would have brought along a pair of woodsman's leather buskins.

She stretched broadly, but showed no other sign of weariness from either their ride out from Dereneyl or their much shorter ride from the Residence.

"Thank you," she said. "It's very gentlemanly of you to hand me down from my horse, but please do get out of the habit of rushing to do it—it makes you look like a servant. I can wait."

"Very well."

She untied the leather provisions bag from her saddle, and looked around. "Should we cut some stakes? For the horses?"

"We?" He raised an eyebrow.

"We," she said, firmly, and reached into her saddle's pouch to produce a short sheathed knife. "I'm not utterly helpless, you know—I'm perfectly capable of chopping a stake."

He tried to decide whether she was really irritated or just teasing him, but gave up. "If the horses won't stay near their riders," he said, "we may as well find out now, and not sometime when we're half a day's ride away from the Residence."

"From home, you mean."

"From home."

He loosened the bits from both horses' mouths and tied the reins to their saddles so that they wouldn't catch in the brambles. After giving Kethol a curious look and snort, his gelding walked a short way off into the meadow, staked out a patch of clover, and began to graze, followed after a moment by the mare, who took a tentative nibble from the same patch, then quickly moved away at the gelding's warning whinny.

He smiled. It seemed that the horse's spirit hadn't been totally cut away when a red-hot gelding iron had taken its cock and balls.

Leria spread the blanket out, flattening the waist-high grasses, and quickly produced a bottle of wine and a half-dozen meatrolls, each wrapped in now-greasy parchment.

She patted at the blanket beside her, and he unbuckled his sword belt and set it down on the grass next to the blanket as he sat.

She frowned at the leather bag. "I'm sure that there's a proper picnic kit somewhere in the Residence, but the cook didn't know where it was, and I'm going to have to have my confrontation with Elda soon enough." She pulled the wooden stopper out of the wine, and gave a quick sniff. "It's Ingarian, I think," she said, taking a brief drink before offering the bottle to him. "I wouldn't say that it's the best wine I've had, but I can swear that it's not vinegar, at least."

"Thank you." He took the bottle and tilted it back. The wine was light and cool, smoother and gentler than he was used to. It tasted of lazy summer days, he decided, although he had never actually had a lazy summer day.

"Confrontation? With Elda?"

She pursed her lips. "A home has to have one mistress, and that's going to be me, not some housekeeper," she said. "The only question is when I have to set Elda straight, not whether, although I'm tempted to say that the sooner, the better. Are you set on keeping her?"

"I hadn't thought about it." That sounded better than saying, *Yes, I have thought about it, but I'm not going to fire the whole staff.*

"Well, please do think about it. I'm sure I could arrange a position for her with one of the nobles minor in town—I'm not talking about turning her out into the night, you know—and I think that a sudden drop in station might actually be quite good for her."

"You decide."

"No. You are the baron, and you have to decide. Even if," she said, smiling, "you decide to do what I think is best. If you're set on keeping her on, though, I'd better have my confrontation with her privately—but if you're not, making an example of her in front of the rest of the staff would probably be the best way to handle things. What do you think?"

"I think," he said, "that I don't have much of any of an opinion, and would very, very much like putting the whole matter off, at least for now."

He was impressed at how her mind was constantly working. And he was impressed at how much there was to the running of a noble household, and yes, he would have to learn all about it.

But not now. Now it was a fine afternoon, and he was in the woods, which only made it better, with the *scree-scree-scree*s of a pair of distant flitterwings boasting to each other of their prowess also announcing that they were alone—flitterwings were even more cowards than they were braggarts.

"I don't think so," she said, primly, folding her hands in her lap. "There's much that you have to learn about being a noble, and little enough time to spare." She raised a finger. "Now, now, don't look like that—you remind me of a little boy, trying not to admit that he's done something that deserves a beating."

She leaned back on an elbow and considered him. "It's quite a turnabout, you know. When we were on the run, it was you who knew everything—how to keep dry in the rain, or start a fire, or when and how to go to ground and let the pursuers pass. But here and now, this is where I'm at home, and—if you'll let me—where I can teach you."

He didn't know quite what to say. "I don't see much choice in it."

"Oh." Her expression grew somber. "Is my company so unpleasant to you?"

"No. It's not that. You know it's not that, not at all." She had a way of putting him on the defensive. "It's just that—I don't think I can *do* this. I'll try, I swear on my sword I will—but it seems to me that anybody can look at me and see that I'm not what I pretend to be."

She shook her head. "I think you give people too much credit. Most people, most of the time, see what they expect to see, what they've been led to see."

"You sound like Erenor." The wizard was perfectly happy to hold forth, at great and infuriating length, on the fallible nature and utter foolishness of both the common man and the noble class.

She nodded, and took a thoughtful drink from the bottle. "Yes, perhaps I do—and perhaps it's not a bad thing to sound like Erenor? As he says, illusions aren't just a matter of magic. If you just remember that you are Forinel, Baron Keranahan, and if you just remember to try to do what Baron Keranahan does, nobody will ever be the wiser." She cocked her head to one side. "You may find that you've come to like it—there are more than enough rewards that go along with the responsibilities."

"But what does a baron *do*? In peacetime, I mean." He spread his hands. "I've served Baron Cullinane, yes, but he's not exactly typical, and his regent does most of the running of the barony—he seems to spend most of his time flitting about, seeing what's wrong and having it fixed, settling disputes, and the like. When he isn't off getting into trouble."

That sounded disloyal, and Kethol didn't like sounding disloyal. But it was true, and a failing of the Cullinanes—they tended to go looking into problems themselves, rather than dispatching somebody else to do it.

Shit, Kethol had been along, years ago, when Baron Nerahan hadn't appeared quickly enough in response to an Imperial summons, and the Old Emperor, Karl Cullinane, had shown up at the gates to his castle leading a company of the Home Guard, loudly threatening to have a following army tear the castle down around Nerahan's ears if the gates didn't open Right. This. Very. Moment.

The gates, of course, had opened right that very moment.

He smiled. The Old Emperor had been very direct, as was his son, and Kethol liked that.

Even better, the tendency of the Cullinanes to do such very unnoble things had given Kethol and Pirojil and Durine extra opportunities to pick up some spare coin—neither the Emperor nor Baron Cullinane ever seemed to notice them going through dead men's possessions, and while there were good things you could say about the Cullinanes, you had to admit that as they went through life dead bodies seemed to sprout in their wake.

He had no complaint about that, or about any of it. It was just that they were by no means usual.

"I'm sure he does that." She pursed her lips and nodded. "In peacetime, that's not a bad thing for a baron to do, although most spend far too little time on everything except settling disputes. You'll want to inspect things—the copper mines, the grain mill in Dereneyl, the buildings in the crofts, the freeholders' armories. Free-holders tend to let their arms—and their tenants' arms—be neglected in peacetime, and whatever you can say against the occupation, it's been peaceful. If it weren't for the occupation, you'd need to be spending far too much time going over the taxes, to be sure that the lords and wardens aren't stealing from you, but right now you have Governor Treseen doing that. Both the going-over and the stealing, I'm afraid."

She thought for a moment. "Treseen will happily handle the nobles for you, as well, to the extent that you let him. Oh, you'll probably want to dispense the middle justice, every now and then—but most of the common freeholders don't push their privileges too far, and you shouldn't have to do that often." She considered it for a moment. "Just make a good example of the first one or two who overreach, and the rest will fall neatly into line."

"But—"

"But mostly, you just live. You can spend much of your time on the hunt—something that I think you can manage without great suffering—and less on managing the lords and village wardens who manage the peasants. I'm not sure when the engineers are going to want to extend the telegraph to Dereneyl, but you'll want to be sure to entertain whichever of them is running the new copper mine and be sure to get him to see how more convenient it would be for him to be able to quickly talk with Ranella in Biemestren."

Her smile broadened, then faded. "It would be more than unusual if you didn't manage to visit the various lords' holdings, from time to time, and allow them to entertain you, while you try to seduce a daughter or two—not that it will take much effort, particularly until we're married. It's easy for a young girl to think that if you like the wine, you'll buy the bottle. Speaking of which," she said, offering him the bottle, "would you care for some wine, dear?"

Her smile made his earns burn red.

"Oh," she went on, as he tilted back a healthy mouthful, "I'll affect not to notice," she said. "As long as you don't flaunt your affairs in my face, and I hope you won't. But you're half-expected to sire a few bastards—and then watch over their upbringing, distantly."

"Forinel's father did that?"

"Possibly, before Forinel's—before *your* mother died, and before he married Elanee." She shrugged. "Elanee watched and controlled him too closely for that, as far as I know. With—with her planning to have you gone, she didn't want to complicate Miron's status by him having even a distaff heir. But it's possible. If my father acknowledged every bastard he sired, I'd be up to my ears in brothers and sisters."

"And you won't mind?"

"Mind? Of course I won't mind." She drew herself up straight, and folded her hands primly in her lap. "How could I possibly mind? I won't even notice," she said. "I've told you—I was raised to be a noble lady, and I'm perfectly capable of doing what's required, and I'll not spend more than a private moment regretting it. Which includes," she said, musingly, "signing my own land over to you—in your person proper, as Forinel Keranahan, and not as the baron. We'd best get that out of the way, sooner than later. Not that that's likely to make much of a difference, but . . ."

"You've changed the subject," he said.

"And you, my dear Forinel, have a keen eye for the obvious." Her fingers idly toyed with the top button of her blouse. "Yes, I will do my duty, all of it. We've applied to the Emperor for permission to marry, and that we will, and the sooner the better. Parliament meets again after the fall harvest—would that suit you?"

There was something distressingly bloodless about the way she said that, at the way her eyes searched his face.

"Unless, of course, you don't want me—you're the baron, after all. There's probably not more than one or two lords' single daughters who wouldn't jump at such a catch. I'm hardly in a position to protest, and it's not like I'd be lacking in suitors."

He was just starting to say something—he was never sure quite what—when a rustling out in the brush had him on his feet, his sword in his hand and the scabbard cast to one side before he half-knew what he was doing.

The bear browsing through the raspberry brambles at the far end of the clearing rose up on its hind legs and turned to look at him, then dropped to all fours and quickly ran off in a curious loping gait, while both horses took off at a gallop down the path, and Kethol had to stop himself from running after them. His two pistols were in the saddle boots, not that he would have wanted to try to kill a bear with something that was barely adequate to bring down a man.

Leria pressed herself tightly against him, trembling. "Did you see that?" Her pulse fluttered at the base of her neck. "Please— don't let go of me. Not until you're sure that, that horrible creature is gone."

"He was more scared of us, thankfully, than we were of him," Kethol said.

"You may speak for yourself on that," she said, her voice shaking. "I'm quite capable of being more scared than a huge bear could ever possibly be."

"Just as well the bear ran away." That edge of the clearing was upwind, and the bear had been unable to smell them at all, and hadn't known that Kethol was there until he stood. Bears were generally afraid of men, which was just as well for all concerned. Taking on an angry bear was a job for at least three men, preferably more— preferably a *lot* more—with rifles and spears, not one with a sword.

"Oh? Wouldn't you have been able to kill it?"

"Kill it?" He snorted. "Me? By myself? Not likely, not even with a real sword, and it would be worse with this little noble-sticker. Not a chance—if I was unlucky enough that it charged, I'd have hoped to be lucky enough to hurt it enough to frighten it away, but . . ." He shook his head. "The right thing to do if you see a bear is to climb the highest tree you can, as quickly as you can, and hope that it doesn't come after you."

She looked pointedly at the old oak across the riding path. "So? Is there some illusion at work? Are you really up the tree and not standing here?"

He didn't understand. "No, I'm here."

If she had started running, he would have taken to his heels behind her without a moment's hesitation. Maybe Pirojil thought that Kethol was an idiot—and maybe, just maybe, Kethol had given Pirojil more than enough excuse, from time to time, to think him so—but he would hardly have confronted an angry bear just for the sake of being able, if he survived, to show the scars.

But Leria had barely gotten to her feet when the bear—and the damn horses, for that matter—were out of sight. Running hadn't been a possibility. Then.

Now, he could try to run after the horses. Possibly they would have slowed and stopped to graze just around the bend. Sure—and possibly the sky would open and rain beef soup on him.

He felt silly just standing there with this little sword in his hand. He tried to take a step back so that he could pick up his sword belt and slip the sword back into the scabbard, but she clung tightly to him, and he couldn't just push her away, after all.

She was still trembling. "I don't think he'll come back, do you?" she asked, her tone much less certain than her uncertain words.

"No—if he's gone, he'll stay gone, more than likely. I don't think that the horses will come back, either," he said. "They won't stop until they reach the Residence." He could blame himself for not hitching them, but in their panic they would have torn a light hitching loose, anyway.

No matter. Thirien would, he was sure, send a party out after them, and, just as a precaution, send to Dereneyl for reinforcements. If a soldier went missing for a while, that was of no particular importance; it was something to be handled by the decurion when he returned, and a few days of mucking out the stables and cleaning out the dung piles beneath garderobes would make him a good example to others.

But the horses of a baron and a noblewoman returning without their riders would—or should, at least—be cause for a search party to be sent out.

Yes, it was peacetime, and the assumption would probably not be foul play—bandits would surely take the horses, after all, and even bandits knew better than to ply their trade close to nobles' residences—but something embarrassing, like a baron and his betrothed taking advantage of a nice afternoon.

After all, Thirien didn't know that Kethol was an imposter, just a simple soldier in disguise, the sort of man no decent noblewoman would bear the touch of.

He wasn't sure why that saddened him. He didn't really know Thirien, after all.

"You're smiling," she said. The trembling had gone, which was good. "I always liked your smile, although I never did see it often enough."

Was she talking about Kethol or about Forinel? He didn't know, and he couldn't ask.

"Yes. I was just thinking about how disappointed Miron will be when a search party turns us up easily."

"Well." She frowned. "I'm disappointed. I was thinking something else, entirely." Her fingers played with her shift's buttons, again. "I was thinking about how you and I haven't had a moment alone since we got back from Therranj." She unbuckled her belt and dropped it to one side. "And I was thinking that perhaps you were thinking that here we are, with some time alone . . . do I absolutely have to put it more bluntly? I hardly know how I *could* put it more bluntly."

He didn't know what to do—every time Kethol had had a woman, it was just a matter of putting a copper in a whore's bowl, and then mounting her quickly, finishing before the next man's turn. The only smile involved was the times he had accidentally put an extra coin in the bowl, and that gap-toothed grin had nothing at all in common with Leria's smile as she stepped out of her riding trousers and came to him, dressed only in her shift, and that fell from her shoulders to the ground even as he reached for her.

Beneath it, she was smooth and perfect, and it didn't seem right for someone like him to have his hands on anyone like her.

But then her mouth was sweet and warm on his, and his clumsiness didn't seem to matter.

To her, at least.

Part 2

PIECE DEVELOPMENT

4

Leria

It's very easy to get what you want. Just think
carefully, work hard, and get very, very lucky.
Okay, I lied: it's not easy. Sue me.
—Walter Slovotsky

Leria kept her smile inside as she threw the uneaten meatrolls into the bush—if the bear returned, it would make him happier than they had made Kethol, although not quite as happy as *she* had made Kethol—then carefully folded the blanket.

She straightened, adjusting her clothes.

Kethol had his virtues, certainly, but he was really no cleverer than most men. Yes, bears were dangerous if provoked, but unless you ran across a bear sow protecting some cubs, they were famous as cowards, and this bear had run away before Leria had even had time to get scared.

And then it was just a matter of doing the obvious. Tremble a little, and play with a few buttons—and never suggest out loud that she was rewarding him for having saved her from the very, very, very dangerous bear—and it had all worked out as she had planned that it would. The bear had simply made things easier, that was all.

Kethol was having trouble meeting her eyes, but she could deal with that.

Erenor had been right, after all.

She had caught up with the wizard in the Residence attic, where he was muttering to himself while clearing space among the stacked boxes and casks.

He had found a battered old tabletop somewhere in the attic, and set it between a pair of wooden boxes that were almost of the same height.

A collection of small jars had been set out on the improvised workbench. Some were made of crudely chipped stone, but most were of plain, dull pottery, and several of those had been glazed in a variety of colors that were probably a key to their contents, although perhaps the unreadable letters on the sides of some of them served that purpose, as well.

Whether through accident or a combination of good timing and Erenor's sense for the dramatic, a beam of light through a gap in the shingles illuminated the small brazier on a cast-iron tripod. While no fire burned in it at the moment, it was filled with enough charcoal to prevent the grill from being fully seated, and the small silver dagger that lay on the grill looked like it would slide off at the slightest shock.

"May one ask what you're doing?" she had asked, her head just above the open trapdoor.

"Oh, just moving things around."

Annoyingly, he didn't stop in his work as she climbed the rest of the way up the ladder to the rough-hewn attic floor. If she hadn't known that his aged appearance was just a seeming, and that he was as well muscled as a peasant farmer, the fact that he was picking up and moving chests that he could barely get his arms around would have told her. Still, while he had apparently been at this for a while, he had just barely managed to clear a space large enough for a bed.

He grunted in effort as he moved another chest from next to the newly cleared space over on top of an already high stack of boxes.

"What this attic needs is some shelving," he said. "But I'm told that there's no carpenter on staff here. Seems they've even been using a cooper from some nearby village—how can they possibly get by without a cooper?—and having Treseen send out a couple of carpenters and apprentices from Dereneyl. Would you mind speaking to him about that?"

She didn't answer. She just stood waiting, irritated at the rudeness, until he looked up, his brow furrowed.

"Oh," he said, "I am forgetting my manners, aren't I?" He produced a rag from—from somewhere, and dusted off the top of a plain wooden box that was about the right height for a chair, then set a folded blanket down on top of it.

She hadn't seen where the blanket had come from, either. Erenor was showing off. That was reassuring—Leria was used to boys and men showing off for her.

"Please, my lady," he said, "would you honor me by sitting?"

If his voice was ever-so-slightly overly formal, she didn't need to take any notice of that.

"Thank you," she said. "I take it you've decided that the attic is the best place for your workshop?"

He nodded. "It will have to do, at least for now. If I don't have good ventilation, it's likely not to be a problem for me, but I can promise you it will be a problem for everybody else. I'm going to be working on, well, on a few things, and some of the preparations are less than pleasant—smelly and smoky." He shook his head. "It would be nice to have a proper wizard's aerie, but, then again, I shouldn't complain, me not being an entirely proper wizard, and all."

"But I'm sure that, oh, by the time that the fall rains come, and root rot breaks out, you'll have learned how to kill it."

He folded his robes about his knees and sat down across from her, seemingly on the air. "I wish I was sure of that, and I wish even more that I could tell if you are being sarcastic or simply overly trusting."

"Why, Erenor, you—"

"—understand you thoroughly." He spread his hands, the picture of embarrassed innocence. "I'm in something of the same position that a friend of ours is in," he said. He thought for a moment, then closed his eyes. "Wait a moment."

He mumbled a quick incantation, and it was suddenly silent around them.

She only noticed by their absence the clopping of horses' hooves, the whispering of the wind against the shingles that roofed the attic, and the far distant screeching of some cook berating one of the serving girls.

"That's better," he said. His voice seemed flat, somehow, as though her ears were not working right, as though she had a cold, and her ears were stuffed. "I don't actually know that the baron's— that *your* servants are spying on their betters, but . . ."

"But you would be doing just that, if you were any of them," she said.

"Well, yes," he said, smiling. "While I usually find it's the case that most people are not nearly as innately inquisitive as I am, I don't particularly think it's sensible to assume that it's always the case. So it seems only reasonable to take a precaution or two. For now, please speak frankly with me. Since it's not my company that you seek, it must be my advice, and if I'm any judge of character— and I'd best be a very good judge of character, all things considered—I'd judge that you want some advice about dealing with how strange Baron Forinel has become in his long absence, am I correct?"

She nodded. It hadn't escaped her notice that Erenor was referring to Kethol as Forinel, despite having made sure that they could not be overheard, and talking around the problem, rather than addressing it directly. Erenor was more of an actor than a wizard, really, and she would have been amazed if he hadn't completely thrown himself into his role. She wouldn't be at all surprised if the collection of jars contained nothing more exotic than salt and dried horseradish.

"Yes," she said. "I'm not sure where to begin."

"Well, let's begin with the obvious—are you pregnant yet?"

She reddened. At least with people she trusted, she knew she was more bluntly spoken than most women of her class, but Erenor was speaking far more bluntly than she was accustomed to, or cared for.

He held up a hand. "My apologies, my lady, my humble apologies. But if we spend too much time chatting by ourselves in private, tongues will start to wag, and I don't think either of us wants that. So, let's get straight to it, and leave both of our blushes aside for the nonce, or even for a couple of nonces. I ask again: are you pregnant?"

She shook her head. "That would hardly be possible," she said.

"Not possible?" Erenor rolled his eyes. "Well, the man certainly does have his virtues, and I've not known him to be overly bright, but I wouldn't think him to be that stupid. Too bad we couldn't use Pirojil for the purpose."

She didn't ask whether by *the purpose* he meant *somebody to substitute for Forinel* or something more crude.

Erenor smiled knowingly. "Again, since we have little time, I'll ask you to forgive my bluntness—do you have reason to think him, err, incapable?"

This was intolerable, but she had tolerated the intolerable before, when it was necessary. The thing to do, she had decided, was to act as though she was talking to herself, and in the privacy of her own mind she never knowingly permitted evasion and deception.

"No," she said. "I, I have every reason to believe him more than capable, but—"

"But he hasn't laid a hand—or, more relevantly, other body parts more to the point—on you." He nodded. "I should have anticipated that. He's trying to be noble, I suspect—or, rather, he's trying to be what he *thinks* is noble. He's spent far too many nights sleeping across your doorstep to easily let himself go through the door, and slip under the blankets. The fool." He pursed his lips. "Let me think on it a moment."

With Erenor, you could usually assume that what he said was not what he meant.

Let me think on it a moment probably meant either *I don't have the vaguest idea of what to do*, or, more likely, *I've a clever plan worked out, and I've just been waiting for you to broach the matter, but don't want to seem as though I've thought things out in advance.*

It would be something devious, no doubt. Erenor preferred things complicated.

He could, after all, have simply presented himself as a relatively young wizard, albeit one who looked overly athletic and well muscled.

But Erenor preferred to look old and withered and weak, and she suspected that was as much because he enjoyed deception for the sake of deception as for the added credibility the added years gave him. It probably had even more to with his ability to instantly drop the seeming and quickly take to his heels, in the disguise that was utterly impenetrable simply because it was no disguise at all.

"I know what you're thinking," he said. "But . . . it's really very simple. So, consider this: Forinel, due to his long absence from polite society, feels out of place. He's not comfortable within these walls, having servants around to wait upon him. He's not used to people ready to bring him clean clothes or a meal, or listening to every grunt and fart he makes on a garderobe, ready to proffer a soft cloth to wipe his noble behind. And the idea of a headboard banging against a wall, well, I doubt that he'd even consider that. At first."

She understood that, in a vague way. But it was unavoidable— no matter where you went, there were *always* servants around. The ordinary details of your life could not possibly be a secret to them. Yes, it was necessary to project a smooth, polished exterior to the world—but the woman who soaked and shaved your legs and arms would no more believe that your limbs were hairless than your cook and serving girls would think that the conversation around your table was lofty, no more than the maid who changed your sheets or the scullery girl who washed them would fail to notice their condition.

"You could just slip into his room tonight, or any night, but I've seen what he does when he's suddenly awakened—that wouldn't be a good idea. So, I think you'll have to create an opportunity to, well, break him in, so to speak. Get him someplace where he's more comfortable than you are, or at least thinks he is, and then handle it, err, directly."

She tried not to blush. Erenor was right, but what sort of place? Kethol wasn't comfortable in the Residence, and they would hardly be alone on Fredensday, in Dereneyl, when Treseen presented him as the new baron to the local nobility.

Of course— "The woods, perhaps?"

The woods to the immediate west of the castle were the baron's private reserve, watched over by a forester who lived deep in them, and while traveling through the woods wasn't technically forbidden, poaching in them very much was, and few nobles and no common-folk would want to try to make their way through the woods when they could use perfectly good roads to skirt them, and avoid any accusation.

He smiled knowingly. "That would serve quite well." He rose from his invisible seat—if it was an invisible seat, if it wasn't just a matter of Erenor having adopted an uncomfortable position for effect—and dismissed the silence with a snap of his fingers.

Sounds returned. The wind whispered across the shingled roof, and off in the distance she could hear Elda berating loudly somebody over something unimportant.

"I think we're done, here." Erenor was, as usual, very pleased with himself. "I hope you won't take it as presumptuous if I wish you a pleasant ride." His smile broadened. "In more ways than one, perhaps?"

She was quite pleased with herself as she and Kethol walked down the path, hand in hand like a couple of children. Their shadows stretched across the hunting trail in the light of the setting sun peeking through the trees behind them.

Rotting corpses of small trees lay on either side of the trail, some covered with mushrooms that Kethol had said were not suitable to eat. The hunting trail had been well maintained over the years—there was no overgrowth to speak of, and while certainly there were some overhead branches that would be eager to snatch at the body and eyes of an unwary rider, there had been few enough that it had not slowed their riding much, and it slowed their walking not at all. Oh, certainly, they had to step carefully where tree roots arched up from the hard-packed soil, but there had been only one tree blocking their path, and that only an arm-thick birch that the horses had stepped over on their way in, and that Kethol had moved to the side of the path on their way out.

The forester was keeping things up quite well. She would have to be sure that Kethol soon had the opportunity to meet the forester, and praise him.

That was not the only praise that would be soon forthcoming, of course, although she would have to be careful. It wouldn't do to seem too experienced—and, in fact, she wasn't overly experienced, at that.

Kethol had been, as she had suspected he would be, even clumsier than Forinel had been, years before, but perhaps he could learn some patience, and, if not, what of it? She had determined to find his perfunctory attentions absolutely ground-shaking and marvelous, and, all in all, it had really been quite pleasant, and he was very sweet.

There were things that were difficult in life, but this was hardly one of them.

Kethol froze for a moment.

"What is—?"

"Shush."

She tried to let go of his hand, but his grip tightened on hers, and he pulled her off the path and behind a pair of old elms.

"It's—"

He clapped his hand over her mouth. He wasn't brutal about it, but he made no effort at being gentle.

"Quiet," he said, his lips up against her ear. "Not a word."

"But—"

His grip tightened, and he released her mouth only after she forced her body to relax against his, and tried to nod against his hand.

Of course, it would just be riders from the Residence, come looking for them when their horses had returned riderless. There was no need to hide.

He pulled his knife from his belt. Reaching up, he chopped

down three small branches, and as he squatted down, he laid them over the two of them.

"I don't—"

His hand was back over her mouth.

This was ridiculous. Could he not simply ask her to be quiet?

"Yes," he whispered, his breath warm in her ear, "it should be a troop from the Residence, it almost certainly is a troop from the Residence—but what if it isn't? Or what if Miron's talked Thirien into letting him lead a search? Now don't talk, don't move, don't even breathe heavily."

Miron?

Granted, Miron was angry at Forinel having—as he no doubt saw it—robbed him of the barony, and she had no doubt at all that he would slit more than a few throats if that would make him Baron Keranahan, but something as clumsy as murdering Forinel, with his own hand? In front of witnesses?

No. Miron wasn't stupid.

She started to protest, but stopped herself. He wouldn't let her talk, and even if he would, he simply wouldn't listen, not now. At the sound of the hoofbeats, he had changed, instantly, from a pretend baron into something else, someone else, a someone with strong opinions, stronger muscles, and the fast reflexes to carry those opinions out without hesitation. She could guide—no, not guide: manipulate; she had to be honest with herself—she could manipulate the false baron easily, but this other person was another matter entirely.

He closed his eyes. "I count three horses," he whispered. "Shhh."

If quiet is so important, she thought, then why are you talking? Just to show off?

She was immediately ashamed of the thought. He was trying to reassure her, and she was more than a little surprised to find that she was reassured. Was it that she thought that Kethol could take on three men all by himself? With them on horseback? She knew that he was strong and tough and fast, but that seemed unlikely, not if they knew what they were doing. He would be lucky to surprise one, and the others would ride him down, baron or no.

She hoped he wasn't going to try anything. But there was no point in trying to protest, since he clearly wasn't going to let her talk.

So she just closed her eyes and leaned back against him, not entirely sure that she didn't resent the fact that he still had his hand clapped across her mouth.

The leaves rested against her face, making it itch, and it was all she could do not to try to raise her hands and brush them away.

The bole of the tree blocked her view as the horsemen thundered by. She had never really noticed before how the ground actually shook, if only a little, under the pounding of their hooves.

The horses slowed, and then stopped, and an unfamiliar voice cried out, "Baron Keranahan? Baron Keranahan?"

There was, of course, no answer.

"I don't see what you're yelling about," another voice answered. "If he's anywhere around, he'll have heard us long before this."

"Yes, but—"

"So shut up and let's ride, Derwin. Or do you want to be in the woods at night and get your eyes poked out when you don't see a branch in the dark?"

The horses moved off, the *clop-clop-clop* of their hooves diminishing in the distance.

She tried to sit up, but he held her firmly.

"No. Wait," he whispered.

She waited for what felt like the longest time, until he finally sighed, released her, and gently laid the branches that had covered them to one side before rising to his feet, and brushing himself off.

He offered her his hand. "I think we can go now."

"May I ask what that was all about?" she asked, as he easily pulled her up.

For once, his smile didn't seem at all forced or hesitant. She liked that.

"I just don't like to take chances I don't have to," he said. "You're probably right—those were probably just searchers sent out from the Residence, looking for us. But why should I bet—why should we bet our lives on it?" He plucked an errant pine needle from his beard, and stuck it between his teeth, then stooped to pick up the branches and throw them off into the brush. "Just to save ourselves a little walk? I don't mind walking, do you?"

He shouldered the provisions bag, and hitched at both his sword and his knife. "Shall we, Lady?"

"Leria," she said, correcting him. "My name is Leria, and I think that, under the circumstances, informality should be the rule between us, and not the exception. Don't you?"

He actually blushed. "Very well. Leria."

"So? What do you think? Weren't those just soldiers from the Residence, out searching for us? They didn't sound like bandits, and while I'm pleased to say I've never met any Dark Riders—"

"I have, Leria, and they're nothing to joke about."

"—those didn't seem like any such. So you think that they were out to kill you? Us?"

"No, I don't." He shook his head. "No, I don't think so. But I'm not sure, and since I'm not sure, it didn't make any sense to me to take a chance. But there were just three riders, with three horses. If they were sent out to rescue us, why only three horses?"

She didn't answer. He was feeling awfully full of himself, which was just what she wanted, and no good at all could come from any answer, except one, so she made that answer:

"Thank you," she said.

He nodded, not blushing now, accepting the thanks as his due.

Good. He wouldn't have nodded so self-confidently if she had pointed out that, of course, two of the soldiers would have been more than happy to surrender their horses to the baron and his lady, so that the nobles could ride rather than walk back to the Residence.

It was far more important to build up his self-confidence than it was to be seen to be right.

And, come to think of it, she might well be able to help to build up his self-confidence tonight, perhaps two or even three times.

She might even enjoy it.

They walked, side by side down the path, talking quietly. Every once in a while, he would stop and stand stock-still, listening or smelling or looking for something, and she obediently mirrored his silence— without the need of him clapping a hand to her mouth.

After a few moments, he would relax and nod, and then they would walk on.

By the time the path broke on the wheat field, the sun had barely set. The waist-high wheat rippled like the surface of a pond in the light breeze, while across the road, a dozen peasant farmers had almost made their way clear across the turnip field in their awkwardly squatting steps, picking the weeds that they thrust into the long canvas bags trailing behind them.

It had always seemed to Leria to be a lot of trouble to go to— just for turnips, after all; she didn't particularly like turnip cake, and absolutely abhorred the way that boiled turnips always gave her gas.

But, then again, it was no secret that different people had different tastes, and perhaps the peasants simply preferred a solid, plain meal of boiled turnips to, say, a roasted chicken, stuffed with aromatic barley, its skin crispy and garlicky to the bite.

A cry from a lookout on the wall around the Residence was echoed throughout, and a party of three soldiers, armored head to foot, emerged at a trot, led by Thirien, who puffed and panted as he ran to greet them, emerged from the gates.

Pirojil and Erenor brought up the rear, walking.

"Balls, boy—I mean, Baron," Thirien said, his eyes searching Forinel's. "You're well?"

"Of course," Kethol said, and the way he said it was indistinguishable to her from the way that Forinel would have. "Leria and I were just out for a ride, and when we stopped to rest, the horses ran away. My fault entirely; I should have staked them out."

Thirien nodded, and while his lips tightened hard enough that it was clear what he was thinking, he didn't ask what the "rest" consisted of.

"I sent three men down that trail," Thirien said, scowling. "Good men, so I would have sworn, although I guess I'd have been a fool to do so. I think I'd best have them posted to extra duty until their eyes improve. Maybe a few tendays of extra night watches will improve their eyes."

Kethol started to say something in protest, but Leria quickly laid her hand on his arm.

"Please, Captain Thirien, don't punish them. I'm sure that they did their best. They probably rode by when we were off the trail. *Resting.*"

She very carefully didn't look at Kethol, and hoped that he wouldn't start with the blushing again. It would be beneath the baron to brag about his exploits, but it would not be in character for him to be ashamed of them, and it was no more unusual that a landholder's daughter's wedding dress would be loosely cut when she and her betrothed were presented to the baron for marriage than it would be if she had started to show when she and Forinel were presented to the Emperor. Yes, there would be laughter at his expense, but it would be familiar laughter.

Thirien gave a slight bow. "As you wish it, Lady," he said.

And if he noticed the two pieces of dried grass that Leria had carefully tucked into her hair, he didn't say anything.

5

✠ Jason and Walter

Jason Cullinane had just handed the big bay gelding's reins to the stableboy when his sister walked into the stable, more dragging than leading her skittish brown gelding.

"Aiea?"

"Hey, you recognized me," she said, grinning. "It's been days since you left Biemestren; I was worried that you'd forgotten me entirely."

The scent of a strange horse immediately had Falsworth snorting and kicking in his stall, and while the stallion wouldn't get out—the last time he had kicked through the gate, Ereken had replaced the too-thin pine slats with thick oak—the noise disturbed all the other horses, as well.

Jason could always trust Aiea to bring confusion out of order. That was the way sisters were, he guessed.

As usual, she was dressed close to indecently: her scoop-necked blouse was cut too low, and her black leather trousers were cut too tight, although he had long since given up complaining about that, since her only response was amused condescension.

"Hunting?" she asked, although she obviously knew the answer. Not that there was any great secret about it—the bloody knees of his trousers were a good indication, and if much or any of the blood had been his, he wouldn't be walking so easily.

"You had some luck, I take it?" she asked, gesturing at his clothes.

"I'll change and bathe right away, I promise," he said. "I just got back, and Taren's got the bathhouse first."

She nodded. "Venison for supper?"

Not a bad guess. His clothes showed every sign of his having messily field-dressed something, and the most likely candidate for that was deer, after all. "No. Orc—but it's not for supper."

She made a face. "I'd imagine not. So why did you dress them out?"

"Just trying to figure if there's a better target to shoot at than the hip," he said. "Since they won't hold still while they're alive, Taren and I have been taking to cutting some up, after."

"Any luck in that?"

"Nah." He shook his head. "But it was worth a try. We even learned a little." He tapped on the center of his chest. "If you ever have to shoot one, don't aim for the breastbone—it's thicker than a boar's."

He was supposed to be surprised to see her—ever since she had married Uncle Walter, something that always seemed more than vaguely incestuous to Jason, she had been spending almost all of her time in Biemestren—but she was expecting that, so he just acted as though it was no surprise for her to turn up.

"How many?" she asked.

"Two. Sow and a buck." He shrugged. "Still some sort of colony of them, up in the hills."

"Not good."

That was true enough. He wished that the orcs weren't getting better about hiding.

When they had first flowed out from the rift between reality and Faerie, they had been preposterously easy to track, if only from the trail of grisly remains that they left behind. Legends aside, most meat-eating animals avoided humans entirely, and only fought men in self-defense—and then, largely, only when cornered. Orcs seemed to prefer human flesh, with pork in second place.

But the orcs were getting smarter, or perhaps they had just killed off all the stupid ones. Jason and Taren had followed the trail that these had left from dawn until after noon until it circled back on itself, and he was confident that the two he and Taren had finally happened upon weren't the ones they were trying to track.

They would go out again tomorrow. The pair that they were hunting had taken to baby-snatching, and that made them a top priority.

"As long as I'm wishing," he said, "I'd wish I were a better tracker."

"Or had a better tracker around?" she asked.

He forced a smile. "Yes, it would be good to have Kethol back."

"Yes." She nodded. "Any word from Pirojil?"

"No." He shook his head. "He's not much for writing."

Pirojil was the most literate of the three—of the *two* of them, and Jason knew that he could read and sound out English letters, and knew at least enough Erendra glyphs to get by, and Jason had had a suspicion that he could read a bit of Low Elvish, as well, although where and how he had picked that up was something that he didn't talk about. Not that he talked about himself much at all.

"Then again," Jason said, "I'm not much for writing, come to think of it."

It would have been good to have Pirojil around, and better to have him and Kethol. But Kethol had gone off to Therranj to retrieve Forinel, and had taken service with the elves, and if there was a tracker or woodsman as good around, Jason had yet to hear of him.

He tried to tell himself that it was just that, and not the sense of betrayal that he felt. Which hurt him more than he thought it would. Fairly silly—but Pirojil and Kethol and Durine had been around, well, forever, almost, and he had been used to the three of them.

But now Durine was dead, and Kethol had stayed on in Therranj to serve some elven noble—and had done that without so much as a by-your-leave. Pirojil had taken service with Forinel—only for a while, so he said—and Jason wasn't sure which of the three he was most angry with, although it seemed both silly and somehow disloyal to be angry at Durine for dying, after all, any more than he should be angry at Father for having done the same thing.

But he was.

While Jason Cullinane had tried to learn that he didn't need to let his every feeling show on his face or in his words, he at least tried to be honest with himself.

She was smiling at him. "Very good self-control, baby brother."

He hated when she called him that. Which was, of course, why she did it.

He could have responded, honestly, that he had been Karl and Andrea Cullinane's son longer than she had been their daughter—Aiea had been adopted, after all, and once, years ago, when she had teased him just a little too much, he had said just that, and he didn't like to remember the look of disgust on Father's face.

"Where's Uncle Walter?" he asked. If he couldn't get a little revenge one way, well, there were others, and if that was a little juvenile for a man of more than twenty, well, his sister, adopted or no, did tend to bring out the juvenile in him, and probably vice versa, as well.

"*Uncle* Walter?"

"Your husband?" He held up his palm, flat, just at his brow level, but off to the side. "Bearded guy, oh, about this tall, smiles a lot, and probably even means it, every now and then?" It was strange that Aiea had ended up marrying Walter—who wasn't really his uncle, and whom he hadn't actually called Uncle Walter since he had been a kid—but they were both adults, of a sort, and what they wanted to do wasn't any of Jason's business.

Even if it was a bit bizarre, given Walter's history.

"*Uncle* Walter, it is, eh?" a familiar voice said, from the doorway.

Walter Slovotsky walked into the stable, his usual, all-is-right-with-the-world-now-that-I'm-here smile firmly in place. His brown hair was thinning a little, these days, and smiles—it couldn't be work or worry—had added some lines around the corners of his lips and at the eyes, but he was, still, Uncle Walter.

And it *was* good to see him, even though it had been only a tenday since Parliament had closed.

Walter Slovotsky stopped a few feet away and gave a quick bow. "Baron Cullinane," he said. "I hope I'm welcome?"

"If not, it's a little bit late for you to be asking, isn't it?"

Aiea snickered. "I'll leave the two of you to talk." She turned to Jason. "Mother up at the house?"

He shrugged. "She doesn't report to me on her comings and goings. Quite the contrary."

"Poor baby," she said, patting him on the cheek, as she left. He watched Walter watch her walking away, and found himself glaring, so he stopped.

"Hey, take it easy," Walter said. "I *married* the girl, remember?"

"Yeah."

Walter looked like he was going to say something—probably some comment about Jason and Janie—but then stopped himself. Which was just as well.

Jason liked Walter, and he trusted him, devious though his mind tended to be, but it didn't help keep their relationship simple that Walter was married to Jason's sister and Jason involved with Walter's daughter—and never mind the strange looks that Walter and Mother passed between them; he didn't want to think about that—

and when you were dealing with Walter Slovotsky, it was always best to try to keep things simple.

Not that there was much of a chance of that.

"Pleasure trip?" he asked.

Walter smiled. "Hey, any time I see you, it's a pleasure." He sobered. "But, more seriously, after the last Parliament, I needed to get out of town for a while"—he raised a palm—"just because the walls were starting to close in on me, eh? Not any kind of trouble, okay?"

"If you say so."

"Well, I do. I figured I'd combine a visit with you and your mother—without having Beralyn glaring at us, like we're plotting treason, every time the two of us exchange a couple of words—with seeing how you were doing. So: how are you doing?"

Jason shrugged, and then cursed himself for it. Trust Uncle Walter to make him feel twelve again, with a shrug for this and a shrug for that, as though he had, yet again, been caught skipping out to go hunting with Kethol when he was supposed to be in the library with Doria.

"I'm fine," he said. "It's good to be back."

Walter nodded. "I know the feeling. Orc troubles, I hear. Getting better?"

Jason shook his head. "Worse, if anything. They're smarter every year, it seems like."

"Evolution in action?"

Jason forced himself not to shrug. "I don't know. I do know that it's . . . getting tougher. Not killing them—"

"I never found them all that easy to kill. Shit, Tennetty never found them all that easy to kill, and she was good at it."

"It takes some practice," Jason said. He tapped himself on the chest. "Don't try for a chest shot, because while that will kill them, sooner than later, it doesn't slow them down enough, not right away.

Hold low and outside," he said, patting himself on the hip. "Break the pelvic girdle, and they fall right over. Gives you enough time to spear them."

A rack of boar spears hung on the wall; he pulled one down, and tapped at the crosspiece, welded to the back of the long, broad head. "It's more like boar hunting than anything else—except that boars don't have hands, and they do."

"Of course, if you miss . . ."

Jason nodded. "I've done that, from time to time. It can get kind of messy. Which is why you need the boar spear—and somebody you can rely on to get around behind, while you're holding on, because even with a spear in an orc's chest, you're not going to be able to hold one off very long."

"And if there's another one of them, as well as another one of you? It could get ugly."

"Yeah. Just as well they don't work together, because if they did, I don't have the slightest idea what we'd do."

"Hmmm . . . then again, if they did know how to team up, they probably wouldn't be hiding in burrows up in the hills, eh?"

"There is that."

Walter nodded. "Well, as long as you trust this Taren . . ."

"If I didn't, I wouldn't hunt with him at all, much less for orcs." Jason frowned. "But more is better than fewer, and I'm hoping that you're not going to try to talk Pirojil into staying on in Keranahan any longer than it takes to get the baron settled. As though that should be his problem, just because he and Erenor brought Forinel back from Therranj."

"I dunno. You're not going to tell me that you need one soldier that bad, are you?"

"No. But—"

"But you're used to having him and Kethol around, and you'd rather hunt with two or three men you know and trust than with a whole company that treats the young baron as though he's baggage, eh?"

"Well, yes."

"I can understand that." Walter seemed to consider it for a moment. "If you want my guess, Pirojil's absence has a lot more to do with Leria than it does with the baron."

"Leria and Pirojil?" Jason cocked his head to one side. "Is there something going on that I shouldn't know about?"

"Almost certainly." Walter smiled. "Why should today be unusual?"

Jason was suspicious. "Something between Pirojil and Leria? That doesn't sound awfully likely. I mean, he's, well—"

"He's terribly ugly, yes, and that bothers him more than it bothers anybody else, I think. Women? Some. Many, maybe." Walter tilted his head to one side. "If women were all that impressed by looks, neither of us would be able to get a date to the prom, eh?"

"Prom?"

Walter Slovotsky shook his head. "Oh, never mind. Then again, it's a different thing—Pirojil is a soldier, and you're royalty, and I'm, well, me. I don't think there's anything going on there—except maybe some unrequited passion on Pirojil's part."

"Which is why I shouldn't be expecting him to hurry back to the barony?"

"Yeah. Give it some time, okay?"

Jason shrugged. Well, if it was that way . . .

"Now, tell me more about these orcs," Walter Slovotsky went on.

"You want to go hunting tomorrow with Taren and me?"

"The chances of me deliberately putting my tender flesh in the way of huge beasts that think of me as an appetizer are zero, zip, and none, Jason." Slovotsky smiled. "Not unless I had to—and I sure don't think that I have to."

As they walked out into the bright light of the noon sun, Walter Slovotsky was keeping his eye on where the tall oaks of the forest rimmed the eastern field. "That said, of course, you never know—you were telling about these boar spears you've been using?"

It was all that Walter could do to keep a smile off his face as the talk turned to matters of orc hunting that interested Walter only in a distant, academic sense, as important as they were to a country baron.

Walter had been in a fight with an orc, once, and once was more than enough, and he had been entirely truthful in telling Jason that he had no intention of ever doing so again.

But he had been right in worrying that Jason would start to get itchy about Pirojil's absence, and maybe begin to wonder why Pirojil had suddenly developed such an attachment to Forinel. That might—might—lead to some awkward questions, and Walter Slovotsky would rather awkward questions never be asked in the first place, rather than answered.

There was no reason that Jason had to know that Forinel was really Kethol, and it was always easier to keep a secret if you never knew it in the first place, and better to supply an answer to a question before it was ever asked.

Besides, Walter Slovotsky thought to himself, if you couldn't fool your friends, who could you fool?

6

Morning at the Residence

If you can manage to sleep until noon, the rest
of the world will have worn itself out solving its
own problems before you have to get involved.

If, that is, they don't get worse—which is,
let's face it, the way to bet.

—Walter Slovotsky

The sun hadn't fully risen over the walls when Pirojil found
Miron out behind the barracks, giving a lesson in swords-
manship to a half-dozen soldiers.

The fencing circle had been cleared in the gravel in the center
of a small grove of old cherry trees. Bent and crooked as only old
fruit trees could be, they trembled in the wind, as though excited
to watch the competition.

Like the others, Miron was stripped to the waist, barracks-style.
While his broad chest held a few scars, including a long, ragged one
over his heart that spoke of a serious wound and the lack of available
healing draughts at the time he had gotten it, it sported none of the
fresh, painful red weals that amply decorated the chests and arms
of all of the soldiers, and proclaimed that Miron had been at this
for a while this morning.

"A good morning to you, Captain Pirojil," Miron said, raising the hilt of his practice sword to his head in a quick salute as he stepped back out of the circle. His boot heel crushed a fallen cherry, its juice red as fresh blood on the graveled ground.

"And to you, Lord Miron."

Turning from him, Miron saluted his opponent, a boy of perhaps eighteen at most, who looked far too young to be a soldier.

A balding, fortyish decurion took up a position between them, his short staff outstretched.

"Make yourselves ready," he said, raising his arm. He didn't quite have the bored tone of a real swordmaster down, and he called out "Fight!" and snapped his arm down before stepping quite out of the cleared dirt circle that served as the practice ring.

Miron and his opponent closed.

It was possible that the boy had simply never held a sword of any sort in his hand before, or that he refused to attempt to score off a noble—Miron quickly beat the blade aside, tapped the boy lightly on the chest, retreated, then instantly reengaged and scored again, even before the decurion could step between them.

"No, no, *no*," he said. "At least *try* to take my blade. Or, if you are too clumsy to do that, just wave your blade around as vigorously as you can, and hope to connect. Such things can happen."

"Yes, my lord."

"Again, please."

"Make yourself ready . . . and fight!"

The boy tried again, with equally useless results. Pirojil counted five, no, six marks on the boy's chest where Miron had scored. All but one of them were directly over the heart, and the other one was just under the rib cage, on the boy's right side. Had they been fighting with real blades, Miron's opponent would be five times dead, and the sixth time, the boy would still be lying on the ground, clutching with white fingers at his gut, trying to hold his body's blood in.

Interesting.

Pirojil had fenced with nobles before; generally, they tried to score on the vulnerable arms and legs. Going for the torso required getting closer to your opponent; it was a soldier's move, not a duelist's. In a real fight, you couldn't count on a superficial arm or leg wound stopping an enemy, and you couldn't afford to leave one enemy who had merely been lightly injured at your back when you turned to face another one. Or two. Or twenty. You had to put them down fast, and hope you ran out of enemies before you ran out of luck.

Of course, in a real fight, you couldn't count on having solid-packed dirt underneath your boots, either, or be sure that if you retreated out of the range of a lunge, you wouldn't stumble over something, and find yourself quickly spitted on a sword. Or a spear. Or get kicked in the head or the balls. Or . . .

"Care to join us?" Miron pointed his button-tipped practice sword at the ground in front of him. "Since the Residence seems to be lacking a master of swords at the moment, I thought I'd give a few lessons."

"Certainly," Pirojil said. "I'm always eager to learn from my betters."

Miron just smiled. "Then let us have at it—the day gets no younger, and neither do you."

Pirojil unbuckled his sword belt, shed his tunic, and picked up one of the practice swords. It was too light, more reminiscent of a dueling sword than of a soldier's saber.

Pirojil felt at the button tip. It was solid, properly welded on, not merely capped. Thin and narrow, the unsharpened blade flexed properly, showing no signs of breaking, although he wouldn't have wanted to try to bend it much farther. It was much more elegant than the wooden practice swords that Pirojil had trained with.

He tossed it underhand to Miron, who snatched it out of the air, raising an eyebrow in surprise.

"I'd prefer to use your practice blade, Lord Miron—if you don't mind."

He had to admire how quickly Miron adapted—Miron simply tossed Pirojil his own practice sword, and gave a casual shrug. "As you wish."

This blade flexed just as well as the other one had, but even Pirojil's blunt fingers could easily detect that the button was loose. It would be a matter of a solid tug to remove it, instantly turning what was supposedly simply a practice weapon into something deadly.

Pirojil didn't say anything about that, or about anything else.

"Make yourselves ready . . ."

Pirojil raised the sword in a quick salute, and at Miron's returning salute, Pirojil dropped into a fighting stance, advancing immediately when the decurion called out, "Fight!"

They touched swords, and then Miron dropped his point and tried a tentative lunge, cutting over Pirojil's sword and trying for a high-line thrust when Pirojil easily parried. He would have easily scored a point on Pirojil's forearm if Pirojil hadn't stepped back.

Pirojil reengaged, extended his arm to offer it as a target, and whipped the side of his blade at Miron's sword arm when Miron lunged.

It connected with a satisfying *smack*. If Pirojil had been using his real sword, it would have cut Miron's arm to the bone.

"Your point," Miron said, smiling. The red weal flared brightly on his arm, but if Miron was in any discomfort, he didn't let it show.

"Another?" Pirojil asked.

Miron's eyes were still on the tip of Pirojil's sword. The button was still in place. "If you please."

"Make yourself ready . . . and fight!"

This time, Miron's attack was more tentative. His weight on the balls of his feet, he danced in and out of the live zone, quickly parrying Pirojil's equally tentative attacks before retreating out of range. But Pirojil pressed forward, and Miron retreated, stopping only when the heel of his back foot touched the gravel surrounding the fencing circle.

Miron started to lower his blade in surrender, but before he could complete the move, Pirojil lunged in, the tip of the practice sword catching Miron on the face. The covered point skidded along Miron's cheek before he could raise his own sword to parry.

"Halt," the decurion called out, stepping between the two of them, his short staff ready to deflect a blow, be it reflexive or intentional.

Pirojil stepped back and lowered his sword.

"Very nice," Miron said, wiping the back of his free hand against his cheek. "You are rather better at this than I would have thought."

"Another, please?"

"Of course."

"Make yourself ready . . . and fight!"

Pirojil raised the sword over his head and played with the tip, then advanced, his left side toward Miron, his right arm and the sword behind him.

Miron hadn't fooled him for a moment, letting Pirojil win two points. But keep the point out of view for a moment, then move the sword back and forth too quickly for Miron to be able to see the tip clearly, and Miron would have good reason to worry that Pirojil had removed the practice tip from the sword, and consider the thought of his own flesh being pierced, and perhaps Pirojil could see just how good this Miron was.

Miron's eyes widened fractionally, and when Pirojil whipped the sword around as he advanced, he wasn't all surprised that Miron easily parried his slashing attack.

Their blades moved faster than any eye could follow, including Pirojil's.

A real fight was different, but in a fencing circle Pirojil always had a detached feeling, as though he were outside his body, watching what was going on, realizing only in retrospect what he had been thinking, what he had been doing.

That was the way of it. You practiced, as much as you could, working through combinations of attacks and parries and counters at first slowly, then faster and faster, until you knew the moves in your balls and bones, not in your mind, because when it was real— even as marginally real as a practice bout was—your mind was never fast enough, and never would be, never could be.

Miron would, of course, try for a touch on Pirojil's arm, or leg, to win the point, from as great a distance as possible, and—

Miron feinted and lunged low through Pirojil's defenses as though they simply weren't there, and the tip of his blade caught Pirojil just below the sternum.

Pirojil's breath went out of him with a whoosh, and his traitor knees turned all liquid and useless. Pirojil tried to bring his blade up to protect himself from a continued attack, but his arms wouldn't work, either. Unable to protect himself, he fell to the ground, the left side of his face pressed into the dirt. He wanted, as much as he had ever wanted anything, to pull breath into his lungs, not caring a whit if it brought dirt and dust along with it.

But he couldn't. All he could do was lie there and make choking sounds, and try to breathe.

"Quickly," Miron said, "bring over the healing draughts—and get him up. Quickly, now, quickly."

Strong hands brought Pirojil up to his knees, and the cold lip of the brass bottle was pressed to his lips, grinding the sand and the grit into his teeth.

He pushed it away, embarrassed at how difficult it was. There was no point in wasting expensive healing draughts on something this minor, no matter how much it hurt.

"He won't—"

"Well, then, leave him be," Miron said. "If he doesn't want it, he doesn't have to have it."

Two of the soldiers helped him to his feet, and held him up straight until his breath returned in ragged little gasps.

Pirojil shrugged the helping hands away. He could stand by himself, or he could fall again.

"Nicely struck, Lord Miron," Pirojil said, cursing at the weakness of his words. A distant, heavy hand wiped at the side of his face, and he was only vaguely surprised to realize that it was his own hand.

Miron nodded. "A good bout, at that. Perhaps some other time we could do this again," he said. He stooped to pick up the rapier that Pirojil had been using, looked closely, too closely, at the still intact tip, then nodded. "Quite a good strategy, all in all, Captain Pirojil," he said.

Pirojil wondered if any of the others had realized what had gone on.

It was just an accident, waiting to happen—on demand. Miron could honestly say, and could produce witnesses, that he had simply been practicing, properly practicing, with weapons that had been made safe, and that somehow the tip had worked itself loose, and, tragically, the suddenly live blade had buried itself in a chest.

Pirojil didn't have any doubt as to whose chest that was supposed to happen with.

Miron nodded, genially. "I think you'd best take this to the blacksmith," he said, feeling at the tip. "Inadvertently, no doubt inadvertently, it seems to have worked loose." He gripped the tip between thumb and forefinger, and tugged on it, and then, when it didn't come loose, pulled harder and harder, his smile only broadening when it didn't come loose. "Hmmmm . . . I don't seem to have quite the strength to pull it all the way, but we ought to be careful. Somebody might get hurt."

At the sound of footsteps behind him, Pirojil turned to see Forinel walking out of the garden. He was dressed in casual blousy pantaloons and loose, flowing shirt, but the image of the idle noble was shattered by the very utilitarian sword belt around his waist.

He gave a nod first to Miron—good, good, he was acknowledging the noble first—and then to Pirojil.

"Some sword practice?" Forinel asked, one eyebrow arched.

Miron nodded. "I would say that I was just giving a quick lesson to Captain Pirojil, but in truth, I think I've learned more from him than he has from me." He drew himself up straight. "Now, if you'll excuse me, my baron, I've promised to visit Lord Melchen today, and I'd best be off. As to you, Captain Pirojil, I'll see you on Fredensday, in Dereneyl, and perhaps we can arrange another lesson."

"I'll be ready for it," Pirojil said.

"Of that, I'm entirely sure."

Miron gave a slight, stiff bow, and then turned and walked away.

At Pirojil's gesture to the decurion, the decurion barked out a quick command, and each of the soldiers gave a quick bow and gathered up the practice gear before heading toward the barracks.

Forinel looked at him. "Some problem?"

Pirojil shrugged. "Maybe."

"I see," Forinel said, although his eyes said that he didn't. But it was the sort of thing that a nobleman should have said. Good.

Pirojil didn't like this at all. It was too clumsy for somebody as deft as Miron. Trying to explain to Parliament that he had accidentally killed his brother in practice? Could that explanation possibly fly?

No. Pirojil had been wrong—it wasn't Forinel that was the target; it was Pirojil.

An accident where a newly promoted captain of march had died was not a parliamentary matter, after all. It wasn't quite as easy to dismiss as slaughtering a peasant, of course, but it would be handled by Treseen, and Pirojil had no doubt that Treseen would simply set it aside as being nothing more than what it appeared to be. Whatever Miron had planned for Forinel could wait until Pirojil wasn't around to be a witness.

Pirojil couldn't help smiling.

For once, it was nice that in order to do his job, he had to protect his own hide.

Forinel watched Miron walk away. "Leria is going over the inventory with Elda," he said. "The whole Residence, from top to bottom. She says it will take some time."

Pirojil nodded. A good idea. He would have been surprised if some valuables hadn't vanished during the many tendays that there had been no noble in residence here, but more than likely most of such would now magically return to their proper places in anticipation of this inventory.

Forinel went on: "She thinks that I should spend the next few days just riding around and visiting the local villages, and perhaps calling on some of the lord landholders—I can get reacquainted with the rest, and some of the nobles minor, in Dereneyl on Fredensday."

Pirojil nodded. "See if the wardens are keeping up repairs and such?"

That made sense. Not that it was likely. But it would be good to see things firsthand. That was something that both a real soldier and a pretend noble could agree on.

"Yes. Do you feel like coming along? Or should I just ride out alone?"

"Alone?" Pirojil shook his head. Yes, of course, Forinel had every right and probably the obligation, come to think of it, to prowl from one end of the barony to the other. But that still didn't make it other than a stupid idea for him to do it alone. "You do need some-body to watch your back, Baron."

He smiled. "Yes, I suppose I do."

And, besides, if Forinel was going to brace any of the noble landholders, it would be a good idea to have somebody handy to change the subject if the conversation turned to awkward matters.

Forinel cocked his head to one side. "Could you tell me what just happened here?" He gestured at the fencing circle.

"Later. We'll have time," Pirojil said. "You sit and have breakfast while I have the cook pack us some lunch, and have the boy saddle us a couple of horses. That gelding you were riding yesterday seems spirited enough, eh?"

"Rather more than enough. If you can find a more docile mount, I'd appreciate it."

Pirojil nodded. "As you wish," he said.

Pirojil headed for the stables, not for the barracks. Thirien would insist on having them escorted by House Guard soldiers, and if the ones Miron had been practicing with were any indication, they would be useless in a crisis.

That probably was unfair, but how could you possibly know in advance of seeing them in action? That was the trouble with peace; it was one thing to be a barracks soldier, and another thing entirely to keep your head about you when the screams of the injured and dying filled the air.

Much better to have a spare horse or two, and be ready to gallop away from any difficulty. Besides, by themselves they could talk freely, something that they couldn't do around an escort.

There wasn't any other reason, was there?

Letting Forinel take a look at the lay of the land made sense. Until Forinel had explored the vicinity of the Residence more thor-oughly, it would quickly be evident to anybody that his only famil-iarity with it was from the maps in the Residence study.

It was, in a strange sort of way, like it used to be, when they used to accompany Baron Cullinane, doing the same sorts of things. Theoretically, it was a chance for crofters and peasants to raise issues with the baron—a noble landholder squeezing them for extra taxes, say—but, in practice, few would take the chance of doing so.

After all, they would have to deal with the village warden or landholder later, and angering their betters was something that few would risk doing.

Then again, when it came to angering his betters, Pirojil had just done the same thing himself with his little comedy with Miron, and only an idiot would feel good about it.

Pirojil smiled to himself.

Being an idiot seemed to be a recurring problem for all of them.

A village? Pirojil sniffed. The presence of the square stone marker at the crossroads proclaimed that it was a village, at least technically. Pirojil would hardly have wanted to call it a village, or call it much of anything, actually.

The roads, bad as they were, were about what Pirojil would have expected. Roads were what tied a barony together, and the roads between the Residence and this village were crooked and narrow, ill maintained at best, and would be hard going on foot or horse, and utterly impassable by anything on wheels for days after a rain.

But there was no real point in maintaining roads between the Residence and a bunch of nothing little villages like this. It would be like using strong spidersilk thread to stitch together a threadbare peasant's tunic. Why bother?

The village, such as it was, was just a cluster of half a dozen one-story, wattle-and-daub shacks beside a stream. Other than the shacks and the barely occupied pigpens, the only man-made structure was a sagging log bridge, its timbers visibly rotting, that spanned the stream.

Pirojil thought for a moment about going upstream to ford where the banks were shallower, but Forinel seemed eager to get across to the supposed village, so Forinel waited while Pirojil chivvied the spare mounts across the bridge. The bridge creaked frighteningly, and some of the dirt and pebbles that covered its surface sifted down through the old timbers to splash into the stream, but still it gave no sign of actually falling into the stream, so he dug in his heels and walked his horse across, Forinel following behind.

By the time Pirojil had retrieved the spare horses' leads, the fields were almost empty.

The children who had been weeding the cornfield had raised their heads and fled in panic for the fringe of woods to the north; one of them, a dirty-faced blond girl who couldn't have been more than ten or twelve, scooped up a wicker basket as she ran, the screams of the baby inside only urging her to pump her bare legs faster and faster—at that, she was barely able to outrun the adults, who had seized up their hoes and run away even more quickly than had the children.

They were almost alone.

The sow pig barely raised her head, and her piglets in the pen were too busy squirming and sucking at her teats to bother about trivial matters like humans riding up, but the dozen or so chickens ran about, some taking to the air in a flurry of wings that didn't get them high, or far.

The only human being who remained was a stocky, sunburned man, his simple muslin peasant's tunic belted with a length of rope.

Using his hoe as a staff, he trudged slowly across the field and up to the road, like a man walking to the gallows.

"Can I help you, my lord?" he asked. He was trying to keep the fear out of his voice, and he wasn't succeeding.

Forinel levered himself out of his saddle, and dropped to the ground.

"Help? No. My name is Forinel," he said.

The peasant ducked his head. "Yes, my lord."

"You?"

That probably should have been something more noble-sounding—*And you would be?*, perhaps—but it mattered only in principle, rather than in practice; if Forinel was going to make mistakes, which seemed more than passingly likely, he might as well make them with a peasant, after all.

"My name is Wen'll," the peasant said, not quite shuffling his feet. "Wen'll, Wen'll's son. Is there anything I can do for you, my lord?"

"He's the baron," Pirojil said. "*The* baron. Baron Keranahan."

Under his mask of sweat-caked dirt, the peasant visibly paled. "Yes, my lord."

Pirojil hated dealing with peasants. It was always the forced smiles, and the ducked heads, and the yes-my-lord, and no-my-lord, and will-that-be-all-my-lord, and, if you didn't watch out, it would probably be stab-you-in-the-back-and-take-everything-you-had-my-lord, as well, more often than not.

Forinel shook his head. "There's no need to worry, Wen'll. I'm not here to take your chickens or your pigs, or," he said, smiling, "your daughters."

Riding down peasant girls had always been a not-infrequent pastime among the young nobility, although Pirojil had never been able to understand it. Each to his own. Pirojil had always preferred a relatively clean, relatively willing whore when the pressure built up enough to bother him. An unbathed, unwilling, garlic-breathed peasant girl was about as arousing as a sheep, and you couldn't even shear them for wool.

"It's just that I've been away from the barony for a long time, and I thought it might be a good idea to see how well the farms and crofts and villages have been maintained in my absence. This is . . . ?"

Wen'll's eyes widened. "This is—this is Wen'll's Village, my lord. Is that—is that what you're asking?"

"Yes," Forinel said. "That is what I'm asking. Which would make you the village warden?"

Wen'll ducked his head again. "Yes, my lord."

He wasn't much of a village warden, but, then again, it wasn't much of a village.

"Well, village warden," Forinel said, "I hope you'll let your people know that when the baron or any of his men ride up, there's no need to take to the woods."

"Yes, my lord. I'll see that it never happens again, my lord."

Pirojil rolled his eyes. He shouldn't have been disgusted, but he was. Well, at least Kethol was sounding like a noble, which meant that he was talking like somebody who could, without blushing, make pompous pronouncements that nobody would ever believe.

Of course mounted men riding up to the village would always be a cause for the villagers' alarm. Even if the horsemen weren't sporting with the girls, they weren't going to ride into a village for the villagers' benefit, after all. And this village, such as it was, lay along the road just east of the edge of the woods that were the baron's private preserve, and was surely fed as much by poached deer as it was by turnips and onions.

While the local nobility couldn't collect their own taxes under the occupation, they could and did insist on their other rights.

Although there were no traces of a deer carcass next to the cooking fire behind the largest of the shacks, anybody with a working nose could smell the rich odor of roasted venison, and wouldn't be distracted by the five gutted rabbits, each spiked neatly through the heel, that hung on the wooden rack near the cooking fire.

Pirojil had little doubt that if he were to stick a spoon in the huge clay pot that sat simmering on the fire, he would pull out more chunks of venison than slivers of rabbit meat. It made sense for a peasant to snare rabbits—even young children could set snares and retrieve the catch—but one poached deer could put a lot more meat on the table than fifty rabbits, and it would take a lot of work to snare the fifty rabbits. Deer and rabbits would let the peasants keep the chickens for the eggs and for trade on market days. The farther you got away from a noble's house, the surer you could be that any peasant meat was caught, not grown.

Yes, of course, perhaps the deer hadn't been poached; perhaps it had been shot while browsing in the peasants' fields, which made it, in the ancient term, "fair game."

But who would witness that it *was* fair game?

With the baronial preserve right there, it was far safer not to be seen to have any deer meat, even if that meant burying bones and burning the skin instead of tanning and drying them. A smooth bone-handled hoe was easier on the hand than splintering wood, but it wasn't worth losing your hand or your neck over a few splinters.

"Well? Since you are the village warden, isn't it your responsibility to see to the repair of that bridge?" Forinel didn't wait for an answer. "But never mind that, not for now—the crofts appear to be in decent shape, although we'll have to see to the thatching, come fall. And we'll let the matter of the bridge be put aside for now, if you can do one thing . . . ?"

"Yes, Lord?"

"If, by the time I can count to twenty, you can put three arrows into an upright of the bridge, I'll just bid you a good day, and ride on—although I do expect that you, as the village warden, will keep things in much better repair than that miserable excuse for a bridge." He hitched at his sword belt, which had been raised a peremptory hand when Wen'll paled again. "No, no, relax, man—I'm just offering to swear on my sword, if you'd like."

Pirojil hadn't actually seen the expression of an animal in a trap for longer than he cared to admit, but he remembered it too well.

"No, no, my lord," Wen'll said, perhaps unintentionally mirroring Forinel's phrasing—although you could never be sure about it being unintentional; few peasants were as stupid as it suited most to pretend to be. "There's no need for any oaths—your word is more than good enough for the likes of me, my lord, more than good enough."

"Then—*one*." Forinel paused a full heartbeat, then continued to count slowly: "*Two. Three. Four.*"

Before he reached *two*, Wen'll was already dashing for the nearest of the shacks, his thick legs pumping madly, and by the time that Forinel reached ten, he had emerged, an already-strung longbow in one hand, and a bundle of crudely fletched arrows in the other. He spread his bare feet widely on the dirt, sideways to the bridge, and quickly nocked an arrow, letting the others fall to the ground.

Wen'll drew the bowstring back quickly, steadied himself, and loosed, not flinching when the string slapped his arm. He didn't wait to see if the arrow struck its mark—wherever that was; Forinel should have picked a target on the bridge and not just let the peasant use the whole bridge as a target—and quickly loosed another, and then another.

The three arrows stood out from the crossbeam, little more than a palm's breadth between them.

Wen'll hesitantly lowered his bow.

"Nicely done," Forinel said. "I don't know that I could have done better myself."

It was easy to read Wen'll's face—the baron was just bragging, although why he would brag in front of such as Wen'll was a mystery the peasant would spend little time thinking on and much less time asking about.

"Yes, my lord," he said.

Forinel held out his hand. "May I?"

The caged-animal look was back, but Wen'll handed over the bow immediately.

Forinel squatted to pick up an arrow. He sighted down its length, shook his head, set it to one side, and then chose another.

"Let's see if I can put this one in between yours."

He drew the bow, and Pirojil noted with some amusement the way Wen'll's eyes widened when Forinel was able to draw the arrow all the way to the fire-hardened tip, his arms shaking not at all.

Forinel held the pose for a long moment, long enough for Pirojil to work out that he was showing off, then let fly, with a smooth loose that had no trace of pluck in it, and, like Wen'll, didn't even wince at the way that the string slapped against his left arm.

The arrow sunk deeply into the rotten wood, just above and to the left of Wen'll's group.

"That wasn't very good," Forinel said, frowning. "I'd best try another." He stooped to pick another arrow, nocked it while still kneeling, and straightened, drew, and let fly, all in one smooth motion.

This time, the arrow spunged into the wood in the middle of the cluster. The crossbeam was beginning to resemble a porcupine.

Forinel handed the bow back to the peasant. "Good bow," he said. "You made it yourself?"

The peasant nodded.

Pirojil rolled his eyes. It was obvious that Wen'll had made it himself—the notion of a peasant, of all things, having enough spare coin to hire a good bowmaker was just this side of preposterous. The shaping and forming of a bow was something that could be done indoors, on a dark night, when there wasn't anything else to do.

But it wasn't a good idea to dismiss peasant bowmen as useless, just because their bows tended toward the crude. Rubbing at an old scar on his thigh, Pirojil remembered just how dangerous a company of Holtish peasant archers could be.

This Wen'll was clearly old enough to have been one such during the war, but Pirojil wasn't disposed to ask, and the peasant would have said no, regardless of what the truth actually was. It wasn't particularly likely, of course, but it was entirely possible that he and Wen'll had been in the same place at the same time during the war, and on opposite sides, and while Pirojil wouldn't kill him over that, he didn't much want to have to think about it, either.

"A good bow, although I think you might want to throw away that warped arrow," Forinel said, as he climbed back on his horse. "Well shot, Wen'll."

"Thank you, my lord." The peasant was beginning to relax, at least as much as he could.

"I'm hoping that the occupation of the barony will be lifted sooner than later. When it does, there will be a regular archer formation after every harvest—and no nonsense about it. The other men in your village have bows?"

"Well, yes, of course, my lord," he said.

Crofters were required to have arms, and be able to use them in service of their lord. While swords were expensive, perfectly serviceable bows could be made in the village, and used for hunting, as well as for war. There were probably no more than a few dozen swords in the barony in peasant crofts and huts, if that many—and those would more likely than not be trophies from the early part of the Holtun-Bieme war, when the Holts were winning.

In a peasant village there were much better uses for a piece of good steel than a memento. Pirojil had been spending too much time around his betters. Not that it mattered much, either way, if a few peasants had a few swords, or a lot of peasants had a lot of swords. An untrained man with a sword was about as useful as tits on a boar.

Pirojil scanned the treeline.

They were being watched, but it was vanishingly unlikely that any of the others would emerge until after he and Forinel were out of sight. Perhaps they could have ordered Wen'll to call out to them to come back, but that would be more of an experiment as to the authority that Wen'll had over his villagers than anything else, and wouldn't have proved anything interesting, either way.

"When I come this way again, I expect that the bridge will be in better shape?"

"Yes, my lord."

"Oh—and one more thing?"

"Yes, my lord?"

Forinel pointed toward the woods. "In my absence, it seems that too many buck deer have decided that the baron's fields are their feeding trough. Next time I come by, I'd very much like to see some good racks—I want you to take some bucks, mind you, not does. And if you were to smoke some sausages from the venison scraps, I might bring my own bow and we could shoot again, with them against a few coppers of my own? I'm fond of venison sausage—good venison sausage, if you don't mind my saying so."

"I'm fond of coppers, if you don't mind my saying so, my lord." Wen'll smiled.

As they rode away, Wen'll was already beckoning toward the woods.

Forinel reached down and brought up the water bag from where it was slung, and took a drink before handing it to Pirojil. Good—he was learning. Kethol would have offered Pirojil a drink, first.

"Not a bad bowman," Forinel said.

"But this competition thing?"

Forinel smiled. "I heard a barracks story about Lord Lerna doing the same thing, except he bet silver to sausage, not just copper, and he paid up. This Wen'll isn't bad—he just might be able to beat me."

"Perhaps." Pirojil was skeptical. A shot at that close range wasn't much of a test of anything, but Pirojil nodded anyway. "I've seen worse. Be interesting to see what he could do with a long shot on a regimental line."

Forinel laughed. "I was thinking that it would be interesting to see what he could do with a long shot on a running deer—and I was thinking that I'd be willing to bet, copper-to-silver or silver-to-gold, that he'd make about nine shots out of ten."

That wasn't unlikely. Pirojil said as much.

"I was wondering something, though," Forinel said. "Did you happen to see the scar on his bow arm? Scars, actually."

"No." Pirojil shook his head. He hadn't been close enough to notice.

"A pair of neat punctures, front and back. Like a couple of extra assholes." He smiled, and started to hitch up his own tunic, then stopped himself.

Kethol had had a similar pair of scars on his left side, just under the rib cage, received when a Holtish arrow had gone right through him. Their idiot captain had decided that it hadn't been serious enough to require the immediate use of expensive healing draughts, and Kethol had been seriously sick, barely able to walk, by the time Pirojil and Durine had gotten him to the Spidersect healer, dragging him themselves in a stolen cart when they couldn't steal a horse.

But not Forinel. Forinel had his own, much smaller, set of scars—a light vanity scar at the point of his jaw, almost completely covered in beard, and a few on his fingers, that spoke of a man not paying attention as he stroked a stone quickly across the blade of his knife.

That was all.

There was something wrong with that. A man should be able to keep his own scars.

Kethol kicked his horse into a trot.

The cave. Forinel's jaw tightened.

Shit. They had been wandering down the roads, always taking the right-hand fork, just to be sure that they could trace their route back, if necessary, and things had started to look vaguely familiar to him even before they came over the crest of the hill.

They had taken the road to the cave.

Forinel shook his head. It wasn't as though he shouldn't have been at the cave—in fact, of course, he should have made a point to visit it.

Kethol, not Forinel. Forinel wouldn't care.

No, that wasn't quite fair. Forinel would care—just not about the same things, or the same sorts of things. He would care that the dragon that Elanee had captured was no longer in the cave, that it no longer threatened the Empire, that the traitoress was dead, that her plan to kill Ellegon and use her hold over the other dragon as a hold over the Emperor . . . that was as dead as the two of them. Forinel would care about that.

What Forinel wouldn't care about was the body buried in the cave. He hadn't piled the stones with his own hands.

"It looks . . . peaceful," Pirojil said.

"Yes. It does that."

There was no guard at the entrance to the tunnel into the side of the hill, and the rockslide from above had almost sealed the tunnel, anyway.

Which didn't matter, either. There was nothing in there for anyone to hide, for anyone to protect, not anymore.

The entrance was human-sized, much too large for a dwarven tunnel. Dwarves built to their own scale, whether they were digging warrens for habitation, or tunnels for mining. Pirojil had said that he suspected it had been an old dwarven tunnel, but that the entrance had been enlarged for humans, and that might well be the case.

The rough corral outside was something the worse for wear. While all of the upright posts still stood, some of the crosspiece timbers had fallen, although whether they had fallen to weather or humans Kethol couldn't tell by looking.

"We could just ride on," Pirojil said. "We're wasting daylight, and there's nothing here that needs attention, is there?"

Even after all these years, there were times when Kethol couldn't tell whether Pirojil was making fun of him or simply telling the truth.

And there was something in that idea, anyway. Soldiers were usually buried in unmarked graves, and there was no reason, he supposed, why Durine should be any different.

But . . .

"I think we ought to go inside."

Pirojil nodded, and without saying a word, kicked his horse into a walk down the slope toward the corral in front of the cave. Each of them tied his horse to one of the upright posts of the corral—these animals would not stay properly ground-hitched, after all—and they walked over to the entrance.

A few green plants were beginning to sprout among the dirt and rocks that had fallen from above.

"Give it a few more years," Pirojil said, "and the cave will be hidden, as well hidden as if we had sealed the entrance." He shook his head. "We don't have to go inside."

"You're not afraid of the dead, either."

Pirojil nodded. "True enough."

A niche for a lantern had been carved next to the opening of the tunnel, but the lantern was long gone. Pirojil found a branch in the rubble and tossed it to the ground, then climbed halfway up the hill to strip a birch of its bark for an improvised torch.

He pulled his fire-making kit from his saddlebags, and while Kethol would have just poured some gunpowder from his horn flask onto the ground, placed the torch on top of it, and immediately brought it to fire with one stroke of the back of his knife against the flint, Pirojil took his time scraping shreds of birch bark into a small pile, and started a flame with just half a dozen quick strokes that sent sparks flying into the tinder.

Kethol wondered if that was just a matter of efficiency, of not wasting gunpowder, or if Pirojil was simply putting off going inside. Kethol shook his head, silently cursing himself for his disloyalty— Pirojil had said that he wasn't afraid, after all, and it wasn't right for Kethol to doubt that.

The birch-bark torch hissed and spat as they walked inside, taking a moment to let their eyes adjust to the dark before they walked farther in.

Kethol's right hand couldn't seem to keep itself from the hilt of his sword, although that was silly. There was no evidence on the floor of the tunnel that any animal was using the cave, after all, and there wouldn't be anything else in there that was dangerous.

The central chamber was as they had left it: large, easily the size of the great hall at the Residence, and almost empty. Three wooden chests lay in a preposterously straight line near the raggedly curved far wall, although one of them was already starting to rot— the crack in the outer wall had let the rain leak in as much as it was now letting a ragged band of light splash into the chamber, making the torch unnecessary.

A cairn of rocks lay squarely in the middle of the chamber.

On the day that they had built the cairn, when they finished it the light through the crack had caught the rock pile full-on, and the blade of the sword that stood at the head of the cairn had seemed to glow with an inner fire.

The sword still stood there, of course, but now it and the cairn itself were cast in shadows.

He took a step forward. Durine's sword was rusty; there was almost no reflection of the light from the flickering torch.

That seemed wrong, somehow.

The sword had cost Durine more than a year's wages. Like Pirojil's, and Kethol's, it had been made of good dwarven wootz. The metal had been heated, hammered, sprinkled with a mixture of glass chips, iron dust, oyster shells, oak leaves, charcoal, and a dozen other things in some secret combination. Red hot, it had been folded over and hammered more, then quenched, and the process repeated more than a dozen times before the dwarf blacksmith had been sufficiently satisfied to begin shaping it. Yes, there were cheaper, easier ways to make swords, but what of that? This sword was light enough to bend rather than break; sharp enough to part flesh on the slash or the cut; and heavy enough to cut through leather armor and flesh and bite into bone.

The pommel was of white bone, not wood like Kethol's, nor brass like Pirojil's.

Durine had always been careful with it, as all of them were with their weapons. Whether the sword got wet from rain, or from having been run through a man's bowels, it was important to clean it as soon as possible, then dry it and carefully oil it before putting it away.

You had to take care of your weapons, after all, just as you had to take care of your companions.

As Durine had taken care of them.

His body lay beneath the pile of rocks, Kethol knew, and dead, he would have no more use for his sword than he had for the massive right hand that had gripped it, and which now was just broken bones and rotted meat lying beneath the sharp stones that caused no pain at all.

"Well," Pirojil said, "I guess he hasn't gone anywhere, has he?"

Pirojil squatted down next to the sword, and touched his fingers to the blade. His ugly face turned up toward Kethol's, as though asking him to say something, but Kethol just shrugged, and Pirojil just squatted there, silently, his fingers resting on Durine's sword.

"Durine," Pirojil finally said, quietly. "We beat Elanee. We didn't just kill her—although we did that, too. But we beat her. The bitch had it figured out, oh so cleverly. Let her little pet dragon be the only dragon in the Middle Lands, with Ellegon dead. The Emperor would have to come to terms with her, and even if not, even if she failed, Miron would still likely inherit the barony. I'm sure that he knew what she was up to, but there's no proving it.

"The thing is, though: we beat her. We won. You, and I, and Kethol. No, the four of us—I have to include Erenor, too, come to think of it. He and I have to remember not to call him Kethol anymore—we have to call him Forinel, and think of him as Forinel, but it's Kethol who is the baron; it's Kethol who will take the lands and the villages and the titles on the taxes and everything that she wanted for her son—even Leria." He smiled. "I know you liked Leria. Right now, she sits in Elanee's garden, eats with her utensils, and sneers at Elanee's son. We've not settled with Miron, not yet, and I don't know if we'll be able to, I really don't. But we'll watch for an opportunity, I promise."

You weren't supposed to take it personally. Soldiers were supposed to die; of the dozen that had gone with the Old Emperor on his Last Ride, only Kethol, Pirojil, and Durine had reached the sands of Melawei, and perhaps it was surprising that even two of them were left.

You had to be careful not to swear vengeance, not even to yourself, because it was important to do what you said you would do.

Ignoring Kethol, Pirojil rose and walked from the chamber, not looking back.

Kethol stood silently for a moment, and thought about something to say, but Durine was dead, after all, and there was no point in saying anything.

Or doing anything. Not really.

All three of the chests at the far end of the chamber were empty, and while they were rotted, they were dry, so it didn't take him much time at all to smash them to pieces against the hard stone, and less time than that to push the pieces into a pile, and touch the torch to that pile.

He threw the torch down and watched the fire grow until the smoke had his eyes tearing, and then he turned and walked down the tunnel into the daylight.

As they rode away, smoke was already filtering up from the hillside, only to be shattered on the light breeze, instantly.

Pirojil was thoroughly hungry by the time that Lord Moarin's castle gleamed in the sun ahead of them, looming whitely above the town below. He caught a whiff of something garlicky roasting—more likely chicken than beef, although it could just as easily have been pigeon rather than chicken—and that set his mouth watering, and reminded him just how long it had been since they'd made their sketchy noon meal.

A few soldiers from Moarin's House Guard lazily stood watch on the walls, although there didn't seem to be much point—the breach that the Biemish cannons had made during the war had not been repaired, and would not be repaired until the occupation was lifted.

The walls had been whitewashed, but not repaired. There was something strange about that. The castle was now just a home to Lord Moarin, and his family and retainers.

It had been something else entirely: a weapon. Weapons didn't have to have a sharp edge or a narrow point; they didn't of necessity have to be able to crush bone and shatter flesh. A weapon didn't need to be able to be carried around by a man on a thick belt or towed by a team of tired horses.

The castle was a weapon. At the very least, the castle had been a collar hammered around the necks of the conquered; occasionally, a weapon thrust by the conqueror into the guts of the conquered.

The Holts had done the same thing when they had overthrown the Euar'dens as the Euar'dens had done to the Tyneareans before them: attack, crush, conquer . . . and then build.

Let the peasants and what remained of the previous nobility revolt. If the nobles couldn't put a rebellion down with their own troops—and, of course, most of the time they could—they could always retreat behind the hard stone walls, sallying forth to fight at times of their choosing, not of the rebels'. Or they could simply wait in safety until armies of allied nobles would arrive, and crush the rebellion from both within and without the castle.

There was no way to tell who had built it, originally, at least not just by looking, but the Holts had improved on it—the outward slant of the plinth was Holtish, not Euar'den or Tynearean. While such a broad base to the wall wouldn't have made it impossible for even human sappers—not to mention dwarvish ones—to tunnel beneath, it did make it almost impossible for any conceivable sapper tunnel's collapse to bring the wall down with it. And while it was always possible, at least in theory, to break a siege by sending troops in through a tunnel, the defenders would have been able to concentrate their defenses on the mouth of the tunnel, pouring a rain of arrows, rocks, and flaming oil on the invaders.

Pirojil hadn't been in this part of Holtun during the war, but he'd seen the same thing elsewhere—once in Barony Niphael, when they had retaken it from the Holts, and three times during the conquest of Adahan.

There had been something detached, almost unwarlike about watching the Biemish cannons that had, hour after hour, pounded away at the stone. Six teams of sweaty cannoneers would grunt as they'd load the gunpowder into the cannons, then grunt as they'd load the cannonball, then grunt as they'd cover their ears when the battery fired, then grunt as they'd start all over again.

While no single cannonball could crack the wall, sooner or later, it would give, it had given, and the stones would tumble, and the cannoneers would fire off a few more salvos before dropping to the ground to watch the rest of the battle, as though they were now just spectators, and no longer participants.

And then the attackers would rush in through the breach.

Pirojil had been one of those attackers, four times. Four times too many.

A soldier couldn't be weak of stomach, so Pirojil didn't like to think of himself as weak of stomach, but even more, he didn't like to think of what he and the others—yes, including Kethol and Durine—had done when they had burst through that breach, into the smoke and the screams, hacking and slashing their way through armor and flesh, ignoring the screams and the smells and the sounds until there was nobody left to kill, and they, too, dropped to the ground, too tired to raise their heads above the blood-slickened stone.

Pirojil wasn't sure why the governor didn't permit the rebuilding of the walls.

Any revolt of the Holtish nobility could be met with those same cannons, again. Rebuilt walls could be broken, again. Armored soldiers—yes, and terrified men, women, and children with nothing to protect themselves save the hands that they imploringly held out—

could once again die, screaming, on the edge of the blade, or impaled on the sharp point of a storming spear.

Still, perhaps the governor was wise, even if only by accident.

Perhaps it was best to keep the walls breached, to let the nobles and the common folk look up to the castle on the hill and remember how vulnerable they were, to see that evidence, every time they looked up the hill, of how nakedly exposed they were to Imperial power.

Maybe, perhaps, hopefully, possibly, that would prevent any revolt, and would let men who otherwise would have been much like Pirojil be able to sleep through the night without seeing all those faces, hearing all those screams, smelling the shit-stink of the freshly dead.

He shook his head to try to clear it.

It was different now. He had to concentrate on how different it was—shit, right now, the only blood that flowed in the narrow streets of the town below the castle came from a butcher's stall.

The Empire had brought peace, and peace was a good thing.

Today was a market day here, and the markets in the town that cupped the bottom of the hill were filled with stalls where peasants hassled endlessly with merchants over the cost of a bushel of turnips; where freshly slaughtered pigs hung from hooks, their rib cages spread wide with wooden laths; where laughing ragged children played their endless games of touched-you-last in the cobblestone streets, ducking under the curses and occasional halfhearted slaps and kicks from tradesmen and merchants; and where, as a pair of Imperial soldiers in their silver and gray walked down the street, locals simply stepped out of their way instead of fleeing and running in terror.

That was, indeed, a good thing, and it was, indeed, a fine day, and he had ridden for hours with nothing more than water to pass his lips.

So Pirojil didn't really understand why he wasn't hungry anymore.

"Both of you will stay this evening and spend the night, of course," Lord Moarin said, smiling. He smiled too much. "I was planning on having to dine alone, and thank you in advance for your company."

His thin gray hair was freshly oiled, and his clean, silver-rimmed silk tunic spoke of a sudden change of clothing at Forinel's arrival. His teeth were far too straight and white, a tribute to the local Eareven priest, no doubt. Spidersect healers were better with wounds, although not as good, of course, as the Hand, but the Eareven were much more adept at smoothing a pocked face, regrowing a lost tooth, and suchlike.

"I'm sorry, but I can't." Forinel softened the words with a smile, as he shook his head. "I promised to be home tonight, and I can tell you that if it's much after dark and I'm not back, old Thirien will have half the barony out looking for me, fearing some improbable disaster."

"Thirien's worries should remain his own, and not bother his betters." Moarin waved the issue away. "I could send a messenger on a fast horse, with a note, perhaps?"

"Please don't. I've been too long away, and I want to get used to sleeping in my own bed, under my own roof."

Moarin gave in with good grace, or at least, with simulated good grace. Which, as far as Pirojil was concerned, was entirely adequate.

On their arrival, they had quickly been brought into the center courtyard of the keep and offered refreshments, and the servants had been dismissed.

The courtyard had surely been ruined when the castle had been taken, but it had long since been repaired. Lamp poles stood waiting for night, and planters were overfilled with an explosion of flowers that left fresh bloodred and sunny yellow petals scattered on the polished marble squares.

Gnarled apple trees rimmed the courtyard; Moarin had, with his own hands, picked several of the fruit, allowing his guests the first choice, and politely taking a quick bite of the remaining apple before setting it down on the stone table where they sat.

Next to the table, two yellow songbirds chirped and sang in wicker cages. Pirojil had assumed that they were captive, and was surprised to see Moarin open one of the cages; the bird had immediately leaped to his outstretched finger, and let him pet it for a moment before it flittered off to perch on the back of a nearby chair.

Now, when Moarin smashed his own apple against the table, the bird leaped into the air and fluttered about, but didn't fly away; it circled above, then again landed on his outstretched finger and waited, patiently, while he fed it a few morsels, then, having had enough, flitted back into its cage and waited for Moarin.

Moarin reached out and petted the bird's head before fastening the cage. "I had four of them until this spring—a cat got into the courtyard, I think, as all I found under the two cages were some feathers and a few bones." He cleared his throat, and his light smile faded as he sat back down next to them. "It's good to have you back, my baron. I'm not one who likes to speak ill of the dead, but Baroness Elanee was too, was too, was too—"

"Busy trying to stage a rebellion?" Pirojil asked.

"—was too busy with other matters to be the barony's advocate," Moarin said, giving Pirojil only a mild glare. He turned back to Forinel. "Keranahan needs a strong voice in Biemestren to argue for the lifting of occupation, and I know you will be that voice. Yes, spend some time reacquainting yourself with the barony, of course—but it's at the capital that you're needed."

Forinel nodded, hesitantly. "Yes, of course. But that's hardly my only concern. I see bridges falling into ruin, roads not maintained, and—"

"I agree, I agree more than I can say," Moarin said, raising a palm. "All that is true, and more. I've two grain mills that need rebuilding, but as long as I can't collect my own taxes, and have to live off the, the barely adequate stipend that the governor provides, I'll hardly be able to do that, and never mind that even if I had the money, I'm not even *permitted* to rebuild the grain mills, for fear that some few grains of wheat might be milled here, instead of Dereneyl, without them being properly taxed. The copper mines in the Ulter Hills have only opened again this last year—and that happened only because some of us were able to persuade an Imperial engineer of the virtue of that obvious necessity." He spread his hands. "There's only so much a simple land baron can do, regardless of his rank and his lineage."

"You seem to be doing well enough," Pirojil said.

Forinel gave him a quick glare. "Be still, Captain Pirojil," he said. "I'm sure that Lord Moarin is doing the best he can."

Pirojil kept his smile inside. He was the pushy one, while Forinel would side with the lord. Just a simple two-on-one strategy, and even if Moarin saw through it, as was likely, what of it?

It was like the old days, in some ways, but it felt different in others. Kethol had always been a better swordsman than Pirojil and Durine, and he was certainly quicker—and it had been a common, almost automatic strategy for Pirojil and Durine to hold a particularly good swordsman at bay until Kethol had freed himself enough.

It wasn't dueling, but, then again, they weren't effete noble duelists.

" 'Be still, Pirojil,' " Pirojil said, as the gates of the city receded in the distance behind them. The wind was from the east, driving the smells of the city away from them, and even the cries in the town markets were almost completely drowned out by the gentle *clop-clop-clop* of their horses' hooves.

"That was good," he went on. "I liked that. Not 'Shut up,' or 'Quiet down,' or even 'Shut your festering gob, or I'll tear off your leg and beat you to death with it,' but 'Be still, Pirojil.' "

Forinel made a face, but didn't meet Pirojil's eyes as they rode, any more than Pirojil met his. It wasn't a matter of avoiding Pirojil's eyes—there was nothing there that he needed to see.

"Well, it seemed like something a highborn would say," he said.

"It was." Pirojil nodded. "That's why I liked it. You're taking to this better, and more quickly, than I'd have guessed you could."

Was it part of the elven magic? Or was it just that Kethol had always been at least somewhat brighter than Pirojil had been tempted to give him credit for? Both explanations seemed improbable, but if Pirojil had had to pick one, he would have picked the magic, and then cursed the magic for not having worked better.

Forinel scanned the treeline to the right, while Pirojil kept a watch on the left, and hated the fact that he was enjoying himself.

Not that there was anything to worry about, as far as Pirojil knew. But that was the way of it—you kept your eyes open, no matter how safe you thought you were. The world was filled with sharp things, and too often those sharp things had an eye for your soft flesh.

But he couldn't keep his eyes open all the time, or watch everything at once, so he split the world into halves or thirds, and paid full attention to his portion, trusting that Kethol would watch his own.

It was a silly little nothing. Just a ride down an unpaved dirt road that was heavily rutted with wagon tracks while the setting sun cast long shadows in front of them, and he and Kethol divided the universe neatly in two.

But the silly little nothing felt good.

That was the thing about having friends. Pirojil hadn't had many friends.

The closest things to it in recent years had been Kethol and Durine, and Durine had died on him—just like the Old Emperor, just like all the others, just like those who had betrayed a young man whose name wasn't even Pirojil then, and whose screams as they died in a burning house, its doors and windows jammed shut, had long since been drowned out in his dreams by fresher, louder screams. He could barely remember what the crackling of burning flesh sounded like, and he had long been able to smell roast pork without gagging and vomiting uncontrollably.

That was the good thing about time passing—the pain passed, too.

There wasn't much that Pirojil liked about the old days, but this was one of them: this silly little thing, this riding down the road, with the universe split in two, was something that he would miss, when this was all over.

And it would be over, and sooner than later.

Kethol would want to keep him around, of course, but there was no good reason that Forinel would, and the best way to quell any suspicions was to be sure that they were never raised in the first place.

He would have to go, and the likelihood that he would now have all three shares of the cache of gold and jewels that he and Durine and Kethol had been accumulating over the years should have made him feel happier than it did.

They had talked about a tavern in Biemestren, where the three of them could painlessly separate Imperial soldiers from their pay with beer and food downstairs and maybe a few whores upstairs.

The Three Swords Inn, they would call it. Pirojil liked the sound of that.

Durine would have kept the peace. Most soldiers, even drunk, would have been more afraid of actually losing their manhood in a serious fight with the big man than they would of appearing to lose their manhood by backing down from the big man, and for those who were too drunk or likely to be too stupid, a man who didn't wait for the other to strike the first blow could end a fight before it had started—and that didn't have to be Durine; Kethol and Pirojil would have been perfectly happy to slap a stick across a drunk's back while the drunk faced off with Durine.

Kethol could spend his days hunting—it wouldn't be difficult for an old soldier to get a hunting warrant or two—and his nights playing bones, further separating stupid soldiers from good coin.

Pirojil would brew the beer. The weak, sour beer of the Eren regions was drinkable, if usually no better than that, but he knew a few recipes that a younger man had learned, long ago, that would put this horse piss to shame.

But now Durine was dead, his body lying rotting in the cave; and now Kethol was Forinel; and now that fine and distant dream had gone where all good dreams go, come morning.

Pirojil doubted that, even with all three shares, he had enough to buy a tavern in the capital; he thought it unlikely that he could run it by himself; and he knew enough about himself to know that he couldn't trust somebody he hadn't bled with well enough. He knew that he didn't have the temperament to watch closely over somebody he couldn't trust, or to stay his own hand when he was betrayed, as he surely would be if he didn't watch closely enough.

So that plan was gone.

Dead as Durine, dead as the Old Emperor, dead as all the others.

Still, if he was careful, perhaps he could buy an inn somewhere cheaper than the capital. Or, perhaps, a small piece of good land, probably up in the Cullinane hills. Land should be relatively cheap in such heavily orc-infested country, and that meant that all he would have to do was kill a few dozen or a few hundred orcs before settling down to the relatively quiet life of a common landowner.

Dirty work, certainly, but he'd done much dirtier.

He wouldn't be the first of the Old Emperor's soldiers to buy a piece of land, and he wouldn't be the last. His ugliness wouldn't prevent him from finding some peasant girl who found that being the mistress of even a modest home was far preferable to spending her days scratching the soil, her evenings cooking and cleaning and washing and mending, and her nights being pounded by some smelly peasant.

Pirojil, at least, knew how to wash. As to his ugliness, if it was a problem for her, she could just spread her legs and then close her eyes, eh?

It would be a better end than most, and even if it all failed, he knew that a loyal retainer would always be able to find a bed and a meal at Castle Cullinane, and be greeted with dignity. The bed would not be particularly soft; the room might well be over the stable; the meal would not be eaten at the table with the baron and his family.

But if he would be, in effect, a beggar coming to the door, nobody would treat him that way.

And that would probably always be true at Baron Keranahan's residence, whether it was the country home or the keep in Dereneyl.

But it would *feel* different. That was the trouble with it. What had Pirojil ever done for the Keranahans—besides help conquer them during the war, besides putting an imposter in the baron's house? Nothing.

No.

He couldn't say anything to Kethol about that, of course.

It was silly. A soldier should long ago have lost any sort of compunctions at all. He was just too tired. That probably was it.

•   •   •

They rode along in silence, and when they arrived at the Residence, Pirojil simply turned down Forinel's offer of help with the horses, too tired to lecture him about how a baron would leave such things to others.

It had been a long day.

Pirojil's legs moved leadenly as he walked the horses to the stableboy.

He went to the kitchens, and got himself a joint of mutton and a huge flagon of beer, and brought it out back.

The mutton was greasy and cold, but he had had much worse. The beer was weak, and tasted more of mouse than of barley, but there was plenty of it, and he drained it and another two flagons quickly. He considered heading out to the bathhouse to wash the road dust off, then decided not to bother. The beer had washed it from his throat, and bathing could wait for morning, after all.

He quietly entered the Residence through the kitchen and climbed to his room on the second floor.

He had slept in worse, and rarely in better. The room was large and airy, and there was a bell pull next to the bed, the rope almost touching the gleaming, freshly cleaned thundermug, clean enough to drink out of. While the hard mattress was of horsehair rather than soft down, that was fine with him. There were no rocks in it, after all, and Pirojil had slept on rocks all too often.

He unbuckled his belt, carefully set his sword and dagger and his pistols in their usual positions, then pulled off his boots, and tumbled into bed.

He was grateful for the beer.

It made his sleep a dark and warm thing, utterly devoid of even a hint of distant screams.

Part 3

MULTIPLE ATTACKS

7

Fredensday

When you write a check that your mouth can't
cash, the only thing do to is go out and do something about your bank account.

—Walter Slovotsky

Skeptically, Kethol eyed the once-again-full glass of wine in
front of him.

He thought that he hadn't had more than one full glass,
which was much less than the tankards of sour beer he was more
used to drinking of an evening—on those evenings when he *was*
drinking, that is, and not pretending to.

But with the way that the serving girls kept sneaking up and
refilling it, he couldn't be quite sure. He thought that he was keeping up his end of the conversation, and he couldn't see any suspicious glances in his direction, but he wasn't sure about that, either.

The only thing he was sure of was that he felt utterly out of
place.

Leria had carefully kept him engaged in quiet private conversation throughout the long dinner—the far too long dinner—and
occasionally would duck her ear close to his lips, and respond with
quiet laughter at whatever he said, if anything, then duck her head
back to put her lips next to his ear and, in whispers, remind him of

the names of all the assembled lords and their hangers-on.

He was beginning to get them straight. Yes, Lord Moarin was easy—and even if he hadn't met him already, it would be hard for him to ignore or forget the wrinkled old husk of a lecher, whose eyes consistently focused on the deeply scooped front of Leria's dress, and whose young wife—Finella? Yes, Finella—was probably half the age of his horse-faced daughter, Brigen. It was interesting that Moarin hadn't brought them out when he and Pirojil had visited the lord—perhaps he wanted to be sure to brief them to be careful about what they said in front of the baron?

Sherrol, short, fat, and bald, had been the lord warden of Dereneyl until the occupation, and while he still was, technically, Leria had said that he spent most of his time these days overseeing loading and unloading from the dockside warehouses. If it hadn't been for the ruffled blouse and the jeweled rings that bedecked his stubby fingers, Kethol would more likely have taken him for a longshoreman than a noble, what with the way that his face and neck were permanently browned from the sun.

Miron didn't seem to think much of Sherrol, which didn't necessarily mean anything more than that Miron wanted Forinel to think that he didn't think much of Sherrol.

Still, the lack of affection was returned.

"How long, Lord Miron," Sherrol asked, "do you think that you'll be staying in the barony?"

"Why, Sherrol—Lord Sherrol, that is—one would think that my company is offensive to you."

"Please." Sherrol's smile was every bit as sincere as a whore's on payday. "I wouldn't want you to think that, not for a moment."

Miron pursed his lips, then gave the slightest of shrugs. "Not long, I think—I came home only to prepare the way for my brother's return, and I've some . . . other matters to deal with sooner than later." He made a self-deprecating moue. "I've some land of my own, yes, in my own right, but those few villages seem to do quite well without me, and since it seems that I'm not to become the baron, it would also seem that I'm in the usual position of a younger brother. I'd like to find some nobleman of good lineage with no son and a marriageable daughter, and while the crop of young ladies in Keranahan has bloomed quite nicely," he said, making a slight bow toward Leria, and another toward Brigen, "so the crop of landed noblemen more than matches it." He sighed. "My guess is that I'll end up marrying some merchant nobleman's daughter, and having to buy into the family business. And I was so looking forward to receiving a dowry, rather than selling my own lands to provide one."

As usual, Miron had talked long, and not said much—except that he was leaving for Biemestren soon, although immediately would have been none too soon for Kethol.

Melphen was the tall, somber-looking one who studiously avoided looking across the table at Miron, while Lord Aredel—supposedly a distant relative of the Biemish Arondael family—was shaped like a beer barrel, but had a preposterously high voice. Lady Ephanie, silver hair bound up with patinaed copper wire, and remarkably firm breasts exposed to the upper edge of her nipples, was the widow of Lord Belchen.

He didn't have to make any effort to remember Miron, who was down at the other end of the table, close to Treseen, and who seemed to spend most of his time in quiet conversation with Ephanie's giggling young daughters, as though he were coppering his Biemestren bets locally.

Kethol—Forinel would have to keep them all straight.

It wasn't enough to lie to himself that he had known them and they him since he was a boy. The best he could do was to keep his mouth working—carefully wielding his spoon and prong with the silly, elegant flourishes that Leria had taught him, and being sure to take absurdly small bites, and letting Leria carry the bulk of the conversation.

"Of course," Lord Moarin said, "everybody here has been wondering about Parliament." He cut himself yet another peasant-sized hunk of the mutton and conveyed it to his mouth with his silver eating prong. For a skinny old man, he packed away food like a woodsman in spring.

"Is there any word about the telegraph line? Or, perhaps, the lifting of the occupation?"

He had asked Pirojil and Kethol the same questions, and so he was asking about that purely for effect, although it was hard to tell who was supposed to be affected, and how. Treseen? Leria?

Kethol sipped some more wine. "Little on either, I'm afraid," he said, choosing his words carefully. "I'm told that the engineers have some questions about the best route from Nerahan—and of course there are higher priorities, the expenses aside."

Except for the telegraph cable itself, putting in a telegraph line wasn't terribly expensive—it was mainly a matter of labor, and while copper wasn't cheap and copper wire was even more expensive, labor was plentiful.

But it hardly made sense, after all, to put up the line near the Kiaran border, when it was a foregone conclusion that Kiaran bandits would simply cut the lines, both for the value of the copper and because bandits had long ago learned that the telegraph enabled Imperial troops to respond to raids in less than half the time it would otherwise take.

"I don't see the problem," Ephanie said. "It's just a matter of, well, of putting up poles, isn't it?" Her shrug threatened to send her breasts popping out of the front of her dress.

"No, Lady, with respect: it's not just a matter of putting up poles," Treseen said, shaking his head. "You need a large team of foresters to harvest trees, and four times that many laborers to dig holes and plant the telegraph poles, and at least one engineer to hang the wires. Yes, if you throw enough workers at it, a telegraph line can go up almost as fast as a man can walk—but the copper is expensive, after all, and copper wire more so, and you want to be sure to put the line along well-traveled roads, not out in the wild, or you might as well simply be handing over the copper to thieves and bandits."

Sherrol nodded. "It's like saying that running a river port is just a matter of rolling the barrels on and off the barges." He gulped another glass of the wine that already had sweat beading on his bald head. "It's true, but it's not a half of it, eh?"

"But why do you not just clean the bandits out from the hills, Governor?" Lady Ephanie's mouth was tight. "I'm not criticizing the Emperor, mind, but it wasn't this way in the old days."

Moarin nodded agreement. "In the old days, for much less offense than we've been given, we'd have sent a couple regiments storming through Kiar, setting every thatched roof on fire for a day's ride around any such."

"And in the old days," Melphen said, "the Kiarans would respond with a couple of regiments storming through Keranahan, setting fields and villages alight, in response." He shrugged. "I'd rather live with the annoyance of a few bandits, myself. Chasing after them gives the Imperials something to do for their taxes, after all."

Treseen cleared his throat. "The Emperor," Treseen said, carefully, "always takes note of what's said, and by whom."

Sherrol frowned over his glass, and shook his head in apology.

"Oh, Treseen," Melphen said with a wave of his hand, "please don't start with that, not again. If the Emperor wants to hang a few nobles for acknowledging that not everybody finds everything he does to be utterly brilliant and wonderful, there are other necks he's more likely to start with than mine." He jerked a thumb at Moarin.

"He might be more interested in, say, the curiously small summer wheat crop that some have been having, eh?"

Moarin was unmoved. "Governor Treseen has thoroughly inspected my holdings, and he's found my accounts completely satisfactory."

Which probably meant that Moarin had paid off Treseen. Or maybe just that he had had a lousy summer wheat crop. The truth was always a possibility.

Kethol didn't care much, either way. As to the politics, Kethol had never bothered much with it himself, but he had spent a few evenings listening to Baron Cullinane and his regent talking about it—well, more accurately: listening to Doria Perlstein lecture Jason Cullinane, while Jason Cullinane tried to change the subject to the Other Side, rather than dull matters of taxes.

Leria looked at him, arching an eyebrow, and at his nod, leaned forward. "The baron and I have been discussing that very matter this morning, over breakfast," she said, "and I think he made some very good points."

That was half-true—they had been discussing it, yes.

"It's different now," Kethol said. "In the old days, if Holtun moved on Kiar or Kiar on Holtun, that would be seen as just a matter between the two countries, and everybody else would have assumed that it would quickly be over, and that Holtun and Bieme would resume hacking at each other. Back then, even Nyphien and Enkiar wouldn't get involved, and you wouldn't even have to think about them bringing in Sylphen or—" He shook his head. "My point is, the power of the Empire, the, well, the existence of the Empire, makes the rest of the Middle Lands nervous, and the last thing that the Emperor should want to do is to unite them against him."

It was Leria's point, not his. But it was true.

Particularly now that the Nyphs were producing gunpowder in

apparently great quantities, and relatively primitive rifles, as well—
Enkiar probably wasn't far behind.

There was an argument—made openly in Parliament, and no
doubt supported in private by the Dowager Empress, among others—that the time to expand the Empire had been before the secret
of the making of gunpowder had leaked out, and that it was entirely
the fault of Walter Slovotsky, who had given out that secret, that
the time was past.

There was also an argument, made much more quietly, that now
was the time to move—while the Empire had virtually all the cannons in the Middle Lands—and that the policy of consolidating Hol-
ton and Bieme could be held in abeyance while the Empire seized
at least one of the surrounding countries. Let the Holtish barons
raise their own armies, and strip the baronies of the Imperial troops,
and let everybody work together to conquer, say, Nyphien, before
the rest of the Middle Lands could fully mobilize.

Of course, that assumed that the Holtish barons wouldn't just
make an alliance with the Nyphs—or with others—and turn on the
Imperials themselves.

Forinel probably should have had an opinion about all that, but
Kethol didn't. Starting a war wasn't something that a soldier had any
business having an opinion about; it was for wiser, and more noble,
heads.

Like, say, the one that he had on his shoulders?

Shit.

"So we just have to live with this?"

How, exactly, are you living with this, Ephanie? he thought, but
didn't say. *You live in your fine house in Dereneyl*—Kethol had
never seen her house, but he was absolutely certain it was a fine
one—*and you sleep safely behind high walls.*

Like others of the city-dwelling nobility, she lived up in the hills
above and to the west, behind walls that surely wouldn't have

stopped and would have barely slowed an invading army, but, together with the nobles' personal guards, kept their possessions and
their bodies safe from simple thieves and more aggressive intruders
alike.

The worst she had to worry about was some maid stealing a
silver eating prong or two, and Kethol didn't doubt that she counted
all the silver every night before going to bed—she looked to be the
type.

But he didn't say that.

Kethol just shrugged. "I wouldn't go so far as to say that there's
nothing that can be done about it. Every problem has a solution, if
you're willing to pay the price." The Old Emperor had said that,
and Kethol liked the way that the words rolled off of his own tongue.
He speared a roasted mushroom and chewed on it for a moment.
"I think—no, I *know* that there are ways of dealing with bandits
from Kiar without having to go to war with Kiar." He forced himself
to chuckle. "We could do it without even having those nervous sorts
in Biemestren worry about it, in fact."

"For example?" Moarin was skeptical.

"Am I hearing you doubt the baron?" Leria asked, quietly.

"Well, yes." Moarin nodded. "Yes, I do doubt the baron," he
said. "I don't for a moment doubt his legitimacy, or his bravery—
I've heard stories of his heroics in the Katharhd—but have we in
Holtun sunk so low that I can't simply disagree with the baron?"

She nudged Kethol's knee under the table.

"Well, of course you can," Kethol said. "My father used to say
something about how a man who can't stand to hear disagreement
should simply take out his knife and cut his own ears off."

He silently thanked Leria for having gotten that phrase from
Forinel's father's journals, and having briefed him to use it immediately if anybody criticized him.

"Yes." Sherrol nodded. "That he did. I can't speak in polite company about what he said a man should do with that knife if he finds it offensive when another noble sports too much with the common girls—can I?" He eyed Kethol over the rim of his glass. "Still, I just want to be sure I understand you: are you saying that you have some way to clear out these bandits without risking going to war with Kiar?"

"Clear them out? No," Kethol said. "It's like trying to kill off wolves—kill as many as you like, and their dams will just breed some more."

"Then what are you saying?"

"I'm saying that it should be possible to kill some number of these wolves, and by doing that persuade at least some others that they can find easier pickings elsewhere than in Keranahan. *Without* starting a war with Kiar, without so much as making a Kiaran noble nervous about Keranahanians setting foot on his lands, as it could be done without even setting foot across the hills into Kiar."

"Now, now," Treseen said, raising a peremptory finger, "let's not have talk of banditry and killing and such on a pleasant evening."

Leria leaned her head close to his. "Do you have something in mind?" she whispered, then quietly laughed, as though amused by a private joke she had told him.

He nodded, as though to himself.

Well, of course he did.

Kethol would no more know how to organize an extended military campaign than he would know how to fly, but this was the sort of thing that anybody could do, if it was worth the trouble and expense. It was like setting a snare for a rabbit, really, except, of course, that snares were cheap and that rabbits couldn't fight back.

It was just that the nobles didn't care. As long as they were safe within the walls of their keeps, what was it to them if a few peasants' pigs and sheep—and daughters, for that matter—were carried off by bandits? Yes, if the raids became heavy enough to seriously cut into their stipends, the nobles would be screaming for action. But, right now, to them, it was just an annoyance, something to complain about to the governor, and to let him handle.

Kethol could do it himself, with a few good men. Shit, if the bandit parties were as small as their take indicated they were, a half-dozen good men would probably be more than enough, if . . .

Hmmm. Yes, there was an obvious way. It was a fairly simple idea, and Pirojil could surely improve on it, but it was, as usual, more a matter of deciding to do something than it was having to be brilliant enough to figure out something clever to do.

It wouldn't occur to Treseen, of course.

Treseen was far too busy being governor to remember what he used to have been, and it was no surprise that none of his captains would step forward, volunteering to take the chances involved. Much safer to ride out in force toward where bandits had raided, and know that they would find no resistance when they got there.

It wasn't like soldiers actually enjoyed exposing their all-too-sensitive hides to enemy blades and arrows, after all, particularly when there was no chance of any loot when it was all done.

There were always risks, yes, but what of that?

Kethol was used to taking risks, after all, and this was the sort of thing that he was good at. The only question was exactly how to bait a trap, but between Pirojil and himself, they could surely work it out. Erenor might even have an idea, although it would probably be extraordinarily complicated and utterly impractical. Best to keep things simple.

"It would be interesting to see," Melphen said.

Leria looked at him, once again, and he nodded.

"Then you shall, of course," Leria said, her voice taking on a decided edge.

"Wait one moment," Treseen said. "If you're talking about me sending out half my troops to hare all over the countryside in search of a few lice-ridden bandits coming over the hills from Kiar, I think that you'll find, Baron, that I'm still the governor here, and I'm not inclined to send even four, five companies out to chase around the barony, looking for these bandits—who undoubtedly have more than enough sense to scatter up and into the mists at the first sound of hoofbeats." He shook his head.

"I wasn't asking you to send out regiments, or even a full company, Governor," Kethol said. "Just give me that Tarnell of yours— Captain Pirojil speaks highly of him—and have him and Pirojil pick out a dozen of your troopers who don't close their eyes when they fire a rifle, and perhaps even know the flat of the blade from the edge—from the point, that is."

"Tarnell? But he's my aide, and—"

"What of that?" Melphen leaned forward. "Surely you can govern the barony for a few days without the help of one old soldier."

"Well, yes." Treseen gave in on that point with good grace. "Tarnell could be made available, at that."

"But to do what?"

Leria leaned forward. "To make the bandits go away, of course. I think you can trust to Baron Keranahan to see to the details of that, can't you?"

"But how—oh, never mind," Melphen said. "I'm sure that a man of action like the baron would much rather show us than tell us."

There was that.

There was also the fact that Kethol didn't quite have an entire plan put together, and he didn't want to talk about the outlines of it with the nobles, at least not until he had had a long talk with Pirojil, who would undoubtedly have some ideas for improving what was, at the moment, only a vague notion of setting a trap and springing it.

Kethol would need Pirojil, of course. It would have been nice to have some solid troopers from Barony Cullinane, and better to have Durine, but a few Imperials would do.

Moarin snorted. "I would pay in good coin to see that," he said.

Leria smiled. "We accept."

"Eh?"

"The baron gladly accepts your kind offer to cover his expenses," she said. "And let me add, I'm grateful, as well." She picked at her food. "It seems that the late baroness Elanee either spent or hid much of the money that should have been in the Residence strong room, and while I can surely come up with a few hundred silver marks, I'm pleased that you've offered to cover that."

Treseen shook his head. "I'm not disposed to allow a special levy for this, this enterprise."

"Levy?" She raised an eyebrow. "Who said anything about a levy, Governor Treseen? As I heard it, Lord Moarin has offered to pay for the baron's expenses out of his normal stipend, and I'm sure that he wouldn't think to try to squeeze an illegal levy on his crofters or landholders."

The table fell silent, and all eyes turned toward Moarin for a long moment.

"Very well," he finally said, with barely simulated good grace. "I'll add fifty silver marks, and cover your"—he snorted—"expenses, upon success, as I know that a gentleman won't take advantage in that. But," he said, raising a peremptory finger, "I do insist upon that success—I'll not pay a copper until presented with at least, say, half a dozen raiders' heads, and the baron's word, sworn on his sword, that that's just what they are. When you can't find these ghosts that flitter in and out of the shadows, I don't want you executing a few upstart peasants as a substitute."

"Done," Leria said. She gestured with her eating prong at the assemblage. "You're all witnesses—particularly you, Miron."

"Yes, we are that, indeed. All of us." Miron raised his glass. "Let us drink to my brother the baron's success," he said.

If there was any sarcasm in his voice, Kethol couldn't hear it.

They stood outside on the balcony, watching the distant pulsation of faerie lights off in the hills. There were only a few of them tonight, and they pulsed slowly through a muted sequence of dull orange to quiet red, to a blue so subtle that it could hardly be seen against the night sky.

They looked tired. He knew how they felt.

"It seems that we do make quite a good combination, Forinel," she said. "In more ways than one." She ran a long finger down the front of his chest, then held up her face to be kissed. Was she kissing him, or Forinel?

He wondered, then wondered why he was wondering. It shouldn't matter. Her tongue was warm and alive in his mouth, and when he reflexively stiffened, she pressed her midsection up hard against him before he could draw back.

"I'll come to your room tonight, again, if you promise to wait up for me." She pulled his body against hers, tightly. "You're just going to have to get used to the servants knowing about us, after all. Unless you'd care to take up sleeping alone."

"I guess so," he said, relaxing against her.

"Guess what? That you'll adjust to the situation, or to sleeping alone?"

"I'll adjust, Leria."

Her cure for his tendency to blush was working, and he was bright enough both to know that he was being manipulated and to not much care. Besides, he felt better about her safety when she was with him. Maybe she wasn't actually safer in his bed than she would be in her own room—probably less; there was nobody who could profit from *her* death, after all, as far as he knew—but it felt like she was.

"Well," he said, "together, I guess, we make a decent baron. You supply the mind, and the style, and all I have to do is kill a few bandits."

"You really can?"

"Of course."

There was, of course, no "of course" about it at all. Any time you insisted on putting your body out in the field, trying to kill men who would be trying to kill you, there was always a risk.

But he could hardly say that to Leria, who was smiling up at him. It was hard to talk. There was still something about the way she looked at him that made it hard to breathe, much less talk.

"Make me a promise, please," he said. "If you will, that is."

"Of course," she said.

"While I'm gone, promise me that you'll keep Erenor near you."

Erenor was devious, certainly, and Kethol never completely trusted him. But Erenor knew without having to be reminded that if he let so much as a bruise come to Leria's toe, Kethol would hunt him down.

That Erenor knew that without having to be reminded didn't, of course, mean that Pirojil wouldn't remind him, as of course he would.

Repeatedly.

She nodded. "I promise."

"Good."

"You must make me one promise," she said. "If you will, that is."

"Of course."

"Come back to me." She reached out and grabbed his ears, not gently. "I mean that: you come back to me. Even if you fail, we can live with that, we will live with that."

He probably should have said something boastful and noble about how failure was not possible, about how he would not permit himself to fail, but that was too much Forinel and too little Kethol, and he was filled to bursting in disgust with being Forinel and not Kethol, so he just put his hands over hers, and she released his ears to hold them, one thumb stroking gently over his scars.

"Of course," he said.

If I can, he thought.

He had always thought that there was something stupid about the way that the Cullinanes always tended to put themselves in harm's way when they could have been sitting, warm and dry, around a table, and he was by no means sure that he had changed his mind about that.

But, if it was stupidity, it was the sort of stupidity that was catching.

He grinned.

"You're smiling," she said. "As though you mean it."

"Yes, I suppose that I am."

"You should do that more," she said.

"I will. I'll try."

There was no need to try to smile, not now. It wasn't just that it was easy—he couldn't help smiling; it would have taken more effort than he could have managed to get the grin off of his face.

For the first time since he had taken on the form and role of Forinel, Kethol actually felt like himself, and it felt better than good.

8

Walter Slovotsky

After you reach forty, it's patch, patch, patch.
—L. Sprague de Camp

Walter Slovotsky more ran up than climbed up the old stone steps to the parapet surrounding the inner keep of Biemestren Castle, thoroughly enjoying the way that his legs, and particularly his knees, obeyed him without any protest whatsoever.

It was his way to enjoy things thoroughly.

It wasn't just the absence of the pain. It was also the absence of the place that he had gone to to make the pain go away, at least for a while.

There was a lot that he didn't like about the Spidersect priest's little shop at the juncture of what were officially known as the Avenue of Pirondael's Treachery and the Street in Honor of Baron Tyrnael's Stand at Lundel, but which everybody still called Dog Street and Cleric's Row.

For one thing, the trouble with the Spidersect was, well, all the spiders.

He didn't like spiders. He had never liked spiders.

He didn't like the little trapdoor spiders that lived in small dugouts along the edges of the walls, although they were generally shy enough not to come out when Filistat had visitors. He didn't like the tiny feather-legged spiders, their bodies no bigger than the size of his smallest toenail, that hung on the walls and seemed to watch him, although he couldn't see their eyes. He didn't like the even tinier Oecobiuses, even though Filistat said that they did more to reduce the flea population than all the others put together.

He thought that the bright green color of the lynx spiders was an interesting contrast to the usual blacks and browns, but he didn't much care for them, either.

But he most particularly disliked Filistat's familiar, a large, hairy tarantula whose slick black body was the size of Slovotsky's fist, and whose fangs were sharp-tipped slivers of what looked like bone, and Walter Slovotsky even more disliked the way that Filistat would coax the spider up onto Slovotsky's leg, step by hairy-legged step.

Filistat had had it climb up that leg until it reached Walter's sore right knee, then slowly, slowly, while Filistat muttered some vague incantations and vaguer assurances, the spider would sink those fangs—painlessly, yes, but they were still fangs—into Walter's right knee, and the swelling would go down almost as quickly as a man's erection would after hearing, "Doesn't that look just like a penis, only smaller?"

He shuddered. Spiders.

Then again, as a kid, much to the embarrassment of Stash and Emma Slovotsky, he would wail when taken to the doctor for a shot, and scream that the needle was hurting him from the moment that old Doctor Menzer touched him with the alcohol-soaked cotton ball.

The spider—and the Spider—took away pain, not even causing a little in so doing, but that didn't mean he had to like it.

What he did like was the way that his formerly swollen knee was working again. Arthritis? Some sort of tear in the cartilage? He didn't know, and he didn't really care—the point was that it didn't hurt. There were other pleasures than the loss of pain, granted, but few were quite as wonderful, and none was quite as stark.

It looked like it was going to be a good day.

The last bits of Parliament business were wrapped up—well, many of them turned over to Bren Adahan, but Walter's role was wrapped up—and the last news along the Nyphien border was that there was no news. Quiet was good, as a general principle, although the Nyphs would bear watching.

Forinel and the rest were, by now, safely ensconced in Keranahan, and since Walter didn't officially know that Forinel was really Kethol, he didn't officially have anything to worry about, and he wasn't much for worrying, anyway. Figuring things out wasn't worrying, after all.

Sure, Kethol and Pirojil would be worried about failing, but at worst it would appear that Forinel, during his long absence from Holtun, had become unsuitable for the job of baron, but probably not sufficiently unsuitable that the Emperor would have to consider replacing him.

And it was a job, after all.

Not the most pleasant of jobs, Walter had long ago decided. If you choose to play king of the mountain, there's always somebody who wants to come knock you off so that he can be king of the mountain. That applied to a bunch of little kids playing out in a construction site at the edges of Hackensack on the Other Side as much as it applied to a baron—or an Emperor, for that matter—here and now, and that made it a lousy job, despite the perks.

Much better to be an assistant to the king of the mountain, and get to go off and do interesting things while others did the dirty work.

Walter Slovotsky was growing old, but he was resolutely determined not to grow up any more than necessary. The only question right now was whether he ought to be waiting around in Biemestren himself, or go off to do some troubleshooting—in New Pittsburgh, say. Aiea liked New Pitt, and while the sounds and the smells of the smelters weren't exactly Walter's favorite things, it was a nice place to visit, and it was a good idea for the lord proctor to pop up there, or anywhere, every now and then, without warning.

Besides, it would really be more of a vacation than anything else. He liked the idea of going out to meet Bren Adahan—and Kirah, alas—in New Pittsburgh, and spending some time with his younger daughter, as well. He and Bren would probably never be friends, not really, but they had actually grown to like each other's company, and that wasn't a bad substitute, all things considered.

The only reason he was still in Biemestren was on the off chance that Ellegon would show up, and that the dragon would have both the free time and the inclination to fly Walter out there.

Granted, there was a delegation due in from Nyphien, but it was best to let Thomen handle it for himself. Walter would just stay out of the way.

Besides, Walter never got along with Nyph nobles, who would spend hours comparing their lineages with each other and with whoever would listen, and there was only so long he could force himself to be patient and polite, what with their Euar'den this, and Tynear that, and Vilikos the other—deathly boring to a kid from Secaucus, New Jersey, You Ess of Ay, eh?

Just clean up a few things, while hanging around to see if Ellegon would show up and be able to take him, and then, dragon or no, he was off.

It was going to be quiet for a while. He hoped.

Derinald was waiting for him at the top of the stairs.

It was hard to read anything on Derinald's thin face, and the way that his ridiculously large mustache hid his upper lip and most of his lower didn't help. Walter wondered if he combed the mustache up when he ate, or just sluiced it off afterward, but didn't ask.

"You asked to see me, Captain?" he said.

"Yes, I did, Lord Proctor." Derinald nodded. It was good to see that he could actually talk and move without Beralyn having her hand stuck up his ass. Walter had wondered about that, from time to time.

"I happened to be walking the ramparts last night," Derinald said, "and I found something that I don't quite understand."

Derinald sending for Walter Slovotsky had been surprising, but Derinald not understanding something was about as surprising as the sun rising in the morning.

Derinald thought himself bright as a shiny new copper, but that was an opinion that Walter Slovotsky didn't share, and didn't think much of anybody shared. Derinald had been a minor disaster as a captain of troops, not knowing enough to leave training and discipline to his decurions, and it had been one of Walter Slovotsky's first brainstorms as Imperial proctor to give Derinald to Beralyn as an aide, secondarily to keep him out of trouble, but primarily to give her somebody instead of Thomen to whisper complaints about and imprecations against the Cullinanes to.

"Please. Show me."

Derinald led him down the Widow's Walk to a buttress. Derinald's name had been chalked there, in thin shaky Erendra letters.

Just his name, and nothing more.

"Well, hey—at least they aren't writing your name in the barracks latrine, right after 'for a good time, call . . .'" Walter said in English, knowing full well that Derinald didn't speak more than a few words of English.

"Excuse me?"

Enough teasing. Walter raised a palm. "So, somebody has written your name on a buttress," he said. "I take it that it wasn't you?"

"If I *had* written my name on a buttress—although I don't know why I would—I certainly wouldn't have asked to see you about it."

Derinald was trying to sound calm, but he was scared, and Walter saw his point.

It didn't make any particular sense, not by itself. Except for castle children climbing up on the ramparts to throw something down the other side into the outer bailey—sometimes garbage for the goats, although pig bladders filled with water were definitely the favorite, as they made a terrific splash—nobody much came up here, except for the soldiers who walked the ramparts on guard.

And Beralyn.

It was, of course, entirely possible that one of the soldiers had, for some reason, scrawled Derinald's name here. But if Beralyn had done it, it was unlikely that the purpose was to memorialize some particular joy.

And who would read the name written there?

As a first approximation: nobody but the House Guard.

"You haven't been irritating anybody in the House Guard lately, have you?"

"No, I haven't."

Which might even be true. Walter Slovotsky found Derinald irritating, and probably everybody in the House Guard did, as well, but it was one thing to find somebody an irritation, and another to make a threat.

It could be some practical joke—sort of like a high school kid writing a Better Dead list, and leaving it lying around—or it could, possibly, have been something else.

"Any idea how long it's been here?"

Derinald shook his head. "I often come up to join the Dowager Empress on her walks, but I hardly spend my time looking for, for such things as chalk marks. It could have been written yesterday, or almost a tenday ago. Certainly it was since the last rain, but, other than that," he said, spreading his hands, "I don't know."

"So . . . you think that the Dowager Empress herself chalked your name there, and you think that that probably doesn't bode well for you, eh?"

Derinald blinked. "I . . . I don't know."

"Take a guess. Take two; they're small."

"Excuse me?"

"Never mind."

Well, if Beralyn wanted Derinald dead, Walter Slovotsky wanted him alive, at least in principle. Rewarding your allies and frustrating your enemies was basic strategy.

Not that he would go far out of his way to protect Derinald, mind.

But . . .

It was a mistake to think of the House Guard as an amorphous bunch. Gold Company, who were now assigned to patrol the inner ward, were housed in the barracks in the inner ward, while Purple, who had the outer wall during this rotation, were quartered in the larger barracks at the foot of the motte. If it had been up to Walter Slovotsky, a barracks would have been built in the outer bailey, but tradition—and maybe a good tradition—was that, for security reasons, the outer bailey was to be kept bare of anything except grass and the herd of goats that kept that grass short.

Except for when the goatherds came out at dusk to chivvy their charges down the hill and out the front gate, anything seen moving in the outer bailey, night or day, had damned well better be moving slowly up the road toward the inner gate.

"Well, I'll tell you what I'm going to do," Walter said. "I'm going to ask General Garavar to switch the inner and outer guard—let Purple take the status post for a while. I won't tell him why; he'll assume that it's just that annoying Walter Slovotsky, shaking things up for the sake of shaking things up. So, if Beralyn has persuaded one of the inner guards to do away with you, that should at least make it more difficult."

Derinald almost pissed himself in gratitude, although Walter Slovotsky was far too realistic to think that the gratitude would amount to anything much or last very long.

"Please," Derinald said, "please don't mention that we talked—not to the Dowager Empress?"

For once, Walter Slovotsky was almost unhappy that he had picked such an incompetent conspirator for Beralyn to conspire with. Was Derinald always such an idiot? Or had fear just driven his brains into his asshole?

They were standing on the rampart in full view of anybody, after all; anybody who knew about the name chalked here would have no trouble guessing what the subject of their discussion had been. If Beralyn had compromised any of the House Guard, which was certainly possible, she would soon know that the two of them had talked, and would have better than a guess as to what they had talked about, within the hour, probably, or by the end of the day, at most.

Idiot.

"Of course," Walter said, "let's keep this to ourselves. No reason to mention it to anybody else." He rested his hand in a comradely way on Derinald's shoulder. "Don't worry about a thing; I'll take care of it all," he said. He looked down at the chalk scrawl. "I'll go directly to talk to General Garavar, while you get rid of the mark. No need for anybody else to see it."

"But—"

"And I'm sure you won't mind spending a few moments, each night, noting down anything that you've seen Beralyn doing, or any conversations you've had with her."

Walter thought for a moment. "Leave the note under the planter at the top of the north staircase, east wing. Daily, mind."

When Derinald started to protest, Walter squeezed his shoulder with more than comradely strength.

"I can't help you if you don't help me help you," he said. "For now, get rid of those chalk marks."

Derinald swallowed heavily, then nodded. "I'll go get some rags and water, and—"

"No," Walter said. "I'm sure," he went on, lying, "that nobody could possibly have noticed the two of us up here, but you want to be sure not to come back here again, not unless you're with the Dowager Empress."

"But how—"

"Well, you can lick it off, I guess," Walter said. "Or," he said, fiddling with the buttons on the front of his own trousers, "there's probably other ways, too. I'll see that first note tonight, I hope."

Walter Slovotsky walked away.

Well, so much for leaving, at least for now. It would be worth hanging around, at least until Derinald was dead.

He shook his head. This shouldn't have been as much fun as it was.

9

Bait

The first ninety percent of the job takes the first ninety percent of the time. The last ten percent takes the other ninety percent of the time.
—Walter Slovotsky

The line of poles snaked out from Castle Nerahan into the hills more slowly than he would have thought it would, so Kethol said.

Pirojil wasn't surprised. That was the way it was with Kethol: when it came to things that he knew about, he always understood both the opportunities and the problems. But with this, he was a fish out of water, trying his best to pretend that gasping for breath as he flopped around on the riverbank was perfectly natural.

Pirojil shook his head. "This is the easy part. Another few days, and then it gets difficult."

"Another few days, and maybe I'll be doing something I know *how* to do," Kethol said.

"There is that."

"Yes, there is." Kethol nodded, and kicked his horse into a slow, hesitant walk down the hill, Pirojil following along behind.

Berten and Ernel were, granted, engineers, but they were very junior, which Pirojil was sure was the only reason that that weasel,

Nerahan, had permitted them to pry them loose for a few tendays.

Prying workers loose had been much easier. It hadn't taken any real prying at all, in fact. With spring planting long over and the fall harvest still several tendays away, the daily maintenance of farms and crofts could easily be left to the women and children for the time being, while the men earned hard copper money. Hearing of work for pay—in hard coin, by the day, and not just in vague, probably empty promises that taxes would someday be offset—workers had streamed from the villages and crofts.

Down the hill, Pirojil could see three teams of diggers working, although he knew that there were twice as many already at work over the ridge. Each team consisted of four men, pushing the wooden arms of a posthole bore around and around, like oxen working a mill. They had to stop, from time to time, when buried rocks prevented the bore from penetrating far enough into the ground. Then they would go to the picks and shovels, sometimes, or more often simply pick up the bore and move it a short way to the side.

But, still, each digging crew managed better than two postholes per hour, and the three-man post-burying crews were hard-pressed to keep up.

He hadn't realized that the job would need almost as many loggers as it did diggers.

The Finster hills were covered with pines, although not quite as thickly covered as they had been. Pairs of woodsmen wielding huge saws were constantly toppling trees, then quickly stripping them of their bark so that hitched pairs of slow-footed dray horses could haul the logs up or down the hill to where they needed to be.

Then it was just a matter of upending the logs into the holes, and tamping in dirt and rocks back around them, while the drillers moved farther up the line to begin boring another posthole.

Everything had turned out to be more complicated than Kethol had thought, just as Pirojil had said that it would.

It wasn't just a matter of drillers and foresters and teamsters to handle the dray horses—there were hostlers to handle the horses, cooks to keep bowls of hot porridge and hotter stew coming throughout the day, and the packhorse teams with their teamsters that kept a solid flow of supplies coming from nearby markets.

And then there were the workers who brought their women, and a few children, and the inevitable whores setting up tents to drain the odd copper from those who were not too tired at the end of the day.

Kethol had guessed that they would be able to do this with fifty to a hundred men, at the most, but he had made the guess privately, and kept his mouth shut in public, which was just as well. Pirojil was in no way surprised to be able to easily count more than two hundred bodies, not including the teamsters who, with their animals, made it a point to stay in the nearest villages, rather than with the moving camp.

That was just fine with Pirojil. The more people involved, the more authenticity the whole thing had.

The whole operation seemed to run on a stream of water and weak beer—Berten had calculated that they would need fifteen firkins of beer per day, and if anything he had been underestimating, and the packhorses seemed to constantly be staggering into camp with filled firkins from nearby villages, or lightly walking away, bringing empty ones back. If it wasn't for the stream cutting through the valley below, they would have had to hire on twice as many teamsters just for the water.

Living off the land only went so far, though; Kethol's notion of shooting game to feed the workers had quickly been dismissed by Pirojil.

It might not be as much fun, he had explained, slowly, patiently, to supply the moving work camp by simple commerce, but it was far more reliable to send agents into town to buy supplies than it was to send hunters, even the Keranahan poachers, into the woods to bring back deer.

Besides, while the deer surely wouldn't be considerate enough to deliver themselves, if you put a ring through a pig's nose or ear and tied a rope to that ring, the pig would willingly, if not happily, trot along behind a packhorse—and there was a lot more usable meat on even a medium pig than there was on even the largest deer.

On the second day, granted, an idiot teamster had tried to help by slaughtering one of the pigs before the others had been properly secured. That, quite predictably, had panicked the rest of the pigs, and a couple of dozen men had wasted half the day chasing the torn-eared pigs up one hill and down another.

Pirojil thought that he understood how the pigs felt.

Well, at least it gave the other teamsters a good story to tell at Felenen's expense.

An east wind brought the piny smell of turpentine and the reek of creosote to Pirojil's nostrils as Berten, stripped to the waist like the laborers, ran up from where a four-man digging team had run into a rock. Two of them squatted on the ground nearby, guzzling water—at least Pirojil hoped it was water; even a peasant soon wouldn't be able to work, or even to stand, after drinking as much beer as these were, if it was beer—while two of the others took their own turns with the pickaxes and the shovels.

"It's a wonderful life, eh?" Berten said. His face was tanned, but his chest and belly held a sickly white pallor.

"Excuse me?"

"I was saying that I think it goes well," Berten said. "If I have my way—and I just might—we can actually put up a telegraph line through here, sooner than later."

He gestured below to where a pair of Nerahan's soldiers stood guard over the long coil of black rope that had been strung across the tops of the poles. Berten had insisted on a team of glassblowers to make what he called "insulators" for the cable, and he and Ernel were barely able to keep up with the pole-digging operation, each taking his turn climbing the poles to install the insulators and then string the next length of cable.

To the extent that it was a cable, of course, which wasn't very much.

As Pirojil understood it—and he didn't pretend, even to himself, that he understood it terribly well—the magic of the telegraph required that its messages travel along pairs of copper wires, and the copper wires had to be protected from touching almost anything, or the message would vanish into whatever they touched. Real engineer cable looked like a very thin rope, but was really copper wires in some slick but flexible substance—sort of like leather, but seamless—that was, so Pirojil had been told, hideously expensive to make.

And, of course, the copper itself was valuable. Cut down the telegraph cable and throw it in a stone crucible on a hot fire, and the covering would quickly burn away, and the wire would melt. You would quickly find that you had a large amount of tradable copper—and the price of copper was going up every year.

Pirojil smiled to himself. Kethol was just being Kethol, after all. He was doing just what a born woodsman would naturally do.

If you wanted to be sure that you could poach a deer when you wanted one, all you had to do was put out a few salt licks in a nearby meadow, and you could be sure that the deer would learn to come there. If what you wanted was wolf, or bear, all you needed to do was to find a good spot that you could observe undetected, and stake out a carcass.

Now, a wolf or bear could smell a rotting carcass half a barony away, but how would the deer know to find the salt lick? Did a rock of salt have a smell that a deer's nose could detect? Did they talk to each other?

It didn't matter. However the deer knew it, they knew what went on in their woods.

The same would be true with the bandits. Pirojil was certain that word of the telegraph line would have reached up into the hills, across the border into Kiar. It was more than possible that, even now, there was some Kiaran woodsman on his belly next to a boulder on a ridge to the north, watching them, ready to report that the line was already complete, and that there was copper to be had for the taking . . . as soon as the Imperials and their servants went away.

He hoped so.

It was just like baiting a trap for any other animal.

The difference, of course, was that you really did have to have salt to interest the deer, and you really did have to have carrion to attract the bear or wolf. But humans couldn't smell copper, and he thought—and certainly hoped—that even the most wary bandit wouldn't suspect that the Imperials had gone to all this trouble and expense simply to bait a trap.

The only question was where they would strike first. Not too close to the towns on either end, and closer to the Keranahan end than the Nerahan one, since there was a small detachment of Nerahan's own troops in Findel Village, at the foot of the hills.

They would start somewhere near the middle, probably close to where the line passed across a saddle between two low hills, and work their way north and east, ready to duck back up into the mists and across the border, trusting to their better knowledge of their home territory more than any unwillingness of Imperials to chase them.

Pirojil smiled. "Another two days, do you think?"

"Then you wait." Berten nodded. "How many of the bowmen, do you think, will stand?"

Kethol drew himself up straight. "They are men of Barony Keranahan," he said.

Berten repressed a snicker.

At least he hadn't come right out and laughed. Master engineers were famous for flaunting their minimal—at best—respect for nobility, and while these two were just barely journeymen, they carried themselves like they thought they were rather more than that. They probably spent the nights in their tent passing a bottle of corn whiskey back and forth and laughing with each other over the pretensions of the nobles.

"I'm not sure that the baron is right." Pirojil shrugged. "It's hard to expect anything more than them shooting off their last nocked arrow, if anybody charges at them. Takes a fair amount of training and more than a fair amount of bones and balls to stand and hold steady when somebody's coming at you. But it's not a matter of whether or not they stand, not when all goes to shit, is it?"

"I guess not," Berten said. "I'd like to have a half-dozen more."

"I" would like? The engineers would be safely back in Nerahan.

"Me, I'd like to have a pretty face, a stiff dick, and more gold than a horse could carry." Pirojil smiled. It wasn't a pleasant smile, but, then again, Pirojil wasn't a pleasant person.

Kethol smiled, too. He wasn't a pleasant person, either.

10

The Residence

I have one good thing to say about travel: it's the
only way I know of to get from here to there.
As for the rest of it, you can have it.

—Walter Slovotsky

A tall pitcher of fresh well water and two glasses stood on the
small table at her side, as Leria sat under a canopy out in
the garden, pretending to do needlepoint.

She didn't much like needlepoint. No, more than that—she
hated needlepoint. But the traditional usages had to be bowed toward, even if she didn't feel obligated to obey them thoughtlessly.

As tradition had it, noblewomen would spend their entire time
during their men's frequent absences sitting around and pining for
them. Pining and fretting, with a little worrying thrown in for good
measure.

Oh, they would be allowed to do minor things. Needlepoint,
perhaps, or knitting—not because seamstresses couldn't do both as
well or better, but because there was considered to be some special
status to something made by a noblewoman's fingers.

Leria had done much of both as a girl—her father had insisted
that she learn and practice all of the useless arts suitable to her

station—and, as far she was concerned, she had done enough needlepoint and knitting for more than one lifetime.

Knitting wasn't bad—she could let her mind wander when she
knitted, although that usually meant that she dropped stitches—but
she really hated embroidery. If she let her mind relax just a little
bit, if she permitted it to wander in the slightest, she always found
herself poking herself in the finger, then quickly having to snatch
her hand away from the wooden frame to avoid staining the work
with her blood. If she didn't move quickly enough, she would have
to start it all over again, since blood simply wouldn't ever come out.

So she had gone through the storage rooms—which she had to,
anyway—until she found an ancient unfinished piece that looked
like it was from some long-dead Tynearean lady. The Tyneareans
always seemed fascinated with the still-life portraits of fruit—for
whatever reason—and Leria kept the bulk of the cloth folded under
on her lap while she poked away at the fringes. She knew full well
that at least one of the maids had examined it—whichever one it
was hadn't quite replaced it on the same spot on her bureau a few
nights ago—but she didn't expect that there would be much loose
talk about that, at least.

In the meantime, there was plenty of real work to do.

The Grand List had been misplaced—probably sometime after
Elanee had died, although Elda was willing to swear all day long
that she herself hadn't seen it in years, and that the baroness kept
it in a lockbox in her bedroom, a box that now contained only some
minor jewelry.

Trying to rebuild the list from the various inventories, what with
compiling the inventories into *the* inventory and checking everything, so to speak, could easily go on for a year, or even several
years. Before the war, the Keranahan family had apparently never
been careful about separating the Residence inventory from the in-

ventories at the keep in Dereneyl. As far as she could tell, the only way that she could reconcile the whole mess would be not only to personally examine and list, in great detail, everything in the Residence, but then to go in and do the same thing at the keep in Dereneyl, as well.

But it had to be done. If you didn't keep close track of what you had, there was no question that somebody would make off with it.

What *had* Elanee been thinking of?

Leria's own inventories, the records of her family's possessions halfway across the barony, just beyond the Ulter hills, were still locked away in the Residence strong room—she had insisted on bringing them along when Elanee had even more strenuously insisted on moving Leria into the Residence.

The inventories were bad, but the worst of it was the tax rolls.

The dead Baron Keranahan—or, more likely, the equally dead Baroness Elanee—had constructed a bizarre, twisty scheme of levies, most of them poorly documented. She had little doubt that the collection of the levies was even more poorly documented in Dereneyl—in part, at least, because of the occupation, and mostly because of the complication.

Silly to blame the Imperials when the Keranahans had brought it all on themselves to start with.

Leria's long-dead father had tried to keep such things simple, but that clearly hadn't been the policy in Baron Keranahan's own lands: why would anybody levy a relatively light farrowing tax in fall and then raise it in the spring? Having the taxes collected by occupation soldiers—rather than the village wardens, lord landholders, and baronial proctors—would only make matters more confusing, and could only add additional chances for theft.

Peasants were sneaky, after all. She didn't blame them, that was just the way they were. This sort of silliness guaranteed that Treseen's proctors would find only cured hams when they made their seasonal visit in the spring, and she had little doubt that herds of pregnant sows would be shuffled, waddling all the while, from crofts that he had yet to visit to crofts that he had already inspected.

She had smiled at the thought of herds of pigs being driven across the landscape while the proctor would make his rounds to find only a few odd sows and boars, and only the occasional sickly piglet.

She would have to figure out how to handle that herself. Forinel was far too soft and sentimental about such things. He would always be that way—and he had always been that way, she reminded herself.

That wasn't new; that was just Forinel. It was Kethol, too, although Kethol was soft and sentimental only in some ways. There was a hard edge to him that she had both liked and been frightened by, from the moment that he and his two companions had walked into her life.

It hadn't been what she had expected, when she had smuggled out a letter to the Dowager Empress, protesting the marriage to Miron that his mother was trying to pressure her into. She had hoped that the Dowager Empress would simply send for her; that was the obvious thing to do.

Instead, for her own reasons, Beralyn had sent Kethol, Pirojil, and Durine to look into matters in Barony Keranahan, and from the moment they had walked into the hall in this very house, the house which was now hers, her life was different.

There had been something in their eyes, something in the way that the three of them never seemed to need to look at each other, but had eyed both Miron and his mother as though the only question was how, and not when, with no soft rationalizations about how the Baroness Elanee was just a woman, because they recognized an enemy.

She had liked that, and the truth was that she had been attracted to Kethol from that moment, although she hadn't expected to actually ever do anything about it.

She smiled. Life would be very different, indeed, if the real Forinel had returned, because he would have expected Leria to be a very proper wife, and to not bother her pretty head with affairs of state and governance, and it would have taken much effort and diplomacy to slowly, carefully, get him to accept otherwise.

Kethol was easier on that score, although there were ways and times when he was utterly inflexible, like when he had peremptorily clamped his hand over her mouth in the woods, not for a moment entertaining the notion that she might understand the situation as well as he did, much less better. It was as though he was made of extremes: utterly compliant or infinitely stubborn, and she had no clue as to how she could possibly bend that stubbornness, when it popped out, surprisingly, on matters that he thought that he knew about.

And, to be fair, he did. She didn't know *how* he would have taken on that patrol, but even though she hadn't thought so at the moment, on reflection she had no doubt that if he had thought that fighting rather than hiding was the better way to protect her from the danger that he thought they represented, it would have been only a matter of moments until he was standing over their dead bodies, and while that frightened her, there was also something thrilling about it, in a way that she couldn't explain, even to herself, and wouldn't have considered trying to explain to somebody else.

It would be more, well, interesting with Kethol than it would have been with Forinel, although she was sure that, eventually, under her tutelage, he would develop enough of the political skills to handle most things, with her advice.

That was fine with her.

Let the men handle matters of war and politics, and think that they reigned supreme, and she would be happy to take care of the real work in seeing that the barony remained solvent. If she was right about how much every peasant and his cousin were stealing from the baron—and she had seen how thick the fields were with golden, growing grain—the barony would be rather more than simply solvent.

Footsteps crunched on the gravel behind her, and she carefully folded the needlepoint in her lap as Thirien walked up, and took up a stiff brace.

"Governor Treseen is here, and he begs an audience with you," he said, formally. "Shall I admit him to the garden, my lady?"

Treseen? She forced herself to rise slowly. Did that mean that there was some word of Kethol?

Was he hurt?

No, please, *no*.

She forced herself to seem calm. Showing panic wouldn't make things any better, and could easily make them worse. Kethol and the others were a full day's ride away—even if she could do anything—and what could she do?—there was nothing that could be helped by panic.

"Shall I admit him?" Thirien asked again.

When the garden had been Elanee's, the baroness had used it as a quiet refuge, and absolutely insisted that nobody enter other than on a true emergency. Leria didn't really need that herself— her mind was always enough of a private refuge—but it made sense and gave her authority to stake out the same territory that the late baroness had, as a way of establishing herself with the staff, and with the governor, and, for that matter, with Forinel.

"No." She shook her head. "No, please. I'll see the governor in the great hall—and would you be so kind as to invite Erenor to join us?"

Treseen might have looked stupid—most men did, and most

men were—but he hadn't survived as long as he had and risen to the position that he had by being utterly brainless, and it would be good to have a reliable witness to their conversation, particularly since she didn't expect that things would go her way.

For now.

Despite that, she found herself walking too quickly into the Residence through the portico, and forced herself to slow her steps as she walked down the hall to the bath room, taking a few moments to wash her face, change her dress, and brush her hair. Anything for an advantage, her father always said, and while he was usually talking about military campaigns, it applied in more areas than that.

She considered, for just a moment, giving a quick spray from the bottle of rose extract to her hair and breasts, but decided that that would seem too calculated, too planned for a lady just coming out of her garden.

The trick was to seem to glide effortlessly through life, and that sort of seeming—as Erenor would have told her was true for most seemings—took much effort.

But . . . had *he* been hurt?

Please, no.

She hurried down the hall.

Treseen was sitting in the large wooden chair next to the cold hearth, as though he was seeking to bathe in its coolness, as he would on a cold night enjoy the heat.

He rose at her approach. His face was gritty and sweaty from the ride, and he held himself back as he bowed over her hand without her having to give even the tiniest of sniffs to put him on the defensive.

"Good afternoon, Lady," he said. "Thank you for receiving me on such short notice—without any notice at all, in fact." He smiled.

She returned the smile as she let her hand fall, and tried not to show her relief.

He was safe.

If Treseen had been coming to report that Kethol—that Forinel had been hurt, or worse, he wouldn't have taken such a light tone. He would have painted a somber expression on his face, and not let her see that he was relieved to now have Miron to deal with, rather than Forinel.

"You're always welcome here, Governor," she said. "Once the governance of the barony is given to the baron, I hope you'll know that you'll always be welcome in our home in Dereneyl, as well."

"Yes, yes." He smiled noncommittally. "I would hope that's always so."

She quite deliberately furrowed her brow. "You seem uncomfortable—I hope you won't embarrass me by telling me you've not been offered refreshment." She was already reaching for the bell rope when a maid appeared bearing a large flagon of beer from the cellar.

"Thirien was kind enough to see that my needs were seen to." Treseen guzzled it greedily, then wiped his mouth on the back of his hand. "I thank you," he said. "It's a hot day for riding."

"Which makes it all the kinder of you to come out and visit me today," she said.

Where *was* Erenor? She could hardly hold off discussing serious matters forever.

Best to start with the obvious diversion. Besides, an empty-headed little noble girl shouldn't have been bright enough to work things out for herself. "Is there word of the baron? Has he been hurt?" She let the concern that she felt—the silly concern; surely, he was fine—show in her face and voice.

Treseen set down the beer and shook his head. "No, of course not," he said.

She sighed in relief, and was only a little surprised to find that the relief was genuine.

"You worried me—your sudden appearance, Governor. It made me think that something might have happened to the baron."

"Then I must apologize for that, as well," Treseen said. "I've not received any word from him, other than a quick message from Baron Nerahan that came along with the Imperial post, complaining about him . . . borrowing a couple of Nerahan's engineers."

" 'Borrowing'?"

"Well," Treseen said, smiling, "Baron Nerahan was a trifle more blunt about it—he's gotten awfully testy since occupation was lifted there. I believe the precise phrase he used was 'something just short of kidnapping,' although I'm more inclined to attribute problems to that Pirojil, myself. I know that all is well with Baron Keranahan— or, at least, I can swear on my sword that all *was* well with him two days ago. Word of any problem before then would have reached us by now—and Tarnell, at least, would have sent immediate word. No, it's not that."

"Then you've come out on a hot day to show me the baronial account books?" She smiled. "How nice of you."

Treseen's lips made a thin line. "Lady, with respect, I haven't, and I don't think that I can or should. The baronial account books are Imperial property. It would be a close matter as to whether the baron himself has any right to see them at this point, and I've sent a message to the Imperial proctor asking for guidance on that.

"Beyond that, my former aide left the accounts in a dreadful state, and with Tarnell gone—and let me remind you he went at your and the baron's insistence, and over my objections—I'm working night and day without any reliable help to try to bring them in order, so that I can at least send the Emperor an honest approximation as to what is owed, and to whom."

Working night and day to try to hide various thefts and perhaps to replace some stolen money, more likely.

The trick was to keep the pressure on, to let Treseen think that he would have the time to restore what he had stolen, before either the Emperor demanded an accounting—which was always possible—or lifted the occupation, giving Forinel an indisputable right to the accounts.

He would either have to put the money back, or flee. Treseen was too fat, too old, and too used to a comfortable life to run, not if he didn't have to. Let him squeeze the noble landholders' estates for the extra, and they would welcome the return of baronial rule as much as they would the lifting of the occupation itself, and—

A breeze blew in from the open door, and swirled dust around the great hall so hard that she had to close her eyes for a moment. When she opened them, Erenor stood before her in his gray robes, his hood back, lying over his bony shoulders, his thin, gray hair tied behind him, withered hands clasped in front of him.

"You sent for me, Lady?" he asked.

Erenor could never resist a dramatic entrance, particularly when it suggested that he was more than he was. She knew—and she was sure that Treseen knew—enough about magic to know that changing oneself into a whirlwind was well beyond the scope of a wizard of Erenor's abilities, and probably beyond the abilities of any wizard in the Eren regions. It was possible, of course, that he had conjured up a small, tame whirlwind, and let it carry him about, and that should have been possible for a wizard who called himself "the Great," but that also seemed less than likely.

What he had probably done was as simple as generating a seeming of a small whirlwind, and then walking in through the door when their eyes were closed. The lack of grit on her face and clothing suggested that had, indeed, been the case.

"No," she said. "I don't recall sending for you." It would be better if it seemed as though Erenor had barged in on the two of them.

"My mistake, and my apologies, as well." He arched an eyebrow.

"Then I'll beg your pardon, and take my leave," he said, bowing.

"Please, no," she said. "As long as you're here, please join us."

"I would never reject a lady's invitation," he said. "I'll be more than happy to."

He pulled the bell rope once, then twice, then once again, in the signal for beer for one to be brought to the great hall—and she found herself more than vaguely annoyed that Erenor had already discovered such things—then seated himself next to Treseen and tucked the skirts of his robe around his knees.

"And what shall we talk about on such a lovely afternoon?" he asked.

"Governor Treseen rode out from Dereneyl to tell me that he's denying me access to the baronial accounts."

"It's only for the time being," Treseen said. "I'm sure I'll get word from the capital, sooner than later. I've sent your . . . request to the attention of the Emperor himself, and I've no doubt that I'll get a response. If he thinks it's as important as I've told him that you seem to, it will be a fast response—perhaps even by telegraph to Nerahan, and rider from there."

She doubted that. Why would Treseen make the request sound so urgent that they would use the telegraph? And, besides, doing that meant that the message would have to go through many hands, and it was unlikely that anybody in the capital would want the barony's financial matters discussed in every town with a telegraph shack between Biemestren and Nerahan.

"No," he said. "That's not why I've come." He reached into his tunic and produced a folded paper from his pocket. "I've received a request from the Dowager Empress, asking me to convey to you her best regards, and then to convey you to Biemestren, immediately—to attend her, she says, and discuss your wedding."

Erenor raised an eyebrow. "Discuss? What is there to discuss?"

"She doesn't say," Treseen said, flatly. "But the wedding of a baron isn't an everyday occurrence—I'm sure she wants to be sure that the preparations are in accord with Lady Leria's preferences, and such."

Leria was sure that it was nothing of the sort. The most obvious explanation was that Beralyn was going to try to throw her and Thomen together, again. Not that she had anything against the Emperor. He was a good man, charming in his own way, and had a more than gentle way with both horses and people. Too gentle, perhaps, but that didn't bother her.

Nor was it that she would necessarily prefer to be Baroness Keranahan, rather than Empress Furnael.

But abandoning Kethol and Keranahan? No. That would be disloyal, and Leria set a high stock on loyalty.

It wasn't just that, and she couldn't pretend to herself that her motivations were utterly noble. Kethol would never become terribly interested in the details of ruling a barony, and he would leave those to her. She would, in many ways, get to be the baron, something that the lack of a stick between her legs would otherwise have denied her.

But it wasn't just loyalty, and it wasn't just greed, either.

There was something about the way that he held her in the night that was more than simply endearing. It wasn't the mad passion that she had had for the young Forinel, and even that passion had been mixed in her ever-practical mind with the fact that he would become the baron.

Until Elanee had driven him off.

Perhaps she had more in common with Pirojil and Kethol than she had thought. She hated the idea of losing.

So she would not lose, and she had long ago set her mind on marrying Forinel and becoming the baroness of Keranahan, and so she would.

The way that Kethol looked at her with adoring eyes, a look that had nothing to do with her station or her lands, had nothing at all to do with it.

It was important to be practical. And never mind that his arms held her, warm and safe, in the night. Such things shouldn't be important.

"I hope you won't mind my company on your journey," Erenor said.

"I'm sure she won't," Treseen said. "Since she won't have it."

Erenor blinked. "I think I have to—the baron was quite clear—"

"Clear or not, the Empress has all the wizards she needs, and she has not sent for you. As to the Lady Leria's safety, I'm sending a full company as her escort, led by my best captain, and they shall travel on interior roads via Barony Adahan. I wouldn't, after all, want to have the lady have to witness the scene of my men cutting down any bandits that might wish to interfere with her.

"It's all been arranged. Once they reach the Adahan border, they'll be joined by another company of Baron Adahan's troops. She'll be quite safe, I assure you." He turned to Leria. "Now, let me be very clear, Lady—you're not some sort of prisoner; I'll not drag you, kicking and screaming, into the coach that will be here at first light. If you choose to spurn the invitation of the Dowager Empress, just tell me now or tell my captain in the morning, and I'll convey word of that to Biemestren, immediately, by telegraph from Nerahan."

She really didn't have a choice. If she refused—no matter how carefully she phrased it—Treseen would be sure that it would widely be bruited about that, as he had put it, she had "spurned the Dowager Empress's invitation."

"Of course," she said, nodding. "I'll be honored to attend the Empress."

Treseen was a good enough politician that he kept his smile inside. He had bought himself more time, and gotten what he surely thought of as a nuisance of a girl out of his way, at least for the time being.

She understood why Treseen was happy.

What she didn't understand was why Erenor was holding himself so still and tight that she was certain that he, too, was delighted. Was it really as simple as him not liking to travel, and enjoying the prospect of being left alone with his study and his spell books, food and drink available at the pull of a bell rope?

Possibly. Erenor didn't have to have complicated motivations for everything.

She thought about asking him later, but decided against it. He'd just lie.

"In the morning, then," Treseen said, rising.

"Yes."

Erenor still was overly pleased with himself as they stood and watched Treseen ride away, but he was starting to let it show.

She tried to keep her voice low and level. "So—you're happy that I've been sent for."

"Well, no," he said, smiling. "I'm not looking forward to that lost-little-child look that the baron will surely display upon his return, no. I'm hoping it's just that, and not a full-scale tantrum. Do you think that smoke will actually pour out of his ears?" Erenor shook his head. "I'm not sure if I'd rather that he comes back here first, or finds out in Dereneyl—and it's perhaps just as well that he's not one for breaking furniture when he's angry."

"I'll leave him a note," she said.

"And I should get how many men to hold him down while I read it to him?" He waved that away. "Well, I'll manage. But yes, I'll admit that I do see some advantages in all this, although I'll freely confess that I far prefer your conversation to that of the guards and the serving girls—except for the little upstairs maid, who is not altogether utterly unpleasant to either ear or eye . . . or the touch, for that matter. And I will admit without any necessity of having hot irons applied to my tender flesh that having to watch so carefully over you has prevented me from being able to freely go into Dereneyl, and seeing if some of the locals can easily be separated from a little coin, and I assure you I will be taking full advantage of that in your absence.

"But I think you're missing the best part of it."

"Oh?"

"A problem is best dealt with the center. Here, we're at the edges. I'm not at all sure what Treseen and Miron have planned—if they have anything planned, as of yet; Forinel's timely reappearance caught them rather off guard, didn't it?

"Tyrnael—and Treseen, no doubt—intended to push Parliament into making Miron the baron, and we've no reason to think that they have any less desire for that now. More, if anything. Tyrnael wanted a Holtish baron who was under his influence, and Treseen wanted to keep his soft, no doubt very lucrative, job as the governor, for as long as possible. A bit of tension there, no?

"Still, the first desire hasn't changed, and the second want is probably more urgent. For them. Particularly with Forinel, right this moment, showing all and sundry that he has quite a lot to offer—I think he'll be at least partly successful with the bandit problem, and I think that will give him some very serious credibility with the local lords . . . although you can expect that Moarin will be more than a little resentful at having to shell out good silver." He raised a finger. "But think on it: the center is Biemestren, and you have just been invited—no, better than invited: you've been commanded to the center, when up until now you had been dispatched to the fringe.

"I think that opens up a whole world of possibilities, don't you? Treseen is anchored here, yes, but do you think that Miron will allow you to whisper into the Empress's ear with nobody around to plead his own case? Don't you think that Biemestren is going to draw Tyrnael, as well? Isn't it at least possible that not only this matter, but others, can be resolved by one very smart young woman, who has the ear of not only the Empress but the Emperor, and is ready to say or do what needs to be said or done, at the right moment?"

He smiled again. "And, who knows? It's not at all impossible that you might, at some point, find that you have some help in one or another matter, isn't it?"

She was going to ask him what he meant—not that she thought that he'd say anything unless it suited his own purposes, though it was, at least, worth a try—but he muttered a few syllables, and the brightness of the afternoon rose up and blinded her painlessly.

And when the brightness was gone, so was Erenor.

"I understand that you'll be leaving in the morning," Miron said, as the serving girl laid another preposterously thin slice of roast lamb on his plate, then ladled a scant spoonful of the horseradish sauce on both the meat and the fried turnip cake. "Pity."

She nodded, and forced herself to smile. There was no advantage to be gained in telling Miron just how much she hated him, and quite a disadvantage to be had in showing that sort of weakness, as she had in Governor Treseen's office, but had not repeated since.

The problem was, probably, that she was too easy to manipulate for fear of being thought weak—after all, she could have eaten in her rooms, or forbidden Miron from joining her at table. But that would have made it seem like she was frightened of him, and she had decided against that.

Ella, the serving girl—she really should be better about remembering names, Leria decided—quickly eyed the level in the mottled-green wine bottle, then walked toward the archway into the main hall. She would be only a pull of the bell rope away, if that. More than likely, she was waiting just out of sight to be summoned, or to eavesdrop on their conversation, or probably both, come to think of it.

Or maybe, just possibly, Ella wanted to be close by in case Leria needed her, but that wasn't something Leria could count on. It wasn't that servants were incapable of loyalty—quite the contrary, in fact—but loyalty had to be earned, by treating them fairly if strictly over a period of time; it couldn't be earned overnight, or purchased with a few coppers. Leria had quite deliberately not picked a permanent personal maid, yet, just for that reason—she insisted on competent service, but didn't want to find herself stuck with somebody who couldn't learn her needs, somebody she would have to live with for years and couldn't dismiss without raising the suspicion among the staff that she was flighty.

She would see. She had told each of the serving girls that they were not to gossip at all about her habits, and had then quite deliberately given each of them different instructions as to minor details, and was watching carefully to see if, say, Ella miraculously discovered that she wanted her hairbrushes laid out in order of size, as she had told Starlen, or her next day's underclothes daubed with a hint of attar of roses, as she had told Tinala.

Making everything appear effortless was, as she had known it would be, a lot of work, but Leria didn't mind work, and in fact reveled in it.

She did not, however, at all enjoy having to put up with Miron, and the truth was that he scared her.

It wasn't a dangerous situation, not really. It just felt that way.

Captain Thirien, she knew—although he wouldn't quite come out and say it—had no love or respect for Miron, and the old soldier was utterly loyal to Forinel; so loyal, in fact, that she knew that it bothered Kethol. She didn't think that it was an accident that Thirien was taking his own supper outside, in the garden, with only a few muttered curses and the occasional dropping of something noisy wafting through the open doors as a reminder that he was only a shout away.

Not that that was necessary, and in practice it was probably as much Miron's protection as her own—although she doubted in Thirien's intent—as she could hardly tear her dress and scream with Thirien right outside.

Although she had considered it.

But Miron would have just sat back in his chair, and looked vaguely alarmed, and not made a show of protesting his innocence, so there was no point in that.

Miron was as dangerous as a poisonous snake, and a country girl, noble or not, knew how to handle a snake: you hit it with something heavy, hard and repeatedly, until you were sure it was dead, and then you hit it a few more times, just to be sure.

What you didn't do was sit across the table from it, which was precisely what she was doing at the small table near the hearth, where the family usually ate.

"You seem very quiet this evening," Miron said. "Which suggests that you're thinking deep thoughts." His smile was a degree short of insulting.

"No," she said, shaking her head. "I was just thinking that the soup was a little thin, and I'll probably have to have a word with the cook about what goes into a proper stock. More chicken, I would think, and fewer dried carrots."

"Very domestic of you," he said, nodding in approval. "It's good to have a firm hand around here, taking pains about such things. Mother, despite her many virtues, seemed to think that paying attention to the details was beneath her."

"She seemed to, yes, but I didn't notice a problem with the food."

"No, you wouldn't have, at that." He chuckled. "Mother was more . . . concerned with results, rather than the process." He sipped at his wine. "A quiet complaint to Cook would always be more than enough, without her having to specify what Cook ought to do about it." He shrugged, and considered the meat impaled on his eating prong as though studying it intently. "Of course, the fact that she'd had Cook's predecessor lashed and then dismissed from her service may have had something to do with how quickly the staff responded to her every need." He looked up. "Not that I'm criticizing you, dear Leria. I'm sure you'll have the house running splendidly in time for my brother's triumphant return—oh, but, then again, you won't be here for it, will you?"

"If you're amused by the notion of Forinel and me being separated again, Miron, I think you'll find yourself not amused for very long."

He shook his head. "You wound me, Leria, really you do. I, for one, wish nothing but the best for both of you, truly."

She nodded, as though she believed that. "Of course."

"Then again, he is off doing something . . . well, soldierly, and that isn't without risk, is it?"

"You hope that he's killed by one of these Kiaran bandits, so that you can be baron."

"Well, of course I do," he said, punctuating the admission with a snort. "If I'd rather be the almost-landless second brother than Baron Keranahan, I'd be an idiot, and I think that one of the few things you and I can agree on is that I'm not an idiot." He shook his head. "Still, that would make you sad, and that would sadden me. Truly it would. So shall we drink to his safe return to this empty house?" He raised his glass, and she couldn't do anything but mirror him, although she drank only a little.

He was not going to get her drunk, if that's what he had in mind.

What exactly was she frightened of? She wasn't certain, not really. Miron had, of course, tried to press his attentions on her back before his mother had died, back when Elanee was trying to pressure her into marrying him, but that had ended when Kethol, Pirojil, and Durine had arrived, and since Kethol—since Forinel had left for Nerahan and whatever he and Pirojil were doing, there hadn't been any of that sort of unpleasantness.

Which was, in a sense, unfortunate. She could have handled that easily.

"Yes," she said. "But the only pity is that I won't be here when your brother returns from Nerahan."

"Returns in triumph, no doubt." There was no overt sarcasm in his tone.

"Yes, it will be just that," she said, her words more sure than her conviction.

"Then since we're both convinced on that, we should probably drop the subject, lest our last evening together is wasted nodding our heads at each other, eh?" Miron conveyed a small piece of lamb to his mouth, and chewed slowly, thoughtfully, his head cocked to one side. "So, since this *is* our last evening together for some time, we should be sure to enjoy it. Would you care for a walk in the garden after dinner?"

"No, but thank you," she said. "I'd best supervise the packing. I'm not sure how long I'll be in Biemestren, and—"

"And there are far better seamstresses there than here or in Dereneyl—fond though I am of Madame Curtenell's shop—and you might as well take advantage of your time in the capital, and travel lightly. Once you settle down to a life of a country baroness, there will hardly be many more occasions for that sort of expedition."

"Country baroness? I think that Baron Keranahan"—she had used the title deliberately, hoping for some reaction, but she didn't get one—"and I will be living in Dereneyl, at the residence there, sooner than you might think."

He nodded, as though actually agreeing. "That's quite possible.

I suspect that Governor Treseen's days are numbered—as governor, that is." He smiled. "It will be . . . interesting to see how well Forinel can actually rule, once the responsibilities, as well as the title, are his." He shrugged. "I, of course, wish him well."

"Of course."

He had the nerve to laugh. "You sound so skeptical, my lady, and I wish you wouldn't. I had best have great faith in his ability to rule the barony, under present circumstances—although he showed scant interest in the details of such things before he left on his . . . little adventure, and it seems to me that it's you, rather than he, who has shown any involvement in such things since his very convenient return."

If it bothered Miron that Forinel had appeared in Parliament just before the Emperor and Parliament were to award the barony to him, it didn't show. Which spoke only to his self-control.

"I think," she said, choosing her words carefully, "that everyone will find that Forinel can handle himself as well in Dereneyl—and in Biemestren, too, for that matter—as he did in the Katharhd."

"Ah, yes, his wanderings in the Katharhd. There were quite a few stories about his exploits floating around the capital, although he's far too modest to retell them himself." A quick shrug. "At least in my presence."

Did he suspect the truth? Was he probing? She couldn't be sure, but there was no way of knowing, and the last thing she wanted to do was to seem defensive.

"If you have any questions, ask them yourself—of him," she said.

"And see if he'll boast to me?" Miron shook his head. "So that I could, perhaps, magnify the stories in my own retelling of them, and use that to embarrass him as a braggart? No, thank you. My brother is a fool—that he left you in the first place proves that beyond a shadow of a hint of a glimmer of a doubt—but he's not that kind of fool." He smiled over his wine. "Whatever he did, I think it's very clever of him to refuse to talk about it, and I've more than a hint as to where that cleverness originates." He saluted her with his wineglass. "Not with Forinel, who has always been something of a dolt, eh?" He drained his glass, then picked up the wine bottle with his own hands and poured himself some more, rather than ringing for the serving girl.

She could have protested, and she wanted to. Forinel had left her, indeed—to go out into the Katharhd and prove himself, as though he had had something to prove—but that had nothing to do with being a fool, unless all men were fools. Miron's mother, Elanee, had had a strange effect on men, something that Erenor described as a latent magical talent. Forinel hadn't been the only one affected—Elanee had had Treseen wrapped about her little finger, and it had been all that Kethol, Pirojil, and Durine had been able to do to resist her attempts to persuade them, when they had first arrived in Keranahan, to leave Leria here. Only their orders and that innate stubbornness of Kethol's had made them able to resist her.

It would have been wonderful, Leria thought, to have that ability, but she didn't, and had to make her way with native wit, sharpened by a lifetime of training, and she sometimes wondered if it would be enough.

He picked up the bottle and refilled her wineglass. "Well, shall we drink to the future true ruler of Barony Keranahan?"

"To your brother," she said, raising her own glass.

As she brought it to her lips it occurred to her how strange it was that Miron had poured his own wine, and that meant that he had had to handle the wine bottle, and—

She let the glass drop from her fingers. It shattered on the floor, splattering her legs.

Miron was on his feet in an instant. "Are you hurt, Leria?" he asked, as he came around the table.

The serving girl ran in through the archway to the main hall a scant moment before Captain Thirien burst through the garden door.

"Some problem, my lady?" he asked, as the serving girl, napkin snatched from the table in hand, knelt down beside her to daub at the stained dress.

She shook her head. "No, it's just my clumsiness," she said. "I dropped a wineglass."

He hadn't had the opportunity to put something in her glass, not directly, but he could easily have slipped something into the wine bottle. Poison? Not likely. Some sort of sleeping potion? She didn't know, but it had been something, she was sure.

Thirien smiled. "I'm sorry to have bothered your dinner, then, Lady," he said, giving a slight bow.

Miron turned to Ella. "Another glass for the lady, if you please," he said, as though he was used to speaking so politely to servants.

"Yes, my lord, and—"

"No," she said. "I think I've had enough. I think there's something . . . strange about that wine."

"The wine?" Miron's brow furrowed. "It seemed fine to me." He raised his own glass, and sipped at it. "As it still does, although I've certainly had better." He shrugged.

"Not the wine in your glass," she said. "The wine still in the bottle."

She hadn't seen Thirien move, but somehow the thick-waisted captain was between her and Miron, his eyes on Miron's. "There's something wrong with the wine in the bottle, Lady?" he asked, not looking directly at her.

She nodded. "I think so."

"Surely," Miron said, "surely you don't think I put something in the bottle, Leria, do you?" He spread his hands. "I'm aghast at the suggestion, and I'm more than a little offended."

"Easy enough to tell," Thirien said. "Wizards are supposed to be good at that sort of thing."

Miron shrugged. "Wizard? I see no need to bother the wizard, but, if you'd like to, you certainly may." Moving slowly, he picked up the bottle and refilled his own glass, then set the bottle down on the table, where Thirien could reach it easily.

"I think you'll find a glassful left, for the wizard to do whatever wizards do. As for me, I prefer a simpler test." He lifted the glass. "To innocence," he said. He drained the glass and set it down on the table. "Perhaps a trifle overly tannic, yes, but a fine bottle of wine, and I most certainly did not put anything in the bottle." His lips were tight as he turned back to Thirien. "Captain Thirien, if you'd call one of your soldiers to accompany me, I find myself in need of fresh air, and I'd like a reliable witness to the fact that I am *not* about to go out into the garden and purge myself of this wonderful wine, for fear of some poison or potion in it. I know a gentleman would do no such thing, and I am, I assure you, a gentleman, but it seems that there are some who do not think me such."

He bowed toward Leria, deeply, too deeply, then straightened himself. "For that, I can only blame myself for whatever it is that I have done that could have raised such an unworthy suspicion in such a lovely head as Lady Leria's, and I'll endeavor not to give such offense again."

She didn't like the way that Thirien was looking at her. "With the lady's permission, I'll accompany you, Lord Miron," he said.

His face was stern, and almost expressionless. She couldn't tell if he wanted to see for himself that Miron wasn't going to make himself vomit, or whether the old captain wanted to absent himself from the company of the flighty girl who had made such a wild accusation, but the two of them walked out through the garden doors, and it looked for a moment as though Miron was going to wink at her.

But the moment passed, and the doors closed behind the two men, and then she was alone with the wine bottle, and with Ella looking up at her, puzzled, as well.

"Should I take the wine up to, to *him*, my lady?"

"Yes, I suppose you should." Leria nodded. "You might as well, although I'm sure it's fine."

She stood alone in the great hall, and cursed herself, since there was nobody there to do it for her. She thought that she had been so clever, that Miron had been trying something—perhaps to drug her, and then pretend to help her up to her rooms?

And what then? Of course, Miron wanted her—that had been clear for a long time, but equally, of course, he wasn't the sort of fool who would risk his own neck just to have an unconscious woman.

On the other hand, he was apparently just the sort who would tempt a foolish girl—who wasn't nearly as clever as she had thought she was—into making a provably false accusation against him, and she had obliged him by doing just that, and in front of a witness.

The next time . . .

Once the word of this got out, the next time that she opened her mouth to accuse him of anything, she wouldn't be believed.

The carriage, accompanied by a full troop of Imperials, arrived at first light, which didn't surprise her at all. Erenor was nowhere to be seen, either, which also didn't surprise her.

She was only half-surprised that Elda reported that Miron's bed hadn't been slept in, and that he, and several of the horses, were gone.

She sighed as she let them help her into the carriage.

It wasn't a day for surprises. She had had more than enough of those yesterday.

11

Bandits

I find it very easy to be philosophical about personal discomfort. As long as it's somebody else's personal discomfort, of course.

—Walter Slovotsky

The night was cold, and the short, hard rains just after sunset had left everything painfully damp.

Cold and damp and dark: now, that was something Kethol was familiar with. There was a real comfort in familiarity, even if it was only familiar discomfort.

Kethol lay, stretched out on the waxed ground cloth, silently cursing himself for not having waxed it himself. Nobles didn't prepare their own gear. Nobles didn't do this, nobles didn't do that . . . nobles couldn't wipe their own asses, probably.

There was a spot just to the right of his right thigh where the rainwater that had soaked the pine needles had soaked through, leaving him miserable and wet.

He had been more careful with the smaller ground cloth next to him where his longbow lay. His body being wet was uncomfortable, but tolerable—but a wet bowstring would stretch more than it ought to, and that would be dangerous. You had to be able to count on your weapons, as much as you had to be able to count on yourself.

The temptation was strong to close his eyes for just a moment, but he had long ago learned—and painfully; the decurion had had a very, very heavy hand—that if he did that, if he allowed his eyes to close longer than it took him to blink, the next thing he would see would be morning light streaming over the horizon.

He was beginning to wonder if this would ever work. After two tendays of planting poles and stringing cable—no, of having others plant poles and string cable; Kethol tried to be honest, at least to himself—he had been certain that word of the new telegraph line would have reached up into the hills and into Kiar.

So where were they? They should have already tried to take the cable, days before.

He hoped it would be here—and it should be. Most of the rest of the twisting path that the telegraph line took went along the tops of the ridges, and that would let somebody trying to cut the cable be silhouetted against the night sky. The Kiaran bandits were cautious enough, at least he hoped, to avoid that.

That would have been less of an issue if the sky wasn't so clear, but tonight the stars shone brightly overhead, and a dozen clusters of distant faerie lights pulsed lazily on the horizon.

Pirojil had announced that they would run this section of the telegraph alongside an ancient streambed in the draw simply to speed things up—it was, after all, both easier and quicker to roll the pine telegraph poles downhill than to have horses and men drag them up the ridge—but their real reason was to bait the trap.

Kethol couldn't see the phony cable in the dark, but he didn't have to. Earlier, he had snuck down, as he did each night, to throw the hooked end of his long coil of line over the top of the cable, and had pulled it tight when he made his way back to his stand.

Drawn taut, staked in place, the line vibrated every now and then when one some bird chose to perch on a nearby length of the cable, and he would instantly come alert.

It was nice to know that he was useful for something.

He hoped that he would detect somebody sawing away at the cable before it went limp when cut, but he wasn't at all sure how far the vibration would carry, and he trusted more to his ears than to the fingers that rested on the line.

Off to the east a hoot owl announced to all and sundry that it had just snatched up a field mouse. That and the twittering of fidget bugs said that Kethol was alone.

Which he was. You could trust the insects and animals to tell you the truth, if only you knew how to listen to them.

They were stretched thin; the nearest one of the soldiers to him was that man of Tarnell's—he said his name was Thorven, but that was an Osgradian name, and the soldier had never quite gotten the Salket lisp out of his voice. There was probably a story there, but it wasn't any of Kethol's business, or of Forinel's, for that matter.

He hoped that none of the soldiers would move around. He had ordered them to remain in place, and he had had Tarnell order them to remain in place, but he was more aware than most that soldiers were not always obedient—particularly not when ordered by some-body they didn't particularly trust.

They were a clumsy bunch, at least by his standards. Not one of them could move to a stand silently. When they took their posi-tions in the early evening, they stumbled up and down the hills, seemingly taking every loose rock and stepping on every dead branch that they possibly could.

He was much more confident of the Keranahan peasants. Wen'll was perhaps the best of them, but they all at least knew how to move silently. And once on watch, poachers all, they knew about being absolutely, utterly still, about waiting for an opportunity.

His only question about them was how well, if at all, they would fight. Which he wouldn't know until it happened, so there was no need to worry about it now.

The light breeze brought a distant, pleasant reek of skunk to his nostrils.

Close up, the smell of the skunk was utterly painful, but off in the distance it seemed to have a comforting, homey smell to it. It made him relax, in the same way that the musky reek of rotting humus on a forest's floor always did, although he wasn't sure why, because they didn't smell at all the same.

It would have been interesting to know what it was that had excited the skunk, but he was confident it wasn't a human—there would have been some outcry. Men who would no more than grunt from an arrow in the belly would still shout, and scream, and dance around when sprayed by a skunk, after all.

He let his mind wander. As long as you kept your ears and eyes open, that didn't hurt any. He tried not to think about Leria, but that never worked; he couldn't help but think about the way that she smiled at him, or about the way that her legs had wrapped around his waist while she groaned beneath him. It wasn't right that somebody like him should be thinking that way about somebody like her, and never mind the fact that it had been more her decision than his.

Erenor had better be watching over her, carefully. But he would, Kethol decided. At some level, he wasn't sure quite why—he trusted the wizard, at least in that. If that made him a fool, he had been a fool before, and would be again.

In fact—

Quiet footsteps sounded behind him. From behind a boulder, a low voice whispered, urgently: "*Baron*. Baron Keranahan—are you there, Baron?"

Yes, he was there. *He* was where he was supposed to be. He hoped everybody else was where they were supposed to be, except, obviously, for Thorven, who instead of being where he was supposed to be was here.

Slowly, carefully, Kethol slid back from the ground cloth, and made his way painfully on his belly, up the rocky surface until he was over the ridge. He rose to his feet and padded carefully to where Thorven was crouching in the dark.

He couldn't make out the expression on Thorven's bony face; it was far too dark for that.

"What is it?" he asked, his whisper pitched low—low enough, so he hoped, that it wouldn't frighten the fidget bugs into silence.

"I heard something."

Wonderful. So Thorven had heard something. The night was filled with sounds—he was *supposed* to hear something. More to the point, he was supposed to stay on his watch post until dawn, when the patrol from Nerahan to Kimball's Village would thunder through the draw below, announcing to all and sundry that the telegraph line would be patrolled—and on a predictable schedule—while giving the watchers a chance to retreat to their camp beyond the next ridge, so that they could sleep through the day and be ready for the next night.

"Well?" he whispered. There was no point in berating him here and now. Leave that for Tarnell, and the morning. "What did you hear?"

"Horses, I think."

Kethol would have snorted at that, but he wasn't going to make any unnecessary sounds.

Still, while there were always false alarms—that was the way of this sort of thing—you had to check them out. He didn't think for a moment that Thorven could have heard anything from the road that Kethol himself wouldn't have heard, but anything was possible, even if it was unlikely.

Horsemen, traveling down the road at this time of night? Unlikely. And there was nothing happening down in the draw.

"Horsemen? On the road?"

"*Not* the road." Thorven tried to hide his impatience. "Off in the hills."

Kethol was skeptical. He hadn't heard anything, after all, and it was hard to believe that some Salke would have ears better attuned to the wild than he had.

"I—"

"Shh." Kethol closed his eyes and listened. At first, all he could hear was the murmur of the wind, and the hooting of that same idiotic owl, and the skritching of the fidget bugs, and, far in the distance, a howl so faint and far away that he couldn't tell whether it was a wolf or coyote.

But then he heard it. A quiet, irregular clop-*clop*, clop, clop, clop, clop-*clop*-clop. No ringing of steel-shod hooves on stone— unshod mountain ponies, perhaps?

Well, it was about time.

He swallowed heavily, trying to clear the bitter, steely taste from his mouth.

"They're coming," he said. "Circle around back—down to the path; don't try to make your way across the rocks—and tell Pirojil. Captain Pirojil."

Thorven crept off, as quietly as he could. Just as well that the wind was carrying sounds away.

The sounds of the horses grew louder, slowly, tentatively. Moving as quickly as he dared, Kethol crept back to where his ground cloth was, and slung his scabbarded sword across his back. It had been the best fit of any of those in the Residence armory—a heavy saber, only slightly curved, and while the basket hilt was inscribed in gold with a complex twisting of lines, the underlying steel would deflect an edge or a point. He wasn't overly enthusiastic about the leather grip, but he had carefully wound it with brass wire, and it fit his hand well enough.

With any luck, though, he wouldn't have to use it, or the matched dagger on his belt.

The bow would be his weapon of choice for tonight.

He emptied his quiver and carefully stuck each of the twenty arrows point-first into the hard soil next to the lonely pine that topped the hill. In daylight, he would have been easily seen, but he thought—and hoped—that their eyes would slide by.

He nocked an arrow, but didn't draw. It was time to wait, to wait patiently, motionless, and hope that his guess had been right, that their path down into the notch would take them directly below him.

He tried to count heartbeats, but it was well past two hundred and he had long since lost count when the first of the ponies topped the ridge across from him, only momentarily visible against the starry sky.

It and its rider began to make their way downslope and into the notch, quickly followed by a dozen more.

A dozen? That didn't make sense. He had expected far fewer. It wouldn't take more than that many to cut the cable at two places, then quickly gather it up.

The best place for them to cut the cable, the most convenient place, the place where an overhang would have given easy access to the top of one of the poles, was directly below him, on purpose. The engineers had carefully arranged it that way at his insistence, over their objections of how that would still leave the cable partic-ularly vulnerable when they actually put in a telegraph wire—and it would be sooner than later, so they said, if this managed to work.

The surefooted ponies made their way down the slope, but they didn't go where they were supposed to; they turned and followed the line of poles east, back toward Nerahan.

Greedy. They intended to cut the cable as close as they could to Nerahan, and then coil it up as they rode back toward Kimball's Village. The fact that there were a dozen or so suggested that they planned another raid on the village before escaping over the hills, although there was little left to plunder there.

He shook his head. He should have insisted on a full company of Imperials, enough for a chase—he had been expecting that he would be able to get one with his first bow shot, and perhaps another before the surviving bandits ran for safety to the west, or went scurrying back up the hill to where, if everything was going right, Pirojil and a team of six Keranahan archers were now quickly working their way, while Tarnell and his men prevented their escape to the west, down the road toward the village.

He settled his sword belt on his shoulder, and stuck the point of the scabbard into the back of his belt, then quickly scooped up his arrows and shoved them into the quiver, tying the drawstring tight across its mouth.

He picked up his bow and broke into a run.

Trying to catch up with the horsemen from behind was pointless—if they heard him pounding and panting down the road, all they had to do was gallop away—but if he could make it over the ridge and down the other side quickly enough, he could get ahead of them, and drive them back, in the right direction.

He ran.

The brush clawed at him, repeatedly making him stumble and almost fall, but he managed to keep to his feet, despite having to hold his bow over his head so that it wouldn't catch on the brush.

He raced along, just below the ridgeline. Their horses should be making enough sound to cover the noise he was making, and he hoped that they either hadn't noticed that the wild had gone all silent, or that they attributed it to their own movement having silenced the insects and birds.

The thing to do was to get there first, and worry about the rest of it later.

And the others? They should be along quickly. Quickly enough, he hoped. Thorven would have seen which way the bandits were heading, and he would have told Pirojil. And Pirojil, of all people, would know that Kethol would chase after them. He would call him stupid for doing that, of course, but Kethol was used to that.

He ran.

As he staggered down the hill, he lost his footing and fell. He slid, digging his heels in to slow his descent, and managed to fight to his feet, using only his left hand, his right hand holding the bow up and out of danger. If he dropped his bow on this slope, it was gold-to-copper that he wouldn't be able to find it in time.

His heart was pounding loudly in his chest and his breath was painfully ragged when he reached the road, just beyond the bend he had been aiming for. The nearest trees large enough to provide any cover were across the road, and he could already hear the soft clopping of the ponies' hooves, so he squatted down behind a rock and tried to force his heart to slow.

Kethol quickly unslung his quiver, and nocked an arrow, swearing at his traitor fingers as they trembled from the exertion.

If only the bandits had cut the cable where they were supposed to, then readied themselves to head in the other direction, all he would have had to do was spring the trap himself. He certainly could have put one down before the others noticed, and probably two. With good enough shooting—and good enough luck—he could have three, maybe four of them down before they even knew what was happening, and rode away in panic, charging into either jaw of the trap.

But not now. Now, what he need to do was get in front of them, and then make enough noise to sound like a company himself, and, if at all possible, put an arrow through the leader, and turn them.

He must have done something wrong.

But not everything. His fingers were steady, and he could ignore the bitter, steely taste of fear in his mouth.

Perhaps they had heard the noise he had made coming down the hill, or maybe, when the wind changed, one of the ponies got a whiff of him, but there was a loud cry as the first of the horsemen came abreast of where he was hiding.

He straightened, pulled back the arrow until he could feel the steel of the arrowhead against his knuckle, and let fly, rewarded instantly by the familiar thunk of it cleaving flesh, and a high-pitched scream as the bandit clutched at himself, then fell from the saddle, to fall, moaning and screaming, to the ground.

He would not have a chance to loose another arrow—they could ride him down while he tried—so Kethol let his bow fall to one side. He freed his sword from his scabbard, and shrugged out of the sword belt, letting the scabbard fall to the ground. His left hand clutched the hilt of the dagger.

The horses were milling about, their riders trying to control them.

Kethol stood himself straight in the middle of the road.

"I am Forinel, Baron Keranahan," he said, letting his voice roar. "And you will dismount and lay down your arms right now, or you'll die, right now."

He didn't really have any hope that they would do any such thing—surrendering was just an extended way of killing themselves—but he hoped that if they didn't simply run, one or more of them would at least say something, giving him a chance to stall until Pirojil and the soldiers arrived. He didn't have any particular hope that the Keranahan bowmen would do anything useful; you couldn't really expect peasants to run toward danger. It was one thing to hide, hoping to shoot from concealment, but another to run toward men with swords and horses, men who were looking to cut your guts out.

But there was no conversation. The bandit nearest Kethol, a skinny little man who almost made his pony look large, kicked the pony into a gallop toward him. Kethol dodged to the right, away from the swinging sword, and barely managed to cut a shallow slice along the man's knee as he rode by, already wheeling his horse about for another pass.

He couldn't ignore the threat from behind for long, but there were still ten in front of him, and it was only a matter of moments before they would collect themselves enough to attack in concert— so he ran toward the nearest, slashing across the pony's chest as he ducked under a wild swing from another of the bandits.

He had to keep moving. To stop was to die, and to slow was to die, and to move not quite fast enough was to die; he lunged at another one of the horsemen, but the horse reared and pranced quickly to the side, out of reach.

And then they were upon him.

A knee or an elbow or a horse—he was never sure quite what— caught him upside the head, and his sword fell from his hand. He was able to fasten his fingers in the tunic of one of the horsemen, but as he yanked the man to the ground, a slash from another's blade sent agony screaming across the left side of his back, and almost made him drop his knife.

It was hopeless, but that didn't stop him. There was no way that he could stop to find his sword, but he still had a knife, and at least that was—

Something hard hit him from behind, throwing him to the ground. He tried to roll away, but a hoof mashed down on his knife hand, and another blow or kick sent him sprawling.

One of the bandits kicked his horse toward Kethol.

A shot rang out, and then another, and as Kethol struggled to get to his knees, something brushed his cheek and an arrow seemed to sprout from the flank of the nearest pony, and it screamed in pain as it reared, sending its rider tumbling to the ground.

And then Pirojil was at his side, and despite the pain, just for the moment all was right with the world, as shots and screams filled the air.

Kethol should have hurt. Not just hurt—he should have still been in agony. He wasn't sure how many fingers had been broken by the hooves, but it was at least two, and it seemed somehow obscene that he could flex them so easily, so painlessly. The almost impossibly bitter Eareven healing draughts had washed away the pain almost as quickly as Pirojil had been able to bathe away the blood.

He stood in the wan light of predawn, forcing himself not to flinch every time he moved.

The road was still filled with death.

Two of the ponies had been captured unharmed, save for a few scrapes, and they had been led away. But four more lay on the ground, their wide, dead, dirty eyeballs staring blankly at nothing.

Just like the men.

Wen'll and another one of the peasants whose name Kethol couldn't remember were already butchering the dead ponies. Piles of viscera gleamed wetly in the predawn light beside the carcasses. Wen'll already had most of the top half of the skin of his off, working swiftly and deftly with a knife that looked too small for the task, but clearly wasn't. A live pony was more valuable than a dead one, of course, and there were far better things to eat than the stringy flesh of a grass-fed pony, but meat was meat, and not to be wasted, and there were a thousand good uses for cured horsehide.

No need to waste.

The peasants weren't the only ones that felt that way. Already the buzzards were circling overhead, and occasionally a particularly brave one would swoop down toward one of the bodies of the men or horses, only to flee, its wings flapping madly as it lumbered back up into the air, when one of the soldiers raised a stick.

Let them eat later.

Kethol straightened.

You got used to this after a while, particularly with a stiffening breeze carrying the smells away. It wasn't really that bad.

Kethol smelled rain coming. Between the rain and the buzzards, and the ants that were already picking their way through the offal, the road would be cleaned in a few days at most, leaving behind only some bones that would bleach white in the sun, if they didn't rot first.

He tried to remember how it all was, how it all really was. That was important to him, although he couldn't have said why he cared. The Battle of the Black Rope would quickly be forgotten, most likely, or else it would grow in the telling and become a legend of how Forinel, Baron Keranahan, waded single-handedly through dozens of giant bandits on huge warhorses, killing right and left with every step.

That was the way it was with battles, even tiny ones like this one. They were forgotten, or they became legends. The reality never was as large or as small—and certainly never as heroic—and the details were always painfully ordinary, and easy to forget.

A peasant archer's arrow had caught one of the bandits in the right eye, penetrating through the skull on the other side before stopping. The dead bandit lay on the ground in a pool of his own blood and piss and shit.

Kethol stooped and tried to pull the arrow loose, but he only succeeded in bringing the dead man to a half-sitting position.

He gave another jerk, and the arrow came free, bringing along bits of congealing blood and little gray morsels of brain with it.

The shaft was plain, without any markings. There should have been markings on the shaft, so that the archer could claim the bounty for his successful shot. Luck or skill, a reward for arrows that reached their mark was important.

But he shouldn't have been surprised at the naked shaft. Peasant archers, after all. Poachers didn't mark their arrows.

"Six," Kethol said, not because nobody else could count that high, but because he thought that he ought to say something. "Only six."

"Only?" Pirojil chuckled as he shook his head. "You are thinking like a noble, Baron Keranahan," he added, quietly. "Besides, one of those who got away did it on a horse that's wounded—look at the blood trail. I don't think he'll get very far, and if any of the others is generous enough to let him ride double, that just means that there'll be two on foot before the morning is over. And the others? Let them escape, and let them talk about how the easy pickings in Keranahan are no longer quite so easy, eh?"

"Yes."

Kethol looked up at Tarnell, who was sitting atop his own horse, the fist that gripped the hilt of his sword economically resting on his thigh, while the flat of the blade rested on his saddle.

"Do you think you can track any of them down before they get over the hills?" Pirojil asked.

"Maybe." Tarnell grunted. "No. I don't think so. Not if they're smart enough to just head right out over the hills. On the other hand, if they stuck to the roads to try to put as much distance between them and us as quick as they could, Fetheren and Arnistead will have had at least some of them hammered to the ground, and there'll be more bodies."

He shrugged. Bodies didn't bother the old soldier any more than they did Pirojil.

"I was wondering where those two had gotten to." Pirojil scowled. "I thought I told you to bring your men. *All* of your men."

"Yeah." Tarnell shrugged. "You did tell me that, as I recall. But my old captain always taught me to keep a reserve, and I wouldn't think you're much of a better soldier than he is, or than I am." Tarnell started to gesture with his sword, but visibly thought better of it and just sheathed it, even though he had to stand up in the stirrups to do so.

"Captain, Baron, Emperor," Tarnell said, "it doesn't matter to me. Doesn't even matter that I was right and you were wrong, not to me. I work for Captain Treseen."

Kethol took the knife from his belt, and walked over to one of the bodies.

Pirojil hurried after him.

"What are you doing, Baron?" Pirojil asked, not gently.

"The heads. We promised to bring the heads. At least six of them, and that's what we have here."

Pirojil nodded. "Yes, we did, and it's not at all inappropriate that the heads should be taken with the baron's own knife." He held out his palm. "But you don't need to be doing that for yourself—Baron Keranahan—do you?"

"I guess not."

"Then leave it to me, and let's get back to the—let's get back home."

Kethol nodded.

12

Jason Cullinane

The bad thing about inherited titles is that virtue isn't hereditary. The good thing is that stupidity isn't, either.

—Walter Slovotsky

What would you say," Andrea Cullinane asked, "about taking a quick trip into Biemestren?"

"Biemestren?"

"You have heard of the city, haven't you?"

He eyed her skeptically. Mother wasn't usually much for sarcasm.

She didn't look directly at him as she finished loading the rifle—not quickly enough, in Jason's opinion, but nobody was asking Jason's opinion, which was typical—and cocked it before raising it to her shoulder.

Despite the heavy barrel, the front sight wavered only a little. She took in a deep breath, let some of it out, and then pulled the trigger.

Bang.

There was another hole in the target, just at the edge of the bull's-eye.

"Not bad for an old woman, eh?"

Well, Mother *was* old—she was well into her forties—but she was well preserved for all of that. There was no trace of gray in her dark brown hair, and while her riding leathers fit too tightly, at least in her son's opinion, that was a matter of her choice, after all. Jason didn't particularly like the way that some of the troops tended to watch her out of the corners of their eyes as she walked away, like she was some sort of peasant girl, or something, but it was a bad subject to bring up. The last time he had done that, she had just smiled, and sighed, and looked at him like he was a little child, which he absolutely hated.

Jason Cullinane shook his head. "Mother, I don't understand you. You're always telling me that it's best if I stay out of Biemestren. Then, when Parliament convenes, you hurry me over to Biemestren—and *then*, the very moment that Parliament lets out, you hurry me out of Biemestren. Now, now you want me to go back to Biemestren? In, out, in, out—why don't I just take a room at Biemestren Castle?"

She laughed. One thing you had to say for Mother was that she had a good laugh.

"Well, you could do that—but don't blame me if Beralyn poisons you."

"She wouldn't."

"Don't bet on it."

He gestured toward the target. "Nice shot, Mother. I'll give you that."

"Your father was better at changing the subject."

"My father, so I hear all the time, was better at a lot of things."

He had seen it, more than once: Father sparring with two, sometimes three opponents—always with a brass flask of healing draughts nearby for their benefit, not his—and it was almost magical the way that he could anticipate a blow, distract one with a feint while kicking out at another, moving and spinning about much faster than any man that large had any right to, and always controlling his touches so that he didn't injure his opponents, save on a few occasions where he decided that one of the soldiers wasn't really trying to score on the Emperor, in which case he would thoroughly work that man over, and hold off letting him use the healing draughts until everybody got the point that the Emperor expected each and every one of his sparring partners to try the best he could.

Jason wasn't nearly that good, and Jason had always had to work at it.

It didn't matter whether it was a sword—and he had spent more time than he cared to think about with a sword in his hand—or with a staff, although why his father and his teachers had insisted that he become so familiar with a peasant weapon still escaped him, or with a rifle.

Father had used to say something about how it was important that a ruler needed to be, if it was at all possible, sudden death in all directions. It was clear from his tone of voice that it was a quote from somebody, although he never did say who that somebody was. A ruler's only other choice, Father had said, was to remain behind his walls all the time, which would only last until somebody brought those walls down around him.

Jason had always worked very hard on his lessons, and considered himself better than most. It would be nice to be right, for once.

She rested the butt of the rifle on her hip, and pointed to the other rifle on the shooting table.

"Your shot. Then we can discuss your upcoming trip, and how you'd better watch what you eat."

She was being ridiculous. The Dowager Empress—well, actually, the *other* Dowager Empress; Mother still qualified for that title, as the mother of the previous claimant, Jason, and the widow of the previous emperor—always looked at Jason as though she wished he would break out into flame, or something, but Beralyn surely couldn't hate him that much, and while she didn't show it, deep down, she probably was grateful to him. After all, he had abdicated the crown and the throne in Thomen's favor.

He smiled. Which meant that while Thomen was having to engage in endless negotiations with Nyphien, and Enkiar, and the other countries of the Middle Lands, not to mention keeping the various barons from each other's throats, Jason could spend his time out in the clean country air.

So who had done whom a favor?

Besides, truth to tell, Thomen was a better choice for emperor than Jason was, and everybody knew it. It might well be possible, someday, to come to some sort of accommodation with Pandathaway—the Council as a whole, if not the Slavers Guild—but that would not be possible for the son of Karl Cullinane, who had, as legend had it—wrongly—single-handedly chased the Pandathaway-based Slavers Guild out of much of the Middle Lands and all of Holtun-Bieme.

Let Thomen run the Empire; Jason had other matters to keep in mind. Like those killers that had been sent to get him on his way to the last Parliament, for example. It was certainly the Pandathaway Slavers Guild, and though there was equally certainly no sign of them anywhere in what he couldn't help still thinking of as Barony Furnael, they would certainly try again.

Unless he cut the snake off at the head.

Give it a couple more years. Two, maybe three more years to settle things in the barony, to hone and polish his skills with a sword, a knife, and a gun, and he would be off to Melawei. He had more than a hunch that the Sword of Arta Myrdhyn would enable him to settle matters with the Guild, even in their stronghold.

He didn't know what, exactly, the Sword of Arta Myrdhyn had to do with him, but it was something, and Arta Myrdhyn, being Arta

Myrdhyn, would not have gone to so much trouble to put it there, waiting for him, if it wasn't important.

Maybe it was the key to Pandathaway, or maybe to something else, but it was important.

Maybe, he sometimes thought, it was the key to the Gate Between Worlds? It would be interesting, if that was the case. He had spent his life hearing stories about the Other Side, about carriages that traveled without horses, and people who flew through the air much faster than even Ellegon could carry them, about pictures that danced in front of your eyes, and cities that were crowded with not tens of thousands, but literally millions of people, who lived and worked in buildings that scraped the sky.

In the meantime, Mother and Doria Perlstein could do most of the running of the barony, which left time for him and Taren and maybe even Ahira to go out and build a few legends of their own.

It was hard being the son of a legend, but it could have been worse.

After all, it was in part because he was the son of a legend that they were spending the morning out at the practice range behind the stables. Not the worst way to spend a morning.

Jason had set up a pair of targets himself, and the two of them had been taking turns with the new rifles that were just in from Home.

The engineer was having fun, again: these new ones loaded at the breech, not the muzzle, and all it was necessary to do in order to prepare one to fire was to push the bullet in by hand until it stuck, then follow it with the small twist of paper that contained a charge of powder, and then snap the breech closed—which also broke the paper cartridge open—and then all he had to do was push a little primer on the firing nipple hard enough to set it in place before it was ready to fire.

The whole procedure was not nearly as quick as it was with the few cartridge-based guns there were around, but it was not nearly as dependent on the brass for the cartridges—there might have been as many as six revolvers in the Middle Lands, and Jason owned two of them—which was apparently difficult to manufacture in any kind of quantity.

Jason didn't know much about that—but he did know that he could reload one of these rifles a lot more quickly than he could a muzzle-loader.

Cleaning it after a practice session was still a bitch of a job, but one of the nice things about being the baron was that he could have somebody else do it for him, and right now he didn't have to listen to endless lectures about how a man was supposed to take care of his own gear, as most of the people who would have given him those lectures were somewhere else. Ahira was playing around in a smithy near New Pittsburgh, and Taren was chasing down orcs in the hills, something that Jason would rather have been doing himself. Jane Slovotsky was off at Home, taking some lessons from Lou Riccetti on the finer points of wootz manufacture, something that he would have enjoyed about as much as he would have enjoyed mucking out a stable. Actually, if you made a point of mucking out the stable regularly, it wasn't that bad, so he was told. But listening to the engineer drone on for hours about temperatures and carbon content and every boring thing under the sun—yech. It was all important, yes, but it was important to engineers.

And Jason Cullinane, thankfully, wasn't an engineer.

He snapped the breech shut, and then cocked the hammer carefully before even more carefully sliding the primer over the little nipple. He had, just as an experiment, cocked the hammer and primed the gun before closing the breech once this morning. The splintered top of the weathered shooting table stood witness to that, and the resulting bang still had his ears ringing.

He raised the rifle to his shoulder, settled it in against shoulder and cheek, and took careful aim before he rested his finger on the trigger, and pulled on it, slowly increasing the pressure until it—

Bang.

His shot was a palm's breadth off the mark. He lowered his rifle, and glared at it.

"Don't blame your tools," she said. "The bullet goes where the rifle is pointed. It doesn't have a mind of its own. You do, and I think you should get your mind back to what we were discussing."

"Why Biemestren?" he asked. "Thomen hasn't summoned me, after all." He raised an eyebrow. "Unless there's something you aren't telling me."

"No, he hasn't sent for you—and he hasn't sent for Willen Tyrnael, either. But I've just gotten word that Tyrnael is planning a trip to Biemestren, and I don't know why. I wish I did."

Jason shrugged. That wasn't particularly unusual. Yes, generally, the Holtish barons stayed out of the capital except during Parliament, but the Biemish ones came and went as they pleased, and that was only partly because there was less travel involved.

Jason was a special case. His presence made the real nobles— the other nobles—nervous. He didn't quite fit in. He was, he supposed, too much his father's son in their eyes, just as he was too little his father's son in some others'. The barons were always preoccupied with the piddling little details of ruling a barony—taxes and inheritance, works and borders, and the absurd issues of protocol and precedence that he found even more boring than the details of steelmaking.

So, if his presence made others uncomfortable there, and he was uncomfortable there, then what was the point?

Yes, it was important to appear at Parliament, to nod in agreement every time Thomen spoke, to—as Walter Slovotsky insisted— appear to be marveling at the gems that dropped from Thomen's jaws every time his mouth opened.

Never mind the fact that he actually liked Thomen; the point was that Thomen was the Emperor, and Jason had put him on the throne, and it was only sensible and honorable and reasonable to do everything he could to keep him firmly there.

Ellegon? he thought. *Ellegon?*

There was no answer.

He hadn't really expected one, although it would have been nice. He had known the dragon all of his life, and somehow or other—he was never quite sure why—that enabled him to communicate with Ellegon farther than anybody else could, but that only amounted to a matter of a few leagues.

Ellegon was probably splashing around the lake at Home, alternating munching up a few trout and playing with the children. Children who had grown up around the dragon—as Jason had—just weren't afraid of him the way that others were.

"How did you get word?" he asked. "You're not telling me that you have spies in Biemestren?"

She laughed. "Oh, I've still got a few connections in the capital. He's not the only one due in. I got a letter, delivered by Imperial post, a couple of days ago. It's unsigned, and I don't recognize the seal, and the proof marks say that it originated in Nerahan, not that I necessarily believe them. It told me that Lady Leria Euar'den— that nice girl who is going to marry Baron Keranahan—has been summoned there, and there's some question about the marriage."

"Why would anybody be going to the trouble to tell you that?"

And more, why would anybody be going to the trouble to tell her that in such a circuitous way?

She shrugged. "It seemed strange to me, and stranger still that this letter arrived even before a note from Walter that said just the same thing." She raised a finger. "So, when you go, don't take the Prince's Road; swing out into Adahan, and ride in with a wagon train from New Pittsburgh."

"All because of some anonymous letter . . . what's your real reason, Mother?" he asked.

She loaded her rifle again before answering. "I don't know. Or maybe I'm just not sure. Intuition?"

You don't have that kind of intuition, not anymore.

He didn't say that. Mother had spent her magical abilities in Ehvenor, burned them like they were gunpowder in sealing up the breach between Faerie and reality, and if the cost ever bothered her—and it had to—she never showed that to the world, and not even to her son.

There was something to admire in that. Father would have been the same, if his own sacrifice hadn't involved blowing himself into tiny little bloody bits on a beach at Melawei. Jason had never heard Mother complain about that, no more than he had heard Tennetty complain about how she lost her eye, no more than he had heard any of the others complain about what they had lost.

Jason Cullinane was the son of two heroes and the companion of others, and he tried to learn from them.

That was hard to do, from time to time, but there were worse fates.

He nodded. "Biemestren it is, then."

13

A Night in Dereneyl

The only good thing I can think of about letting
two idiots settle a controversy with a pair of
sharp, pointed pieces of metal is that it *does* settle the controversy.

—Walter Slovotsky

Erenor had tried to talk him out of it, but he had thrown up
his hands in frustration when the most he could do was to
get Kethol to change clothes before riding into Dereneyl.

Pirojil hadn't even tried.

It was just as well that they had ridden straight back to the
Residence, and not stopped off in Dereneyl in the first place, as
Pirojil had wanted. When Kethol had found that Leria was gone—
and Miron, as well—he had gone suddenly cold and distant, and
couldn't seem to keep his fingers from clutching the hilt of his
sword.

Pirojil thought that he would have been happier if Kethol had
broken furniture.

At least he wasn't fingering his sword now, as they waited for
Treseen. Instead, he was constantly kneading his right hand with his
left, as though he had hurt it. That wasn't perfect, but it was better.

Tarnell had taken up his usual position at the door of Treseen's office, and waited, presumably to make sure that they didn't rifle through the governor's papers while they were waiting.

Treseen bustled in, all smiles and handshakes. "Congratulations, Baron, and thank you for coming to see me," he said. "Tarnell's just been telling me about the success of your . . . great adventure, and I've sent for both Lord Moarin and Lord Melchen, to join us at dinner tonight."

Kethol opened his mouth, closed it, opened it again. "Leria," he finally said.

"Yes." If Treseen had been beaming any more brightly, it would have been hard to see anything in the room. "Isn't it wonderful?" He spread his hands. "I wouldn't be surprised if it's only a few tendays before you're summoned to the capital, as well. With any luck, the two of you will be married before the fall harvest, and I'm very much looking forward to the celebration." He tapped at the papers in front of him. "Work is important, but it's these sorts of things that bind us all together."

He pushed himself back from his chair, and rose. "Now, if you'll excuse me, there's been some minor trouble down by the riverfront, and I'm not at all happy with the chief armsman's report on it. It's one of those things where I'd best go see to it myself, unruffle a few ruffled feathers, if it can be said that dwarves have feathers, and—"

Kethol shook his head. "No. We need to settle this, now. You can try to distract me later."

Treseen's lips tightened, and Pirojil could more feel than see Tarnell stiffen out of the corner of his eye.

"Distract?" Treseen sat back down heavily. "I'm not sure I understand your meaning, Baron, and if you don't mind my saying so, I'm a little offended."

How could he be both? Pirojil wondered. If he didn't understand, after all, he wouldn't be offended—and Treseen very clearly did understand.

Well, honesty was not a major tool of statecraft, after all.

"I'm sure that no offense was intended, Governor," Pirojil said.

It was the thing to say. It was the thing that Forinel should have said, of course, but Pirojil would have been able to grow old waiting for Kethol to say it. The idiot—just this side of calling the governor a liar?

"I'm sure none was," the governor said.

Pirojil glared at Kethol.

"No," Kethol finally said, "of course not." He shook his head. "It's just that I was . . . disappointed."

Treseen nodded. "That's more than understandable, and you've had a rough few tendays. Yes, of course. You and she were separated for so long; I was heartless not to see how coming home to an empty house would be disappointing, even under the circumstances." He frowned. "Although I would have thought that that fast-tongued Erenor would have made matters clear to you, as he well should have."

"I'll speak to him about it," Kethol said.

"Good."

That was better. There was a time and a place for open warfare, but this wasn't it.

Having Leria in the capital was a *good* thing, at least at the moment, as long as Kethol didn't screw things up here. Let her talk around court about how quickly on his return Forinel had immediately set to handling a bandit problem that Treseen hadn't been able to touch. The more she bragged, the more anybody expressed any doubt about what Forinel could do, the better—surely some in Biemestren would doubt, quietly if not openly, that he would succeed. Then, when reports filtered in through both official channels—and the travelers' gossip that always made things bigger than they were—Forinel's reputation would grow.

What they should be doing now was simply letting Treseen do

what he obviously wanted to do this evening: praise Forinel's success with the bandits in front of Moarin and the rest of the local nobles.

Perhaps Treseen would even offer to send a joint letter on the subject to Biemestren. Moarin would see the virtue of that, and if it didn't occur to him, Pirojil would suggest it.

Moarin would, of course, be less than entirely happy to have to pay the costs of building the decoy telegraph line, much less plunking down a bagful of silver marks to pay off his bet, but, of course, he would be enough of a politician to conceal any unhappiness, and to praise Forinel's courage and strategy to the skies.

It was in his own interest, after all. The more competent the baron had demonstrated himself to be, the stronger the case could be made in Parliament for the lifting of the occupation, which would let the local lords get back to the business of squeezing the peasants and landholders themselves, rather than living off stipends from the governor. It would be a tricky matter, of course, to advocate for that without alienating the governor, but Pirojil could rely on the likes of Moarin and Melchen, and all the rest, to do what came naturally to them—the lot of them had been suckled on intrigue more than milk from their mothers' tits.

Not that intrigue couldn't be learned.

"I'm sorry to hear you've been distracted, Governor," Pirojil said. "It seems to me that you are far too busy to handle something like this 'small unpleasantness' at the waterfront, what with all the demands on your time." He gestured at the governor's desk. "Those many accounts to reconcile, and all."

Treseen spread his hands. "Yes, but what am I to do?" He turned back to Forinel. "As you'll see when you take over the barony, when you're in charge, your life is not your own, and people are usually more interested in persuading you that everything is fine, regardless of the situation, than they are in telling you the truth.

Back when I was just a captain of troops, it was my experience that the best way to find things out was to do it myself, and—"

"Or rely on somebody trustworthy," Kethol said, interrupting. "Like, say, me?" He rose. "You won't mind me looking into this little problem along the waterfront myself, will you?"

Shit. There he went again.

It was clear to Pirojil that Kethol didn't believe that there was any problem at the waterfront at all. Kethol obviously thought that Treseen had merely invented a story about problems in the interest of getting the baron out of his office and out of his way, at least for the moment, and would try to find some way to be sure that Forinel didn't simply go straight to Dereneyl's chief armsman until Treseen had time to get word to the chief armsman about this fictitious problem.

That might work, in the short run. But it wouldn't work long, not if a suspicious Forinel simply asked around. Which he would.

Which is why it was even clearer to Pirojil that Treseen wasn't lying. Overstating a problem, quite possibly—but Treseen wasn't stupid enough to make up a lie that could be so easily checked.

So he wasn't at all surprised when Treseen smiled, and immediately reached for his pen and a sheet of vellum.

"Would I mind?" Treseen asked. "How could I possibly mind when you've offered to do me such a service, Baron? If you have any questions, Wellum is the chief armsman, and while I'm sure you'd find him most accommodating in any case, with a note from me, I'm doubly sure."

His smile broadened as he began to write.

They had missed the bar fight—which was fine with Pirojil—and almost all of the aftermath of the bar fight, which wasn't nearly as good.

At their approach, the two battered dwarves supporting the

badly injured one had limped off quickly down the street, and a couple of Imperials running after them would likely only have scared them into a full run, if they could have managed it.

The tavern was almost empty.

All of the dwarves were gone, as were the human brawlers. Anybody with a lick of sense, of course, had lit out when the fight had started. The only people remaining in the Spotted Dog were the tavernkeeper himself and a preposterously ugly woman, presumably his wife, whose unrestrained dugs waggled beneath her stained muslin tunic in counterpoint to the sweeping of her broom.

The rough-sawn floor of the one-story tavern was still littered with broken shards of pottery, and more than a few puddles that Pirojil hoped had come from upended bowls of stew, but could just as easily have been vomit. The scrawny, brown, torn-eared dog that was greedily feasting at one of the pools probably wouldn't have cared much either way.

Broken stools had been haphazardly shoved over into the corner, but none of the low tables seemed to have been upturned or broken, which pretty much guaranteed that they were bolted to the floor.

Whether by design or accident—Pirojil would have guessed it was accident—the floor visibly sloped toward the rear of the tavern, where steps led down to the dock below, which meant that it was easy for her to sweep the detritus off the back porch, and let it fall. What didn't just splash down into the river could be swept off the dock later.

The tavernkeeper bustled over to them, wiping his hands on his none-too-clean apron.

"Good evening, Decurions," he said, ignoring the fact that their borrowed Imperial livery held no rank insignia at all. It never hurt business to inflate a customer's rank. "Beer?" He rubbed a dirty rag on the dirty surface of the table. His faded red hair was braided behind him in a simple sailor's queue, and bound up with a wooden fillet that would keep it from being easily snatched in a fight. He was awfully skinny for somebody who daily hauled kegs of beer up all those steps from the dock below—even if he used a block-and-tackle rig, it would still take solid muscle—but he probably was stronger than he looked. Lots were.

Pirojil raised two fingers, and pulled up a pair of stools for himself and Kethol.

The tavernkeeper emerged from behind the rough-hewn bar with two clay mugs of beer and stood, looking expectant, until Pirojil produced a copper, and set it on the table.

"Some trouble here tonight?" Pirojil asked, leaving his finger on the coin.

The tavernkeeper shrugged. "None to speak of, Decurion—and nothing involving Imperials, no need to bother yourself. It was just some of those Ulter dwarves starting another fight with a few of the noble boys, and the dwarves just got some of what was coming to them, although it wasn't much, and it was all over by the time that the armsmen arrived. A little damage to the place, sure, but that's been taken care of."

"Oh." Pirojil flicked the coin across the edge of the table; the tavernkeeper snatched it out of the air and scurried away, busying himself behind the rough-hewn bar at the other end of the room.

"Dwarves," Kethol said, his mouth twitching, "causing trouble." He tilted the beer mug back, but when he set it down, it was still almost as full as it had been. Some things never changed.

"You heard it," Pirojil said, then took a deep pull on his tankard. It wasn't very good, but it was beer.

"Yes, I heard it." Kethol pretended to drink more.

In their time, they had spent thousands of coppers and more than that number of hours in taverns like this one—few worse, some better—and Kethol's habits were well enough established that he didn't even consider not nursing a beer when he drank in public. A soldier who wasn't busy trying to get himself drunk could find a game of bones every bit as easily as one who was, and regardless of the myths about drunken fingers being more steady than sober ones, a sober man was far more likely to come out a winner at the end of the evening—both at the gambling and at the almost inevitable fight.

A wise captain always had issues more pressing than punishing his men for minor misbehaviors on their off hours, after all.

Like Kethol, Pirojil never had seen much pleasure in recreational brawling, but there were others who did, and Kethol had been known to take advantage of that, every bit as much as he did of his skill at bones. A reasonably clever, sober man could make off with a few dropped coins or even snatch a purse while making an escape when a fight broke out, and while that wasn't nearly as lucrative as looting a battlefield, there were a lot more tavern fights than battlefields available these peaceful days.

"Have you ever known a dwarf to start a fight?" Kethol asked.

Pirojil pretended to think about it, although there wasn't really much to think about.

Warfare was one thing—humans had long ago learned that trying to invade the dwarven warrens was a particularly painful form of suicide; if there was a stupider way to die than crouched in a tunnel so that you couldn't even swing a sword properly, while some dwarf with an ax hacked you to bits, Pirojil couldn't think of one offhand.

Brawling?

Brawling was about as much a dwarven activity as swimming was, and dwarves were famous for never being willing to enter water deeper than their knobby knees. It was more than a little strange that a creature that would work its way through a narrow mining tunnel, the weight of a mountain pressed down on its chest, would shake and tremble at the thought of water up to its hairy belly, but that's just the way that it was.

Brawling? Dwarves? The word for "dwarves" in their own language meant "the Moderate People," and the appellation fit, by and large. While dwarves tended to be a noisy bunch, particularly after a few beers—if Pirojil never, ever heard another dozen low voices raised in a guttural dwarven drinking song, that would be fine with him—fighting for pleasure was almost unknown among them.

Unless, of course, you counted wrestling—but ceremonial wrestling, the way that the Moderate People saw things, wasn't really fighting. It could be and was used to settle disputes, but dwarves more commonly wrestled just for the sake of wrestling. An accomplished dwarf wrestler had about as much status among them as a master blacksmith did. Wrestling was somewhere between a sport and a religious offering, like a Hand priestess burning bay leaves before the altar.

Burning bay leaves did smell better than a bunch of sweaty dwarves did, but that was another matter. Brawling dwarves? Not likely.

"No," Pirojil finally said, "I haven't."

"Be interesting to find out who they fought with, and why, wouldn't it?"

"Well, yes, it would." Pirojil nodded, and gestured with his mug toward the tavernkeeper. "Be interesting to see what he'd say if it was Baron Keranahan who was asking him, instead of a pair of Imperial soldiers."

"Want me to try?"

Pirojil shook his head. "If anything is going on tonight, it'll stop quickly as soon as word gets out that the baron is prowling around the riverfront."

"It might have already stopped if Tarnell has spread the word." Kethol frowned.

"Possibly." Pirojil shrugged. "If he does, then we've learned something interesting."

"How interesting is it if Treseen's catamite has a loose tongue?"

"Please—Baron. Go a little easy, eh? Tarnell's not a bad man, just because he's got a different set of loyalties than some other people."

Besides, Pirojil didn't think that Tarnell would talk, except to Treseen, who would probably just find the whole thing amusing.

Tarnell had offered to have their clothes laundered and be ready by morning when they had gone to borrow some soldiers' livery, but Pirojil had declined, and just tucked them in his bag. If they were going to be nosing around town, they would draw less attention as ordinary soldiers, but particularly in a rough part of town it could easily become more than a little convenient to be able to become Captain Pirojil and Baron Keranahan again with a simple change of clothing—say, if they had to blow one of the armsman's whistles that Tarnell had also provided.

Tarnell had just smiled and nodded. While noblemen really didn't often take to common dress to pass among the common people the way they did in legend, it wasn't entirely unknown. Shit, the Old Emperor probably would have done it himself, if the fact of an all-too-good likeness of his face being emblazoned on every Imperial coin hadn't made that impractical.

Pirojil had hoped that the tavernkeeper would come back, and maybe they could engage him in some conversation about the fight, but he didn't, so they left their beers largely undrunk, and themselves entirely undrunk, and headed out of the tavern and into the night.

Dereneyl was, as most cities were, different by night than by day.

The day-busy streets were almost empty, for a start. As it was said, the day is for honest men, but the night is for thieves.

The more prosperous tradesfolk, common merchants, and nobles minor that made their living along the riverfront had left for their houses or estates up the hill, leaving servants and apprentices behind to keep the streetlamps lit and the doors barred shut. Those who lived in their shops stayed inside behind shuttered windows and barred doors.

Cities draw thieves and robbers the way that an open wound draws flies, and at night even the burly longshoremen who worked the riverfront warehouses and docks traveled in groups of four or more and carried their loading hooks with them, and when a bunch of them stopped to get themselves serviced by a whore working one of the alleys, they would be even more careful in looking down the alley to make sure that she wasn't a decoy than they would in feeling up the whore's dress to be sure that the whore wasn't—or, in some cases, was—a boy.

Pirojil and Kethol made their way down the steep steps to a walkway along the river. Between here and Riverforks, to the southeast, and Stormsend, to the west, the Nifet was slow and broad enough for barges to operate, and shallow enough to make that desirable. A dozen barges of various sizes lay a short way out in the river, tied to pilings, their distance from shore a guarantee to a would-be thief of a difficult swim. Yes, the barges would have to be hauled in to shore in the morning, but the time and effort of setting them safely out in the river was cheap insurance.

Two of the barges didn't have cabins at all, and the cabins on another nine were dark, but in one the light in the window and the sounds of a flute and drunken laughter carried across the quiet river, and on another, hobbled horses shuffled in their open-air stalls. The only barge with visible guards on it was one of the cabinless ones—it was piled high with bags, and rode so low in the water that Pirojil suspected it was filled with copper from the Ulter mines, destined to be hauled upriver by teams of mules stumbling along the river-bank path.

As they walked along the path beside the docks, a scurrying sound in the alley to their right sent Pirojil reaching for his sword, quickly flattening himself against the nearest wall.

He wasn't surprised to find Kethol next to him, his sword in one hand, his dagger in the other, and his smile warm in the dark.

They waited, listening, but there was no other sound, and when Pirojil stooped and picked up a pebble to bounce off the wall in the alley, the only thing that he could hear was the sound of the pebble bouncing on the ground before it came to rest.

Just as well, and just as likely. It could have been rats, or it could have been thieves; whoever it was, was gone. A pair of soldiers might well have some coin on them, although not much, but the cost of earning it was likely to be excessive, all things considered.

Pity.

There would be advantages to adding another couple of heads to the collection, all in all, and it wasn't unknown that thieves would have some valuables on them. That might not matter to Kethol, not anymore, but it did to Pirojil.

Blades back in their scabbards, they walked on.

"Any idea where these dwarves might be lodging?" Kethol asked.

"I've something more than an idea," Pirojil said. "Tarnell told me that there's an inn on Cooper's Way, just north of the Hand temple, but I figured that if I got into the issue of how I don't know where Cooper's Way was, he'd just tell me to ask the baron."

There were likely to be maps in Baron Keranahan's study of every street in town, accurate at least as of the time of the war—maps were a necessary part of maintaining tax rolls. But the study was in the Residence, and even if the two of them were in there, Pirojil had no confidence that he and Kethol, even working together, could have found them in a few hours or a few days. They could have had Treseen order Tarnell or the chief armsman to give them a walking tour of Dereneyl, but that really ought to wait for Leria's return. She would help Kethol cover any lapse far better than Pirojil could—by pleading exhaustion, if nothing else, or maybe by fainting. She wasn't really much of the fainting type, granted, but Pirojil had no doubt that she could fake a swoon with the best of them.

"Well, if you were a dwarf, staying in Dereneyl, and you had to pick an inn, where would it be?" Kethol asked.

"Elsewhere."

"I was thinking about how it would be away from the water," he said.

"Yeah, but . . ." But that sort of thinking was next to useless. Yes, a dwarf would want to stay as far from the river as possible, but in Dereneyl, that meant the walled houses near the top of the ridge, as far out of the smells and sound of the riverfront as it was possible to be, and it was a foregone conclusion that there would be no inns or taverns up there, where the land was dear and the neighbors were nobles.

A group of four men, the foremost holding a lantern on a pole, turned a corner ahead, and began to walk toward them. Pirojil didn't actually have to see their brassards to know that they were armsmen from the nightwatch.

They approached Kethol and Pirojil slowly, and came to a halt.

"Identify yourselves, if you please," one said. He was the tallest of the four, by a head, which was typical. "Promote the tallest" was a common form of silliness. The best field decurion Pirojil had ever worked for had been a scrawny little man, the top of his head barely coming up to the bottom of Pirojil's neck. But he had a booming voice, a hard hand, and a forceful way with words that could bring even a lumbering Osgradian recruit to a full brace.

"Your names, if you please," he said.

It would have been easy to pick a name and a unit—under Emperor Thomen, the Imperials had become meticulous in their naming conventions.

But what if the armsman knew who captained that troop? Honesty was the safer bet.

"I'm Pirojil," he said, "captain of march, Emperor's Own, seconded to the Keranahan Home Guard."

There should have been a snicker, and a further challenge, but the leader just nodded.

Shit. Well, so much for Tarnell keeping his filthy hole shut.

"I guess I should have guessed, from the look of you," the armsman said. "And since you and the baron are walking about in ordinary soldiers' livery, and don't want to be recognized, I guess I'll be standing tall in front of the chief armsman if I give a proper bow?"

Kethol gave an entirely noble-sounding chuckle. "I wouldn't be surprised," he said. "Although I am surprised that you were told to expect us."

The armsman's mouth twitched.

"Go ahead," Kethol said. "You've got something to say, so out with it."

The armsman cleared his throat. "Begging the baron's pardon, but the chief's a good man, and he watches out for us, and we watch out for him. You and the captain prowling around dockside looking for all the world like a couple of Imperial soldiers is a perfectly fine thing, really it is, and it wouldn't be for me to say otherwise if it weren't.

"But if you and the captain was to decide, say, to honor a local girl or something, and say we was to come across you while you was busy taking your turns honoring her, and then she was to scream, if we didn't know, we might do something wrong, and the chief would not want to see us triced to a whipping post—or worse—for doing what we just thought was our job. Begging the baron's pardon," he added quickly, touching a hand to a forelock, forgetting for the moment that he wasn't supposed to be acknowledging Forinel's rank.

The other armsmen looked straight ahead, pretending, as they no doubt were wishing, that they weren't there. Even discussing laying a hand on a noble—at least, discussing it to the noble's face—was a risky thing, at best.

Pirojil felt Kethol stiffen at his side. Kethol had a thing about rape, and the armsman had just suggested—shit, he had practically winked at the idea—that the two of them were just looking to jump some common girl.

Kethol was always an idiot when it came to that sort of thing. He had gotten himself and Durine jailed in Riverforks when Kethol had jumped a couple of young noblemen who had been drunkenly busying themselves with some girl that they had snatched off the street, and Pirojil had had to break the two of them out of jail.

Pirojil didn't understand it, himself. He didn't have a taste for rape, no. But if he made judgments about those who did, and he did, he kept them to himself, as long as it was none of his concern, which it usually wasn't, and never was if it was a noble man and a common girl involved. Shit, it wasn't rape, except in practice, and any commoner girl with a lick of sense would just lie back and enjoy it, if she could.

Of course, if somebody, anybody, had laid an unwanted hand on any of the Cullinane women, or on Leria, Pirojil would have cut that hand off at the crotch, instantly. Not because he liked them, of course, although he did. In this life, who you liked and what you liked had damn little to do with what you had to do. But when you took pay from a man—be it a commoner, a minor noble, a baron, or the Emperor himself—you had the obligation to protect what was his, whether it was his horses, his peasants, or his women.

But Kethol surprised Pirojil by relaxing. "No offense taken, err . . ."

"Bendamen, Wat's son," the armsman said. "Is there something I can do for Your Lordship and the captain, or should we be getting out of your way?"

He didn't have to add, *and getting away from the sort of person who can have me triced to a whipping post.*

"Well, there is one thing. A little information?" Pirojil raised an eyebrow. "I heard that there's some dwarves lodging somewhere in town. Wheelwright's Road, was it? No, that isn't right."

"It's on Cooper's Way—there's an inn that caters to the dwarf trade, although I don't know why, the way that they keep getting themselves into trouble, of late." Bendamen shrugged. "Guess everybody's got to be somewhere, Captain." He turned to Kethol and drew himself up straight. "It would be an honor, of course, to escort you there—or anywhere else you'd like to go, my lord."

"Escort us?" Pirojil shook his head. "Why would you want to escort us? We're just a couple of soldiers, off duty, out looking for something to do on a quiet evening. But if your patrol would just happen to take you past that inn, it might be that a couple of ordinary soldiers would just happen to be wandering along behind, and not have to worry about thugs lurking in any of the alleys."

Bendamen smiled as he touched his knuckle to his forelock. "I'd say, if you don't mind me saying so, that the thugs would have more to worry about—but I think a turn down Cooper's Way wouldn't be a bad idea, at that. Honored-to-be-of-service," he said.

Pirojil and Kethol stood aside to let them pass, then followed along.

Daherrin Brokenose eyed them suspiciously as Kethol squatted down in front of the other dwarf, the one who lay on the flat stone next to the hearth.

Daherrin Brokenose was broad across the chest as a muscular man, but stood barely chest-high. Despite the name, his broad nose

showed no sign of a break, old or recent. Daherrin Brokenose hadn't
been badly injured, although two of the fingers on his left hand were
clearly broken, and twisted off at odd angles.

The one on the floor—Dahera, his name was—looked like shit.

Somebody had given his face a serious working over. His pur-
pled right eye was swollen tightly shut, and his left barely open a
slit. His nose had been broken badly enough that his gasps for breath
came through his mouth.

It wasn't just the face.

Blood stained the bandages that had been wrapped around his
preposterously broad chest, and the skin on his right shoulder was
flayed almost to the bone, as though he had been dragged across a
road. His hands were unmarked, save for the scratches across the
palms.

Of the six dwarves crowded into the tiny, smelly room, this one,
Dahera, was the worst, although all had been beaten badly enough
to make somebody more gently raised puke at the sight of it.

Pirojil had seen beaten and injured before. But it was the
dwarves' beards that were strange. They had all been crudely hacked
off, just below the heavy chins.

"We don't want any more trouble," Daherrin Brokenose said,
again. He spoke Erendra with a thick accent that made Pirojil suspect that he was from Endell. His thick fingers couldn't help but
stray to where his long beard should have been. "Just go, please."

Pirojil didn't know much about dwarves, despite having picked
up the language back—back a long time ago, but he knew that a
dwarf would never cut his beard unless the beard reached his waist,
at least, and that a dwarf boy wasn't considered to be an adult until
he had forged his own pick—starting with ore—dug himself a chamber in the warrens with it, and grown a beard down to his chest.

"*Shasht*, Daherrin," said another, in dwarvish. "Speak more gently to the Emperor's skinnylegs, lest you arouse their anger, as well

as that of the other skinnylegs." He shook his massive head as he lay stretched out on a cot that was almost twice as long as he needed. "Have we not had enough dealings with the skinnylegs for one night, or for an entire lifetime? Let them revel in the damage that their children have done, and we can be gone in the morning."

Pirojil nodded; he had been right about the accent. Definitely Endell. Humans were "skinnylegs" to dwarves from the Endell warrens, rather than the more common "smallnoses" or "tinybeards," or what the Devenell dwarves less than charmingly called "needledicks."

The one by the hearth was the only one with wounds serious enough to worry about. He would probably be able to make it to morning, and a trip to the Spider—dwarves were tougher than they looked, and they looked tough—but you could never be sure.

Kethol looked up at Pirojil. "How bad is it, do you think?"

Pirojil shrugged. He didn't know, either. The Spidersect compound was across town. The Spiders were renowned cowards, who would probably have to be dragged at swordpoint to cross into lowertown after dark, which was a bad idea—cowards that they were, a Spider healer could inflict injury just as easily as he could cure it. The Eareven were a better bet, but Pirojil didn't know where the Eareven were, if there even *were* any Eareven in Dereneyl.

The best thing to do would be to go down the street and knock on the gates to the Hand temple and try to beg the novice on duty to get a healer to come over, but Hand priestesses made Pirojil nervous. Their eyes always seemed to see far too much, and it wasn't beyond possibility that one could take one look at Forinel, smile, and say, "Hello, Kethol." Yes, the elves had said that the transformation was complete, and far beyond what any human wizard could not only possibly do, but detect—but Pirojil didn't know if they were right.

For now, Kethol had a flask of healing draughts in the bag, and while Pirojil considered for a moment spending a sip of that on Dahera, he didn't consider it very hard—even Eareven healing draughts were hideously expensive, while the services of a healer were relatively cheap.

"We mean no harm," Daherrin Brokenose said. "And we meant no harm."

"Tell me," Kethol said, quietly.

"No, Lord, there's no point in it. Please, please, just leave us be."

"You had best not say more, Daherrin," the old one on the bed said. "Remember what they said."

Daherrin Brokenose looked at Pirojil and Kethol, and at their blank stares turned back to the other. "But these skinnylegs are the Emperor's men, and the Emperor himself treated with the king for our services."

"You heard the other skinnylegs. They vowed—one swore on his sword!—to find us if we made protest to the Emperor's men, and swear that once the Emperor's men leave, as they surely soon will, they will remember us and our brothers, having marked us, and throw us into the river. The river, Daherrin Brokenose, the river." The old dwarf shuddered.

Pirojil looked over at Kethol, who clearly hadn't understood a word. He crooked an eyebrow at Pirojil.

"It was some of the local noble boys," Pirojil said, in Englits. It was unlikely that any of them could speak much Englits. "I'm not sure what happened, or why, but they said that if the dwarves go to the governor, nothing will happen—which probably isn't exactly true—but that when the occupation is lifted, they'll remember, and take their anger out later, on these or others."

Daherrin Brokenose's massive head was cocked to one side. He had apparently been able to follow at least some of the Englits conversation, and was wondering how the skinnylegs could have understood him. It wasn't utterly unknown for skinnylegs in the Emperor's service to speak dwarvish, but surely Pirojil would have commented before.

Pirojil took a deep breath.

"Yes, this skinnylegs speaks the language of the Moderate People, although not as well as he would wish," Pirojil said in dwarvish, not minding at all the way that, save for poor Dahera's, all the dwarven eyes suddenly became wide and round. It had been vaguely insulting to be taken for granted, and speaking in their own language was revenge of a sort, and cheap revenge, at that.

"This skinnylegs," he said, "has shared beer and spilled blood and wrestled for sport and honor with Ahira Bandylegs, himself the godfather to Baron Cullinane."

It was all he could do not to say that Kethol had done the same. But there was no Kethol, just Forinel.

"And the other skinnylegs," he went on in Erendra, so that Kethol could follow, "is Forinel, baron of Keranahan, and this talk of his children embarrasses and angers him, because those who cheat at bones and beat on others without cause and for supposed sport are no children of his, but mere bastards, fathered by goats."

Kethol's face grew impassive. Anybody who had known him less well wouldn't have known how angry he was.

Kethol reached into the bag and pulled out the brass flask of healing draughts, viciously twisted the top off, and poured half of it into Dahera's mouth, then stoppered it and tossed it to Daherrin Brokenose.

"Split this rest among yourselves, and then tell me everything that happened," he said. "*Everything.*"

They had been accompanying the wagons from the Ulter mines, both to swear before the tallier as to how much copper had been weighed at the smelter out in the hills, and to accept a portion of their pay in Imperial silver.

Most of that pay was, of course, still safe at Dereneyl Castle, in the strong room; they hadn't been foolish enough to carry all that money on their persons when they had gone down to lowertown, picking the least appealing tavern they could find in which to wash the taste of the mines and the roads from their mouths and their minds.

But then a party of six skinnylegs, all of them dressed far too finely for lowertown, had come into the place, a drunken girl with them, and after getting themselves even more thoroughly drunk, had decided—insisted—that the dwarves should gamble with them, and one of them had pulled a finely carved box containing a set of bones out of his bag. Playing for a half-mark a game seemed to be a cheap price to pay in order to get the skinnylegs to let them leave—as they had promised to do, after one game—so Dahera had sat down, and managed to lose that one game, which quickly became a second, a third, and then a fourth.

But when it came time to pay, and Dahera produced two copper marks, the skinnylegs had been insulted.

Copper?

Copper?

Did these impudent dwarves think to pay a golden bet in copper—in ordinary copper that had probably been soiled by the touch of a thousand peasant hands—when it was known that dwarves had half the gold in the world and all of the gold in the Eren regions?

Two of them had started beating on Dahera, and when the other Moderate People moved to intervene, all six of the skinnylegs had drawn swords, and held all of the Moderate People at swordpoint while the two finished with Dahera, and then started on the others, and then the skinnylegs had hacked off their beards as trophies.

Trophies.

•   •   •

"Name," Kethol said. "Give me a name."

"Linter. One of the others called the one who played at bones 'Linter.' And another was Felesen, I think?" Daherrin Brokenose spread his hands. "Please, don't make any more trouble for us. We leave for the Ulter Hills in the morning, and we don't—"

"Shhh." Pirojil looked over at Kethol, and raised a palm. "We just needed the name. We'll go back to the castle, and have some words with Treseen in the morning."

It was irritating, but it wasn't really that bad. The right thing to do was something safe and political. They could talk to Tarnell in the morning, and work out something reasonable with him, and then present it to the governor. Treseen would probably just fine the boys' fathers, and issue a stern warning against bothering the dwarves that would likely be obeyed, coming as it did from the governor.

It should be easy to persuade Treseen. After all, it was one thing for some local commoners not to get along with the dwarves, but the work of the dwarves in the mines had been negotiated at Biemestren, in the name of the Emperor.

Granted, a few incidents, even incidents provoked by local nobility, were not going to endanger that agreement. It was in everyone's interest that the dwarves work the copper mines—they could work happily for long hours in tunnels smaller than humans needed, at temperatures that would make humans faint, and their darksight made it possible for them to see by their own body heat, at least far enough to swing a pick or shovel. The Empire needed the copper, and dwarves could certainly mine it much faster than humans; the dwarves were more than greedy not just for payment in silver, but to trade that silver for as much New Pittsburgh wootz as they could get their huge, knobby hands on.

A few bruises, broken bones, and slashed beards wouldn't make much of a difference.

Unless, of course, somebody with sufficient influence said that it would.

A baron, say, who had discovered that one of the injured dwarves was the cousin of the Endell king—whose name was Daherrin, too, come to think of it, although that was a common enough name in Endell. That would put a scare into Treseen, and Treseen could put a scare into the local lords.

That was the right thing, the sensible thing, to do, and Pirojil prided himself on being sensible.

Kethol was already on his feet, stripping off his soldier's tunic.

"Would you just—" Pirojil started, knowing full well that he wouldn't be allowed to finish the sentence.

"No," Kethol said. "I *wouldn't* just. I wouldn't just for a moment—go whistle for the armsmen."

"Baron—"

"*Now*, Pirojil."

Kethol pounded on the thick door with the hilt of his dagger, ignoring the brass gong that hung on the chain next to it.

Wham. Wham. Whamwhamwhamwham.

His pounding set the thiefwire along the top of the door ringing loudly, and even some of the much greater lengths strung along the stone wall seemed to vibrate in a quiet warning, one that would have just been attributed to the wind in other circumstances.

Wham. Wham. Whamwhamwhamwham.

"You in the house—*open the door*."

The squad of armsmen stood to one side, as though they wished they could avoid the whole matter, which was more than almost certain.

There were sounds of movement from inside—booted feet

pounding hard on the stones, a few muttered words, and the whisks of at least two swords being pulled from sheaths.

The cover of the barred viewing window slid back with a loud *thunk*, but remained dark; no face presented itself in the lantern light. Whoever had opened it was probably sensibly standing to one side, not wanting to risk a sword coming through it and into his eye.

A harsh voice called out, "Who goes there?"

Bendamen swallowed heavily, and then brought himself to attention several steps back from the barred window, either to let who was inside see out better, or because he didn't want a sword or a spear stuck through the hole and through him, either. "I am Bendamen, Wat's son, senior armsman." He pulled the brassard off his arm and held it out in front of him as though it was a shield. "Open the door."

"We didn't send for any armsmen, and Lord Sherrol is not going to be happy about any armsman pounding on his door in the middle of the night."

Kethol stepped toward Bendamen, who quickly moved aside to let Kethol face the viewing port.

"Then you'd best tell him that Baron Keranahan is here," Kethol said. "In case you haven't heard, I've just returned from the border with a collection of bandits' heads, and I'm telling you that if these doors don't open by the time I count to three, yours will be joining the set."

"But—"

"Two."

The doors opened, without any protest about how he had started with two instead of one.

One of the guards was just finishing lighting the last of the lanterns that ringed the courtyard as the front door to the two-story stone house opened.

The house had been built to deter thieves, not as a stronghold in time of war—there were no storehouses visible inside the walls, and although the walls themselves could probably have stood for quite a long time against a battering ram, the top of the wall was utterly naked of any walkway for defenders.

Still, there were already three guards, armed and armored, that had made their way from the servants' wing down to the stones of the courtyard, and that probably meant that there were at least again as many who were at the moment standing beside their beds with swords in their hands, stepping into boots before they even considered pulling on their loose breeches, because in a fight you needed to be sure you could protect your feet a lot more than you worried about your balls swinging in the wind.

"Put your swords up," Bendamen called out. "It's the nightwatch, and the baron."

Kethol wouldn't exactly want to count on the armsmen in a fight, but the chances of a noble's private guard taking on the nightwatch in a fight were low. But not zero.

He knew that it should have bothered him that it could all break loose at any moment, but it didn't.

Sherrol lumbered down the front stairs and into the courtyard, dressed only in a long nightshirt. He walked straight across the garden, not seeming to notice how the sharp stones cut his feet.

"Baron?" His eyes were wide, and his fingers kept reaching to his waist, as though to cinch up the belt that wasn't there. "Please—what is this all about?"

There were faces peeking out of the darkened doorway, but Kethol ignored them.

"Get your son out here. Now."

"My son? But—"

"You have a son named Linter?"

"Yes, I do—"

"Get him out here, now."

"But, can't you at least tell me what this is all about, please don't—"

"I'm here, Father."

A young man stood in the doorway. His hair and short beard should have been mussed from sleep, but he had clearly taken the time to brush them into place, dress himself in a bright yellow blouse and dark linen trousers, and belt his short sword around his waist.

He was a handsome enough lad, not quite filled out, and more lean than skinny-looking, and he walked with a definitely arrogant swagger as he made his way down the front steps.

"Linter, what have you been doing?"

"Nothing discreditable, Father." Linter shook his head. "I'm not sure why this man—"

"Mind your mouth. 'This man,' as you would have it, is the baron."

Linter accepted the correction with a humble nod, and a slight crook of a smile that said that he had already known that. "It's kind of you to visit our home, Baron Forinel," he said. "I'd hoped we'd soon have the honor of it, but I would have hoped that you would visit us properly, in the daytime, not at night like—"

"Watch your mouth, Linter."

Linter's lips tightened. "As you wish, Father." He turned back to Kethol. "My apologies, Baron; I meant no disrespect."

"I suppose you meant no disrespect in lowertown tonight, when you cheated and beat those dwarves?"

"Dwarves?" Sherrol's forehead furrowed. "What would my son have to do with some lowertown dwarves?"

At a signal from Pirojil, Daherrin Brokenose walked into the courtyard, looking for all the world as though he would rather be anywhere else.

"Is this needledick the one that beat you and your companions?" Kethol asked.

Daherrin Brokenose didn't say anything until Pirojil said something in dwarvish, then added, loudly, in Erendra: "I say again, so that all can hear it: that if you speak the truth, the baron swears that no harm will come to you from it."

"Yes." Daherrin Brokenose nodded. "It's him. He is the one."

Linter didn't quite sneer as he turned to his father. "It's true enough that some friends and I had some unpleasantness with this filthy dwarf, but—"

"It's Felesen, isn't it?" Sherrol turned to Kethol. "Felesen has a taste for the worst of lowertown, and it's a miracle that he and my, my idiot son haven't fallen to some footpads, no matter how good they think they are with their swords."

"I think we'd best see just how good Linter actually is with his sword," Kethol said. "Now would be a very good time."

Sherrol shook his head. "Over some problems with a few dwarves? Surely that's not—"

"You don't understand, Lord Sherrol," Pirojil said, stepping forward. "When Baron Forinel was off in the Katharhd, his life was saved by a dwarf, a distant cousin to Daherrin Brokenose—who himself is cousin to King Daherrin himself. You could ask Lady Leria about it, when she returns—she's heard the baron talk about it, and how . . ." Pirojil raised a hand and stopped himself. "It's a long story, but the point of it was that he swore an oath that he would never suffer to see his friend, or his friend's kindred, abused."

That, of course, wasn't true. It had nothing to do with the truth, whatever it was.

"But the baron didn't see anything," Linter said, smiling. "I could flay a thousand dwarves to their preposterously heavy bones and his oath would be safe, as long as it wasn't in his sight."

Sherrol turned to his son. "You take such things very lightly, Linter," he said. "Hear this: I swear—you have *my* oath—that if you do not apologize to the baron, you'll depart this house, and not return while I live. We're not of the most ancient of lineages, you and I, and yes, you'll hear lords like Moarin talk about us as though we're but a generation or two up from the common ruck, but if you think that the word of a nobleman of Holtun is something to laugh at, you'll learn the better of that, one way or another."

"Father—"

"I may even be saving your life if I have to send you away. He's sworn—don't you understand that he has to challenge you? Do you think a paltry few little so-called affairs of honor among your friends have prepared you to face a man who went out into the Katharhd with nothing but the clothes on his back and the sword in his hand— and came back a hero?"

Sherrol reached out and fingered the scar on Linter's cheek. "Yes, it's one thing to play at swords with the other boys—and boys you are, even if a stiff dick fools you into thinking yourselves men— and to be sure to have your little affairs of honor in the daytime, out behind the Hand temple, knowing that if you get a wound that hurts too much, or that endangers your life, or that won't leave an attractive scar, help is but a shout away. It's another to face a real man with a sword, one who knows how to use it, and whose honor won't be satisfied with a few drops of blood on the point."

Nobles were big on oaths, although a common soldier had to be more practical.

Kethol himself was more practical, most of the time.

But maybe he had spent too much time around the Old Emperor, and Pirojil and Durine, too, for that matter. Or maybe he had simply been too long a soldier, and had seen and done too much. It had been one thing to fight in a war, to push back the Holtish invaders and then finish with them before they could regroup to attack Bieme. It was another to fight in order to eat, and when he had killed in self-defense, the only thing he had ever regretted was the smell of the dead.

But sport?

For fun?

An idle evening out cheating and beating on some dwarves while others held them at swordpoint so that they couldn't even defend themselves? But he was sure that this wouldn't stand. He might be a false baron, a phony noble, but there was a limit to how false and phony he would be, and letting this young braggart pound away on those who were prevented, at swordpoint, from defending themselves . . .

Not in my barony, he thought.

"Get your sword out, Linter," Forinel said, quietly.

Kethol wouldn't have said anything. He would just have launched himself at Linter, beaten him until he lay broken and bloody on the stones. Hands, knives, sword—it didn't matter. And it didn't matter what the results were, just as it hadn't in Riverforks, back when Durine was alive and at his back.

Yes, he knew that Pirojil thought he was an idiot about such things, and perhaps he was, but . . .

Linter drew himself up straight. "If the baron is offended, I offer my apologies for having offended him, and no matter that it was just an innocent little evening."

"Well, then." Sherrol visibly relaxed, and turned back to Kethol. "I'll have words, with him Baron, I promise—he's probably too old to strap, but he's not too old to see how much joy he can have persuading a seamstress to sew him a fashionable new tunic when word gets out that I'll not be settling any accounts for him until after the harvest."

"*Father.*"

"Better—until spring. Would you care to try for next harvest?" Sherrol turned back to Linter. "I don't care much one way or another about dwarves, and I don't mind throwing a few coppers, now and then, to some commoner girl who claims that the squalling, smelly baby that she carries on her hip is your bastard, but I'll not have anybody in this household offending the baron."

He turned to Daherrin Brokenose. "I offer you my apologies, as well, good Daherrin," he said, adding just a fraction of a bow.

"Father!"

No. Words were not enough. Words, promises, apologies, oaths—they might matter to Forinel, but Kethol paid and collected in steel and gold and blood, not in words.

"I think mine is the better idea," Kethol said, stepping forward, his hand on his sword. "You and I will settle this matter, Linter, now. Here."

"Please, Baron, don't—"

Even in the flickering torchlight, Linter was pale. Perhaps he had thought that the worst that the baron would do would be to idly challenge him, and what was another little nick? A noble family would surely have a flask of healing draughts handy, after all.

But it was as clear to him as it was to Sherrol that a little nick wouldn't satisfy this baron, and the fact that Linter didn't know that the baron was an utter fraud only made it worse, not better.

Linter was a braggart and a bully, yes, but Kethol had to give him credit: he swallowed once, heavily, and nodded, and stepped back, reaching for the hilt of his own sword.

"I am at your service, of course, Baron Keranahan, now and at any time."

"*No.*" Sherrol stepped between then.

"Your son claims to be a man, and carries a man's weapon," Kethol said, as gently as he could. "Let's see how he handles it, and himself."

He could more feel than see Pirojil throwing up his hands. Well, Pirojil could disagree with him, and they could discuss it later, after Kethol had cleaned the blood from this sword.

"Wait. Please." Daherrin Brokenose stepped forward, reaching for Kethol's arm, then stopping himself. "This is not right."

Eh?

"No; you must not." The dwarf shook his head. "I was fooled by the beard—you humans have such silly little beards," he said. "I thought that this was an adult—but I've listened: this Linter is barely a child, despite the beard. It is not right to kill a child for what is just a childish tantrum, after all. I have children, myself, in my home warrens, and they often behave foolishly. I'd not wish to see one of them spitted on a sword for that."

"I'm man enough," Linter said.

"Yes," Daherrin Brokenose said, "such a man you are, indeed, Lord Linter. Such courage and bravery are truly an honor to your line."

Linter went for his sword, but Sherrol was even quicker than Kethol was. His thick hand gripped his son's wrist, and after a moment's struggle, Linter ceased.

"I've a solution," Pirojil said, stepping forward. "There is a way among the Moderate People to settle such disputes, to restore honor. It might not be as interesting as watching the baron run an arm's-length of steel through Linter's guts, but it might be . . . educational."

He turned to Daherrin Brokenose. "The Moderate People call it *shach-shtorm*. In Erendra, we call it 'wrestling.' "

Daherrin Brokenose shook his head. "There's no honor in *shach-shtorm* with a child. Teaching children, of course, is one thing, and for them to play at *shach-shtorm* with each other is only natural, but for an adult . . ."

"Adult?" Pirojil smiled. "I mean no disrespect, Daherrin Brokenose, but doesn't an adult of the Moderate People have a full beard?"

It took a moment for the dwarf to see what Pirojil was getting at, but then, slowly, a smile spread across his broad face.

"Yes, that is true. I am but a child, at that, it would seem," he said, turning to Linter. "Let us two children contend with each other, shall we?"

The combat, such as it was, was remarkably short.

While the top of the dwarf's head barely came to the middle of Linter's chest, he weighed more than twice what the boy did, and he was, after all, a dwarf. Dwarves were much stronger than humans were—Kethol had seen Ahira, more than once, start a fire by quickly bending a piece of iron bar back and forth in his massive hands until the center glowed a dull red, then tossing it into a pile of tinder.

Linter tried to kick out at Daherrin Brokenose, but the dwarf simply seized the foot in one hand and unceremoniously dumped Linter to the ground, then waited in a half-crouch while the boy rose to try again. This time, Linter made the mistake of closing with the dwarf, who seized him at the shoulder and waist, and lifted him above his head, ignoring the way that a flailing arm or leg would occasionally make contact.

It would have been trivially easy for Daherrin Brokenose to have brought Linter down over his knee, snapping his back, but the dwarf simply spun him about and lowered him to the ground and gave the human what looked like a gentle push, but which sent Linter sprawling across the stones.

His shirt hung in tatters from his chest, and his trousers had split toward the knee. The dwarf had gone easily on him, but there was a nice bruise growing on the side of his face, and he held one hand pressed against his die.

"Shall we have another fall, young skinnylegs?" Daherrin Brokenose asked.

Kethol had to smile. Daherrin Brokenose was definitely getting in the spirit of this, despite the fact that this wasn't real *shach-*

shtorm, not to him, but just the discipline, and education, of a wayward child.

Linter started to edge toward the bench where he had placed his sword belt, but Pirojil, with Sherrol at his side, was in between him and the bench.

"If you want to play with swords, little boy," Kethol said, "you play with me."

Linter shook his head. A few bruises had knocked the bravado right out of him.

Kethol nodded. "Another fall, please."

The next morning, Treseen was not happy with Pirojil. That seemed to be an ongoing problem.

"Again?" He shook his head. "Is it ever possible for you to spend a night in town without getting into a fight, *Captain* Pirojil?" He looked back down at his plate, and toyed with the fish compote, then stabbed at it with his eating prong as though it was Pirojil.

Pirojil kept his face impassive. It wasn't the first time that a senior officer had had him stand at attention while he chewed on him, and Treseen was out of practice—although Treseen having had Tarnell come to Pirojil's room and shake him awake while Kethol was still asleep in the next room wasn't a bad start.

Treseen looked up at him. "Well?" He made a stabbing gesture with his eating prong. "I think that I asked you a question, Captain Pirojil?"

Pirojil kept his eyes studiously fixed on a spot on the opposite wall. "Yes, Governor, it is possible for me to spend the night in town without getting into a fight. In fact, Governor, I didn't get into a fight at all, and neither did the baron—"

"Don't you argue with me." Treseen stabbed at the air with his prong. "You may be wearing captain's braid, but you and I both know that you're just a poor excuse for a line soldier, who just happens to have some noble connections. You're an imposter, Pirojil, that's all." He tapped at the table. "I've got a letter on my desk, addressed to the Imperial proctor, Walter Slovotsky, telling him that I think your usefulness here in Keranahan is done, and asking to have you sent back to wherever it is you belong, which I suspect is digging latrines for field troops, at best. Those other two you were with last time you were here—Durine and that Kethol—now those were a proper pair of soldiers, and even at their worst, looking at them didn't make a man want to gag on his food."

Pirojil didn't like the way the discussion had gotten to the question of an imposter—and it didn't seem to be wise to pursue it, or to anger Treseen further.

What was he so angry about? Granted, Dereneyl seemed to be a little on the crime-ridden side, but it was not much worse than most, and certainly better than Biemestren or New Pittsburgh, for example.

Not that there was any benefit to be had in arguing the matter, not here and now.

So Pirojil just stood, arms at his sides, and didn't say anything.

"Now get your ugly face out of here—and since you and the baron have seen fit to spurn my hospitality, I would very much appreciate it if you would get out of Dereneyl before you start some other incident with the dwarves, or with the nobles, or start a fight with some longshoremen, or do whatever stupid thing you insist on doing. And I do mean you, Pirojil; I don't blame the baron. He's been absent for years, and what he should be doing is settling in on his estates, and reacquainting himself with the local nobility—not trying to start duels with every nobleman in the barony."

"Yes, Governor, and—"

"Don't you dare talk back to me. Just get out of my sight. Now."

•   •   •

Erenor was waiting for them out in the courtyard. One of Tarnell's soldiers was busy attaching several muslin bags to his packhorse's rigging under Erenor's supervision.

He turned quickly at their approach.

"A pleasant morning to you, my lord the baron, and to you as well, Captain Pirojil." He folded his withered hands across his waist and bowed so quickly and so low that it flipped the hood of his robes up over his head, and he had to pull it back off when he straightened.

Kethol cocked his head to one side. "What are you doing in town?"

"Well, nobody told me that I had to stay out at the Residence, and there were a few odds and ends that I needed. You know, the usual sort of a wizard's supplies—the odd eye of frog, tongue of bat, some powdered pig liver, and particularly some Salket tea."

"Tea?" Pirojil wasn't terribly familiar with what wizards used in their preparations—when the preparations didn't simply consist of impressing the symbols from their spell books into their brains, which they mostly did—but he had never heard of tea as an ingredient.

"Well, of course—have you even tasted that vile brew that that lying Elda claims to be tea? My guess is that it's a mixture of rotted oak leaves and pig shit, and probably boiled in the same loathsome vat where the serving girls boil their crotch straps. But—" He stopped himself. "Never mind; I'll brew you up a proper pot this evening. After I rejoin you at the Residence."

"You're not coming back with us now?"

"No." Erenor shook his head. "I've a little more business to finish in town."

"Tell me," Kethol said.

"I'd rather not."

"He wasn't asking," Pirojil said. "Neither am I."

Erenor shrugged. "Very well, if you insist. I heard about your little . . . escapade of last night, and it occurred to me that little Lordling Linter got off with nothing more than a few bruises that the Spider will have made to disappear by now, and just a minor loss of dignity, which his young mind will quickly forget. I thought it would be, well, not unpleasant to add something to that, even if that means standing in the hot sun for a while, waiting for him to come out from behind his walls."

He raised a palm. "Oh, I'm not going to do anything terribly serious, although I do need to sneak into Lord Sherrol's house and, er, retrieve a few minor items to make it work. Just the smallest of spells, the slightest of glamours, and for the next few tendays young Linter will be unable to, er, exercise his manhood."

He brightened. "And if there's poison ivy down by the river— and I'm sure there is—he might well find that he breaks into an itch every time he's within sight, sound, or smell of a dwarf."

"And why are you doing this?" Pirojil asked. "I don't understand."

"True enough." Erenor smiled sadly. "You really don't understand me, Captain. Not even a little."

14

✠ Beralyn

The delegate from Nyphien was even more arrogant than Beralyn would have expected. Although perhaps she should have expected as much, or even worse.

Or perhaps not. It wasn't like all the Nyphs were troublesome. Derinald had reported that the margrave's escort, a full company of Nyphien cavalry, were behaving themselves with impeccable manners in the city.

Which was all well and good, but why was Derinald still alive? Somebody had erased his name from where she had scrawled it, which meant that whoever Tyrnael's agent was inside the castle had read it, but what was taking him—or her, or them—so long?

In the meantime, Derinald seemed to be avoiding her, and she couldn't figure out quite why—she was going out of her way to speak softly and gently to him.

There was no point in berating a walking dead man, after all.

Derinald was accurately reporting that there had been no trouble with the margrave's soldiers, though; she had heard Garavar say the same thing to Thomen. It might just have been because Biemestren's lord chief armsman had seconded some of the Emperor's Own into armsman service, and made it a point to keep both Imperial and baronial troops out of whichever taverns the Nyphs happened to be using at the moment, knowing that, regardless of orders, drunken Nyphs and drunken Biemish troops would fight.

Men.

But this margrave was another matter. He didn't say anything objectionable, not exactly, but his whole attitude was of a major lord paying a visit on a minor one, when he should have been showing more respect for the Empire as a whole, and for Thomen himself.

Thomen didn't seem to notice. He just chatted with Margrave Den Hacza as though the two were old friends, while the rest of the nobles gathered in the courtyard were watching the jugglers, while a band of silverhorns played.

She didn't know where the juggling troupe had come from, but she had seen worse.

Their leader, whose fringe of dull gray hair was braided in a sailor's queue, kept a shower of knives going, while a barely decently clad young girl and a shirtless boy—they looked like brother and sister, and they had the same sort of folds to their eyes; probably all Salkes—ran and capered and tumbled on a slack rope that was supported only by being tied around the thick waists of two almost impossibly large men. From time to time, it looked as though the boy would fall—not that a fall from waist height to the ground would have been dangerous or anything more than embarrassing. But then the girl would give a clever twitch of her feet, and the swaying of the rope would stop long enough for him to regain his balance.

The grand finale of their performance involved throwing at least a dozen lit torches back and forth between the leader and the boy and girl, while the silverhorns took up a low, mournful wail, as though foreshadowing an awful burn.

But the finale came off without injury; one by one, the elder juggler picked the flaming brands out of the air and planted them in the sand at his feet, and then the brother and sister flipped themselves into the air, landing beside him in perfect unison, while the three jugglers bowed to scattered applause.

"Very nice," the margrave said. "Do you keep these about?"

"No," Thomen said. "They're just traveling performers—although I think they are quite good, don't you?"

"Very good, indeed."

"But you were asking about our troops," Thomen said, "so I thought that they might provide a little entertainment, as well?"

"Oh? Do they juggle or sing?"

There it was again. Not quite obviously offensive, but just shy of it.

"Neither, I'm afraid," Thomen said. He looked over at a servant and gave a signal, and another servant brought out a wicker basket that appeared to be filled with gourds.

"I thought you might enjoy watching some of what our lancers can do."

The basket was filled with green and purple gourds; the servant lined up more than a dozen on a low table near where the jugglers had been performing, then quickly set the basket down and walked away.

"I am, of course, interested in whatever you have to show me," the margrave said.

Her son was an idiot.

What he should have been doing was lulling the Nyphs into a sense of security, while as quietly as possible raising armies. It took a preposterously short time to take a shit-footed peasant and turn him into a soldier—as long as you could give him a rifle, and not expect him to learn how to use a sword, or spear, or bow. You couldn't expect, so Garavar said, peasant soldiers to stand against a cavalry charge, or to close with even a broken army in the field, but the massed fire of hundreds of them could prepare the way for the real soldiers.

Peasant levies, after all, had been instrumental in breaking Holtun.

It was only a matter of time. Guns could as easily be turned on the Empire, after all, and they would be. Right now, they were rare—although she was sure that every aged dung pile in the Middle Lands was being turned over for saltpeter, and there were constantly trains of wagons leaving the Waste of Elrood, piled high with foul-smelling sulfur. It would certainly be a long time before any other country had any quantity of rifles as well made or accurate as those that the Imperial engineers made in their shops, not to mention the more elegant ones that were made in Home, but even this Nyph noble had arrived in Biemestren with a company of Nyph riflemen.

That traitor, Walter Slovotsky, had let the secret of making gunpowder slip from his lips, and now there were rifles—cruder than the Imperial rifles that were manufactured by Home engineers, granted, but rifles nonetheless—and soon there would be cannons all over the Middle Lands, and the whole Eren region, for that matter.

The time to strike was soon, and the sooner the better. Let Thomen grab the border Nyphien baronies, say, and perhaps some of Kiar and Enkiar, and nobody would even dare to think that anybody other than Thomen Furnael belonged on the throne.

Instead, of course, he put on a show.

Hoofbeats thundered from the direction of the front gate. That Greta Tyrnael stiffened, and started to rise, but desisted when Thomen laid a hand on her arm.

"Please keep your seats," Thomen said, raising his voice, "there's no need for concern."

While the nobles forced themselves to sit back down on their chairs on the grandstand that cupped the edge of the inner courtyard, a full dozen of the Emperor's Own galloped through the open gate and into the courtyard. Save for their helmets, which were lashed to their saddles, they were in full armor, from head to toe, and each of their shields was decorated only with the Imperial dragon.

Hooves beating hard against the gravel, each of the cavalrymen galloped in through the open gates, circled the donjon, and at a full gallop, each one snared a small gourd on the tip of his lance, then brought his horse to a prancing halt in line in front of the grand-stand.

It wasn't quite as dramatic as it should have been—several of the gourds had simply split on the lances, and one had fallen as the decurion had raised his spear, and splattered his right pauldron and haubergeon with orange gourd guts that quickly leaked down onto his greaves.

"Very nice, very nice indeed," the margrave said. Den Hacza's hand fluttered at the end of his wrist like a butterfly. "Such precision is impressive."

Instead of waiting for the Emperor to speak, that annoying Lord Miron fluttered his own wrist back at the margrave.

"It's not precision, I would say, as much as it is the . . . intensity of it all. It's one thing to see it on a nice, sunny afternoon—but I remember, as a boy, seeing the Emperor's Own bearing down on our good Holtish troops—and I'll tell you, Margrave, that our own Holtish troops were every bit as good as any you'll find in Nyphien— and watching men turn and run that I and my father had sworn would have stood steady in the face of anything."

He was sitting close—too close—to both Leria and that annoy-ing Greta Tyrnael, leaving Thomen looking more abandoned than regally alone.

If that Greta chit carried, as she did, a feminized version of her father's good looks, she had none of the focused intensity that Ber-alyn had always admired in Willen Tyrnael. Beralyn would have rather that her every move be calculated, from the polished sardonyx stones that bedecked her hair to the way that the hem of her dress revealed too much smooth, shapely ankle, but Beralyn had the distinct impression that it was all just random, mindless, like the way she giggled loudly—too loudly—at every one of Miron's japes.

It had taken no great effort for Beralyn to say a few unkind words about that Greta to Thomen, although she had had to be careful to not be too transparent. This Greta would be an acceptable match—and if Thomen didn't choose her, there were easily a dozen young ladies of perfectly acceptable lineage in the capital at the moment, and more available on demand. Leria Euar'den had, surprisingly, been very useful in helping to arrange social occasions for visiting young nobles—she seemed to have quite a knack for it.

"Oh," Greta said. "I so dislike hearing talk of war on such a pleasant day."

Thomen smiled, and reached out and rested his hand on hers. "Then we shall have no more talk of war," he said. "Peace is not nearly as good for building legends, but much better for the building of nations."

The margrave mirrored Thomen's smile as he reached for his glass. "That's worth inscribing on the castle gates, if you don't mind my saying so. Still, that was very impressive." His hand fluttered again toward where the horsemen still stood in line.

The goo from the shattered gourds still dripped down the side of the decurion's face, but he stared unblinkingly ahead, as though not noticing.

"That aside, there are much more pleasant things to talk of than war," Miron said, "and even more entertaining to talk of than trade and treaties, if the Emperor doesn't mind me saying so."

"Like, for example, the various marriages that are in the offing?" the margrave suggested. "I understand that the lovely Lady Leria is soon to be married to your brother."

"Yes, the Dowager Empress was kind enough to summon her here to discuss the arrangements." Miron nodded. "It's quite a touching story. They were childhood sweethearts, you know, and Forinel took it into his head to abandon his duties in the barony, and hared off to the Katharhd, having all sorts of just wonderful adventures, although I've never quite heard all the details, and if there's some reason why they have . . . decided not to wait until the autumn Parliament, I—"

"I don't think you have ever asked your brother for any of the details," Leria said. "I think you've been far too busy complaining to everybody with a title, here and in Keranahan, that Forinel is unsuited for running a barony, and that you ought to—"

"Enough." The Emperor raised a hand. "I have no objection to us airing our minor disputes out loud. In fact, I insist on it—although I also insist that we don't do it in front of Margrave Den Hacza. After all, I wouldn't want any of you to give the margrave the impression that Holtun-Bieme is other than united."

"Of course it is not," Miron said. "It's utterly clear that the margrave is far too wise to not fail to think anything other than otherwise."

Miron's compounded double negatives were hard for Beralyn to follow, which was no doubt intended.

"Please." The margrave waved the issue away. "It's of no import—in fact, I find these open discussions something of a relief from the . . . strictures of King Belerus's court. It's far more free, and frankly more interesting, here. We have all these visitors from Pandathaway, Kiar, Enkiar—it seems that one can hardly take a step without tripping over some visiting envoy, delegate, or ambassador."

The fact that the margrave was mentioning that meant that he knew that the Emperor knew about those visitors. Not that Thomen had seen fit to mention so much as a word about it to his own mother.

Den Hacza took a pastry off a tray and nibbled at it. "Still, I'm curious as to the subject of this demonstration, if you don't mind my saying so. It's long been understood by all that the Empire's cavalry are perhaps even the equal of our own—our horses are better, of course, and I think I see more than a little Nyphien breeding in some of their mounts—but as for me, I'd find it much more entertaining to see a demonstration of rifle marksmanship. I think that my own troops have taken quite well to this new thing—although I must tell you that we've now more than a few deaf decurions; it's quite noisy.

"But one hears so much about your soldiers' accuracy with rifles, and while I'm not a skeptical man, I've always thought that it's much more interesting to see something myself than it is to hear tales."

Thomen nodded. "If you wish it, then it can surely be arranged."

"I'd like that very much," the margrave said. "Could we arrange for that, perhaps, tomorrow, before I have to take my leave? I—"

"Why not now?" Thomen pushed himself to his feet, and smoothed his tunic down around him, then held up a hand, fingers spread, when the rest started to rise. "Please, sit—this is just for . . ." He stopped himself, and shook his head. "No, perhaps everybody should see. It might be entertaining."

He turned to Beralyn. "Mother, would you be kind enough to lead anybody who is interested up to the ramparts—the eastern walk?"

He turned about, picked up another gourd from the table, and walked over to where the horsemen were still waiting.

Beralyn plodded slowly up the steps. Let the others follow at her pace. Everybody in the courtyard had, of course, decided to be interested, which was just as well for them.

The margrave was quickly at her elbow. "May I offer my arm?"

She forced herself to smile. "Why, of course, and I thank you."

She took hold of his offered arm, but didn't rest any weight on it. She was perfectly capable of walking, after all. She was old, yes, but she wasn't a cripple. She would have snapped at any Biemish who had dared to suggest that she couldn't walk up a flight of stairs by herself—she had had to do that once, only—but if somebody was going to offend the margrave, it wouldn't be her. Control was important.

What was Thomen doing, though?

The margrave asked the same question out loud. "I'm curious as to what the Emperor has planned. Would you consider enlightening me?"

She forced a smile. "I think that the Emperor would have told you, if he didn't want it to be a surprise." She tried to nod knowingly. "My son is a very straightforward man, generally, but he does like his little surprises."

The margrave didn't make any comment.

The party spread out on the walkway, looking down into the courtyard. They had passed the rampart where she had, far too long ago, scrawled Derinald's name in chalk, and she watched carefully to see if anybody glanced down toward it.

"You seem preoccupied," the margrave said. "If you don't mind my saying so."

"Not at all," she said.

"To which?"

"Excuse me?"

"Are you not as preoccupied as you seem, or do you not mind my observation?"

Smiling at him was easy. It was nice to be flirted with, as though she were a girl. It would have been nicer if the margrave weren't distracting her from watching the rest of the crowd that had spread out across the ramparts.

Nobody seemed to pay much attention to the buttress, one way or the other, as far as she could see. Which was unfortunate—if Tyrnael's agent in the castle was one of the local nobles, or one of the visiting ones, he or she was well disciplined. Which, she supposed, was to be expected.

The horsemen still stood there, and the servants were moving
about, removing glasses and plates. What was Thomen up to? And
where was he?

"Your attention, if you please," Thomen's distant voice called
out from—from *behind* her?

It took all her self-control to force herself to turn slowly and
look out onto the outer bailey.

Braying and snuffling, the herd of goats scattered madly as Thomen brought his borrowed horse to a prancing halt at the far end
of the bailey, almost under the outer wall.

"Your attention all, if you please," he said, again. His voice carried easily over the light breeze. "I'm pleased that my friend the
margrave Den Hacza has asked to see a demonstration of Imperial
marksmanship." He held up the gourd, off to one side. "I'm even
more pleased to be able to provide him with one that I hope he will
find entertaining."

No. He couldn't be.

"*Now!*" Thomen shouted.

A shot rang out, and the gourd exploded, fragments splattering
Thomen's purple tunic.

There was silence. Thomen reached down and pulled a cloth
from his belt, and wiped his face.

It was all very quiet, the silence shattered only by applause from
the nobles.

There should have been an alarm. There had been no announcement of rifle practice, and the guard held rifle practice outside the keep, anyway. The alarm bell should have been ringing
madly, and the Home Guard, every man of them, should now be
running frantically to their posts, armoring themselves as they ran.

But it was all very quiet as Thomen finished wiping his face, then slowly turned, and rode off, back toward the road from the outer gates to the inner ones. The whole guard had known that there was going to be an unscheduled shot fired.

Beralyn looked around, trying to see where the shot had come from. It couldn't have been from any of the guards on the outer ramparts—she would have seen it. And the shot had been distant enough—she could have sworn it had come from behind her—that it couldn't have been from any of the guard stations on the inner ramparts, either.

The only indication was a puff of smoke, carried across the inner courtyard.

The rifle shot had come from the donjon itself.

Beralyn didn't know much about this whole riflery thing, but she knew enough to know that even a good marksman, even the best marksmen in the Empire, would have found putting a shot into something even as large as a head to be difficult at that distance. The gourd was much smaller. The shot could easily have gone wide and low, and hit Thomen in the chest or even the head, and all the healing draughts in all the world could not bring back the dead.

Thomen was an idiot, to risk his life just to make such a point with the margrave.

Although the point had been made, granted.

The margrave shook his head. "Amazing." He was visibly shaken. "I've heard about how accurate the Empire's soldiers are, but I hadn't realized . . ."

Beralyn nodded slowly. "I hope that you never see how good they can be in the field," she said.

She left the obvious unsaid: that if the Empire and Nyphien ever went to war, it would not simply be a matter of noble officers sitting on a hill, out of the range of the nearest Empire bowmen, directing the carnage below. Even a man should be smart enough to worry about a rifleman, hiding behind a tree, able to put a bullet in a head from an almost unbelievably great distance.

Her son was still an idiot to have so risked himself, but he had made his point.

Beralyn would have some very strong words for him. Perhaps this time he would even listen. This sort of idiotic heroics was what had gotten that horrible Karl Cullinane killed. That didn't bother her for a moment—she would rather that his mother, if he had even had a mother, had drowned him at birth—but Thomen idolized that terrible man, and maybe he would see . . .

No. She would try, but he wouldn't listen to a useless old woman.

But that was for later, and would be private, and for now all she could do in public was to smile and nod, and pretend that it was all a typical sort of thing in the Empire.

15

The Assassin

There are things you never notice until they're gone, the assassin thought.

Like breath, say. He could breathe, at least. Or the freedom to move your arms and legs, which he couldn't do.

There wasn't much else to do except breathe and think, as he crouched motionless in the darkness of the castle garden, waiting for the guards to pass by again.

You can go tendays without even thinking about breathing, but the moment you duck your head under the water in the cut-off barrel you're bathing in, or take in a lungful of smoke from a campfire, you're reminded of how much you miss it.

Stretching and moving around were like that, now. He hadn't thought much about how good it was to be able to move, even a little, since the last time he'd been on an ambush. The body, it seemed, needed to move, and he simply couldn't, not until he was sure that the guard had passed by.

The baron was not cooperating; he was going to have to do this the hard way.

The cool night was cloudy, only a few stars peeking through breaks in the dark masses, while off in the distance faerie lights quickly pulsed from a bright red to a muted orange and an almost actinic blue, then back again.

He could have done without the faerie lights, but they were far enough off that they couldn't reveal his position, as long as he didn't move.

And he didn't move. He had been crouching long enough that his thigh muscles were complaining and his back muscles were doing worse than that, but he had long since learned to accept—and, if possible, give—far worse pain as simply a fact of life.

It was all just a matter of space and timing, after all. He had memorized the map of the castle grounds and the keep's floor plan long before, of course, and had, of course, immediately destroyed it as soon as he had. A mercenary soldier in the pay of the Empire would have no reason to have such a thing on his person, and once he had committed it to memory, there was no need for the map.

The gold had been a different matter. He couldn't leave it in his footlocker, as it was not at all uncommon for a signature knot to be learned by a thieving supposed comrade or a momentarily empty barracks taken advantage of by one less clever who would simply use a knife—what would Dereken, a private soldier, be doing with so much gold?

Some questions were best not asked, and if they were not asked, it would be easy not to have to have an answer. It had been much easier to keep the gold coins on his person until he could arrange a stint in the barracks saddlery, and stitch most of the coins inside his saddle, with a few substituted for the lead weights at the hem of his cloak, just in case he had to abandon the horse and saddle.

If everything went right—and he was determined to make it go right—he would ride away on his pay this night.

He smiled to himself. Yes, of course, only half the money had been paid in advance, but that half would have to do. The merchant who had hired him had sworn that the rest of his payment would be made when Forinel was dead, and he had dutifully agreed on a meeting time and place, several days hence.

He would, of course, be long gone well before that.

A hired killer was a loose end, and whoever it was who wanted the baron dead would have an easy opportunity to tightly tie up said loose end with sharp steel across Dereken's throat rather than tie it up much more loosely, with gold in Dereken's pocket.

Leaving him dead might solve the problem more neatly than that—Dereken's company, after all, was in the pay of Governor Treseen, and his dead body would point toward Treseen.

Which probably meant that Treseen had no involvement.

Who was his real employer?

Lord Miron was the obvious suspect—killing Forinel would as much as give the barony to him—and Miron was said to be spending his time in Baron Tyrnael's court these days, five or six baronies away, across into Bieme proper.

But who was supplying the gold didn't matter. What did matter was the gold in his saddle, and the geas that made it literally impossible for him to try to ride away from Keranahan until he knew that Forinel was dead. He had tried, of course, but he had found himself unable to take the eastern road; his fingers and feet wouldn't give his horse the commands, and he couldn't even try. He couldn't even find himself able to believe that he could leave without killing Forinel.

Well, that was part of the bargain, and while he would have broken his side of the bargain without remorse or hesitation, he had been unsurprised when his employer had left the room, and sent in a masked wizard to lay on hands and murmur words that could not be remembered. Actually, he was relieved about the implications of that mask, how it suggested that they wouldn't kill him when the job was done—it had actually made him consider, just for a moment, risking collecting his pay.

As, no doubt, it had been intended to.

He smiled to himself. You'd think that—

He froze in place, forcing himself not to breathe, not to move, not to look up at the ramparts. He had once avoided a night ambush when a flash of starlight on the eyeball of a hidden killer had alerted him, and he didn't intend to pass the favor along.

But there was no hesitation as the even footsteps sounded above; the two guards didn't even pause in their muttered conversation, and he more felt than saw that their attention was directed outward.

The man who called himself Dereken—shit, that was his name; his name was whatever he called himself at the moment, and never mind what they called him in other places—moved closer to the northern portico.

Peace had made them all lazy. There were square indentations in the ground where the barding would have been installed, turning the opening into a solid oak wall, and making the portico entrance even less accessible than the massive oak door on the front end of the keep. He wouldn't have been at all surprised if there were murder holes in the room above this entrance, as there surely were in the keep's foyer, giving defenders one last, probably pointless chance to hold off an enemy that had breached the outer walls.

But that wouldn't give the baron and his wife-to-be—and damn the geas for preventing him from taking the obvious opportunity after he killed the baron; the closest he had ever come to mounting a noblewoman had been that fat town warden's young wife in Enkiar during the cross-border raid two years ago—the opportunity to walk out of the great hall on a cool evening and smell the roses.

It would have been nice if the baron had done that himself this evening.

One quick looping of that spiked Therranji garrote over the baron's head, a sharp tug that would have probably broken the baron's neck and surely would have crushed his windpipe . . .

. . . and the man who called himself Dereken could have been on his way up the stairs to the ramparts, and down the outer walls, sliding down the rope much more quickly than he had climbed up.

But, of course, life never was easy, and a mercenary soldier should be used to that.

The keep itself was relatively quiet, but not completely. That was to be expected, even out here in the hinterlands. Dereken had served in Biemestren, and liked the constant noise and bustle of the capital. Standing guard as part of the Keranahan contingent, even at the outer ramparts of the castle, had been less boring than such things usually were, what with servitors from the castle kitchens bringing meals and tea—iced or hot, depending on the season. And some of those servitors had been young and female.

As he made his way into the great hall, the only sounds he could hear came from the kitchens. He kept near the walls—his employer had told him that there were more than a few squeaky floorboards between the old long table and the archway that led to the stairways up into the Residence proper.

He would have said this was too easy, but as a matter of policy and temperament he had never really accepted the notion of something actually being too easy, and this didn't seem like a time to start.

The Residence had originally been a three-story, fairly slim tower—built during one of the pre-Holtish dynasties; Euar'den, perhaps—but it had been expanded by a series of attached structures that included the great hall and the kitchen on one side and a combination servants' residence and officers' barracks on the other, and nowadays it was just a staircase, a widdershins spiral of stone blocks set into the wall of the castle itself, that opened on the second and third floors.

Every ten steps or so, a steel spike had been driven in between the immense blocks that made up the structure, but oil lamps were hanging from only about half of them, and of those, only two were lit, hissing and sputtering as they shed a wan, weak light that De-reken would just as soon have lived without, despite its weakness.

Light was not his friend tonight.

He blew out each of these as he passed. Darkness was his friend and ally, and while it was difficult to admit it to himself, it was good to have a friend and ally, for once.

He passed through the archway and into the hall, keeping close to the edge of the archway more out of superstition than reasoning. After all, if there was anybody awake to see him framed in the doorway, he was a dead man.

But there wasn't. No guard stood or even slept on watch outside the half-open door at the end of the hall. Dereken stood next to the doorway, and listened, silently, to the quiet sounds inside. It took him a moment to be sure that there were two in there—one barely snoring, the other simply breathing slowly, in sleep—before he walked in.

Under a rumpled pile of light sheets that were more than were needed on such a warm night, two forms lay, intertwined.

He closed his eyes for a moment, and tried to imagine strangling the baron, then—after gagging her, of course—quickly mounting the woman sleeping with him. It would be a stupid thing to do, but . . .

But he couldn't even get excited at the prospect; the geas bound his mind too tightly. He couldn't even produce a distant relish at the notion of slitting her throat quietly, which is what he would rationally have preferred to do, all things being equal. A quick poke would be available for a few coppers in the nearest town, after all, and if he found that inconvenient, there was always a peasant's shack.

Unless, of course, it wasn't Lady Leria.

The thought of that made him smile above and stiffen below. Hmmm . . . well, of course it wasn't the Lady Leria; it simply couldn't be a noble lady. Naturally, unless there had been a marriage, a noble lady would be keeping her noble hymen intact for her wedding, and as long as Dereken could make himself believe that, he could mount her, kill her, and be gone, and no matter that his supposed employer had made it clear that she was not to be touched.

Rumor had it that before Baron Keranahan's reappearance, there had been serious talk in Biemestren that she might even marry the Emperor himself. Her bloodline was certainly adequate—she was, by some accounts, rightfully the Euar'den heir to what had centuries before been conquered by the first Prince Holt and renamed Holtun. And the drawing Dereken had seen and the rumors he had heard about her face and form were intriguing enough. It would be interesting to poke a noble lady and see if they actually were any different.

But it wasn't worth risking even a few gold coins, and it certainly wasn't worth his life.

A bulbous oil lamp stood on the nightstand on the right side of the bed—the baron slept on the right side, so Dereken had been told—with the wick trimmed to the point where it barely flickered.

One of the forms mumbled something, then shifted on the bed, although the mattress itself didn't seem to move. You could never quite figure out nobility—if Dereken could have, he would have slept on the softest of soft down mattress that ever there was, but it looked like this idiot had one stuffed with horse hair or something.

Well, while Dereken was, by nature, a curious sort—his long-dead father had often beaten him for asking too many questions, and that, of course, had merely made him ask even more questions—he had learned, painfully, that there was a time and place for everything, including curiosity, and this clearly wasn't one of those.

He reached behind and loosened his spiked Therranji garrote with one hand, while he unsheathed his dagger with his other hand.

Loop the garrote over the baron's head, jerk it tight, then slip his hand over the baron's bedmate's mouth—surely not the Lady Leria, of course, of course, it simply couldn't be her, of course, of course—and it would all be over in a matter of the few final heartbeats.

He didn't waste any time as he stood over the baron's sleeping form; with one hand he yanked the pillow away, and slipped the garrote over—

It slipped through the baron's neck, slowed down no more than if it had been sliding through a wisp of smoke, a flame, or a bad dream.

Dereken tried to turn and run—but found that his muscles wouldn't obey him. The baron wasn't dead; he had just turned into some sort of intangible phantom, and the geas wouldn't permit Dereken to flee just because of that.

Light flared from behind him, impossibly bright, unreally silent.

He might not be able to run, but he could defend himself with his knife—and his feet, fists, elbows, and knees, if it came to that.

But as he started to turn, dropping the garrote to reach for the forearm-long dagger strapped to his back, the two bodies in the bed simply disappeared, gone in an eyeblink, like the flame of a candle that has been blown out.

"Stand easy, man, and it's just possible that you might live out the night," sounded from behind him.

He finished his turn, his fingers clutching at the dagger's hilt.

Standing in the doorway were two men. One of them, sixtyish and in gray wizard's robes, held a short stick—much shorter than the usual wizard's staff; it was about the length of a typical truncheon—out and to the side, not squinting in the incredibly bright light issuing from its tip, bathing the room in painful brilliance.

The wizard was about Dereken's height, and his thinning gray hair was bound back, tight to his head. His too-well-trimmed beard seemed awfully short and stylish for a wizard, and his smile revealed overly even, too-white teeth.

"My name is Erenor," he said. "Some call me Erenor the Great. Then again, others call me Erenor the Barely Adequate, At Best. I'm not offended either way."

The other one snorted at that. Half a head taller than the wizard, he was simply the ugliest man that Dereken had ever seen. His thick face was heavy-jawed, with sunken, piggish eyes under heavy brows that almost met his hairline. His mouth was too small for him, and his double chins should have belonged to a rich merchant, and not a soldier with the blue and gray piping of Keranahan at the hem and cuffs of his jacket, and a pair of singlesticks clutched firmly and easily in his hands.

A beard would have covered the double chins and the twisted mouth, but there was nothing much that could have been done about the sunken, piggish eyes.

The right thing to do, the only thing to do, would be to run for the window, to get away, and every instinct told Dereken that that was exactly what he should be doing, but . . .

But there was no baron here. Of course—the baron had been made to vanish, transported elsewhere. And that meant that this Erenor was something rather more than some local hedge-wizard, even more than the masked wizard that this employer had brought in to place the geas on Dereken.

But spells took preparation, and Dereken knew enough about wizardry to know that they could keep only a small number of spells coiled in their minds at one time, ready to be shot forth like the quarrel of a crossbow. Surely this wizard would have some spell ready to protect himself . . . but perhaps if Dereken threw something at him—his knife would do—to distract both him and the ugly man for just a moment, and then leaped through the open window and hoped that he didn't shatter his ankles on the stones below . . .

It was a slim chance, but his only one.

Until Baron Keranahan stepped into the room, a pistol in his hand, as well.

Dereken might be able to distract one long enough to flee, but the window was easily five, six steps away, and the other would surely cut him down before he made it halfway.

And Baron Keranahan? As a boy, he had fled his title to make his name adventuring in the Katharhd, and had returned just before the Emperor and Parliament were to award it to his half-brother.

Dereken could not leave him alive.

Forinel, Baron Keranahan was taller than either of the others, with the broad jaw and sharp cheekbones of the Keranahan dynasty, leavened perhaps by the dark eyes topped by almost feminine eyelashes that he must have inherited from his mother. He held a pistol leveled at Dereken, as well, but he held it awkwardly, unlike the short sword that he held in his right hand.

"I'm known as Forinel, Baron Keranahan," he said. "You have my word that if you'll tell me who sent you, you'll depart a free man. An outlaw, mind, guaranteed death if you don't flee the Empire. But a free man."

The wizard smiled at that, his eyes twinkling in the light from his faerie torch. "But there's plenty of world beyond the Empire, and some of us, at least, have been known to flee a town from time to time."

"Shut up," the ugly one said. His voice was higher-pitched than Dereken would have guessed it would be, but there was no anger or heat in his voice.

"But, I—"

"Shut your hole, Erenor."

Dereken was stunned at the wizard's reaction: he just bowed, albeit sarcastically, in feigned apology, although his eyes never left Dereken's face as he spoke.

"Yes, Pirojil, of course. I live but to obey."

Fleeing wasn't possible, and Dereken had no illusions that his geas would permit him to tell what little he knew. There was only one solution.

With no hesitation, no windup, he flipped his knife at the baron, hoping that it would land point-first.

But, just as the garrote had, it passed through the baron's neck, and clattered against the wall beyond.

And then the ugly one was upon him, the sticks swinging swiftly.

Dereken ducked under the first blow and launched himself at Pirojil, the ugly man, lashing out with fists and elbows and knees and head. He simply couldn't be taken—they would have him tortured to extract what little he knew, and since he would be unable to talk, all he had to look forward to was an eternity of pain.

But the sticks moved more quickly and deftly than they should have in the hands of such a clumsy-looking man. One battered his hands away to his sides, while a poke from the other caught him in the middle of the gut, sending him, retching, to his knees.

Distantly, he felt his hands taken behind him and bound, and he was dragged upright to his knees. The smiling wizard took hold of his shoulders—his grip was far stronger than Dereken would have guessed—while the other one lifted him by his hair, the length of one of his sticks resting against Dereken's throat.

"He's been made safe, Forinel," Pirojil said.

Again, the baron walked out from behind the door, holstering the pistol behind his back.

His face was emotionless, in a way far more frightening than anger would have been. He unsheathed a knife from his belt and took a step forward.

"No," Pirojil said. "You gave your word."

"Well, actually, no," Erenor said, "he didn't."

He held tightly to Dereken's right ear with one hand while the other lightly fluttered up and down Dereken's tunic, removing his purse and his spare knife, but missing the hidden garrote and small, scabbarded knife that Dereken had tied to his upper thigh. "It was my seeming, after all, and not really the baron."

"He would have killed *her*, too, Pirojil," the baron said. "He would have slit *her* throat in the bed, while she slept next to me, Pirojil."

Why the baron was pleading with an ordinary soldier was something that Dereken didn't understand. Enough to understand that, appearances to the contrary, this Pirojil was in charge here, and if Dereken was to bargain for his life, it would be with him, and not with the baron.

Erenor shook his head. "He's just a tool, no more than a knife. You don't blame the tool—blame the man who uses it. If you need to destroy a tool, go out into the hall and break his knife, and let's see if we can get some answers out of the man. At least he can talk."

"That is, of course," Pirojil said, "if you agree to that, Baron Keranahan. It's your choice, of course. It's your word."

"If he's not just another of your seemings, wizard," Dereken said. "I'd not take the word of an illusion."

This Erenor didn't look like a wizard—from his manner and the cut of his clothes Dereken would have guessed him to be a guard officer, possibly, or more likely a minor noble.

But . . .

"Oh, this one's no seeming," Erenor said. "Your little toys—and such nasty little toys they are, aren't they?—went right through my seemings. They're just illusions, after all. But the baron is solid enough, and that's easy enough to prove. You want to persuade him of that, Baron?"

Keranahan's brow furrowed.

"Please. I think he's still skeptical." Erenor jerked his chin at Dereken. "Touch him."

A vague smile crossed the baron's lips. He took a step forward and backhanded Dereken across the mouth so hard that lights danced in Dereken's eyes. His hand seemed harder than any noble's hand had a right to.

Dereken's own blood tasted salty in his mouth, but somehow the feeling was reassuring rather than frightening. It wasn't the first time he had tasted his own blood, after all.

"If you tell us everything you know, you'll live. Just as the seeming said." The baron's lips tightened. "Unless you ever, ever take a step in *her* direction. Just once, take just one step toward her, no matter how far away you are, and if you have time to look around you'll find me behind you."

Pirojil's face was impassive, but Erenor rolled his eyes.

"Always the hero, our . . . baron is," Erenor said. "Still, don't think he doesn't mean it—although how you're expected to know where she is all the time escapes me, as does how, if you're off in, say, Pandathaway, you're supposed to know which steps might lead you ever-so-slightly closer to her. But you get the idea."

"Do you swear it?" Dereken asked. "Will your wizard here put you under a geas?"

Erenor chuckled. "A geas? That's not my specialty. They're far too real and substantial for an illusionist like myself. And, other than that, if the truth be known—and it is, from time to time, if not often—when it comes to anything other than illusions, I'm not very much of a wizard at all."

Keranahan eyed him levelly. "I don't need spells to bind me to my word, and you do have my word."

"Take it or leave it," Pirojil said.

"Please leave it." Erenor chuckled. He was enjoying himself by all appearances, although Dereken didn't trust the appearances much. "I want to see how he does this." His eyes hardened. "And, truth be told, and even a liar tells the truth now and then, I'm ordinately fond of the lady myself, and don't much take to somebody who would have slain her in her betrothed's bed." He patted Dereken on the cheek, and the gentleness of that was more frightening than the baron's meaty slap. "You're quite lucky that she's not even in Keranahan at the moment, or the baron wouldn't be so generous."

Dereken would have shrugged, but Pirojil probably would have taken that as some sort of attempt to escape and beaten him senseless, so he didn't.

So be it.

I am under a geas.

He could say that, and they would understand why he couldn't say any more. He wouldn't have to say any more—they'd find some wizard to break it, like a locksmith opening another's lock. It would take time, and perhaps a trip to Biemestren—the Emperor's wizard was, understandably, the best in the Empire—and perhaps during that time there would be a chance to escape.

He would certainly try.

"I am under a—"

There are things that you don't miss until they are gone, the assassin thought, as his heart stopped.

He would have sworn that he had had rarely either heard or felt the gentle *thud-thud-thud* as it beat within his chest, but it had always been there, and now it was gone.

He'd always thought that when your heart stopped you were dead, immediately, right then and there.

Oh, he had heard stories about soldiers continuing the fight with an arrow or a spear or a bullet through their heart, and he had certainly learned early that a man didn't die right away simply because you'd run him through.

But it wasn't so.

He couldn't breathe, and if Pirojil and Erenor hadn't been holding him upright, he surely would have fallen, but he wasn't dead, he wasn't gone. He was still there. He couldn't breathe; he couldn't speak; his heart couldn't beat, and he missed breath and speech and heartbeating, but he was still there.

And then, slowly, the blackness swept up and over him until it became a light as white as that of Erenor's faerie flare, and his last thought was not to wonder if he was the only person ever to notice that a man didn't die instantly when his heart stopped, but rather to wonder how many before had learned this just before it all went—

16

Night in Castle Keranahan

Pirojil wasn't the one who liked to take chances. The man looked dead, yes, but . . .

He eased the tip of his belt knife into the dead man's neck, right over the artery, to let the blood ooze—and it oozed, not spurted, which meant that the assassin was indeed dead—before he let the body drop to the carpet.

He didn't even feel badly about it.

After all, the castle servitors would have had to take the carpet out and wash it anyway, after the way the would-be killer had voided himself in death.

Well, at least he hadn't gotten any on Pirojil. That was something.

Pirojil had smelled the shit-stink of men fouling themselves in death more times than he probably could count, and of a surety more times than he cared to count, but, still, he tried to avoid breathing through his nose until he led the other two out into the hallway. The fact that he was familiar with the smell didn't mean that he had to endure it unnecessarily, after all.

And killing?

There were times when killing bothered him, at least some, but not when the intended victim had been Kethol, and—

Not Kethol, he corrected himself. Kethol was gone, disappeared, lost somewhere in Therranj, living with the elves, maybe dead.

But definitely gone. The baron was not Kethol. The baron was Forinel, Baron Keranahan, who had recently returned from Therranj to the Empire of Holtun-Bieme to claim his barony, and if the connection would seem suspicious to anyone—and there was no reason why it would—why, the two men didn't look the same. Kethol—wherever he was, which certainly wasn't here, of course—was about the same height, but lanky and rawboned, with a shock of red hair that had lost only some of its fire over the years. Forinel was about the same height, but built solidly, and with features far more regular, and a much smaller collection of scars.

This wasn't Kethol. This was Forinel. It was getting harder and harder to remember that, and while Pirojil was certain that he would never speak it out loud, he had to constantly watch himself. This supposed Forinel's swordfighting technique was identical to Kethol's, but of the few swordsman Pirojil knew who were familiar enough with Kethol's style—not to mention good enough to detect that—none were here, after all.

And, also granted, his skills with a longbow were far beyond what Leria had remembered of Forinel as a boy—but it wasn't impossible that Forinel had learned the Way of the Bow while off in the Katharhd and Therranj.

Remember, he thought. This is Forinel, not Kethol.

It was important to keep reminding himself of that even in private. That way, there was less of a chance of him making a mistake in public, and he had come far too close to that the other night in Dereneyl.

Erenor looked insufferably smug as he tucked his lightstick away into a hidden pocket in his robes. Not well hidden enough—wan, yellow light shone through like a firefly that couldn't seem to turn itself off. Noticing that, Erenor muttered a low, guttural phrase and the light died even more quickly than the assassin had.

He shook his head. "Well, the only good side of this I can see is that it does give the baron some additional legitimacy."

Pirojil had decided, some time back, that it was easy to waste time trying to figure Erenor out. Half a heartbeat was far too much time trying to figure Erenor out—whatever else you could say for the wizard/swindler, his mind twisted in unpredictable directions.

"Very well," he said, "why is that a good thing?"

Erenor laughed. "You really don't see?"

"No, I really don't see," Pirojil said.

Erenor had taken to laughing a lot at Pirojil lately, and Pirojil would have found that irritating if he didn't already find just about everything about Erenor irritating. There was always the temptation to improve Erenor's attitude with a few cuffs and kicks, but Pirojil felt that if he started in with that, he'd never know where to stop.

Not that that was, necessarily, a bad idea.

"It's a good thing," Erenor said, his tone insulting in its patience, "because it guarantees that whoever sent our late, lamented friend is . . . well aware that the baron is home, and not elsewhere."

As usual, Erenor had a point, and, also as usual, he'd expressed it in a way that would probably make no sense to other ears. If somebody outside of the very small circle that knew of the deception and substitution had been listening in, they'd not have gotten a clue.

The noise had finally brought the guard—two soldiers, clad in light leather armor, were making their way cautiously up the staircase, the leader holding a lantern in one hand, and the other still had his sword sheathed.

Idiots.

Too afraid to disturb His Lordship's slumber to do their fucking job.

Pirojil blamed them, and Thirien, the idiot senile captain of the House Guard, and would have blamed himself if Erenor hadn't noticed the bad security and decided that—at least while Leria was in

Biemestren, answering the Dowager Empress's summons to attend her—Kethol should room with them while Erenor baited a trap with a seeming.

It had, at the time, seemed overly cautious to Pirojil. After all, you simply couldn't protect yourself from all dangers, everywhere, but you could wear yourself down to a nub worrying about it.

If it had been anybody but Kethol, his longtime com—if it had been anybody but Forinel, Baron Keranahan, Pirojil would have been more annoyed with Erenor for having been right than he would have been upset at another dead body.

Pirojil was used to dead bodies, after all.

"Is there . . . is there some problem, Captain Pirojil?" the taller asked. Pirojil tried to remember his name, but he didn't try too hard. The possibility of getting friendly with the Keranahanian troops was small, and the idea had less appeal.

"You know," he said, keeping his voice level with some effort, "that I once served as part of the Emperor's bodyguard. The Old Emperor—Karl Cullinane himself."

"Yes, but—"

He had intended to surprise the guards with the body, but a waft of air from the room brought the smell into the corridor. Nostrils flared and eyes widened.

"I don't know about you, but I always figured that letting an assassin in to kill the man I was supposed to protect was a bad idea.

"Don't send for the servants. Clean it up yourselves."

Their discipline had been ruined by somebody, Pirojil decided, when they looked to Forinel for confirmation. Well, at least they were looking to Forinel, and not Erenor.

Forinel just nodded. "Tell Captain Thirien we'll be out in the garden."

•   •   •

Kethol didn't know what he had expected to find out in the garden.

Another assassin, perhaps?

That would have been nice. Killing another assassin would at least have given him something to do, instead of standing around in the dark, wishing there was something within the range of his sword to kill.

Irritated, he flicked the tip of his sword at one of the rosebuds, shattering it into a brief shower of petals that were carried on the stiff breeze, leaving only a heavy scent behind.

He instantly regretted it. It wasn't the rosebush's fault, after all.

Kethol—he knew he was supposed to even think of himself as Forinel, but in private he had long given up on the idea—was out in the garden with Pirojil and Erenor when the guard captain approached, his sword belt clutched in his hand. Thirien looked more comical than military in his white sleeping shirt, bandy legs revealed from the mid-thigh to the tops of the boots that he had hurriedly thrown on.

Under the light of the flickering torches, the old man's hair was mussed from sleep, and his beard was flattened on one side, as though he had been sleeping on it, which he probably had.

His mouth worked once, twice, three times, and then he shook his head.

"My baron," he said, bowing. "It's evident that I've failed you." He held out his sword. "I'll have my things packed and be gone in the morning." He turned to Pirojil. "I know you'll immediately have the guard posts and schedules changed, in case my foolish tongue wags where it shouldn't. I'd swear to it that it won't, but it seems that my oath is worthless. You have my apologies, Captain Pirojil," he said. "As you know, I spoke openly against His Lordship keeping you on here. You will forgive an old man for listening too much to wagging tongues, I hope."

Even after all these years, Kethol couldn't read Pirojil's expression.

"I remember. Something," Pirojil said, "about how Keranahan didn't need to hire on any Cullinane-loyal lackeys, I seem to recall."

"Your memory fails you, Captain Pirojil." Erenor smiled. "No, I don't recall it was that kind, and I do remember what Captain Thirien said about a wizard who can't even come up with a death spell to kill the rats in the stables."

Which Erenor hadn't, not quite directly. But eating bowls scattered around the floor of the stables, filled with some horrid poison that, with a few muttered syllables, suddenly smelled like a particularly ripe Rumushian cheese, had served as well, although they had had to kennel all the dogs, who liked the cheese just as much as the rats did.

It had worked for a tenday or so—then the rats came back. The rats always came back.

Thirien eyed both of them levelly, and nodded. "Yes," he said, quietly. "It's clear that I . . . made too much of my years of service, and not enough of the way that age has sapped my wits."

Quite a change in his manner from just a few tendays before, when he had objected both openly and privately to the new captain—who had never served in Keranahan; who had been fealty-bound to, of all things, a Biemish barony; who had been given a rank that he had earned without ever having raised so much as a company to command; and who was so butt-ugly that it was said that even the two-copper whores in town wouldn't have anything to do with him.

Granted, Pirojil hadn't been brought on as an equal to the captain of the House Guard; his title—and the Imperial warrant that went with it—was intended to keep him out of the chain of command of both the relatively small House Guard and, more importantly, the occupying Imperial troops in town, under the command of Governor Treseen.

Thirien turned back to the baron, and held out the sword—still scabbarded—on the palms of his hands.

"I received this at the hands of your father," he said. "I swore to him, and I swore on it, that I'd serve him and his family with loyalty and devotion. It's clear that I've failed, and if it wasn't for your wisdom in ignoring the prattlings of an old man, my failure would have cost dearly. I'm sorry, boy."

The right thing to do would have been to accept the sword, to dismiss the captain from his service; the real Forinel would have done that.

But the truth was that Thirien hadn't betrayed his oath. He had promised to protect the real Baron Keranahan, not some imposter. Thirien could have even sat in a room and watched while somebody whittled on Kethol from ears to crotch to toes, and not been forsworn.

So Kethol shook his head. "You didn't swear to be right, and you didn't swear to be successful," he said. He reached out and folded the old captain's fingers closed, and squeezed them tightly over the scabbard. "Will you betray your baron now by walking away simply because you happened to be wrong this one time?"

Maybe that was the right thing to say, even if an imposter was saying it: Thirien drew himself up straight.

"It's not my loyalty that's in question."

"No, it isn't. Nor is the loyalty of any of the House Guard," Erenor said.

"Eh?"

Erenor was pleased with himself, as he usually was, when he had figured out something faster than somebody else, and Kethol had long since gotten used to that, although it didn't make him feel any less like wiping the smile from Erenor's face, preferably with a grinding stone.

"The killer," Erenor said, "was expecting Lady Leria to be here—he made that much clear before he died."

"But—"

"In fact, he expected that she'd be sleeping in the baron's bed. So did whoever sent him."

Even in the torchlight, the old captain's face seemed to redden. His lips were a thin, tight line. "If I can find the name of the man who thinks to speak in front of others of, of, of how the baron and his lady conduct themselves—"

"Oh, *please*." Erenor's smile broadened. "None of us are children here, and with the exception of the baron, none of us are nobles, either—just save that indignation for a moment. My point is this: is there anybody in the Residence—soldier, serving girl, stableboy or the like—who doesn't know that the Lady Leria left most of a tenday ago, summoned to visit the Dowager Empress?"

"No, but—"

"But the killer thought that she'd be here. I was watching—he had to overcome some resistance against killing her. Probably a poorly constructed geas."

"Powerful enough," Pirojil said.

"Pfah." Erenor wasn't impressed. "Powerful enough to persuade him to stop his heart beating, yes. But why would anybody go to the bother to protect the lady if he knew that she wasn't going to be here? Geases are tricky things—this one slowed this fellow down, had him spending too much time dealing with it, and not enough time to slit a throat."

"Which wasn't there," Kethol said.

"Not that he knew that. Which indicates that this was set up before Leria was summoned to Biemestren."

"Miron." Pirojil nodded. "Who is conveniently in Biemestren, too."

"Well, he's the obvious candidate—but just try to prove it." Erenor cocked his head to one side. "Although it is fairly suspicious, and should seem fairly suspicious to anybody. But you're missing the other part of it—it was as important to whoever sent him that she wasn't killed as that you *were* killed, Baron. And I think that's very . . . interesting, don't you?"

Kethol found it more reassuring. They weren't after *her*. Just him.

That was different.

He had always expected to die violently, ever since he had gone a-soldiering. Oh, the three of them had long been trying to squirrel away money to buy a farm or a tavern to support themselves when they hung up their swords, but he had never really expected to live to spend the money.

"Or, perhaps," Erenor said, thinking out loud—Kethol had always thought that Erenor liked the sound of his own voice too much, "perhaps that's what we're supposed to think."

"That may be." Thirien nodded. "But it's all too complicated for the likes of me," he said. "I always prefer something simple." He turned to face Kethol again. "If you're going to be generous enough to keep me on, my lord, then I'd best get back to my duties."

Walking away under the light of the flickering torches, the old man in the nightshirt with the bandy legs sticking out of his boots should have looked ridiculous, and perhaps he did, but Kethol couldn't help but find a strange sort of dignity in him, as well.

Which was, immediately, ruined by Erenor raising his voice.

"Captain?" He beckoned him back.

Thirien took being ordered around with the best grace he could muster at the moment. "Yes, Erenor?"

"You'd best take to more than your duties—we're going to have to leave the baron in your care for some time."

At a quick private glare from Pirojil, Kethol managed to keep quiet.

"I don't understand."

Erenor shrugged. "Well, when somebody sends a killer after, say, Jason Cullinane or his father, or even the Emperor himself, it's hard to figure out how to limit the field. We don't have that problem in this case. The only problem we have is in making the accusation stick."

"Treseen," Pirojil said. "It could be Treseen."

"Just because Leria has been pressing him on the account books?" Erenor shook his head. "He doesn't impress me as being that scared, that bloody-minded, or that stupid. And Treseen, of all people, knows well that Leria isn't here. Don't you think he would have mentioned that to some hired assassin?" Erenor stretched out a hand toward Kethol. "Do you really think that, say, Lord Sherrol or his idiot son are behind this?

"No. When somebody tries to kill the baron—and tries to be sure not to kill Lady Leria—we can be sure it's not somebody local, at least not somebody both noble and local. The lords are delighted that the baron has returned, after all, and they should be. Oh, maybe Lord Sherrol is a little irritated over that . . . unfortunate event the other night, and certainly his son isn't an admirer of the baron's, but this isn't their sort of thing. I can think of only one candidate, and he's in Biemestren." His smile broadened. "Which makes it all the more interesting that Lady Leria is at court, isn't it? I guess we could always include the Emperor—"

"—who is a fine and honorable man," Pirojil said, interrupting. "He's decent, and whether or not he had intended to marry the Lady Leria before Baron Keranahan's return, he'd no more have the baron killed to remove him as a suitor than he would, would—"

"Would bugger a baby in broad daylight?" Erenor suggested.

Kethol didn't like the image, but he had to agree. Nobles were by no means always noble, but the Emperor?

No.

"So it's not the Emperor," Erenor said. "But it's somebody noble, and the place to prove who it is isn't here—it's in the capital. It would be interesting to see just what Lord Miron has been doing there, wouldn't it?"

Thirien nodded. "Governor Treseen will have it looked into—"

Erenor interrupted him with a snort. "Governor Treseen is a thief—which doesn't matter, not in this—and an idiot, which most certainly does. I think Pirojil and I had better look into this ourselves."

Pirojil nodded, and Kethol silently agreed.

It made sense. It wasn't even unprecedented. He and Kethol and Durine—solid, reliable, dead Durine—had been used, after all, first by the Dowager Empress to rescue Lady Leria, and later by Walter Slovotsky to find Forinel.

Of course, things hadn't worked out the way anybody had planned, either time.

But there was something about being at the center of something important that seemed to have started appealing to Pirojil, despite his protestations that he preferred to be simply a private soldier.

Kethol knew how he felt; Kethol, after all, felt the same way. There was something about handling a problem himself, and not having to trust to his betters to see to it for him.

It was best that they look into matters themselves.

"I think you'd draw far too much attention," the captain said. "Wizards don't tend to travel much, and—"

Erenor held up a finger, silencing him.

"Then, perhaps, I'm not a wizard."

He muttered a few syllables, and he *changed*.

Kethol had to admire the gradualness with which it happened: thin, gray hair thickening and darkening into a warm brown while wrinkles smoothed and a bent stature became firm and upright. There was, of course, no hint that it was an illusion, no intimation that he might not be a strong man in his thirties, well muscled like a laborer, not an ancient, ascetic wizard.

"And that will hold how long, after someone so much as lays a finger on you?" the captain asked.

"Oh," Erenor said, "I think it may still work." He reached out and took the scabbarded sword from the captain's hand, and slowly drew the sword.

Strong fingers gripped it both at the hilt and near the tip, and Erenor seemingly almost effortlessly bent the sword into a shallow arc, then slowly let it go straight again.

He smiled. "I wouldn't think that Baron Keranahan would have given you a sword that could easily shatter or bend without springing back into shape; I'm pleased to be right, as I usually am."

"Pfah," the captain said. "Just another illusion. The sword never bent, eh?"

"Then, if you will," Erenor said, "grip my hand in both of yours, and squeeze."

Thirien belted the sword around his waist—it still looked silly, over a nightshirt—and gripped Erenor's hand in both of his.

The captain was in his sixties, yes, but his shoulders were broad, and his forearms thick. He squeezed; only the set of his jaw and the way the tendons on his arms stood out, drawn tight, like a bowstring, showed how much he was attempting to crush Erenor's fingers.

Erenor simply smiled more broadly and squeezed back, smiling and squeezing and squeezing and smiling until the captain, with a muttered oath, released his hand and nodded.

"Well, it's apparently a day for me being wrong," Thirien said. "I've never seen such an illusion."

Kethol would have been more impressed if he hadn't known that this was actually Erenor's real appearance, that the old, wizened wizard was just a seeming that Erenor—never much of a wizard, except for his illusions—assumed to give himself some stature.

And, for that matter, it had served Erenor to lure unwary travelers into making foolish wagers, as Erenor had done the first time he had met Pirojil. Kethol was vaguely irritated with himself that the thought of Erenor swindling the usually difficult-to-fool Pirojil brought him more amusement than the anger that it should have.

He wasn't surprised that the idea appealed to Erenor. Erenor was far too tricky for his own good, and liked things complicated.

Still . . .

"I'll be going with you," Kethol said.

Pirojil wasn't surprised. That was the problem with Kethol.

Heroism.

The idiot.

It always had been and it always would be. Kethol had his virtues—he was by far the best tracker and woodsman that Pirojil had ever known, a good horseman and a better swordsman, and there was nobody alive that Pirojil would rather have had at his back in a fight—but he had one horrible, constantly frustrating weakness: he always had to be a hero. His idiocy in trying to stop a dozen bandits single-handed was only the most recent example. It was only through luck, and because Kethol had long been partnered with Pirojil—and Durine, for that matter—that Kethol's insistence on being a hero hadn't yet gotten him killed.

Yet.

"Eh?"

"I said," Kethol repeated, "that I'll be traveling with you to the capital."

Erenor's smile was conspicuously absent. "I'm not surprised. Lady Leria is there, after all."

Thirien nodded. The explanation satisfied him.

The best way to lie, Erenor always said, was to tell a little bit of the truth. And there was some literal truth in what Erenor had said—it was no secret that Forinel had gone adventuring to prove himself to his childhood sweetheart, and it was no secret to Pirojil that Kethol was in love with her, as he would have been with any woman who would spread her legs for him without having first heard the sound of coins clinking into a wooden bowl.

Still, it made sense—absent Leria to guide him, Kethol/Forinel didn't know much about running a barony in general, or any more about the barony than a casual visitor to Keranahan would. Most of that, of course, could be explained by his long absence, and vague references to injuries, or simply avoided. But it was always best to keep the necessity for explanations to a minimum, and zero always did make the perfect minimum.

Besides, two ordinary soldiers—even if one of them actually was a wizard in (or was that out of? With Erenor, you could never be quite sure) disguise—wouldn't have much influence in Biemestren. Oh, certainly, they could get the ear of the Imperial proctor—Walter Slovotsky seemed to have some respect for both of their talents—but there was no guarantee that he would be in the capital, and while Pirojil thought that he probably could get a message passed to Leria, there was no guarantee. Imperial livery or not, you couldn't just walk into Biemestren Castle, not without a pass.

But, on the other hand, a baron, even a Holtish baron from an occupied barony, would not be turned away at the door, and could surely get an audience with the Emperor. Hang this around the neck of Miron—or his absent neck, if he wasn't in Biemestren—and that would go a long way to making things easier around here.

Pirojil wondered if that had been Erenor's plan all along.

"If the line is still up in Nerahan," Erenor said, "we can have a telegram to the proctor by late tomorrow."

Pirojil shook his head. Even if he wasn't known to Berten and Ernel, his captain's warrant should be good enough to get a telegraph message sent, but announcing their coming?

No.

Shit. After that little excursion along the border, Pirojil had been looking forward to some quiet time, helping Kethol—damn it, Forinel, Forinel, *Forinel*—to adjust to life as a baron. Nothing more dangerous than a deer hunt, he had thought, or maybe a boar at worst, and killing a boar, as long as you were hunting with somebody you could trust, was mostly a matter of paying attention and hanging on to the spear.

And there was every chance that by serving a baron—a phony baron, but one nonetheless—some coin would end up sticking to his fingers, to be added to the stash that he and Durine and Kethol had been building for years. In his mind's eye, he could see the size of his homestead in Barony Cullinane grow, tenday by tenday.

He didn't trust Kethol's judgment—baron or soldier, he was always too inclined to be the hero—and he didn't trust Erenor at all.

So why, he wondered, did he feel like somebody had breathed life back into him?

Pirojil decided that he wasn't only ugly, he was stupid.

But he still smiled. "Let's see . . . we'll need to raid the strong room for some coin, and I'm sure that you can find some Keranahan livery for all three of us," he said, thinking out loud, "and a message for the Emperor, sealed with the baron's seal, should explain to any Imperials what we're supposedly doing if we get stopped on our way. If the governor or any of his men show up here . . ."

"Since my loyalty isn't in question, you can leave that to me." Thirien shrugged, then smiled. " 'Good morning, Governor,' " he said, addressing the air in front of him. " 'The baron is out hunting boar or deer or more bandits, and is not expected back for a few days, at least, and can I offer the governor some refreshment?' "

He thought for a moment before he turned back to them. "In fact, it would seem to me to be best if the three of you equip yourselves with boar spears, and some packhorses, and cut through the forest until you reach the Nerahan road."

He chuckled as he clapped a familiar hand to Kethol's shoulder. "It won't be the first time I've let you sneak off to hare about, eh, Baron?"

Part 4

FINAL ATTACKS

17

Thomen

When the student outsmarts the teacher, it speaks well for the student—and probably better for the teacher.

—Walter Slovotsky

A h, to be Jung again," Walter Slovotsky said, "as Freud said with his dying breath."

As Aiea set down the serving tray, she gave him one of her not-quite-patented he's-making-obscure-references-again looks. She had taken to doing that a lot, lately.

Looking, that is.

She looked pretty, she looked at him, and she looked like she wanted something, which was also something that she was doing a lot of lately, so he did the obvious thing, which was to take her in his arms and hold her.

Which was also something that he had been doing a lot of lately.

She had been spending a lot of time with Thomen, of late. That actually bothered Walter a little, and it bothered him that it bothered him at all. He wasn't the faithful type, himself, although he had been far too busy for any dalliances at the last Parliament, and maybe he was slowing down, or maybe it was that he was just, finally, a happily married man. Hard to say.

He had just become a creature of habit, he decided. Habits were bad.

Just as well there was no assassin looking for *him*—at least as far as he knew—at the time. It wasn't like he hadn't ever had people trying to kill him. And not just people, either.

He guessed that that sour-faced Sister Bertha had been right when she wrote down "doesn't play well with others" on his report card, closer to four decades ago than he was comfortable thinking about.

Then again, if the universe—this one or the one on the Other Side, assuming they were different—had been designed for his convenience, he figured he was long due for a refund on defective merchandise.

Aiea had brought him lunch on a tray at his new office. It was a suite of three rooms on the third story of the Imperial Keep, just down the hall from where a trio from the House Guard kept a watch on the Emperor's bedroom—killing a man while he's sleeping is one of those old faithfuls that never quite goes out of style—and perhaps more than a little on the Imperial proctor.

She plopped down in his lap. There were moments when he didn't revel in how comfortable she was with him, but those were few and far between. Not at all like it had become with his ex-wife, Kirah, who had gradually grown to the point where she couldn't stand his touch.

"I've heard," she said, "that you've gotten a telegraph from Nerahan."

"The barony, or the baron?" he asked, trying to keep his voice light.

"Please." She frowned, and shook her head. "The baron. Which is surprising. As we all know, Bob," she said with a grin—she had apparently been spending too much time with her mother, Andrea, again—"Baron Nerahan has no particular love for you."

That was true enough. On the other hand, Nerahan was smart enough to know that word of Baron Keranahan's disappearance had to get to Biemestren quickly, and unfond enough of Treseen to mention that it had been closer to a full tenday since Keranahan had disappeared from there, in the wake of some unpleasantness that Nerahan was probably honest in saying that he didn't know anything about—but which meant, in any case, that it would be any day now that Forinel would be knocking on the castle doors.

He wasn't the only inbound baron, either—Jason Cullinane was on his way in, and Tyrnael, as well.

Not exactly Walter Slovotsky's idea of a good rump Parliament session, but nobody, apparently, was asking his opinion.

"And I'm not the only one who has heard. Garavar craves an audience, and Bren Adahan has wired you to stay put until he gets in, day after tomorrow."

"Is he bringing Kirah and Doranne?"

"He didn't say, which probably means that they are staying in New Pittsburgh." She smiled. "Which is fine with me—"

"I thought you like my daughter. Both of my daughters."

She ran her fingers gently down the side of his neck. "If you want to change the subject, that's fine with me. Yes, I like both of them. I don't even mind Kirah, not much."

"So—"

"But you should know that *he* says *he* wants to see you, too. At your earliest convenience, which means, I think, right now, or he'll send for some guards to march you over."

"You didn't want to mention that right away?"

"Well, you seemed to have other ideas. I thought Thomen could wait for a little while."

"Wonderful."

Not that he had any problem going to talk to Thomen. For once, he and Beralyn were in agreement about something: that stunt that Thomen had pulled with the margrave was something that Walter had been looking for an opportunity to chew His Imperial Highness out over, in detail, and with as much heat as it was safe to muster when chewing out the Emperor.

The shot had been impressive, granted. But, coming from the keep, it was a good hundred, hundred and fifty yards, at least, and it had just been pure, dumb luck that the shot hadn't gone totally wide—which would have ruined the effect of it all—or taken Thomen's fool head off, which would have been worse.

If Thomen was going to do something that risky, he should have consulted with his lord proctor, who would, Walter Slovotsky devoutly hoped, have been able to talk him out of it, and surely would have tried.

Walter wasn't one to quibble with success—and surely the margrave had gone back to Nyphien very impressed with the quality of the best of the Imperial marksmen—but shit, that had been stupid.

Walter Slovotsky was stunned by the abilities of whoever that marksman was—that had been a miraculous shot—but nobody was talking to him about it, although he had asked around, and Derinald was about as useful as usual, which was to say that he managed to occupy a body-volume full of air.

Well, things had already gone to hell, anyway, what with the still-living Derinald sending him daily notes about nothing much, and Walter watching and waiting for Derinald to show up dead, which he hadn't yet been considerate enough to do.

"The life of an Imperial proctor is never a quiet one," he said, straightening.

It could be worse. He rubbed his back, and tentatively straightened his knee—time to see the damn Spider again. Still . . .

It was good to get up and move; he had been working in just trousers and a blousy shirt, going over reports.

An empire—even a small one, consisting of just two countries that had been united in a war—flowed on a river of paper. There was the steel production in New Pittsburgh to go over, and the curiously small taxes just in from Niphael, despite what appeared to be a bumper crop of wheat and oats, and requests for Imperial troops to be moved from Adahan to Tyrnael, and never mind the Biemestren master-at-arms's report of increased brawls in the city and a particularly ugly rape-and-murder in Kernat Village, just down the river, that the armsmen were having no success at all in solving, and probably never would.

Someday, with any luck, reporting of such things would be done on some sort of regular basis, so that somebody could sit back and take a look at the whole picture. But it was hard to figure out how to plan a forest when you spent all your time pissing on little wild-fires.

He sighed as he stood and stretched, then picked up a leather vest from where it hung on the chair next to his desk. Long practice kept him from letting it collide with the desk. The thunking sound would have revealed at least one of the throwing knives just under the hem, or the slash pocket inside the vest that kept his revolver at just about the same position that a shoulder holster would have.

"So," he asked, "do you want to come along?"

"He didn't send for me."

"If he doesn't want you to stay, he'll ask you to go."

"No; but I thank you anyway, good Lord Proctor." She shook her head as she sank into his chair. "If you're not going to eat your lunch, I may as well." She picked up a meatroll and popped it into her mouth.

Damn. She even chewed prettily.

Thomen Furnael, Baron of the Prince's Barony, Prince of Bieme, and Emperor of Holtun-Bieme, was in the garderobe when Walter was admitted to the east wing.

Which didn't particularly surprise Walter. Even an emperor has to take a dump, every now and then, after all.

Walter waited until Thomen emerged from the garderobe, dressed only in a silken robe, belted loosely around his waist. He washed his hands in the washing bowl on the wall, then splashed some water on his face, and accepted a soft towel from the serving girl, dried himself, and handed it back to her.

"Thank you," he said.

She smiled back with very nice dimples, gave a light bow, and walked away down the hall.

Thomen retied his robe belt and stepped into a loose pair of slippers.

Put a pipe in his mouth, and a large-breasted blonde on each arm, and he'd look like a young Hugh Hefner.

"So nice of you to come to see me, Walter," he said. "You wouldn't have time, this fine afternoon, to go for a short ride with your emperor, by any chance?"

"I haven't been on a horse for a week or more," Walter said.

"Then I think it's about time. I seem to recall somebody telling me that I needed to get out more into the fresh air, not all that long ago. In fact, if I recall correctly, that somebody climbed into my room in the middle of the night—scaring me half out of my wits in the process—to tell me that, among other things."

"The Emperor must be mistaken. Everybody knows that the castle is far too secure for any such thing."

"It is now. I think. The north field?"

"Dealer's choice."

They had been speaking in English; whether Thomen preferred talking in English with Walter because they were less likely to be understood if overheard, or just to show off, wasn't one of those questions that you could ask an emperor. It probably wasn't out of any worry that they would be overheard. There are always security concerns about the emperor going for a ride, but the fallow fields to the north of the castle should be safe enough, as long as he didn't make a habit of doing it too often, and kept his habits irregular.

Walter didn't really think that any of the barons would be stupid enough to try to have the Emperor assassinated—everybody knew full well who would grab the crown if that happened—but it was never a particularly good idea to rely on anybody else's intelligence, and dangerous enough to rely on your own.

"As you wish."

"I'll go change into some riding clothes—" Thomen held up a peremptory palm. "Nothing in Imperial colors, mind—and then we can go saddle our own horses."

Yippy skippy. We can saddle our own fucking horses. Yay. "If I'm really good, can I muck out the stalls, too?"

"We'll see."

They were almost out of sight of the castle before Thomen said anything other than a few pleasantries.

It was a nice enough day. Birds chirped in the trees, and the wind came across the fields, carrying a nice, sunbaked smell, rather than the stink of the city. To the extent that Walter could ignore the company of Imperials on the road to the east, and the other one to the west, it was almost like they were alone, a couple of friends out for a pleasant ride.

"So?" Thomen asked. "Aren't you going to berate me for that 'silly little stunt' of the other day?"

"I kind of figured that your mother had already done enough of that," he said. "Not that she said anything about that in public—if you listen to what she's been telling Leria and Greta and all the rest of her attendants, it was a brilliant political move."

"You don't think so."

No, he didn't think so. It was the kind of fool stunt that Karl would have pulled. But maybe it was best to let Thomen work that out by himself.

"I don't like to argue with success. You sent the margrave home worrying more about the quality of our marksmen and our weapons, rather than trying to compare the numbers—although those are still in the Empire's favor."

"For now."

"And will be, for the foreseeable—unless you think that a bunch of clumsy Nyphs can start making rifles as quickly as Riccetti's engineers."

"You know, that's the one thing that I've never liked about you, or even Karl. You always tend to assume that we—we 'natives,' isn't it?—that we natives can never be as clever as you Other Siders."

That wasn't true. But there was no sense in arguing about it. It wasn't a matter of cleverness, but of knowledge, that had shaken up the Middle Lands—and most of the knowledge hadn't been even Karl's or Walter's. Take some basic sixteenth-century—Other Side reckoning—knowledge about how to make gunpowder, add in enough resolution to make some changes, and there would be changes. It wasn't as though Karl had thought he was some sort of Che Guevara—and Walter knew enough about the reality of that to know that that myth was bogus, too: he knew about Guevara running around like an idiot across Africa playing revolutionary, while the CIA had been busy making sure that everything he did failed embarrassingly.

Things had just happened, year by year, until Karl's revenge on the Slavers Guild had ended up putting a crown on his head.

Besides, Walter did think he was cleverer than most. That was just because it was true, after all.

Thomen shook his head. "I would have thought that your time at court would have taught you a little about how devious us primitive types can be."

"I noticed."

Thomen laughed. And then his expression grew somber. "I don't like conspiracies. I guess I'm more like Karl than you—I like things out in the open. I like it when there's a problem that you can solve by smashing something flat, or building something up, or even just making a deal. But too often it all gets . . . so complicated." His fingers played with his mare's mane. "An emperor should try to stay above it all, don't you think?"

Walter shrugged. "I guess that's what you have me for, in part, isn't it?"

"Perhaps. And since that's what I have you for, perhaps you'll tell me why Baron Keranahan is on his way here, with—so I'm told—blood in his eye."

"Probably to kill his half-brother. Not that I blame him. Not that you should try to stop him."

"Oh?"

"You know as well as I do that Miron was every bit as involved as Elanee was in that attempt on Ellegon."

"Know? Of course I *know*. I'm not an idiot, no matter that that's the only thing that you and Mother seem to agree on. It only makes sense—but if I start killing off nobles for things I can't prove, I am going to have to start worrying rather more about assassination attempts on me. I'd have to have something close to proof, and I don't."

"Proof might be provided. Good enough proof, that is."

"From you?" Thomen shook his head. "I don't think so. What are you going to do? Write up a confession and sign his name to it?"

"I don't think that would work, do you?"

"No, I don't think that would work."

Then again, maybe Derinald might be of some use after all. Perhaps Miron had made some sort of late-night, drunken confession? The trick would be in the details—but the details could be worked out.

It was something to think about. "Well, at least I'm not idiot enough to risk my life just to make a silly little point about Imperial marksmen."

Thomen smiled. "Oh, that."

He reached into his saddlebag and pulled out a metal tube. It looked like a pistol barrel—it *was* a pistol barrel, complete with a little nipple at the breech.

Thomen curled his fingers around it.

"If you put a small powder charge—it doesn't take much; a quarter-charge will do—and stick a gourd on the end of it, then mash down on the primer with, say, a ring that you're holding in your hand, it does make a fairly impressive display, as long as you time it correctly. You have to watch for the flash from the supposed marksman, and not wait for the bang." He looked at the tube for a moment. "Gift from the Engineer—he thought that it might be nice for the Emperor to have a little something he could hide in his sleeve, just in case, say, somebody . . . untrustworthy slipped into his room one night."

"Lou didn't say that."

"Not in those words. But it was a nice gift, and while he did say he hoped I'd never use it, it's nice to have. Particularly with all these guests we're about to be having, eh? You never know."

It didn't surprise Walter that Thomen's information was as good as his own.

"Willen Tyrnael is here, already," Thomen said. "He got in late last night, so here. He's staying with Lord Lerna."

That Walter hadn't heard. Why was Tyrnael staying in town with one of the nobles, rather than at the castle? It would be interesting to know. Not that that necessarily meant anything—Tyrnael and Lerna were thick as thieves.

Thomen smiled. "Well, it appears that, for once, I've heard something before you do. What do you think that's all about?"

"Maybe Tyrnael just wants to see *Birth of an Empire*, again. I've heard that the fellow who plays me is really very good."

Walter hadn't seen the play all the way through. He had tried, mainly because Aiea wanted him to, but it wasn't his cup of tea. He doubted that he ever would develop much of a taste for local theater—the actors seemed to have to bray every line out at the top of their lungs, and if Walter was going to sit in a darkened room, he just preferred it to be a private darkened room, and his companion to be solitary, and female.

"And Jason?" the Emperor asked. "Why is he on his way in?"

"Well, you can blame me for that—when I heard that Leria had been summoned by your mother, it was only a matter of time until Baron Keranahan was on his way, so it occurred to me that having Jason around as a moderating influence might be a good idea. Besides, anything that a Cullinane says will sound to Pirojil like it's coming from a burning bush, and Forinel does seem to value his opinion."

More to the point, both Kethol and Pirojil could be counted on to listen to and obey anything that Jason said. But since Walter didn't officially know that Forinel was Kethol—and he very much hoped that Thomen didn't know it at all—that probably wasn't a good thing to bring up.

"Good enough of a reason, I suppose." Thomen nodded. "My mother thinks that he's coming here to take the crown, although I haven't heard of him bringing an army with him, and, then again, my mother always thinks that any time he comes into the capital, it's to kill me and take the crown." Thomen seemed to consider it for a moment. "That doesn't seem to be terribly likely—at least, not to me."

"No. Your mother's wrong." Walter shrugged. "But beyond that, if I told you I knew what was going on, I'd be lying."

"And you wouldn't ever want to do that, of course." Thomen seemed to consider it for a moment. "Well, I've got an explanation. Let's just assume that Lady Leria is pregnant, and that we—note the Imperial 'we,' Walter—have decided to sanction her marriage to Forinel and perform the ceremony now, rather than waiting until the fall Parliament, by which time her condition will be obvious."

"Some of the other barons won't be happy about that, and they—"

"We'll make that up to them at the fall Parliament." Thomen nodded. "I think that the marriage of an emperor should be an even better social event, don't you?"

This day was full of surprises. Thomen's self-destructive stunt had turned out to be nothing of the sort, and now he was getting married.

Walter thought about saying something to the effect of, well, *since Frankenstein could find a bride, it shouldn't have taken you so long*, but Thomen was unlikely to understand the Other Side reference, despite his long acquaintance with Walter and the Cullinanes, and probably wouldn't be amused even if he did understand it.

There are so many wonderful times in life to keep your mouth shut.

"Do I get to know who the new empress is? Or do I have to wait until you lift the veil?"

Thomen smiled. "I had a thought. It occurred to me that one way to cement my hold on everything would be to marry into the Cullinane family, joining the Old Emperor's line with my own." He cocked his head to one side.

Aiea?

Thomen held a hand. "Oh, Walter, relax—I'm just teasing. I'm not going to divorce you from your wife so that I can marry her. Besides, she said no." Thomen was enjoying this too much. "It would have made sense, though—if I could have gotten her to go along with it." He shook his head.

"No, I'll be marrying Greta Tyrnael, come fall. My mother assures me that she is fully capable of bearing children, and she's pleasant enough, at that." He tilted his head and looked carefully at Walter. "All you have to do is make sure, after she does bear me a son, that her father doesn't have me killed so he can be regent until his grandson is old enough to take the throne on his own."

"That can probably be arranged."

"Good. For now, though, I'm giving you a job: keep the peace. There are to be no problems between Forinel and his brother that might mar the pleasantness of the ceremony, and I think I will have you make the announcement about my own pending nuptials. Or do you think it should be Bren Adahan?"

"Is that a serious question? Or are you just having more fun with me?"

"Pretend it's a serious question."

Actually, that made sense. The Furnaels and the Adahans were hereditary enemies, although in truth both Thomen's father and Bren's father had put that aside, during their time. Bren Adahan had been the first Holtish baron to have his barony returned to him—although as Thomen's chief minister, he had been more involved in Imperial matters than baronial ones.

We are an incestuous little bunch, Walter thought. Walter had married Karl's daughter, and Bren Adahan had married Walter's ex-wife, Kirah. Walter had finally gotten to the point where he could think about Bren and Kirah in bed, and just hope that they had a good time, rather than resenting that Kirah could bear Bren's touch without screaming, something that had been impossible for her with Walter in the last years they were together.

"Bren," Walter said, "I think. I'm called a lord proctor even though I'm no noble—"

"You are the lord proctor because I say you are."

"That's my point. Bren has his own lands, and a title that goes back to the first push in the bush in Holtun. I'm an outsider, and I always will be. Title—and authority that goes with it—or no. So it should be Bren, and not me."

Thomen nodded. "I can go along with that. So we'll keep this all in a low, gentle key. You be sure to greet Baron Keranahan when he arrives, and I'll hold you responsible for his conduct. We'll just have a sudden marriage, and let all the barons giggle and chortle quite privately about why that's necessary, and—"

"The ones who aren't invited aren't going to be laughing."

Thomen smiled. "Why, Walter—I think I have put another one over on you. *All* of the barons will be here. I've sent word to the ones close enough to get here on their own within the next three days, and I've enlisted a little help to collect the other barons. And a few others, who aren't quite nobles, as well." He seemed to consider the matter for a moment. "In fact, if matters of security weren't quite so tight at Lord Lerna's country estate right now—if that cook of his hadn't been unable to have a note smuggled out—you might have heard about all the people there, and others arriving every day."

Walter was getting too old for this. Thomen had arranged all of this without him having so much as suspected, and he even knew who Walter's spy in Lerna's estate was—well, one of them, anyway.

Walter nodded in admiration. The student had indeed surpassed the teacher, and if Walter had been wearing a hat, he would have taken it off.

Wait a minute.

Even with the telegraph it would take days to get—

"What do you mean, 'a little help'?"

Thomen touched at the dragon symbol emblazoned on the medallion around his neck. " 'I have friends in high places,' isn't that the way it's said?" he laughed. It was a good laugh, a sincere laugh, and Walter couldn't help but join in.

"You take care of Baron Keranahan," the Emperor said, "and you let me take care of . . . of everything else. Like the Empire, say?"

Walter was trying to think of a comeback and failing miserably, when Thomen kicked his horse into a fast canter.

"Now, see if you can catch me," he called back, over his shoulder.

He gave a quick tug on the reins, and barely touched his heels to the big gelding's side. He was halfway across the field before Walter could even start his horse galloping.

Part 5

ENDGAME

18

A Reception, Of Sorts

A small troop of Imperials picked them up a few dozen leagues
outside of Biemestren.

Pirojil had been expecting that—neither he nor Erenor
had missed the way that that armsman in Kernat had ridden off in
the direction of the telegraph station just a little too quickly, although Kethol hadn't noticed.

He had barely spoken an unnecessary word in days. He was
probably preoccupied with figuring out how Forinel would have
called Miron out, and rehearsing the words in his head. Over and
over and over and over.

Pirojil hadn't argued with him. There was no point in arguing,
not when Kethol had made up his mind—distracting him, on the
other hand, was another matter.

What he had planned to do was to get the three of them settled
in in some inn down in the city, and then himself go up to the castle
and make arrangements for the baron's reception.

But this was just as good. Better, even.

Regardless of what Kethol thought he was going to do, he could
hardly go up to the gates of the castle, bang on the door, and call
Miron out.

Days of hard riding hadn't done anything to calm him down,
but that was to be expected.

It had actually been a pleasant few days, in a strange sort of way. Their Keranahanian livery had proclaimed them to be three ordinary baronial soldiers, and it was nice for Kethol and Pirojil to pretend to be something that they actually were, even if it was only for a while, rather than pretending to be something that they weren't.

And it was probably even nicer for Erenor to be pretending to be something he wasn't while looking entirely like what he was, although, with Erenor, you could never tell.

The Imperials' armor gleamed brightly in the sun, despite the light coating of road dust. The stylized golden dragon on the shields that lay slung across their horses' withers proclaimed them to be from the Emperor's Own, Gold Company.

"Greetings, Baron Keranahan, Captain Pirojil," the captain said, tilting his cap back to wipe the sweat from his brow, "and I take it this is the wizard, Erenor, in a clever disguise."

It was a hot day for wearing full armor, and they wouldn't have been wearing it on an ordinary patrol. It was the sort of ceremonial greeting that Forinel would have to get used to, when he visited the capital.

Pirojil knew the captain. Gaheran, one of Garavar's sons. He had his father's oversized head and large nose, and his nostrils seemed to flare in time with his horse's.

"A good day to you, Captain Gaheran," Erenor said. "I'm flattered that you recognized me."

"I hadn't. But I've been told by the lord proctor to expect three of you. I saw the baron at Parliament, although briefly, and I've known Pirojil, albeit slightly, for years. I was told by the lord proctor that if there is one of you who doesn't look at all like he could be a wizard, I could be sure that it was Erenor."

His smile revealed teeth that were too white. "Since you look even more like an ordinary soldier than the baron and captain do, you would have to be Erenor, wouldn't you?"

Erenor touched his knuckle to his forehead. "Well, somebody has to be."

Lord Ellermyn's city home was a small compound that wasn't really within the city proper, although Pirojil could have probably lobbed an arrow over the city walls from the decorative outer gates.

It was newly built—the Ellermyn family was apparently doing quite well in the mercantile trade. The trees that lined the entry road would someday arch over the road in a green canopy, but for now, they just looked small and naked and silly, and he could have kicked any of them over as he rode by.

Ellermyn himself greeted them at the front gate, and dismissed their escort. Gaheran gave in with surprisingly good grace, but it was no surprise to Pirojil that he and the rest of his troop waited patiently while Pirojil, Kethol, and Erenor dismounted, and didn't turn his troop around and ride away until after he had himself witnessed the horses being led away.

"I'm honored, of course," Ellermyn said, "that you'll be gracing this little cottage with your presence until the wedding.

"I've already some guests waiting for you—in the sitting room. We'll have, I hope, ample opportunity to chat later. But all—*both* of them insisted on seeing you the moment you got in, and well, now appears to be that moment."

Walter Slovotsky and Bren Adahan were waiting for them in the sitting room.

Kethol reminded himself that he had met them only once before. It wouldn't do to seem to know too much about either of them, and Pirojil had cautioned him that if Slovotsky went to scratch at himself, he was just to act as though the proctor was scratching at himself, and not smile when he noted where the hidden weapon was. *Kethol* knew that Slovotsky habitually walked around with enough knives to equip a company of peasant field-dressers—but *Forinel* shouldn't know that.

The proctor and the baron made an unlikely pair: Slovotsky, pleasantly homely—although he always carried himself as though he thought otherwise—in his typical, middle-class blousy white shirt, leather vest, and trousers, without so much as a signet ring decorating any of his fingers, ran those fingers through his thinning hair, mussing it even further; Adahan, impeccably dressed in a well-fitting cream-colored linen tunic and matching leggings that set off his shock of perfectly combed brown hair and dark eyes, sat back in his chair with his fingers tented. Two seals hung from almost preposterously thin golden chains looped around his neck, as though declaring that he couldn't go through an hour without finding some document that needed either his ministerial or baronial seal.

Both men had taken off their swords, and looped their belts over the backs of their chairs; they had apparently been sitting, sipping at whatever was in the dew-beaded glasses on the tables next to their chairs.

"You've had a long few days—and they are about to get longer, over the next few," Slovotsky said, waving the three of them to chairs.

What would a baron do? Kethol was getting tired of asking himself that question, so he just sat. Pirojil and Erenor should be waiting for the baron to say something—and the two of them were looking at him, waiting for him to say something—so he did. "It's a strange welcome to Biemestren, to be accosted by a troop of the Emperor's Own."

Slovotsky smiled. "Well, it's strange enough for a baron to be trying to sneak into the capital."

Bren Adahan nodded in agreement. "I know you've been away

for years, but the . . . conventionalities need to be followed." He sipped at his drink.

Pirojil made a face. "What's so conventional about Miron trying to have the baron killed?"

"Yes, there is that." Slovotsky nodded. "I see your point. I've only gotten the bare bones of the story—I'd like the full details."

Erenor rose and poured himself a glass from the pitcher on the side table. He took a sip and nodded. "Hot or cold, there's always better tea in the capital—and you'd best ring for some more. This may take some time."

Kethol let Erenor talk. Erenor liked to talk, and it took some time.

"The problem," Walter Slovotsky said, "is a matter of proof. And all the proof is dead."

Kethol didn't like hearing that, but Pirojil saw the point, and so did Erenor.

The wizard nodded. "I'm so very sorry that this assassin inconvenienced us all by dying, but we had other concerns at the time."

Slovotsky laughed. "I can see that. But the point is, I've gotten orders from the Emperor himself that the baron is not to get himself involved in a duel with Miron." He tilted his head to one side. "A fight that I'm not entirely sure you could win, anyway."

Kethol leaned forward. "Everybody knows that Miron—"

"No." Bren Adahan—Baron Adahan—held up a hand. "Everybody *knows* nothing. Many people *suspect* many things; I think you're probably right.

"I *suspect* that Miron was involved with his mother's plot. I *suspect* that Miron carefully set up the assassination, and then left for Biemestren, so that he could be here and not there when the news arrived. I *suspect* that he's thick enough with Tyrnael and enough of the other barons that he could reliably have counted on getting the title—particularly since there is no other candidate with a good claim. I more than *suspect* that would be a terrible precedent—there's lots of younger brothers of baronial heirs around, and I don't think it would be a good idea if it became easy for them to improve themselves simply by getting their big brothers knocked off.

"I had a brother, once." His eyes closed for a moment, then opened. "He was supposed to inherit my barony, and I'd give up all of it, every bit of it, if only he was here today."

They all were silent for a few moments. But then Walter Slovotsky grinned. "I think your brother would have given up dying, too, in exchange for Barony Adahan."

Adahan's lips tightened. "There are times when you press me too far, Walter."

"Then I'd better stop, eh?"

Adahan gave him another glare, but it had the feel of him doing something that he had done a thousand times before, a man reacting to a habitual irritation with a habitual frown.

He shook his head. "What I don't understand is Beralyn's role in all of this, and I can hardly ask her."

"I don't think she was involved in this," Slovotsky said.

"That's unusual," Adahan said. "You're usually ready to accuse her of anything from a deep conspiracy to being the cause of too many mosquitoes in spring."

Slovotsky grunted. "I just don't believe in things being that much more complicated than they appear. If she and Miron were somehow conspiring—and why she should want Baron Forinel dead—"

"Other," Pirojil said, "than that she had seemed to have picked Leria to be her new daughter-in-law. I heard that from you."

"I remember you when you were just an ordinary soldier, Captain; it wasn't all that long ago. You didn't used to interrupt your betters so easily." He looked over at Kethol. "If you're going to keep him around, I think you'd better have some words with him." He cleared his throat and took another drink. "As I was saying—before I was so rudely interrupted—she and Thomen have already picked another winner of that beauty pageant, and while I think she'd have been more than bloodthirsty enough to have Forinel bumped off to get him out of the way, I don't think there's any reason to believe her that reckless, not with the matter settled.

"So that explanation is out, unless you want to assume that she is one of those people who likes to complicate things just to make them more complicated, and she isn't." He nodded, smiling in agreement with himself. Walter Slovotsky was always his own best audience. "And since the new empress is going to be Tyrnael's daughter, that should pretty much quiet Tyrnael down. And with you marrying Leria in . . . two days?"

"Three," Adahan said. "Arondael and Forsteen just wired that they won't be able to get in until the day after tomorrow, so we've pushed it a day back." He shrugged. "It's all going to seem unseemly hurried, in any case."

Slovotsky's smile broadened. "But that's the best part—we marry Forinel off to Leria, and then we announce the marriage of Greta and the Emperor. The giggling—and these nobles giggle like a bunch of schoolgirls—about the reason for the rush should persuade Miron that his chance to end up as Baron Keranahan will be over in less than a couple of dozen tendays.

"The Emperor's marriage gives Tyrnael what he wants, which means that he doesn't need any support from Miron, as Baron Keranahan, and a little bit of politicking on your part, Baron Keranahan, should solidify that—you've got yourself a new best friend at court: Willen Tyrnael. Let him think that you're just trying to ingratiate yourself with the Emperor's future father-in-law." He spread his hands. "I'm not like my late friend, the Old Emperor. I don't like things that end with a bang, and a boom, and a river of blood on the floor. We end this with a marriage, and an announcement, and some laughter, and then we get on with our lives."

There was an obvious problem with all that. Even Kethol saw it, but Pirojil spoke up first.

"But that still leaves Miron thinking that he is in line for the barony, if the baby is a girl, or if Leria and Baron Forinel happened to get killed—"

"Oh, I think there have been far too many assassination attempts around here, of late. Never mind who was responsible for the one on Jason, or the one on Ellegon—which also easily could have killed me, for that matter, although nobody ever seems to make a point about that!—and never mind who was responsible for this latest attempt on Baron Forinel.

"I think that, properly pointed out, the rest of the barons will start to look more than a little askance at this whole . . . epidemic, and will make it clear that they and the Emperor would be none too eager to reward all this promiscuous assassination with lands and titles. Bad precedent.

"The only question is how to make that clear to Lord Miron, and give him something else to think about."

Erenor nodded. "You have that all worked out, I take it."

Slovotsky nodded. "Which means that somebody with some credibility just has to have a few words with Lord Miron, and somebody with some credibility has to arrange for him to be more than a little busy with other matters." He looked over at Baron Adahan. "Baron Minister, do you happen to know anybody with that sort of credibility?"

Adahan smoothed a hand down the front of his linen tunic as he smiled back at Walter Slovotsky. "Well, yes, Lord Proctor, I happen to be a person with that sort of credibility, and I've got a little surprise in store for Lord Miron. A particularly ugly surprise, with a foul temper, and a very newly noble father who needs a son-in-law to berate—but we can save that for tomorrow night, at the castle," he said, walking over to the bell rope.

He pulled it three times, then twice again. "In the meantime, Captain Pirojil, if you and Erenor don't mind joining the proctor and me out in the garden, I think that Baron Keranahan might be interested in other things."

"I don't think I want to be left out," Kethol said.

"Oh, I think you do, all things considered." Walter Slovotsky smiled.

The hallway door opened, and *she* stood there, smiling.

19

The Widow

Beralyn suffered through the long meal without complaint. The table in the great hall was far too crowded. It seemed that each and every minor noble within three days' travel of the capital had decided to grace the castle with his presence, and their appetites, and it wasn't just the main table—the side tables in the great hall had been pressed into service, as well, and other tables carried in from elsewhere in the castle.

Beralyn didn't have much of an appetite. That had been an ongoing problem, of late.

It wasn't just the meal. The long table was crowded with food, dozens upon dozens of serving dishes piled high with baked yams and turnips, roasted meat from any animal that could walk or fly; fish baked whole, and stewed.

Everybody else seemed to be eating like a bunch of famished peasants, but it was all she could do to pick at her plate. Food seemed to have lost its appeal.

While they had not made the formal announcement, yet, nobody had failed to take note of the fact that Greta Tyrnael was presiding over the head of the table with Thomen, her father beaming at the two of them. She chattered and laughed much, and ate little. Probably the moment that she was married, she would swell up like a poisoned thumb.

Willen Tyrnael was obviously happy. He had gotten what he wanted, and he hadn't even had to do what he said he would.

He murmured something into his daughter's ear, and then excused himself. While she had noted that he had had his glass refilled from the water pitcher, not any of the wine bottles, she was surprised it had taken him this long. The man must have had a bladder made of good steel.

That little weasel, Derinald, was still somewhere around, although he had not, of course, been invited to dine with the nobility.

Which was fine with her. What wasn't fine with her was that what she thought of as the Cullinane delegation had all been seated near the head of the table, along with the happy couple. She included Baron Keranahan in that—he was far too friendly with them. Forinel listened much and spoke little, while Leria smiled, and chatted, and laughed with that horrible Jason Cullinane—and his sister, and his mother—like the lot of them were old friends.

There was far too much Cullinane presence in the hall, and particularly near the head of the table. They had even seated that Pirojil character with Forinel, although at least they had relegated his wizard, Erenor, to one of the side tables, where he and Henrad conversed in low voices while Henrad's apprentices acted as servants, keeping an almost impossibly large stream of food and drink coming.

It was, apparently, too much drink for all of them, particularly Erenor.

He should have known better, a man his age. Both of the wizards rose, Erenor even less steady than Henrad was, and more staggered than walked out of the hall, Henrad bowing toward the Emperor and making some comment about how the two of them were going off to discuss some fine points of magic.

She caught that Lord Miron smiling. He wasn't fooled, and neither was she. The two of them were just going to sleep it off. Henrad was bad enough, but from the way that Erenor staggered, she would have been willing to bet that he would be on his knees, vomiting, before he was halfway to his room.

Beralyn was relegated to the foot of the table—supposedly also a position of honor, but it didn't escape her notice that Thomen kept her surrounded with minor city nobles, with the only person of any substance nearby being Vertum Niphael, that fat, word-slurring drunk.

"A lovely couple," he said. She ignored him, but he pressed on. "Has it been decided when the formal announcement is going to be?"

"No."

Nobody has asked me, she thought. If it had been up to her, of course, the announcement would already have been made. What did it matter to her if that took all of the excitement out of the immediate wedding? It might even be better for Forinel and Leria, although she didn't much care about that—people were laughing behind his back about their carelessness, and any distraction would have been in his interest.

She pushed herself away from the table, and walked, wordless, to the main entryway, servitors and soldiers alike scattering in her wake. At least somebody was showing her some respect.

Just a little longer, she thought. If she could just push this ancient, pain-ridden body for a couple more years, long enough to see a grandson, she could close her eyes forever.

In the meantime . . .

She walked outside, into the courtyard, and headed for the stairs up to the ramparts. The night was cool, but not so chilly that her shawl wouldn't keep her warm, as long as she walked.

Below, the river sparkled in the starlight, and a distant pair of faerie lights were playing touched-you-last on the horizon, one of them lazily pulsing through a series of greens and blues, while the other rapidly flashed from red to yellow to green, always settling on red again after it had made contact with the other.

Somebody was waiting for her at the next buttress, his face hidden in shadow. Not that she had any doubt who it was.

"Good evening, my Empress," Willen Tyrnael said.

"It is an evening, at that," she said.

"And you see nothing good about it? Our families about to be joined? That doesn't please you? That saddens me more than I can say."

She nodded. She understood the implied threat. "I'll make no objection. Truth to tell, I have no objection to the girl. Just to her father."

"Me?" He started to place a hand, fingers spread, on his chest, but stopped the motion. "You object to me?"

"You didn't keep your word to me. That Derinald is still alive, and you said you'd have him dealt with."

Although she never should have believed him. Derinald was the best evidence of her involvement with the attempted assassination on Jason Cullinane. She had been an idiot to think that he would remove that evidence, and the hold that it gave him over her.

"My word? I don't recall ever giving my word that I would have Derinald, or anybody else, killed."

"You said—"

"I said, my Empress, that if you wanted somebody killed, you should chalk the name on this buttress. As, I take it, you did. I think you assumed that I had some agents in the castle, who would report that to me, but I don't think I ever said that I did. In fact, I'm quite sure that I never said that at all." He smiled. "Just as I never said that, if you chalked somebody's name on this buttress, I would have that somebody killed, and I chose my words very carefully. I told you that I am your friend—and indeed I am. I told you that I would wish to protect you from your own recklessness—and indeed I do."

He laid a gentle hand on her arm. "There's only one minor matter to be attended to with regard to that, and we can attend to it shortly. But for now, there's no need for all this concern. It's all worked out very well, for your family, for mine, and for the Empire. I would wish that your son was half as taken with my Greta as that Forinel is smitten with his Leria, but I don't insist on it. Do you?"

"No." She shook her head. "But—"

"But that may come, in time. I hope it will." He shook his head. "But enough of that. You and I have one more task to perform, this evening, and then we can take our ease. I'll see you in the hall, in but a few moments. Let's eliminate this problem, you and I, once and for all."

He quickly turned and walked away before she could ask what he meant.

20

✠ Pirojil

Pirojil was alone in his room on the third floor of the barracks when there was a knock on the door.

"Yes?"

The door opened, and Erenor stood there. He looked like a wizard again: his lying face was lined with age, and there were grease stains on his beard. He had a bundle under his left arm, something about the length of a sword, wrapped in a blanket.

"A pleasant evening to you, Captain Pirojil," he said. "You've been missing a lovely dinner."

"I don't remember being invited."

"Well, you weren't, not exactly—but, after all, you are a captain in the Emperor's Own. A captain of march only, granted, but a captain nonetheless. I think you ought to think seriously about joining the festivities, and now would be a very good time—and I'm not just talking about having a few sips of wine while pretending to drink more than a few glasses; I've done enough of that for all three of us this evening."

He produced a folded piece of parchment from his robes. "Here's a pass, although I doubt you'll need it. I don't think that anybody will stop you—people are coming and going under the watchful eyes of the House Guard all the time right now, and while you might need a pass to get into the keep, you are within the keep, after all. Aren't you?"

"What is this all about?"

"I think you ought to go to the great hall," Erenor repeated. "You might bring this along with you." He smiled. "And your own sword. If you please. It's not necessary, by any means, but there's a certain . . . sentiment attached."

He tossed the package onto the bed, and turned to go.

"Wait."

Erenor shook his head. The smile was gone. "No, I don't think I want to wait, not anymore. The time for waiting is over."

Pirojil reached for his arm, but Erenor muttered a single, utterly unrememberable syllable, and vanished.

Pirojil stood, for a moment, in silence, alone.

There was something wrong here. Yes, Erenor liked to act mysterious—but most of that, most of the time, was just an affectation.

What was this . . .

Pirojil's blunt fingers pulled at the knots that held the package shut, until he just gave up, and retrieved his mind and slashed the twine.

A sword lay inside the blanket.

Pirojil had seen that sword before, many times. It was similar to his own: the blade was thin, but heavy enough to cut as well as thrust; the hilt was plain, wrapped with brass wire, and the pommel of polished bone, not brass like his.

It was Durine's sword.

Somebody had taken great pains to polish the rust out, although there was nothing that could have been done about the pitting of the surface of the blade. But the edge was sharp, sharp as a razor, sharp as Pirojil's own sword.

What was—

Pirojil quickly belted his own sword around his waist, and wrapped Durine's sword back up in the blanket. It wouldn't do to move faster than a fast walk—that would draw attention from the guards—but it was all he could do to keep from running.

21

Kethol

It takes a lot of time to make things go right,
but they can all go to hell in a heartbeat.
—Walter Slovotsky

It was wrong, but you could get used to something being wrong, Kethol decided.

There were some things right about it, though, or at least that felt right. Like the way that Leria sat to his left, maintaining the flow of conversation around them, bringing him in and leaving him out just as deftly as Durine and Pirojil would have used their bodies and their swords to make an opening for Kethol.

He had talked about the trap that they had set for the Kiaran bandits, and had pushed the dishes away so that he could draw a little map in beaded water on the polished table, and while Leria had pretended to chide him for taking on the bandits all by himself, the Emperor had been impressed, and seemed to accept Kethol's explanation that all he had been doing was stalling until help arrived.

He had tried not to brag—he had given most of the credit to Pirojil and the peasant archers, and made sure to mention Wen'll by name, but nobody had seemed to take that very seriously.

"You think," the Emperor said, "that these peasant archers

might someday be as useful in defense of the Empire as they were in opposition to it."

Leria nodded. "He certainly does. We were just talking about that this afternoon, about how regular formations and watches—and bounties on any bandits—would let the peasants deal with things themselves, probably without any need to call in Imperial or baronial troops—"

"Except to count the bodies," Kethol said.

"Please." Greta Tyrnael interrupted. "I'm sure that the two of you have much better things to talk about than some smelly peasants."

"I would hope so," the Emperor said.

Kethol would have said something, but Leria, without looking at him, had laid her hand on his thigh and given him a peremptory squeeze.

"We talk about many things," she said. "And I know he's already decided, once occupation is lifted, to hold regular peasant archer formations."

"Not the worst idea I've ever heard." Walter Slovotsky nodded. "I've been saying for years that's the trouble with the occupation— you don't want to beat the peasants down, and that's what the occupation has done, all too often. Shit, that's what too many of the Biemish nobles do, by habit more than anything else."

"I don't know." Jason Cullinane shook his head. "When I ride into a village, I'm not entirely sure I want to be greeted by a bunch of armed men."

"Get used to it, kiddo—it's going to happen. In fact . . ." Slovotsky stopped himself. "But let's save that discussion for another day, shall we?"

Willen Tyrnael had rejoined them while Walter was speaking; he nodded, and sat, patted his daughter gently on the hand, then reached for his glass. "It sounds like quite an interesting discussion; let's do have it, sooner than later." He turned to the Emperor. "If I may . . . ?"

Thomen shook his head. "I know we agreed that we would save the other announcement until after tomorrow. I think it would be unseemly to preempt this evening's celebration with any other—"

"No, I wasn't going to talk about that. But I do have a confession to make, and I hope that I can get the attention, and perhaps the forgiveness, of the entire party." The smile was gone from his face, and his expression was grave. "Please bear with me for a moment."

The Emperor cocked his head to one side. "Willen? What *is* this about?"

"Indulge me for a moment, please," he said, rising. "If I may have everyone's attention, please," he said, raising his voice. "There is a matter that needs to be discussed now, and not later."

The room got very quiet.

Kethol looked around, and noticed that Pirojil had, without him noticing it, entered the hall. He stood near the door, a blanket-wrapped bundle in his arms. He looked like he wanted to say something, but Tyrnael had already started talking.

"As you all know, after his mother's attempted rebellion in Keranahan, Lord Miron sought and found shelter with me.

"He swore to me—and I believed him then and I believe him now—that he had nothing whatsoever to do with Elanee's treachery. It hasn't escaped my notice, or the notice of anyone else, I'm sure, that there are those who don't believe him."

Like me, for one, Kethol thought.

He wanted to say something, but Leria was shaking her head, and he trusted her instincts in this better than his own.

Miron smiled. "I thank the baron for that, and, of course, what he said is true."

Tyrnael nodded. "And he's also been accused of having tried to assassinate his brother, recently. I don't believe that, either." He turned to Kethol. "For the sake of us all, I am going to ask you to believe that."

Kethol shook his head. "So who was it?"

"I don't know. I just ask you to accept that. I ask you to hear me out on another matter before you decide whether or not I can be trusted.

"I ask that, because I, in an indirect way, have broken a trust. Baron Cullinane, I owe you an apology. I know who was behind the attempt on your life before Parliament. That person let it slip, once, in a drunken moment. That person thought—wrongly, I swear—that I would see an attempt on you as in my interests, as a way of bringing me closer to the throne. My line is the oldest, save possibly for the Furnael line, of the Holtish barons. If—and I hope that it never happens—the Emperor were to die without leaving an heir, my claim would be, I think, the best. Save for only yours, Baron Cullinane."

"I gave up the throne," Jason Cullinane said. "I did it because I thought that Thomen would be a better Emperor than I could be, and I'm pleased to say that he's proven me right."

"I believe you," Tyrnael said. "And I believe—as I hope all of us believe, from the lowliest noble minor, to the Dowager Empress herself—that you meant it when you abdicated, that you understood that there was no going back." He nodded, in agreement with himself.

"Without going into other matters—yes, Emperor, this night should be free of that other announcement—I make no apology for my willingness to see my grandson, someday, on the throne. I make no apology for having thought, once, that I was the proper heir to the throne.

"But I do apologize for this: I let this matter rest, this matter about which I need to talk to all of you. I didn't want dissension among us. We have challenges, and dangers to face, and I thought that—"

"Wait." Beralyn stood. "You promised—"

"Yes, Dowager Empress, I promised. When I discussed that with you just this evening, you told me that I was wrong when I had decided to let this matter go, that we could not just let the common belief that it was the Slavers Guild who attempted to kill Jason Cullinane be believed.

"You brought me to my senses, my Empress, and I will always be grateful for that. Didn't you? Did you not say that Miron must be called to account?"

Miron was on his feet. "That's not true—"

Tyrnael faced Miron. "I swear, on my honor as Baron Tyrnael, on the honor of my family, that you confessed to me. That you thought you would ingratiate yourself to me, and though I found what you had done to be disgusting, I confess to this company— and I ask the forgiveness of you all—for not having dragged it out into the open before now."

He turned to Kethol. "Your brother has brought disgrace upon your family, even as my silence has brought disgrace upon mine. My weakness—no, my cowardice—stopped me from acting before, and I'll understand if you don't choose to forgive me for that cowardice."

Jason Cullinane was on his feet, and he was smiling. "Baron Tyrnael's word is good enough for me. Shall we have a trial, or," he said, "would Lord Miron be good enough to step outside for a moment?"

"No." Kethol stood. He didn't need to see Leria nodding to hope that she was. And if she wasn't, it didn't matter. His eyes were fixed on Miron. "He's mine."

He didn't know what Forinel would have done, and it didn't

matter. Maybe Forinel would have wanted Miron to stand trial, or maybe he would have taken this shameful assassination attempt as a blot on the family's honor.

Kethol didn't know much about honor, and less about trials.

But he knew a little about loyalty. Kethol and Pirojil and Durine had served Karl Cullinane, the Old Emperor, and the three of them had been the only survivors of the Emperor's Last Ride, which had cost Karl Cullinane his life.

Kill the Emperor's son?

No.

Not even over Kethol's dead body—Pirojil would be there to follow through if Kethol failed. It would end here, and it would end with Miron's body on the floor. And if there were more bodies than that, that was fine with Kethol.

Leria seized his arm, but he shook it off.

No.

He'd defer to her about many things. She was smarter than he was, and better educated, and she had a feel for things that made his head ache.

But *she* hadn't stood on the sand in Melawei, among the bits of bone and flesh that were all that had been left of the man that Kethol had served. Kethol had. And *she* hadn't sworn, flat of her sword balanced on the palms of her hands, that she would protect that man's son and daughter—and Kethol had done just that.

This disguise of too-solid flesh didn't change that, not for a moment.

The whole hall was silent until Thomen nodded. "So be it: it's your privilege, Baron Keranahan. It's your decision. Shall we sit in trial, with your brother being judged by me, or—"

"No." He turned to Miron. "You and me, right here, right now."

Miron smiled. "And if I win? When I win? Will all agree that these vile charges are untrue?"

"I guess you'll have to wait and see," the Emperor said.

Like all the others, both Kethol and Miron had hung their sword belts on the back of their chairs. A sword was not just the right of a noble, it was the badge of a noble.

"If I may," Pirojil said, stepping forward. "I have two matched swords here, one of them mine. I have befriended the baron, and I hope he will honor me by using my sword." He drew his own sword and laid it on the blanket next to the other.

Miron quickly walked over to the blanket and picked up Pirojil's of the swords. "I think I'll take your sword, Captain Pirojil. I suspect that the other one has been tampered with."

Pirojil picked up the other sword, and gave it a few practice swings.

"No," he said. "It's just fine. There was some rust on it, I think, but that's been polished off. Tampering with swords is your sort of thing, Lord Miron, not mine." He turned to avoid putting his back to Miron, and walked backwards until he reached Kethol.

The sword felt right in his hand. And it was familiar.

Pirojil nodded. "This used to belong to a friend of mine," he said. "I think he would want you to have it, don't you?"

Pirojil didn't have to show him the bone pommel for Kethol to know that it was Durine's sword.

Why Pirojil had retrieved it from the cave, and why he had arrived in the hall just in time, was something that Kethol would ask him later. If there was a later.

Pirojil leaned forward. "Forget everything else," he said, as though he had read Kethol's thoughts. "Kill him now, and we'll have time to talk about it later on."

Leria was nodding, too.

Miron shrugged himself out of his short jacket, and tossed it to one side. "Well, I wondered if it would come to this, although I probably should have been wondering *when* it would come to this, eh?" He raised his—Pirojil's—sword in a quick salute, then gave it a few practice swings. "A bit heavy and clumsy, but it will do, it will do."

The whole world, the whole universe, became Miron.

The marble floor was clear from the main table to the side tables.

A noble would have said something. The real Forinel would have said something. He would have talked about how his brother had disgraced their house, their line, perhaps. He might have challenged him or taunted him, or both. He would have said something.

But Kethol just walked, slowly, quietly onto the floor, and took up a ready position, not bothering with a salute at all.

He wasn't even angry, not at the moment.

Fighting had nothing to do with being angry. He didn't believe for a moment that Miron hadn't tried to have him—and worse, much worse, her—killed. But it wasn't a moment for anger, and it wasn't about him.

They engaged tentatively in a high line, then Miron feinted low, but Kethol met the flat of his blade with the flat of his own, and slashed at Miron's arm as Miron retreated.

Miron dropped the point of his sword, and beckoned with his free hand. "Come on, come on. Surely you can do better than that. Try me—let me see if I can beat you as easily as I did when we were boys."

A noble duelist would have felt Miron out, probed his defenses, tried to lure him into an attack, seeing if he could manage a stop thrust on an extended arm.

But Kethol ran at him, in full extension, and batted Miron's blade out of line, not caring for a moment that its tip pierced his sword arm, paying no attention to the agony that shot through him, at the way that his fingers refused to grip the hilt of the sword, at the way that it fell from his fingers.

Because Kethol had another arm.

He snatched the hilt of Durine's sword with his left hand, twisted it away and into his own hand and gripped Miron's shoulder with every bit of strength that he had in his wounded arm, and ran him through, then twisted the blade, back and forth, over and over and over again, ignoring the way that Miron's deafening screams became weaker, and weaker, until he fell silent, and Miron slipped from the blade, to fall to the floor.

Kethol tried to take a step, but he slipped on the blood-slickened floor, and fell, hard on his side.

Leria was at his side, trying to hold his wound shut, careless of the way that blood was spattering across her arms and chest. He wanted to say something, although he didn't quite know what.

It was just as well, perhaps, that the darkness came up and washed over him.

He probably would have said something stupid.

Part 6

POST MORTEM

22

✠ Farewells

Leria looked down at his sleeping form. He was so awfully pale. Filistat, the Spidersect priest, laid a reassuring hand on her arm. "I'm sure that he will be well," the priest said, smiling genially, as he twitched his fingers to beckon his familiar back toward him.

The huge spider walked across Kethol's chest, and, preposterously silent, made its way down his right leg before scampering into the ample recesses of his brown robe, peeking several eyes out from between the folds of the robe, from where it perched on top of the priest's ample belly.

"Not even a scar, and he will probably be awake shortly," Filistat said, giving a quick look at where Pirojil stood by the unlit hearth. "You could wake him now, I suspect, but I think it's best to let him sleep." He looked over at Pirojil, again, who was sitting at the table, still cleaning the swords, and frowned. "If you had gotten the healing draughts to him quickly enough, he wouldn't have lost so much blood. Still, that's the only thing that I can find wrong with him. Hand healing draughts?"

"No." Pirojil shook his head. "Eareven—but I used a lot."

"Apparently." Filistat ran a thick finger down Kethol's shoulder. "I can barely feel where the wound was, and even the healing structures beneath the skin are fading—I don't think he'll have any loss of motion, or any pain, for that matter." He smiled. "Not that the pain would mean much to a man like him, but a man should have two good arms." He nodded, agreeing with himself. "He'll be well."

Forinel's—no, she would call him Forinel, but he would always be Kethol, inside, and that was more than fine with her—Kethol's face was still deathly pale, and his chest only slowly rose and fell as he breathed.

But he *was* breathing, after all, and the priest said he would be well, and what more could she ask for?

Pirojil didn't respond to the priest other than by nodding. He had been at Kethol's side more quickly than Leria would have thought he could move, and he had gotten the small brass flask of healing draughts out very quickly, and even giving Miron's head a final kick hadn't slowed him down.

But the blood had been spurting in a red fountain from Kethol's arm. Pirojil had pressed down on the wound, stemming the flow long enough for Leria to pour the sick-smelling liquid over his hands, and into Kethol's shoulder.

They made a good team, the three of them.

She drew the blanket up over him. He was so cold and pale that, for a moment, she had to lay her hand on his chest to be certain that he was still breathing.

The priest smiled. "He just needs to sleep, and eat, as much as he can, until he can restore the blood he lost. Rare beef, broth—any kind of broth, as long as it's salty—and he should be up and around in a day or two." He looked up at her. "He'd best not travel until he's fully recovered. Give him a tenday of rest, though, and he should be well enough for travel, and other . . . strenuous activities."

He looked like he expected her to blush, but she just stared levelly at him, until he looked away.

"I guess," he said, "that I had best be going, as there's no more need for me here." With that, he gathered his robes about him, and bowed himself out.

The three of them were alone, although maybe she should just have thought of it as the two of them, given that Kethol was asleep.

Pirojil looked for a long moment at Kethol's sleeping form, then went back to the small table where he was busy cleaning the swords. A small pile of clean rags lay on the table, and a growing heap of bloody rags lay on the floor next to him. He ran a clean cloth down one of the blades, then examined the cloth thoroughly, nodded, and ran his thumbnail down both of the sword's edges and gave the bone pommel a final quick polishing before setting it down, and picking up the other, the one with the brass pommel, shaped like a walnut.

"Is there something I can do to help?" she asked.

"If you'd like." He nodded. "You might want to oil that sword," he said, gesturing at the glass bottle on the table. "Have you ever done that before?"

She shook her head. "No, I can't say that I have."

"Don't stint—you want to be sure you get the oil into every crack, because if you don't, water will find its way in, one way or another, and it will rust. I think that Forinel will want to keep that sword, all in all. You might even find that it's what he usually chooses to carry, rather than a noble's rapier. A little more awkward to carry about than a smallsword, perhaps, but . . . I don't think anybody would question his choice of it, do you?"

"No, I don't think so, either." She shook her head as she accepted the sword, hilt-first. It was lighter than it looked, although the grip wasn't quite right in her hand; the finger impressions in its wire-wound leather surface were too large and widely spaced for her, and probably for Kethol and Forinel, too. "It is the sword that he dispatched his traitor half-brother with, and I can see how nobody would question why he would choose to belt that sword around his waist."

"Yes." A thin smile played across his thick lips. "That's what I was thinking, my lady."

" 'My lady'? Really, Pirojil." She arched an eyebrow. "After all we've been through together, don't you think you can call me Leria?"

"I don't think so." The smile was gone. "It wouldn't be a good idea to get in the habit of first-naming my betters, all things considered, my lady," he said, gesturing at the seat across the table from him. "More than a little unseemly, perhaps."

"If you insist."

"No." He shrugged. "No, I don't insist about much." His lips twitched. "Insisting isn't the sort of thing for the likes of me, or Kethol, or Durine or Erenor. But . . ."

"But?"

"But I think, as I said, that getting into bad habits is, well, a bad habit in and of itself, my lady."

"As though Forinel or I would ever call you to account for being too informal with us, or permit anyone else to do so." She snorted. "Really."

"Well, I don't know if I'll have any occasion to worry about that," he said casually—too casually. "Not in the near future, in any case."

She sat back. "Why not?"

"Because, well, when the two of you go back to Keranahan, I'll not be going with you."

His eyes never seemed to leave the surface of his own sword, and he wrapped a bit of cloth around his index finger and rubbed heavily at a spot that she was sure was utterly free of anything except gleaming steel and oil.

"It's not just that questions might be asked—as they would, eventually." He found another clean spot and rubbed at it, as well, and still his eyes wouldn't meet hers. "I think that Forinel has the right . . . partner to lean on, in more ways than one, and another old

soldier who should be off soldiering isn't going to be of any real
help, not in matters political. Besides, Governor Treseen is not overly fond of me, as well, and it would be a bad idea for me to be in
his way—I'm getting a little tired of every damn thing going wrong
in Dereneyl being my fault."

What is the real reason, she couldn't ask. *Is it me?*

He might as well have read her mind: his ugly face split in a
smile as he shook his head.

"I'm about done in, my lady." True enough, his face was lined,
and if anything the wrinkles had deepened in recent days. "I've had
enough of blood feuds, and enough of killing people I don't know
well enough to have any grievance with—and I don't need to make
any new enemies at the moment." He tapped at the captain's tabs
on his shoulder. "Besides, I'm spoiled—I've gotten used to having
some rank, but I'm not vaguely qualified, not even as a captain of
march. Governor Treseen was right about that—I've never even
raised a company, after all, much less commanded one. It would be
a bit hard to go back to being an ordinary soldier, after all this."

But you don't have to, she didn't say.

"So what are you going to do?" she asked. "Back into Baron
Cullinane's service?"

He chuckled. "Jason Cullinane was born to go look for trouble,
and I'd just as soon he have somebody else watch his back, somebody a little younger, and a lot faster—both of wrist and wit. Better
for him. As for what I'm going to do, I'm not sure, but I do have
some ideas, and I'll just have to see if I have the money I need to
do something about them."

"If it's a matter of money," she said, then stopped herself.
"Please. But money can be come by, if . . . ?"

He shook his head. "No. Kethol and Durine and Erenor and I
managed to put some gold aside, over the years, and I had occasion
to take it out and look it over the other day, and it's gotten to be

a fair amount. It's starting to be too heavy to carry around, if the truth be known, as it sometimes is. Even after I give Erenor his share, there's probably enough for me to buy the tavern that the three of us used to talk about, as long as I don't insist on it being in the capital, and I don't. Maybe over in Cullinane, or perhaps in Adahan.

"The Three Swords Inn, maybe? That was the name that we always talked about, the three of us. Durine would have liked that, and, well, with Kethol off in Therranj, I don't think I'll hear an objection to me using his share of the money, or the name." He looked up at her. "If he ever shows up to claim his share of the tavern, that would be fine with me, but I somehow doubt that he will, eh?"

"There are other possibilities, you know," she said. "Dereneyl, for example—"

"Dereneyl, my lady, is governed by Treseen, and even after the baron takes over, I've made a few enemies there. I seem to have that habit. It would be difficult for Lord Sherrol and his son to hold a grudge against the baron, but an innkeeper? I think that settling in Dereneyl would be asking for trouble, and well, I'm trying to give up asking for trouble, aren't I?" He shrugged again. "It really takes more than one person to run a tavern, but I think I might cut Erenor in, for a small piece." His grin was back. "Probably not as small as he'll agree to, but I can live with that."

He had still been rubbing at the same spot on the sword, all the time he had spoken, and he glared down at it, stopped himself, and stood.

Pirojil picked up his sword belt, and slipped the sword into the scabbard, pumping it a couple of times as though to make sure that it wouldn't stick, before he belted the sword around his thick waist. "Back to normal, eh?"

"So when . . . ?"

"When do I leave? And for where? As soon as I can. I've got to go take my leave of Baron Cullinane, and tell Walter Slovotsky that the next time that he has some dirty job that he needs to rope some poor fool into doing for him, he'd best find somebody else." He sighed. "And I should talk to Erenor. There's . . . some matters he and I need to discuss, particularly if I'm going to let him buy into the Three Swords, wherever it ends up being." He frowned for a moment. "We'll see," he said, as he drew himself up straight. "But that's nothing that you need to concern yourself with, my lady."

He reached out and took her hand, and bowed deeply over it. His hand was rough and callused, but he held hers gently, as though he was afraid that it would break. "This shouldn't need to be said, not really, but I'll say it anyway: if, well, if you ever do need an ugly old soldier, you know that you have but to send for me."

His words were quiet, but there was an intensity behind those piggish, sunken eyes that frightened her.

Send for him? Why should she have to send for him? It wasn't right. Why couldn't he just stay?

Yes, of course, he would come if she or Kethol sent for him, and if there was anybody in the way . . .

"I've never been one for long goodbyes," he said, "and this one has already been more than long enough for me." He gestured at Kethol's sleeping form. "Give Baron Keranahan my best wishes, my lady."

His shoulders twitched, and just for a moment, she thought that he was going to reach out to her, but he just brought a knuckle to his forehead.

He left, closing the door softly behind him.

She watched the door for a very long time.

23

Beralyn

It's not over until it's over, and maybe not even then. (A fat lady singing just means that you're at the opera, or maybe listening to Kate Smith.)
—Walter Slovotsky

Beralyn couldn't even think of sleep. Walking the ramparts was, at least, better than pacing up and down in her room, which is all she would have done.

She didn't understand it, not any of it. Tyrnael had refused to have a quiet word with her, and had begged to be excused, bowed quickly, and walked off to his rooms.

It was quiet now. Even most of the nobles minor who should have been honored and pleased to have been offered residence in the castle had excused themselves and found other accommodations in the city.

Even Forinel and that Leria had not reappeared, closeted up in their rooms with his injuries as an excuse, although the healing draughts that Thomen, himself, had poured into his wounds had sealed them up almost instantly. Yes, he had had some loss of blood, but she doubted that that was the real—

"Nothing quite like a sudden death to end a party, eh?"

She started. She hadn't seen Tyrnael come up to the ramparts.

He bowed deeply, too deeply.

"I thought you were in bed," she said.

He shook his head. "Well, there is some truth in that. Baron Tyrnael does lie sleeping in his bed—sleep spells, combined with wine, are most effective. I'm going to have to sneak in and wake him up—and I assure you, he will take some waking—before I can explain to him what a reluctant, belated hero he's been this evening, having exposed—belatedly, but exposed nonetheless—Lord Miron. I think he will accept it as an accomplished fact. As will you, Beralyn."

What?

Tyrnael muttered a quiet phrase, and he *changed*.

The man who stood in front of her was the wizard, Erenor. Gray-bearded, stooped with age, much like herself.

"I have been your friend, Beralyn, albeit a friend under false pretenses." His smile was far too self-satisfied. "I had always thought it more than a little convenient for you—the timing of that assassination attempt on Jason Cullinane. In my business you have to have a feel for timing, after all."

"You."

"None other." He gave a slight, mocking bow, then straightened, smiling broadly. "I thought you had me for a moment, the first time we met up here. That talk about the gift that I had given you—for a moment, I thought you were testing me, as I was surely testing you.

"It never was about you, my Empress. May I call you my Empress? No, don't answer; I will, anyway. There was no question in my mind that Miron could not be deterred, and that he would find some way to harm, preferably kill, Forinel. And I haven't known Forinel very long, but I like him. I've never had many friends." He shrugged. "It's part of being a swindler, a liar, and something of a thief, I guess."

"I don't know what to say."

"Then you should probably say little, or, better, nothing. I don't think I need to explain myself completely to you—we're not really friends, after all—but I think I should point out some obvious things.

"Such as, for example, that you don't want this whole matter looked at any more than it already will be. Three of us—you, me, and Derinald—know that Miron was killed for something you did. Let's leave it at that."

"And then there's the men that Derinald hired."

His smile broadened. "Really? I suspect that they are long gone; I could swear honestly, if I cared to, that I've never seen them—but I thought that added a little bit of verisimilitude to the story." He spread his hands. "I doubt that those men ever have, or ever will, set foot in Biemestren. Fear does make a powerful motivation, doesn't it?"

"You—"

"Shhh." He raised his finger. "Not that it's hard to hire someone, if you've got enough gold, to kill almost anybody. I even did it my-self, in Dereneyl. I could excuse it by saying that Forinel isn't really a friend of mine, but that's of no matter—Dereken was intended to fail, anyway. He was completely expendable, and I quite completely expended him.

"I don't have many friends, but I do have one. His name is Pirojil. For whatever reason, he's terribly fond of the Cullinanes, and I think he would be very unhappy if anything—*anything*—bad were ever to happen to any of them. I don't think you would want to make him unhappy, do you?"

She shook her head.

"A good choice, as it would make me unhappy, and I would make you very, very unhappy.

"So let it all go. Jason Cullinane has no designs on your son's throne, and you don't need him as an enemy; you will soon have a grandson of your own—I do have a little foresight, you know?—so just let it be.

"You can talk privately with Tyrnael, if he wants to, and apologize to him for having been taken in by such a clumsy imposter.

"But you probably want to advise him to let it be, too. You all get what you want, don't you?"

"And what do you get out of it? Why did you go to all this, all this . . ."

"Trouble? Those who know me even little know that I like things to be complicated. Leave it at that, if you will."

The smile was gone now, vanished completely. "Or, if you decide to, think of it this way: Miron didn't just endanger one of my friends. He and his mother were responsible for the death of another one of my friends, and, as I told you—and I don't always lie, simply because I often like to—I haven't had many friends.

"My friend's name was Durine. He never seemed to like me much, but, as I say, I'm used to that.

"His name was Durine. You remember that name, Beralyn, and every time you put your head on your pillow, before you fall asleep, you would serve yourself well if you remembered that name, and made it a point to remember what happened to the son of the bitch that killed my friend."

He raised a finger. "You can think of Forinel and Pirojil as my friends, if you like, and their friends as my friends by concatenation."

Erenor took one step toward her, and gripped the front of her muslin dress, just below the neck. His grip was much stronger than it should have been. "You wouldn't *ever* want to hurt my friends, my Empress."

He released her, smiled, and then he bowed—one last time—and muttered a quick spell.

And then he was gone.